SUNRISE LIBRARY
ROCKVILLE, MD

POTOMAC JUNGLE

Other books by David Levy:

The Chameleons
The Gods of Foxcroft
The Network Jungle

POTOMAC JUNGLE

A NOVEL BY
David Levy

KNIGHTSBRIDGE PUBLISHING COMPANY
NEW YORK

Copyright © 1990 by David Levy

All rights reserved. Printed in the U.S.A.

Publisher's Note: This novel is a work of fiction. Names, characters, places, and incidents either are the product of the author's imagination or are used fictitiously, and any resemblance to actual persons living or dead, events, or locales is entirely coincidental.

No part of this publication may be reproduced or transmitted in any form or by any means, electronic or mechanical, including photocopy, recording, or any information storage and retrieval system now known or to be invented, without permission in writing from the publisher, except by a reviewer who wishes to quote brief passages in connection with a review written for inclusion in a magazine, newspaper, or broadcast.

Published in the United States by
Knightsbridge Publishing Company
255 East 49th Street
New York, New York 10017

Library of Congress Cataloging-in-Publication Data

Levy, David
   Potomac jungle / by David Levy. — 1st ed.
     p.   cm.
   ISBN 1-877961-34-5 : $19.95
   I. Title.
   PS3562.E927P6   1990   90-4084
   813'.54—dc20   CIP

Designed by Stanley S. Drate/Folio Graphics Company, Inc.

10 9 8 7 6 5 4 3 2 1

First Edition

This book is dedicated to my friends in the television industry, particularly to each member of the Caucus for Producers, Writers & Directors; and to my brothers, Charles and Abner; and especially to my wife, her mother, and her daughter:

VICTORIA   JO ANN   KATE

With special thanks for editorial and technical advice from Mary H. Claycomb, Donald L. Keach, Lance M. Lee, Dr. Myles E. Lee, Joan B. Sanger, Shelly Usen, and especially to Dr. Charles Lee.

The Constitution of the United States
AMENDMENT 25 (1967)

SECTION 1. In case of the removal of the President from office or of his death or resignation, the Vice President shall become President.

SECTION 2. Whenever there is a vacancy in the office of the Vice President, the President shall nominate a Vice President who shall take office upon confirmation by a majority vote of both Houses of Congress.

SECTION 3. Whenever the President transmits to the President pro tempore of the Senate and the Speaker of the House of Representatives his written declaration that he is unable to discharge the powers and duties of his office, and until he transmits to them a written declaration to the contrary, such powers and duties shall be discharged by the Vice President as Acting President.

SECTION 4. Whenever the Vice President and a majority of either the principal officers of the executive departments or of such other body as Congress may by law provide, transmit to the President pro tempore of the Senate and the Speaker of the House of Representatives their written declaration that the President is unable to discharge the powers and duties of his office, the Vice President shall immediately assume the powers and duties of the office as Acting President.

Thereafter, when the President transmits to the President pro tempore of the Senate and the Speaker of the House of Representatives his written declaration that no inability exists, he shall resume the powers and duties of his office unless the Vice President and a majority of either the principal officers of the executive department or of such other body as Congress may by law provide, transmit within four days to the President pro tempore of the Senate and the Speaker of the House of Representatives their written declaration that the President is unable to discharge the powers and duties of his office. Thereupon Congress shall decide the issue, assembling within forty-eight hours for that purpose if not in session. If the Congress, within twenty-one days after receipt of the latter written declaration, or, if Congress is not in session, within twenty-one days after Congress is required to assemble, determines by two thirds vote of both Houses that the President is unable to discharge the powers and duties of his office, the Vice President shall continue to discharge the same as Acting President; otherwise, the President shall resume the powers and duties of his office.

POTOMAC JUNGLE

Sunset. In the Oval Office of the White House, his face pale and lined with fatigue, eyes closed, H. Stephen Thompson, President of the United States, slumped back against his oxblood leather chair. His bony hands gently massaged the thin blue veins of his temples. The nagging headaches, absent the past few weeks, had returned, now with increasing intensity.

"One second, Betsy . . . in a moment or two. . . ," he sighed, pushing a few hairs from his clammy forehead. "I'll be all right." Then, fumbling with the buttons of his brown cardigan sweater, he added, "I should relax a bit more, maybe take a couple more coffee breaks. . ."

Betsy King, straitlaced and prim, her gray hair neatly held in place by tortoise-shell combs (a legacy from her mother), had been Thompson's secretary for years, starting from the time he joined the prestigious Washington law firm Cabot, Henderson, & Vail. Some of the firm's clients, then and now, were among the giants of international industry and finance, those multinational corporations that wielded economic power greater than that of many of the nations of the world. Betsy had served him through his days as chief executive officer of Universal Corporate Investments, a holding company with worldwide interests, and later still through his years of public service on a variety of assignments for the United Nations as well as on confidential missions for Presidents and Cabinet officers.

In rhythm with the President's movements as he settled back in his chair, Betsy quietly placed her pad on the edge of his desk, then rose from her stiff-backed cane chair to pour water from an eagle-etched carafe into a tumbler. She shook two white pills from one of the three vials on the President's desk, handed them to him, and waited patiently at his side for him to take them.

He reached over for the pills and water as he glanced up at Betsy. "Always ready," he said softly, swallowing the pills. A moment or two later, color returned to his cheeks. "Margaret always said, 'Never lose Betsy, never, *never*. When I'm not there, she'll know what to do and when.'" He handed the glass back to Betsy. "She was right."

"She was a marvelous woman, so very easy to work with, so very kind. I'll not ever forget her," Betsy said, and Thompson noticed the tension and tautness of her compressed lips. In that movement he detected a subtle disapproval of the second Mrs. Thompson.

"Betsy, you're *always* at the ready, thank heaven."

"Practice," she said, resuming her seat and picking up the pad. "You set the rules, we follow them."

Rules. A faint smile crossed Thompson's face as he thought of the younger man down the hall in the corner office. Clifford Hawley, Vice President of the United States. He pictured the handsome tanned face suddenly creasing with concern, even anxiety, as Hawley read the terse memorandum Thompson had directed twenty-four hours earlier to his top three aides and to him, instructing them that, henceforth, the privilege of free access to the Oval Office must be terminated, except in emergencies, so that the President might use his time more efficiently. The time had come to let his once-close association with the Vice President wane. There was the upcoming political convention, plus vital decisions he had to make. And coupled with them the whispered insinuations levelled privately by his son that had startled him and raised disturbing, even distressing, questions of character about Hawley.

Thompson returned his attention to the matter at hand. "Where were we, Betsy? Would you read the last section, please?"

"Starting with 'You and I know, Mr. President, that we might survive in the deep shelters provided for us, but what about outside, what about up above the shelters'? There?"

"Yes. What about up above? Up above," he repeated as he rose slowly and moved to the window, gazing out at trees that had been planted by the first resident of the White House, John Adams. Thomas Jefferson had followed that tree-planting tradition, as had all of Thompson's own recent predecessors. "They'd all be gone, of course," he mused, his hands clasped behind his back, "the trees, the garden, the plants. All of the animals. The monument out there. This White House. Their Kremlin. Work all that in," he said as he returned to his chair. He leaned forward and pointed a finger at Betsy, saying, "How, in heaven's name, despite all of the cutbacks both sides have made, how do we ever contain it if it ever once gets loose?"

Betsy straightened up, certain that the question was merely typical Thompson rhetoric. She would simply wait without responding.

The President picked up a pencil and began his familiar doodling on a White House pad. "A paper edge means nothing. We know it. They know it. And yet we both play those endless, even quite dangerous, war games. Especially underwater. Their submarines. Ours. Constantly stalking each other, listening and waiting. There's where we need verifiable security, and being sure of the psychological steadiness of every man in every submarine. Theirs and ours," he emphasized. "We worry about slipping back to life in a jungle. The truth is we already live on the edge of one." He tossed the pencil aside and looked across at Betsy. "I don't have the right handle yet," he said abruptly. "Better tear it all up."

"All of it?"

"Yes, all of it. I think I'll have Alice Curtis work up a draft on this. If she has a few free moments in Geneva—although I doubt that the Soviets give her much free time—I'd like her to wrestle with this, to see if there's a chance to employ the one faculty that can save us." He tapped the side of his head. "Reason. Pure, simple reason. And trust," he added. "The hard kind—mutual trust." He settled back in his chair. "We'll pick it up another time."

All of her movements quite precise, Betsy King folded her notebook, straightened her black wool skirt, placed her chair against the wall, glanced back and bowed, and then let herself out.

What, he asked himself, could trigger a renewed beginning,

one that would be positively verifiable, one that would guarantee mutual survival, not mutual assured destruction? The instability of Eastern Europe, precipitated by the initial unshackling of democratic reform, had created new problems that were still volatile after a decade of internal nationalistic and ethnic struggle. Then, too, he'd always thought of Reykjavik back in the mid-eighties as the true jumping-off point of all subsequent summits. He'd picked up on Ronald Reagan's basic theme of greatly reduced offensive systems tied to each side's deploying minimum defensive forces as a national goal. It was a subject that occupied him at some time every day. He was certain it also occupied the mind of his counterpart some six thousand miles to the east. He stood up, feeling a mild dizziness as he gripped the edge of his chair. Thinking could come later. Time to rest.

Thompson felt a flush of intense anger as the door to his office opened. He had given the order only twenty-four hours earlier that no one should walk in unannounced. Standing in the doorway, however, in a plaid wool jacket and navy blue skirt, was the one person to whom the ban did not apply—Kathy, whom he'd married shortly before he'd assumed office almost three years earlier. The radiance about her open smile, the brightness and alertness in her dark eyes always gave a lift to Thompson's spirits.

"It's time, Stephen. Past your time. You promised." She crossed the room and kissed him lightly on the cheek.

"I know, I know," he said, a trifle impatient, "but I'm only fifteen minutes late."

"And I told you I'd come and fetch you if you were."

"*Fetch* me, is that it?" he said, chuckling. "I like that word. I remember old Cardinal Brannon—he's gone now—and his great red setter out on the Main Line, Paoli actually, and I can hear him and see him, tossing that gnarled Haitian nightstick he always carried just to stay in good with the old setter. 'Fetch, boy! Fetch!' That's what he'd say." He slipped his hand into hers. "Just like you, Kathy, come to fetch your old setter of a husband, that it?"

She started to protest. "No, that's not it, and you're not old, Stephen, you're not to say that—"

He led her to the door. "I know, I know," he said reassuringly.

"I only came—"

"And I'm coming, little girl, I'm coming."

She stopped and thrust her hands into the pockets of her

jacket. "Stephen! We agreed you'd never—" There was a note of exasperation in her voice.

"Kathy, look around, there's no one here," he said, interrupting her. "No one."

"Some women might think it belittling," Kathy insisted, "especially these days."

"Now, Kathy, would anyone really think I'd make a demeaning reference to you? Could I really be guilty of such conduct?"

"Not purposely, of course not," she admitted, then added, "but would you have said it about Margaret?" The moment she spoke she was angry at herself.

"No, I wouldn't have," he said, a testy touch in his voice.

"I'm sorry I asked that."

"Because," he went on, "it would have seemed preposterous, even ridiculous. With you, I only mean it as a compliment." He repeated the words softly, almost to himself. "Little girl." Then he stepped toward her. "Is it really so offensive?" he asked.

"All right," she said as though to settle the issue. "Just don't let it slip if others can hear you, that's all. Please?" She smiled as she held open the door.

Sunset was the scheduled time for the meeting of the Committee, the inner group of the new National Security Council, limited to six members including himself: Clifford Hawley had wanted to attend the meeting, but he'd recognized the awkwardness that his presence at this particular meeting might create. When two Committee members, Richard H. Daniels, Director of the CIA, and Edward Jaggers, Secretary of State, expressed caution, he had to respect their concern. He would spend the time in his office in the massive old EOB, the Executive Office Building across the road from his White House office, out of sight of the President's staff. In a way, the vice presidential suite served as a private retreat. Hawley was glad that protocol had kept it available, gladder still that when the President insisted (at the beginning of his term) that Hawley occupy space near the Oval Office, he had discreetly arranged to retain the vice presidential quarters that a century before housed the Navy Department's top brass. His privacy was important to him, and there was a lot to think about: the President's memorandum, the Committee's agenda, the convention now only months away.

Clifford Hawley, the youngest man ever to be elected Vice President, sat sipping a Bristol cream sherry, toying aimlessly with the drawer of his desk, amused, as always, at the signatures scrawled on the inside surface by previous occupants of the room—Nixon, Mondale, even Truman—and his own. Then he glanced at the open book on his lap, Freeman's definitive biography of Washington. He knew that his friends in the Senate and the White House, even more so his ladies in Hollywood and Washington and Manhattan, would be surprised at his continued study of the lives of all the men who had occupied the offices of President and Vice President. He'd learned much from those studies; he'd been likened to Burr, also slight of build; in fact, he'd often been told he resembled the bust of the controversial Vice President peering down from the Senate gallery. To many, his magnetic black eyes flashed like those of Burr in old engravings. He was never unmindful, though, that some meant their comparison to carry an unpleasant connotation in view of Burr's dubious place in history.

He had moved smoothly from being a congressman from Los Angeles to occupying a key role in the political battles that had led to the nomination of H. Stephen Thompson and to his surprising reward as Thompson's running mate. Now he sat wondering what Daniels would think of his exclusion from the President's office. Word was bound to leak out, would probably be deliberately leaked. Henry Kraus, the President's cagey Chief of Staff, had probably already planned it. He'd felt immediate concern when he read the President's memorandum, intensified by his own awareness of a growing coolness in the President's manner toward him. In recent cabinet meetings, he'd noted that Thompson had occasionally treated his remarks with indifference, on one occasion actually silencing him abruptly. Hawley had not been able to conceal his surprise and vexation, and that had prompted a presidential retreat. "It's not that I don't want to hear you, Mr. Vice President," Thompson had said almost apologetically, looking up and down the long table. "It's that Mrs. Thompson says we're all too long-winded here, especially me. So let's say that I'm only relaying orders from upstairs." Everyone laughed good-humoredly, but Hawley's annoyance lingered. And in the eyes of some he recognized the cunning attitude of a pack of jackals picking up the scent of rejection, and with it he sensed troubles looming.

Yesterday he had discussed some of his misgivings with Daniels, taking care to characterize the latest incident as unimportant, as probably only the action of an aging man who had recently fought off a bout of pneumonia and who, in addition, was famous for a presidential temper that, like Eisenhower's, could burst forth like a summer storm and just as quickly recede. An older Californian who had sat in the House years before and who had for some years now occupied the post of CIA Director, Daniels paid a visit to Hawley's office soon after testifying before a Senate subcommittee dealing with appropriations. His soft voice and heavy-lidded gray eyes belied his coldness and toughness.

"You're correct, Mr. Vice President, not to take umbrage. The President deserves your consideration—especially," he added, as he leaned forward to drop the ashes from his ever-present cigarette into an onyx ashtray, "especially considering the possibility—I stress *possibility*—that his recent illness is only, shall we say, the tip of the iceberg?" A mirthless smile crossed Daniels' face. "That's why I dropped by, as a matter of fact. The illness, even the potential illness of the President—and I might add, that is one thing I know a little something about—is why it might be the better part of judgment to absent yourself from the Committee tomorrow?" Daniels' speech often included statements ending as questions requiring no response.

Daniels coolly lit another cigarette, studying Hawley's face through the swirl of smoke. He knew that in making sensible suggestions, in winning acquiesence even on small points, a pattern would emerge that would assure success on more important decisions ahead. Daniels, who had read Machiavelli, could now write his own set of principles, not only on the art of achieving power but also on the art of securing it, something that had eluded Machiavelli's efforts. His few words of caution were not lost on Hawley.

Hand delivered only moments after Daniels' departure, a brief confidential message from the Secretary of State, one of Hawley's most trusted political allies, had, in effect, seconded Daniels' motion and confirmed Hawley's decision. It read: "Committee subject at tomorrow's meeting, review of Twenty-fifth Amendment, specific clause pertaining to presidential disability. Absence will allow more open discussion and your own contribution can be more effective later, if required. E. J."

At first, Hawley had recoiled from the thought of missing the meeting. Attendance at Committee meetings was more than de rigueur, it was mandatory. He had never been absent, but quick reflection persuaded him that, with Daniels and

Jaggers both recommending it, his interest would be fully protected.

Now in the privacy of his office, Hawley turned his thoughts to less weighty matters. If his reading habits were little known, his amorous activities were fun and games for the press and for his political enemies. He had been photographed, two years earlier, in Beverly Hills, dancing with Vivien Lessing, the dazzling new Hollywood sex symbol—she in a daring, backless gown in the elegant L'Escoffier Room atop the Beverly Hilton. And even though he'd been with a large party, and even though he'd danced with every other woman in the group, the media's exclusive attention had been paid to those few moments with her. Perhaps it had been the instant when he'd felt the flamboyant star's hand touch the nape of his neck, and he'd whispered in response, "You do that, it can lead to other people's misunderstandings—"

"A lot of things can," she'd said, pulling back to stare at him, tossing her blond mane and venting her famous throaty laughter. Then, carefully, dropping the exploring hand, she had moved even closer into his arms, whispering, "Are you some kind of old-fashioned prude, Mr. Hawley?"

He disavowed prudery later that same night when a smaller group accepted the star's invitation to her Bel-Air mansion, a pretentious building with Ionic columns and a pediment full of statues representing Greek gods at its front entrance. Set back behind high wrought-iron gates on a quiet cul-de-sac, the house gave Vivien Lessing the kind of privacy her life-style demanded. Hawley acted as though he would leave with the last couple, but on an impulse he momentarily waved them on as he stepped back into the circular foyer, presumably for a forgotten raincoat. The retrieval led to four hours of a new and steaming romance in a pink and white room that commanded a view of the endless green lawn.

She told him that she wondered if she'd gone too far. She hoped not; she was weary of the tradition that stars had to exchange sexual favors for their stardom. Moreover, she bluntly confessed how she despised the studio heads, her leading men, and every agent she'd ever accommodated on her climb to fame. But, keeping her thoughts to herself, she had to admit that a handsome young Vice President could be both a challenge and a stepping-stone to new power. The price, she decided, was worth the experiment.

Then there was the image of Gloria Whitney, the diminutive

daughter of the Chief Justice—a saucy package of feminine charms and wiles, green-eyed, irreverent, apparently totally liberated despite the puritanical speeches of her learned father, and determined (so gossip said) to seduce the entire superstructure of government. That had been worry enough. Then came the rumor of her problems with pills and alcohol, which grew persistently until he heard it, or so it seemed, at every party and political function he attended.

He remembered escorting her to a Kennedy Center opening. She'd been insistent on his coming in for a nightcap in the large dark house she shared with her widowed father in the stately Kalorama area of the city. "Old Marble Bust retires very early," she said cheerfully, tossing a mink stole across the railing of the curved staircase. "In here," she added, swinging open one of the carved double doors, turning coquettishly as she leaned back against it and held out a hand to him. He glanced at his watch. "Nothing to be afraid of, and no one to be afraid of, Mr. Vice President. Only little me. And we have all the time in the world," and with that she wrapped her arms about his neck and kissed him, pressing tightly against him. When she released him, she said, "You've been wanting to do that all night, admit it!"

It was true. But it was also disconcerting for him to notice a photograph of young Harry Thompson, the President's son, staring up at him from beside a Tiffany lamp. "That's all over," she said with a dismissive laugh, turning the picture down. But her affair with Harry wasn't over, and that was one of the problems Gloria Whitney brought with her.

And then there was the tall, sensual figure of Felicia Courtney, her tawny hair styled in an elegant French braid, whose physical assets were remarkably counterbalanced by her imposing business and intellectual attainments—magna cum laude from Radcliffe, onetime senior editor at Random House, and now the new publisher of *Insider's Washington*, a magazine launched initially by her late husband, Ted, and already the official arbiter of the capital's younger social set. The impact of the magazine had begun to confirm Felicia as the doyenne, despite her own relative youthfulness, of *what* was in, *where* was in, and *who* was in.

Hawley, followed by his Secret Service guard, had bumped into her in the cocktail lounge of the Four Seasons Hotel a few weeks after the untimely death of her husband. He remembered her first words when he stopped at her table and greeted her. "Nice to see you out," he'd said.

"You haven't called," she replied, extending a hand.

"I apologize," he said, taking it. A friend of Ted's, Hawley had been among the first to pay his respects to the young widow at the old brownstone Victorian home located just a stone's throw from famed Dumbarton Oaks.

"You've been too busy, I'm sure."

Hawley was momentarily flustered. "Frankly, I guess I thought. . ." He stopped and looked down at her. "I'd heard you were at the magazine, but it didn't occur to me. . ." He shrugged his shoulders.

"I'm meeting a shareholder, a very dull investor," she said helpfully. "Can you join me until she arrives? Or am I keeping you from something?" she added with a smile.

Hawley sat beside her and signalled a waiter. "Whatever the lady's drinking, please," he said. Then turning to her, he added, "It's good to see you, Felicia." His eyes swept over her fashionable dark green suede suit. "And seeing you looking so very well."

"Thank you," she replied.

As Felicia lifted her glass to him, Hawley sensed from that gesture, her silence, and her steady gaze that Felicia Courtney was someone he could know better. But he also suspected that she was someone no one could ever take for granted, and that her playfulness could be just that and nothing more.

"Dinner next week, this weekend, tomorrow?" he suddenly ventured, amused at his own impetuosity.

"Dinner tomorrow," she said at once, as a heavyset woman, Felicia's shareholder, burst in upon them, claiming her attention.

That first dinner had been followed by two others. After the last, as they sat in his car outside her home (the Secret Service contingent discreetly parked some distance away), he decided the time was at hand to make a move, but as he turned to put his arm about her she shifted deftly. "We have time, Cliff. We don't want to rush anything." He made an effort to protest, but without a word, with a soft smile, a touch of a finger to her lips and then to his, she was gone.

The final image that rose before Hawley was the lithe and enchanting figure of another woman. Their first meeting seemed so long ago: he, still an aspiring congressman; she, a bright, eager, stylish young journalist doing free-lance pieces for national magazines. Those brilliant dark eyes of hers had mesmerized him. And he liked the crispness of her voice, her confidence. As they sat in the stately, oak-panelled cocktail lounge of the Hay-Adams, a stone's throw from the White House, Kathy Bryson's questions were pointed and insistent. And the two of them were on a first-name basis almost from the start.

"And your ultimate goal, Cliff?"

He raised his glass to her. "Let's start with *your* ultimate goal. Okay?"

She smiled, shaking her head. "Later. This is my interview. So shall we try again—*your* ultimate goal?"

"I'm sorry," he said, settling back in his chair. "Okay. My ultimate goal. I'd put it this way. I'd like to try my hand at governing."

"But you're doing that right now."

"Not exactly. One member out of 435 House members is not my idea of governing. Participating, yes, but not the real thing."

"You've already achieved a great deal in the House," she said. "So, what about the Senate?"

"Not even the Senate." He watched her as she made her quick notes. "I'd rather that none of this part be for publication, if you don't mind."

"You don't want just a bland story, Mr. Hawley—" And then, noticing his mock disapproval, she smiled and said, "Cliff. Okay. Just a parade of facts, no opinion, no plans, all pap—you really don't want that, do you?"

"I'm really still something of a freshman Congressman, and the old rules say that children are to be seen, not heard. If I said exactly what I want to be when I grow up, it might frighten my elders. It might make them set up barriers that would keep me under surveillance in a playpen they can control."

"You're full of metaphors."

"Not for publication?" He stirred his drink, studying her. "We trade ultimate goals?"

She hesitated a moment and then let her notebook rest on her lap. "Okay, deal," she said smiling.

"Good. Then how about the White House?" he responded.

"The White House? After only—what is it—two terms in the House?"

"I may not be an Abraham Lincoln, but he managed to do just that after only one. But look, it doesn't have to be the White House itself. Maybe something close to it?"

"The Cabinet? Chairman of a big agency?" She pointed her pen at him. "You were a communications major at college. How about the Federal Communications Commission?"

"Sure. Something along those lines."

"Not the Supreme Court?"

"I'm not an attorney."

"You don't have to be," she said.

He was impressed. "I see you're a student of the Constitution."

"I studied political science at college. Once I even thought of doing graduate work at Georgetown."

"Really? I've given special lectures there, at night, on the real world of politics," Hawley volunteered.

"What does that mean to you, 'the real world of politics'?" she inquired.

"Well, it's not the day-to-day wheeling and dealing you might think I'm referring to. It's more—if you don't mind my puffing up like some pseudointellectual, which is what I've been called by some left-wing writers—geopolitical. You deal with basics: geography, populations, economics, political systems. There's been a new world shaping up ever since the Cold War went out of fashion with the Berlin Wall. And we're still trying to understand it. That includes its instability and its unpredictability."

"But we are making progress, aren't we? And the Russians are, aren't they?" she asked, curious, too, to have the opportunity to probe his mind.

"We don't know for sure. Not even after all the Gorbachev years, *glasnost* and all the rest. That's because the new Russians aren't synonymous with the old Soviets. We tend to forget our history—my father teaches history at Penn and he keeps reminding me—the Russians were always repressive, which accounts for the frequent expansion of their frontiers throughout all their history, all for the purpose of protecting their own security."

"Anything wrong in that?" Kathy asked.

"When it's repressive, yes. And this withdrawing we've witnessed these past years—is it just the ebbing of the tides or is it something permanent? We don't know that for sure either yet, and we won't know for some time, which means that *we*, of necessity, must retain a powerful military posture especially in a world where there are still thousands of nuclear weapons around. We have to be concerned with who's in charge of that stockpile. That fact alone has to be paramount in all of our thinking."

"And meanwhile? How do we proceed?"

"Cautiously. It will be a long time, if ever, before the Soviet state has a true pluralistic democracy or a free-enterprise system, even with the gestures they've made in both areas. All we can do is to hope for stability. Theirs. Remember, as Dr. Kissinger once remarked, with the exception of the still-debatable departure of Mr. Gorbachev, no Soviet leader has ever retired voluntarily."

"While up to a short time ago we once had four former Presidents all leading their own pursuits: Reagan, Ford, Carter, Nixon," Kathy observed.

"That says something about the two systems right there," Hawley said with a smile.

"Are we back to old-fashioned balance-of-power strategies?" she asked, favorably impressed with Hawley's thinking.

"Quite possibly," Hawley replied. "And that's what today's geopolitics is all about, and that's why I like the course I teach."

"Does it also have something to do with countering the image you have of being—how shall I describe it—a playboy?" Kathy said with a mischievous look.

Hawley shrugged. "I've read that charge. I live with it."

"But giving courses at night with your kind of schedule? You are trying to build a new image, aren't you?" she asked.

"It's part of my heritage. Teaching. Like I said, my father's a teacher."

"So politics comes natural to you?"

"Political science," he emphasized, smiling. "Now how about you? You said you were once thinking of graduate work at Georgetown. That means you want to try for the foreign service?"

She nodded in vigorous affirmation. "I know it would be exciting and meaningful; besides, there's all that implied power plus the traveling."

Pointing an accusing finger at her, he asked, "Do I detect, maybe, a little desire on *your* part to do some governing?"

This time it was she who sat back comfortably, crossing her legs. "Yes, but less as a participant, more as an observer."

"Well now," he said, "we're running along parallel lines here. I want very much to be a participant, you want to be the spectator—"

"Observer. I like observer better."

He paused. "On second thought, I'm not sure I like that figure of speech, parallel lines." He reached across the table and let his fingers rest on hers. "I prefer lines that intersect, don't you?"

She smiled as she withdrew her hand. "Perhaps. I don't know. But I think we'd better get back to my doing the questioning. Example: if it's a higher office, you might travel farther with a wife. Buchanan was the only one who ever made it to the White House single."

"Cleveland. You're forgetting him."

"He was married," she said.

"*After* he became President," Hawley replied.

"Really? I must have forgotten. You *do* know your history."

"Like I said, I should. I was raised on it," he said, "my father teaching, writing. So I'm always reading it."

"And I've been reading about *you*," she replied smiling, changing the subject. "You and that Felicia Courtney. Anything to that?"

"Friend," he said with a smile. "And she doesn't sound like one of yours. Not the way you say *that* Felicia Courtney."

"She's turned down everything I've ever submitted. Close friend?" she asked, as she sipped her drink.

"I don't know about that. Not yet I don't."

"Special?"

"Let's just leave it 'friend,'" Hawley said. "You were talking about the FCC, remember?"

"Right. Okay. So let's start with the FCC. Why do you see yourself there? Can we mention that?"

"Sure. For one thing, I spent considerable time in the world of television, at Time, Inc. and at Young and Rubicam. And one of my friends—and I say that with some reservation because he makes a point of not having any real friends—was and still is Joe Gratton, the head of Federal Broadcasting. Difficult bastard—he'd be the first to admit it—but probably the best-informed man on the future of communications in the country: broadcasting, the new networks, UHF satellites, direct broadcasting, pay TV, cable, you name it. We used to debate it for hours over our occasional lunches. Gratton knows his stuff, so I made a point of listening and learning. Matter of fact, he'd make one hell of a good chairman himself except that he likes the network money and the perks and the power he has more than he'd like the FCC."

"And you?"

"You may discount this, but if you want to know the truth, I think I'd welcome the opportunity to do what some political appointees sometimes forget—serve the public interest. Maybe I'm a frustrated maverick!" he said, suddenly striking the table, eyes flashing. "For one thing, Kathy, I don't happen to consider the invention of television as just another means for advertisers to get their damn irritating repetitive ten-second and fifteen-second commercials into America's homes! And then, sometimes, I also think of the god-awful comic-book junk that's stuffed into our kids' brains night after night, the terrible waste—" Abruptly, he leaned back in his chair, letting out a sigh. "Didn't mean to sound off like that, but it's a subject I think about."

"Here I was, when I started this interview, thinking you were all ambition, pure and simple. I'm impressed," she said as Hawley rose to greet Edward Jaggers, then chairman of the House Committee on Foreign Affairs, who was beaming down at the two of them over his long, aquiline nose and his bulging waistline. Hawley had begun to introduce her as Jaggers sat down.

"Know all about her, Hawley. Smart as a whip. Doesn't go after us establishment fogies. She's got a nose—a very pretty one, as you can see—for smelling out the comers. Her blessings can do as much for you as the Speaker's—well almost. Keep on her good side. And remember, I told you." Then, turning to Hawley's companion, he said, "And you remember this, my dear. This young comer can probably do the same for you. In his two terms in the House he's authored more legislation than any member in our entire history. Quite a record. Says something. Keep in touch with each other, that's my advice. Oh, waiter? Scotch and soda—Cutty Sark, if you please. . . ."

Now, seated in the vice presidential office, Hawley knew that in her present position Kathy Thompson might be able to furnish a clue as to why the President seemed to be excluding him. The first problem would be one of contact, of reaching her without being too direct; he would have to be patient, and careful.

Or perhaps, he thought, studying the intricate patterns of the elaborate marquetry floor of his EOB office, there might be a more immediate clue later in the evening when he was scheduled to meet the President's son for a fencing workout in the White House gymnasium. He hoped the President would keep his word to his son and show up to watch the match.

☆ ☆ ☆

Sunset. Gloria Whitney, her layered hair complemented with blond highlights and contained by a blue scarf, snuggled close to Harry Thompson, the President's only child. As they walked slowly along the Tidal Basin at the foot of the Jefferson Memorial, his dark thick hair blew about in the light wind.

"I don't know what the hell we're doing here," he said, glowering down at her.

"Because I love statues. I live with one, remember?" She looked up at Harry's grim face. "And that doesn't mean you have to put on an act with that famous scowl of yours, Harry."

"It's not an act."

"It doesn't scare me, Harry."

"This place is for tourists. Look at them, gawking. Jefferson, the Tidal Basin."

"Some of those gawkers are your own damned Secret Service guardians," she fretted. Then, in her abrupt way of changing the subject, she whispered, "The Tidal Basin is something I've always wanted to swim in."

"It's not deep enough," he said.

"Maybe not right here, but farther out, in the middle, it's maybe thirty feet deep. Besides, if one of those paddleboats can float here, then it's deep enough anywhere." She pushed closer against him. "You can hold my hand. No one knows who you are."

"Thanks."

"Do you think he really had a slave as his mistress?"

"Jefferson?"

"Who else?" she asked.

Young Thompson glanced back at the towering bronze figure. "Probably. They were all available."

"Do you think your father ever slept with a black woman?"

Harry Thompson pulled away from her with an angry gesture. "For Christ's sake, Gloria, is that all you ever think of?"

"Oh, still wrapped up in your public halo and your old man's holiness, are you? Well, take it from me: anyone who's slept with Kathy Thompson—who always looks like a cake of ice to me—might welcome a warm, thick-lipped, big-breasted black woman who knows all the tricks. That even includes his holiness."

She looked up at him. "Admit it Harry. You like Kathy, don't you—just a little?"

Harry Thompson walked along in silence.

"You don't have to answer, Harry, because I've seen you staring at her." She shrugged. "Maybe you don't like her. But maybe you dislike her only because you can't have her. Anyway, she's too old for you, although I'll admit she's got great eyes and not too bad a figure. What she ever saw in his holiness I'll never know except to go down in history books as a First Lady. Can his holiness really get it up?"

Thompson stopped and placed his hands firmly on Gloria's shoulders as she leaned back against the slender metal railing that circled the Basin. "Look," he said, a note of exasperation in his voice, "I know you like to say any damn non sequitur that pops into your crazy head. Maybe it's the pills. And those things you should lay off of. Maybe it's your way of getting attention. But if we're going to see each other, one of us is going to have to change." She began to laugh. "I'm serious, Gloria. I respect my father. Yours, too."

"You mean dear Old Marble Bust?" she asked, feigning surprise in her voice.

"Okay. I don't always agree with his decisions, that's for sure, or the court's, but for God's sake, he *is* the Chief Justice. Doesn't that mean anything to you?"

"It means he's a bore. B-o-r-e. Unanimous decision. No dissents."

"Very smart. Something you're full of, smart-ass talk."

"Clifford Hawley thinks I'm smart, no matter what *you* think." She looked up at Harry archly.

"Hawley," he said with a touch of derision.

"You've never objected when he's been my escort," she added.

No, he hadn't objected, and Hawley had been that and nothing more. But some public speculation about the bachelor Vice President and the Chief Justice's daughter in a gossip column had begun to irritate him.

"Hawley," she repeated. "Handsome, available, lascivious Mr. Hawley. I like him."

Thompson walked along in silence.

"He likes me," she said provocatively.

"Sure he does. You like every good-looking thing in pants, and he seems to like anything in skirts," he blurted out. "Truth is you two might really make a good pair."

"Don't push it, Harry. I could have him. Easy."

He started to walk away, angry at her, more angry at himself for the growing awareness of his newborn hostility toward Hawley. "You're hopeless," he said as she ran to catch up with him.

"And you love me, Harry Thompson," she said as she thrust her hand around his arm. "If you didn't, you wouldn't just walk away—you'd run. Shall we go to your place, baby?"

The sea was quiet at sunset, its long gray swells rolling out toward the darkening slate-colored skies. A lone giant tanker, capable of carrying half a million tons of cargo, its black bow rising and falling slowly, exposing its rusted waterline, slid easily across the gentle cresting of the ocean. In the distance a few yellow lights gleamed from the receding shore; two fat, grayish sea gulls swooped down and glided toward the freighter's churning white wake. High in the sky, miles above the weathered face of the captain standing on the bridge—and even farther from his thoughts—the penetrating eye of a Soviet satellite automatically probed the surface of the Atlantic, searching for American submarines.

The ship's captain, puffing contentedly on his pipe, sniffed the sweet aroma of his tobacco. Below decks a poker game was in progress. The blue and white cards were crisp now, but their snap would be gone and their edges worn before the ship lay anchor at its destination, Murmansk.

Beneath the keel of the huge, lumbering tanker lay a giant American ballistic-missile submarine, the USS *Colorado*. During the night of a violent storm some weeks before it had left its New England base and for thirty days had moved to a greater and greater depth at a stately pace within a carefully prescribed set of coordinates, waiting for its secret rendezvous, finally gliding to a fixed position under the thousand-foot merchant ship, its captain hopeful that it was secure and beyond detection by Russian trawlers, or by Russian satellites whose cameras and intelligence-gathering sensors were tuned to catching the thermal wake of American submarines.

Inside the vast submarine—it measured almost the length of two football fields—its captain, Commander Jeffrey Whitney, was tamping his own pipe as he sat absorbed in studying a batch of naval scientific reports. He knew that the Soviets had long ago achieved the ability to obtain 365 days of complete photographic coverage of the United States by means of overlapping flights of their forty-eight reconnaissance satellites. His mission was to determine whether they could detect his submarine at sea; he knew that, submerged anywhere off the coast of the United States, his ship had enough firing power to reach Moscow and dozens of other Russian cities with its package of twenty-four nuclear missiles, all of them carrying eight ballistic warheads, each one precision honed to zero in on its appointed target.

At a prearranged hour, his submarine would leave the protective cover of the huge tanker above, dive deeper, more quietly, and at a faster speed than any of its predecessors in the fleet, then take a position close to the ocean bottom, waiting, as it once again began its slow circling routine. The husky young officer reached across his small desk to straighten a family photograph of his father, the Chief Justice of the United States; his younger brother, Lane; and his sister, Gloria.

Jeff Whitney (all-American in his Navy football days) studied his secret orders. For eight more days he would maneuver his ship deep in the ocean, testing its new sound-absorbing hull and the quiet of its pumpless nuclear power plant. Then he would take up his final position some miles off the Spanish coast to test his men's psychological and mental stamina for at least three more months of deep underwater duty.

If special orders came via a low-frequency series of coded sound, he would consult his code book to interpret the orders and possibly, he knew, become but one part of a potential Armageddon. In his mind's eye he had a sickening vision of his latent power—and theirs.

He stepped out of his small cabin, walked down a narrow passageway, and nodded to a sailor standing at a watertight door, who swung it open as Whitney headed below to the crew's quarters. He caught a glimpse of members of his crew playing poker. One of the card players had just told a joke and the others were laughing. It was clear that none of them was thinking of where he was and why he was there. The captain was pleased. That was the way it was supposed to be. Messengers of death should be relaxed, feel no psychological tensions.

At sunset, a hooked-nosed old man, his skin laced with wrinkles, gazed at his clean-shaven face in the mahogany-framed mirror above his antique porcelain washbasin. His lips parted in a crooked smile and he shook his head; he had never won any beauty contests, and it had never mattered. He was Admiral of the Fleet Kenneth G. Hornwell, onetime Chief of Naval Operations and now Chairman of the Joint Chiefs of Staff. That was enough for any man.

He stepped into the spartan office in his quarters aboard a reconditioned relic of World War II, the *Decatur,* a destroyer upon which he'd once served as an ensign, now permanently anchored in the Potomac. Hornwell had always resented the decision that had converted the historic Admiral's House, standing on the twelve hilltop acres of the Naval Observatory, into the official residence of the country's Vice Presidents, beginning with Rockefeller and extending down to the incumbent, Clifford Hawley, toward whom Hornwell felt a strong antipathy.

He picked up the paper stamped TOP SECRET, and his smile—less a sign of affability than a mark of calculated shrewdness, a quality that had carried him to the apogee of personal power—stretched back his cheeks like the folds of an accordion. The flat of his left hand rhythmically struck his desk, an old worn board he'd used as a naval architect. Once more he read the cold print of the dispatch. The breakthrough by which American forces should be able to pinpoint the exact location of all Soviet submarines would be operative within a maximum period of ninety days. The Defense Department's Red Dye Day, the code name given to the Navy's secret plan to proclaim its superiority in nuclear warfare, was imminent, awaiting, at an appropriate moment, only the President's final approval to be implemented.

He pushed himself away from the desk and stepped over to a porthole, rubbing his fingers together, a telltale sign of inner contentment. In ninety days he would have the power, technically, to wipe out the Soviet submarine fleet. The deadly game of underwater hide-and-seek, whose details the American people were unaware of, would be over. America's armed forces had long played this game against their Soviet counterparts, a relentless military-scientific struggle raging in a stillness from hundreds and thousands of miles above the earth down to the deepest recesses of the oceans. Neither side recognized the new Soviet openness in those dangerous, dark waters. Now at last one side finally had the means with which to tag the other. To tag was to win the game; to win was to control the planet.

For a moment Hornwell visualized Alice Curtis, America's chief arms negotiator, her black hair streaked with thin bands of gray pulled tightly back from her high forehead, seated with her team at the current Geneva Arms Control Conference, and he saw her emotionless face revealing in a split second a look of surprise mixed with satisfaction as Hornwell's naval emissary passed a confidential dispatch to her confirming the Navy's scientific advance. What a bargaining chip he would deliver!

His thoughts abruptly turned to the President. He scowled as he scanned the dark swirls of the Potomac from the porthole. He had common interests with the President: both loved the sea, both were students of history, and both had lost their wives almost to the hour of the same day, although he had chosen to remain a widower. Suddenly he compressed his thin lips, his decision made. First word of the breakthrough engineered by naval personnel—a breakthrough that dimmed even the achievements of the legendary Rickover—had to go to the Committee. He was uncomfortable at the thought that he was withholding vital security information from the Chief Executive. But under present conditions, with the unending series of crises within the Soviet Union requiring constant evaluation, that was the way things were now done.

A room, housed deep in the bowels of a small unimposing building set at the end of a tree-lined street on the southern edge of Alexandria, was the regular meeting place of the Committee, although it maintained three other nondescript surface structures across the country, each with bombproof meeting rooms.

The Committee consisted now of Admiral Hornwell, Chairman of the Joint Chiefs of Staff; Edward Jaggers, Secretary of State; Oliver Moran, Deputy Secretary of State; Anthony Clauson, Secretary of Defense; Richard Daniels, Director of Central Intelligence; and Clifford Hawley, Vice President of the United States.

What had given the Committee its own decisive status was its de facto assumption of powers, powers that were necessary in a world where a few minutes might mean the difference between peace and annihilation, where the illness of a single human in a position of authority could imperil a nation's security—powers that were deemed essential where the internal stability of the Soviet Union was still an unsettled issue, as that nation struggled to accommodate democratic ideals with centuries of autocratic rule, whether Czarist or Communist.

The threat of proliferation of nuclear capability in the hands of Third World countries dominated by capricious and dangerous zealots provided further justification for the Committee's assumed position.

Members were always careful to arrive in ordinary cars, aware that the more unceremonious they were, the less attention they would attract. As Hornwell stepped out of his blue Chevrolet and approached the red brick building, its front door swung open. He nodded to the Marine doorkeeper and headed for an elevator that led down to an open doorway at the end of a corridor, where a few carefully selected staff aides stood quietly against the walls. Meticulous about punctuality, Hornwell was always the first to arrive for these meetings, contributing to the secrecy of the occasion by wearing civilian clothes, today an old gray suit that was now a bit large for his thin frame.

A few minutes later the Deputy Secretary of State, Oliver Moran, arrived. An imposing man with skin of a rich chestnut brown, Moran wore thick-lensed pince-nez and was always sartorially correct. Today his outfit was completed by a black and orange striped Princeton tie. Some had begun to think of this quiet thinker, who had made his way up through the ranks of the foreign service, as presidential timber.

"Good evening, Admiral."

"Mr. Secretary." Hornwell never allowed himself to assume any kind of familiarity with any member of the Committee.

Anthony Clauson, the white-haired genial Secretary of Defense, was the next arrival. Always affable, he immediately circled the table, shaking the hands of some of the Committee aides and greeting his two colleagues.

The three men chatted informally until the portly Secretary of State entered the room. Edward Jaggers, a heavy gold chain crossing his ample front, was the most loquacious of the group. He stroked each side of his full, dark British-cavalry moustache. "Am I late? I don't think so," he said, looking at Clauson as he pulled out an antique watch from his vest pocket. "I only hope we have a good menu tonight, and I'm not referring to the agenda, I'm referring to our dinner. I'm not sure that Mr. Daniels cares, I mean about food, but as the saying goes, 'It's not the horse that pulls the cart; it's the oats.' That's an old Russian proverb. I'd always thought it was French, but I checked it out a year or two ago. Pure Russian. Never would have guessed it." Without a moment's pause he kept talking. "The Vice President's not going to be here, which I think is a mark of, shall we say, statesmanship?" he pulled out his watch again. "I'd say *he'll* be here any moment."

The reference was clear to each of them. Only when Daniels actually arrived did they begin to form a group in the large windowless room, moving purposefully toward the round mahogany table designed to equalize their ranks. There was, however, an unacknowledged recognition that in this Committee, among these leaders, and in spite of protocol, one was more equal than others. No one would take a seat until Richard Daniels, head of the CIA, dropped his gangling body into one of the identical black leather chairs. When he sat down and hunched over the table, the other Committee members took their places, the staff aides sitting down in chairs set against the walls.

Daniels, speaking in his customary soft voice, opened the meeting without formalities. "We have some delicate matters to discuss here this afternoon. Red Dye Day, for one. The news from Admiral Hornwell's scientific team is good—" he looked at Hornwell, the latter flinching because he recognized that what he had considered private knowledge of the Joint Chiefs was already known to the CIA. "We have a report on the President's health," Daniels continued, "which brings up the Twenty-fifth Amendment." He glanced to his left, at the unoccupied sixth chair. Then, in the peculiar questioning manner in which he announced decisions, he said, "As you know, I suggested to the Vice President that in view of the nature of our conversation here today, it would—would you not agree—be somewhat inappropriate for him to participate?"

Hornwell snorted. It was no secret he felt some personal resentment toward Clifford Hawley, if only because, when Hornwell's reappointment was being considered, Hawley had favored a younger officer as Chairman of the Chiefs. "He's been here before, Mr. Daniels," the Admiral said, "when the Twenty-fifth was discussed. In fact, the amendment makes it obligatory for him to initiate clearly defined steps should he ever deem it advisable to replace the President."

Daniels pursed his lips. "Correct, sir. And we could reach him if that were the desire of the Committee. . ." Daniels let the statement hang there for a moment, and when there was no response forthcoming, he said, almost self-deprecatingly, "It may be best this way, Admiral."

Hornwell felt the opposition of the other four. They knew

he was the President's man and would remain so unless and until he honestly felt that the President could not discharge his duties efficiently. And he felt that Daniels was very much Hawley's man. But what worried him most was whether Hawley might one day, in fact, become Daniels'. He tapped his knuckles rhythmically on the table, his reedy voice betraying a trace of sarcasm. "Since you have evidence of the Navy's new submarine-detection system, perhaps you should be the one to place it before the Committee—"

Daniels' hands went to his lapels. He smiled sardonically as he said, "I have no doubt, sir, that Naval Intelligence is generally satisfied with the internal operations of the CIA—as we are with theirs. Shall we let the issue rest there, sir? And shall we get to the crux of the meeting, which is the potential dilemma of the President vis-à-vis the Vice President?"

"Yes, I know it's on the agenda," Hornwell said tartly, "but I'm not at all certain that we have any crisis to debate."

Moran clasped his hands together. "I tend to agree with you, Admiral," he said, "but the point is we don't want to wait until we do have a crisis, do we?"

"No," Hornwell responded tersely, "of course not. But I can still recall even when President Reagan was shot, there was no outcry in or out of government that he had to be replaced, permanently or temporarily."

"Except, Admiral," Daniels cut in, "the matter *was* discussed. Even more to the point, it was discussed long after the attempted assassination when his forgetfulness, his dozing off at meetings, had sent a few chills through his key staff. It was debated, sir, and properly so, which is why, in the case of President Thompson—where there are even more visible signs of fatigue—we have a right, a duty, to weigh all of the evidence. Particularly with the stakes so high with the imminent activation of Red Dye Day. Now, with your permission, sir, may we, I repeat, get back to the crux of this meeting, our potential dilemma of the President vis-à-vis the Vice President?"

☆ ☆ ☆

Kathy Thompson, in a severe-looking chalk-lined gray business suit, stood in the center of a group of teenagers and high-school teachers in her East Wing office, cameras grinding away. As she caught the discreet signal of her efficient secretary, Anne Koyce, whom she had brought to the White House when Anne was working for Federal Broadcasting's Washington office, she reached down to her desk to pick up a framed citation.

With an economy of words, but with the right degree of warmth and interest, she presented it to the spokeswoman of the group, a young, smiling, pretty black teacher from Trenton, saluting her and the others for the dedicated leadership all of them had exhibited in the still-ongoing battle against drugs, a program initiated by one of her predecessors, Nancy Reagan. In a moment the citation was in the teacher's hand. Kathy listened politely and with practiced intensity to her response. Then the cameramen started packing while Anne moved in to lead the assembled group into the outside reception area.

Kathy slipped into a floral-covered wing chair as Anne returned. "That's the last one of the day," Anne said.

"Amen."

"It'll make the local news. Maybe even one of the network shows," Anne added reassuringly.

"They'll have to be hard up."

"It's important."

"Important? Well, it is, of course," the First Lady acknowledged. "But I thought what we used to do back at Federal was really important. This was the kind of material a Joe Gratton used to scoff at as pure filler."

"What makes you think most of what's on the news programs isn't just plain old filler? What the First Lady does is news to women and very important to them. Just ask the President."

"What the First Lady wears may be even more important."

"You're being cynical, Mrs. Thompson."

"Kathy."

"Kathy." That was a routine repeated almost daily, Kathy Thompson's insistence on Anne's calling her by her first name, Anne compromising and complying for the most part—but shrewd enough never to display an intimate relationship when others were around.

"I haven't done today's mail," Kathy said, glancing at her desk.

"It can wait," Anne said.

Kathy riffled through the small pile. "I never thought so many women—men, too—would want to contact the First Lady."

"Remember, you only get the tip of the iceberg out of almost two thousand letters a week."

"Do you think the others enjoyed it?" Kathy asked.

"It goes with the territory. You may not expect it, you just accept it."

"Are they always comparing me to Margaret Thompson?" Kathy asked abruptly, almost immediately regretting the question.

"When they do, you have nothing to worry about. Even I remember, if dimly, she had a reputation of just not being the most feminine of women. If you want it short and to the point, the way we summed up ladies like her when we were at Federal, she was what you'd call ballsy. But she was also clever. Nobody ever said she was stupid. Shrewd, yes. Calculating, too."

Kathy stood up. She liked Anne; Anne had come as close to being a friend as anyone she knew in Washington, but there were areas she considered privileged. Margaret Thompson was one of them. "I'll clean up the rest," she said, going to her desk. "See you in the morning."

"Right," Anne said as she headed for the door. "First thing tomorrow we have that delegation of grandmothers. Their week or something like that; I'll have the facts on your desk in the morning. Good night."

Kathy wondered what Stephen Thompson was doing at the other end of the White House, if he had any idea of the sea of trivia she had to deal with every day. But of course he did, she reflected, thinking about the many sessions the President endured every single week as he was photographed—as even she was photographed—with deputations from all over the country, even the world, each group representing hundreds, thousands, even millions of fellow Americans pledged to one cause or another. It was an endless routine.

And that was it, the routine of it all, after more than three years as First Lady. Yes, there had been trips to Europe and one to Brazil, one to Bermuda. There was the excitement of being famous overnight, of being sought after, deferred to, and complimented; the endless parade of galas and banquets and receptions and interviews.

It was Clifford Hawley who had told her that meeting Thompson that very first time might lead to a valuable contact, one that could fulfill her ambitions to travel, to have a post overseas. Now she had begun to wonder what she might be doing after her days as First Lady ended. Most of all was the nagging question not of whether Clifford Hawley had used her to further his own ambition, but whether she, in turn, had taken advantage of Hawley's suggestion, one that had led to her own dilemma. The truth was that being First Lady had actually ended her goal of foreign service and had actually doomed her, ironically, to a life of wealth and prestige, and the increasing problems of an ailing husband, whether he was President or, eventually, ex-President.

☆ ☆ ☆

At that moment Clifford Hawley was standing in a corner of the blue-and-cream-colored White House gymnasium, carefully taping the sharp tip of an Italian-made épée. Hawley, trim, shorter than the other two men who stood on either side of him, said, "Lane, why don't one of you use the tipped foil over there in the case?"

The tallest of the three, Hawley's aide Lane Whitney, a red-headed, cheerful, gregarious man, opened the case and handed an épée to Harry Thompson, who was standing in place on the lined six-by-forty-foot fencing area. Thompson, one-time captain of the Princeton fencing team, eyed them both in his inscrutable way, his only response being to limber up by lunging at an imaginary adversary.

Whitney chuckled. "Great talker when the mood hits him." He turned back to Hawley. "Some day he's going to put his intercollegiate trophy up for grabs in a match with you, and if by some miracle he should win, he'll challenge you for your Olympic medal." He turned toward his opponent. "You ready, Harry?"

Thompson, his voice muffled by the mesh of his helmet, called out, "On guard!"

Both men lowered their weapons, the taped points aimed at each other's heads. For a moment they were in a frozen tableau, and then, just as Whitney prepared to move, Thompson lunged forward with a direct thrust, a move that surprised his opponent, though not enough to prevent him from warding off the blade.

Hawley's mind was far from the sharp clash of the blades and the nimble footwork both men displayed. It disturbed him that the President had, at the very last moment, cancelled his appearance at the match. The thought entered Hawley's mind, as he kept score of the touches made by both men, that this deliberate act was just another in a growing and irritating list of small events involving him.

As Hawley watched, he knew that the two fencers were unevenly matched. Harry had run up a four-to-one lead over Lane Whitney as they moved back and forth. The touching of their blades, the snap of sole and heel on the hard floor, the sharp intake of breath were the only sounds in the room. Whitney, hanging in tenaciously, decided to make a direct thrust, but Harry, parrying the attack, and following up with a series of fast lunges, scored the final touch.

Hawley slapped Whitney on the back and then strode over to pat the still-lunging Harry Thompson. "Good form, Harry, and clean hits."

Harry lifted his mask. "He got one on me. That alone proves I'm not ready for you yet, sir."

Hawley shook his head and said, "Harry, how many times do I have to tell you to can all that crap, the 'sir' business. We're alone." Then, taking another tack, he added, "I'm just sorry your father couldn't come down to watch you."

"I am too, but I appreciate your coming," he said, hesitating for a moment before adding, "Cliff."

The easy familiarity of the evening was something Hawley had long cultivated with Harry and Lane Whitney. It was simply good political sense to stay on close terms with two young men who had worked so hard with him to help elect H. Stephen Thompson some three years earlier.

Hawley had no problems with Whitney, but, as with the President, recently he'd sensed a withdrawal on the part of young Thompson, subtle but nonetheless visible to a discerning eye. Some of this he attributed to his earlier attention to Gloria, whom he'd barely known before the election. Hawley had dated Gloria only on occasion and even then basically as an escort, a role he quickly dropped when he finally came to realize how much she meant to Harry Thompson.

What Hawley didn't know was that in Harry Thompson's mind there was a growing resentment of Hawley, propelled by his own father into the Vice Presidency, and that—whether justified or not—Thompson had come to view Hawley as one who'd moved in on his private turf—Gloria Whitney. There were other reasons, but for that alone Hawley had to be brought down.

☆ ☆ ☆

Upstairs in his second-floor study, the President sat gloomily fingering a small key. For three weeks he had thrust it from time to time into the keyhole on the left side of the desk, and slowly opened the drawer, only to close it. Tonight it was different. He reached in with his left hand, and for a brief moment fingered the slender audiotape that lay inside. Abruptly, he dropped it as though it were a hot coal, slamming the drawer shut. From the moment he'd allowed Harry to play it—and then it had been played for only a few seconds–he'd regretted it. Then and even now, he felt sudden despair and fear surging through his body, coupled with anger, and worse, the insidious evil sting of jealousy.

He remembered how Harry had stood uncertainly before him, some weeks before, in this very room. "You remember," Harry had said, "how you wanted a personal tape system set up, not as elaborate as Nixon's back in those Watergate days—"

"Yes, I remember. Just something if I ever felt the need, the absolute necessity, of having an accurate report, a record, of some complicated discussion—that's what I asked for," Thompson had said. "In *this* room, when I might be alone, no witness, no secretary, only a phone message."

"Right. I put Jeb Rossmore on it."

"Jeb Rossmore?" the President repeated, eyebrows raised.

"Lieutenant Rossmore. Signal Corps. He checks out the system."

"I understand."

Harry shifted uneasily as he took a seat opposite his father.

"What's on your mind, Son?" the President asked.

"Well, it's just that when you and Kathy were in New York a month or so ago, I took the liberty of expanding the setup." Harry shrugged. "Just a bit."

"Meaning?"

Harry rose nervously from his chair. "It's just that you're not always in this room, Dad. You move about upstairs. I've seen you get calls in other rooms up here." He turned to face his father. "That's what it's all about."

Thompson crossed his arms and looked up at his son. "Secret taping, in other rooms, up here?" He shook his head with distaste at the very thought.

Harry pulled out a small pocket-size tape recorder and set it on the President's desk. "You came back from New York a day *after* Kathy, remember?"

"Go on."

A cunning smile crossed Harry's face as he reached down and switched the machine on. The President was startled upon hearing Kathy's voice. "But, of course you're free to call. Cliff, why in heaven's name would you give it a second thought?" And then he heard the voice of Clifford Hawley. "Only because I thought the President should never know that, in fact, you and I, before you—" Thompson's hand shot out and abruptly turned the machine off. The veins stood out at his temples and he turned on Harry, his eyes dark with anger. "I won't have it, Harry! Do you hear? I won't have it! I won't listen!"

Harry was startled by his father's vehemence. "Look," he said defensively, "it wasn't anything I expected. Rossmore was checking the system for *you*—"

"I don't want the system! You understand?!"

"You're not going to listen? Look, when you hear it—"

"I don't want to hear it and I don't want you telling me what you heard, is that clear?"

"Okay, okay, I only thought—"

"I know what you thought, Harry. What you're thinking. I want it undone, all of it, except for this room. My study. Clear?"

"Clear, but—"

"No buts."

Harry had left the room, not only shaken by his father's anger, but resentful at the thought that his plan had backfired. With great disdain the President had tossed the recorder and the cassette into his desk drawer.

Now, as Thompson slowly turned the key and checked the drawer to make certain it was locked, he again felt the flame of jealousy and the ugly suspicions it created. He knew there was something implicit, something of significance in Hawley's few words, something that indicated a relationship between Clifford Hawley and Kathy that had been kept secret by the two of them. The very thought repelled him. He admired Hawley, enjoyed his company. But now he sat hunched in his chair feeling a cloud of mistrust and doubt enveloping him. What exactly was it that Hawley felt the President shouldn't know?

3

Hornwell, on this occasion in uniform, felt himself squirm in his chair as Daniels lifted a file out of his worn leather briefcase and placed it on the table before him. It had the familiar insignia of an official medical report from the Bethesda Naval Hospital.

Only forty-eight hours ago Hornwell had accompanied the President to the hospital, reassuring him during the entire limousine ride that Bethesda provided an atmosphere as discreet and comfortable as it was efficient.

Hornwell relived the quiet dinner he had shared with the President and First Lady in the President's dining room on the second floor of the White House the day before Thompson entered the hospital.

"I have to be sure, Admiral. I don't want my health to be a matter of public debate," the President had said. "Not with the convention beginning to press down on all of us."

Hornwell had noted the slight slur in Thompson's speech. "Bethesda's the place, sir," he replied, his eyes admiring an elegant mahogany sideboard set against a wallpaper scene of Revolutionary-era Boston.

"The public must know eventually, but I want the initial results to be private. I want to study them first." Perspiration appeared on Thompson's forehead, and he dabbed at it with his napkin.

"Of course." Feeling uneasy, the Admiral looked down at his plate, then glanced up at the First Lady. Dressed in a black velvet suit and white satin shirtwaist, Kathy Thompson had sat quietly through most of the dinner, looking to Hornwell the epitome of grace and style. Hornwell had to acknowledge she'd grown in the years he'd known her, and while at first he'd been discomfited by Thompson's marriage to her, he'd quietly come to admire Kathy's intelligence and her affectionate attachment to the President.

Hornwell remembered the first Mrs. Thompson's steely manner, the speed and authority with which she spoke, and the dinners he'd attended at the Thompson estate in Kalorama, sometimes drawing her as his dinner companion. He remembered her unpleasant habit of chewing food, blowing smoke through her mouth and nostrils from an ever-present cigarette, and talking—all at the same time.

If Margaret Thompson, with her short, plump figure, tomboyish face, and clipped hairstyle, paled beside Kathy's classic beauty, her intellectual drive had been enough to attract and hold a younger, more impressionable, and less secure Stephen Thompson. No one ever doubted where Margaret Thompson stood on any issue; the strength of her convictions was always supported by a fiercely articulated logic and an astonishing range of knowledge. People always said she was the one who pushed Thompson on to his greatest achievements. It was the same unrelenting pressure she placed on their son, though some whispered that Harry had wound up as the confused, dour product of a domineering mother and an acquiescent father.

The President reached over to take his wife's left hand. "Kathy's had some reservations." Hornwell was surprised as he looked across at her.

"I'm concerned that Stephen does too much. You know the enormous energy he gives to everything. I sometimes worry—" She stopped abruptly, and turned toward her husband. "I can't tell you what to do, Stephen—the President is the only one who can decide." That, Hornwell, thought, would never have been Margaret Thompson's response.

"You see, she worries, Admiral," Thompson said, smiling broadly. "You and I aren't the youngest bulls in the arena, and yet, here *you* are, carrying on with your own heavy responsibilities, a tremendous load that would challenge a much younger man who might have every qualification for the job. Yet you continue to do it. Why?"

"Duty, Mr. President. Duty. Nothing more or less. Plain, simple duty."

"Well now, that's just about the way I see it in my own case. I can easily understand what made Roosevelt run again when he knew his health was shot, and others, too. It wasn't power or honors that drove them. It was just what you said—duty." He looked at Kathy and then back at the Admiral. "Duty. Kathy understands. Margaret would have, too."

Hornwell noted Kathy's slight flicker of annoyance. As he watched Thompson rest his head against the back of the chair, he detected no joy in the President's face or in his pronouncement, only a sense of resignation.

"Bethesda it is, Admiral. Why don't you arrange matters?" Thompson abruptly leaned in closer toward Hornwell. "Let's do it quietly. Meanwhile, I have no hesitation in telling you that I intend to seek a second term."

"I'm very glad to hear that, sir." Hornwell beamed his approval.

Thompson smiled again and fixed his eyes on him. "If you find the news useful. . ." he said, reaching out to touch Hornwell's arm. "You understand what I'm suggesting, Admiral?"

Hornwell hoped Thompson would say more, but the President rose, terminating the discussion.

Now, sitting with the Committee and its dozen carefully selected staff aides in its panelled room, the portraits of a half dozen Presidents looking down at him, Hornwell was distressed to think he was a participant, no matter how unwilling, in a breach of medical ethics. National security, he knew, was an old euphemism covering many sins. He would have to live with it.

Daniels' cigarette dangled from his lips as he spoke. "We've become increasingly aware that the President's health is slowly deteriorating. I think that the nearest comparison might be to Franklin D. Roosevelt. I know from my reading that those who were close to him were astonished at how he managed to carry on, because he was a *very* sick man. I've been told that there were times he left his guests absolutely bewildered by his inability to complete sentences. To me, that appears to suggest some signs of brain damage."

"That was President Roosevelt you were speaking of, not President Thompson," Hornwell said sharply.

Daniels slowly extinguished his cigarette. "But wouldn't you say, Admiral, that you've noted similar signs of debilitation in the President, some unusual fatigue, even an occasional mental lapse?"

Hornwell straightened himself in his chair. "The President is a good deal younger than I am, and I've never seen him when he wasn't in full command of his intellect. Completely composed. There is absolutely nothing remotely similar to Roosevelt's condition. That's a fact."

"You're not suggesting that you see no reason for concern, are you?" Daniels asked as he leaned back in his chair, with a glance at the others.

Hornwell was uncomfortable as he studied his colleagues. Though it pained him to admit it, he had indeed noticed a touch of slurring in the President's speech and an occasional aphasia, sometimes embarrassingly revealed by his inability to utter a simple word. The pasty coloring of the skin around his eyes was increasingly alarming. Hornwell had done his best to classify these symptoms as external products of presidential fatigue, because there had always been sufficient evidence that the President could summon his full powers when required.

"Mr. Chairman," Hornwell said, with a quiet deliberateness matching Daniels', "we should deal only with facts, not my opinions or yours. Hard, incontrovertible facts."

"Which is why we are gathered here, sir, isn't it?" A quick synthetic smile crossed Daniels' face. He removed his glasses from their leather case and carefully adjusted them for reading. "This report indicates the following: One: the President's blood circulation is slow, which points to potential failure of the circulatory system. Two: his vascular system is strained because of developing arteriosclerosis. Three: the blood vessels in his eyes reveal developing arteriovenous problems." He glanced up at Hornwell and said, "Fact: his heart is enlarged and one valve does not quite close properly. Fact: his blood pressure remains high." Daniels removed his glasses. "Gentlemen, my own medical sources tell me that a man of the President's age, sixty-nine, with heavy executive responsibility, may, possibly—mind you, only possibly—expire at almost any given moment, or may live for perhaps three, maybe four, years. Perhaps longer with proper medication."

Without further comment he passed the report across the table to Hornwell.

The Admiral neither looked at the papers nor touched them.

"I'd say you not only gave us some facts, but also added a great many conjectures. The President could die at any given moment, you say. So could you. So could I. So could any of us."

Peering over his round glasses, Jaggers broke the silence. "Isn't there a possibility for the President's rehabilitation through surgery?"

"You must remember the President had a triple bypass five years before taking office. With that record, I'm told that the pathology of the patient's arteriosclerosis is now realistically beyond further surgical repair," Daniels said.

"Well, then," Jaggers persisted, "he can be treated medically, can't he?"

Daniels lifted another paper. "This report shows that the President is taking digitalis. He's also receiving injections of Lasix to speed up the functions of lungs and heart." He paused for a moment as he searched the record. "Oh yes, here it is—he has another pill mentioned in the report which he takes regularly or when he senses extreme hypertension. And still another which I'm told he jokingly refers to as 'the bomb' since it's designed to prevent cerebral hemorrhage."

"Does he know all this?" Jaggers inquired.

"He's seen this report. I understand he instructed the doctors at Bethesda to do whatever they deemed proper to—as he put it—quote, 'hold me together,' unquote."

"I'm familiar with those words, Mr. Daniels," Hornwell interrupted. "The President was making a little joke when he entered the hospital. I was there. Everyone laughed—as they were meant to." He pushed himself away from the mahogany table and stood up. As he talked, he began to circle the room.

"Gentlemen, the President has this report. Let's remember that. And let's not forget something else—the President is first and foremost dedicated to duty. I've never known a finer man." Hornwell leaned on the table to direct his remarks to Daniels. "If he couldn't handle the job, he'd be the first to admit it. To find his like, we have to go all the way back to Eisenhower, who always placed his country first. Even ahead of family."

Daniels lit another cigarette. "I believe you want to remind us that Eisenhower ran for a second term after his heart attack. Am I correct?"

"You are, sir! And he survived that second term!"

"True, true, he did. And fortunately for the United States," Daniels replied softly, "we had a clear-cut strategic superiority over the Soviets in nuclear arms during his eight years." He glanced up at Hornwell. "Can we risk our security now when that kind of superiority no longer exists?"

In the quiet that followed, Hornwell resumed his seat, perching on the edge of his chair like an angry eagle ready to pounce on any of his four colleagues if he were further challenged. Anthony Clauson, the handsome white-haired Secretary of Defense, smiled before he spoke. "Gentlemen, the issue isn't about the President's patriotism. No one doubts it for a moment; we're unanimous on that score. The issue is simply presidential capacity." He turned toward Hornwell. "You asked for facts and the facts are before us. We should now come to a policy decision. Preferably a unanimous one." Looking toward Daniels, he said, "I'd like to know what the Director has to propose."

Daniels nodded. "Quite right, Mr. Secretary. Which brings us to the crux of the problem." He looked about the room, his gray eyes searching the faces of the others. "In doing our own duty we have to consider every contingency—ultimately perhaps, assuming, of course that the facts warrant it, even the possibility of the removal or the resignation of the President, wouldn't you agree?"

Hornwell frowned, his eyes fiercer than his voice. "Do you really think, Mr. Daniels," he said, softly, "that the President of the United States is voluntarily going to transfer his duties and powers—to a man like Hawley?" He pointed to the empty chair. "Hawley?" he said, repeating the name with a touch of contempt, as though such emphasis would underscore the absurdity of the thought.

"Mr. Hawley is Vice President of the United States, Admiral Hornwell. Elected by the people."

"I don't need to have it spelled out, Mr. Daniels," Hornwell said acerbically. "I'm quite familiar with the role he played in bringing about the President's election. He's a politician. Ambitious. Nothing wrong in that. But being a politician doesn't qualify him for the presidency. Maybe the President owed him the vice presidency. He doesn't owe him anything else."

"I wouldn't dismiss him so casually, either. The man has grown in his job," Clauson interjected. "I've seen it, listened to him in Cabinet meetings, read his speeches, which I understand he often writes himself."

"He could become President overnight, Admiral," Jaggers murmured. "We have the medical report before us."

Oliver Moran, whose government service dated back longer than that of anyone else at the table except Hornwell, spoke out for the first time. "I'd like to suggest that we forget our personal feelings. We all respect the President. We know that the Vice President has been kept informed on all sorts of matters of the most sensitive kind, and he's handled himself extremely well, I might add. Now fate could intervene and silence our arguments, or worse, complicate matters. If—God help us—the President were incapacitated, we would be in a most difficult, a critical position. The Soviets may still conceal their ailing leaders as soon as their infirmities are obvious, but our society just won't permit that kind of secrecy. We must have a fully functioning head of state. We may require his decision to implement Red Dye Day in the very near future. And in that area we will want quick authorization. In the meantime, I must confess it disturbs me that we have so many key vacancies from the Supreme Court to the military, even some sub-Cabinet posts that need filling—that must come from him. Patience has an end, gentlemen."

Hornwell sat quietly as the others murmured a general assent to Moran's comments. It then dawned on him that Thompson could be aware of this meeting, but whether by intuition or a leak from staff or even one of the others was immaterial. The President had taken Hornwell into his confidence about a second term, and Hornwell was suddenly certain that the President had, in fact, intended him to spread the news. The moment to do so, he realized, was at hand.

"Gentlemen," he said, "if I may have your attention. It may interest you to know that the President intends to have his name placed before the convention in some four months' time. He's going to run for a second term, and there's an end to your debate."

Jaggers instantly asked, "Are you certain of that?"

"The President told me so himself."

Suddenly the room erupted, each member of the Committee having something to say about Hornwell's news. Daniels rapped the table with the flat of his hand. "Let's settle down, gentlemen, and go to the Constitution. If Secretary Moran would read section four of the Twenty-fifth—the exact words of the first paragraph, if you please, sir?"

Oliver Moran's lips tightened. He didn't like being a member of a cabal that might at some future time be accused of usurpation of power. Even as he spoke, he wondered just what would actually happen if a President were legally removed from office against his will. Would force be used? Where would a President so removed be taken, and could he be prevented from seeking immediate redress?

Moran, looking at each of the others in turn, read in a low, solemn voice. "Section four of the Twenty-fifth Amendment to the Constitution states: 'Whenever the Vice President and a majority of either the principal officers of the executive departments or of such other body as Congress may by law provide, transmit to the President pro tempore of the Senate and the Speaker of the House of Representatives their written declaration that the President is unable to discharge the powers and duties of his office, the Vice President shall immediately assume the powers and duties of the office as Acting President.'" Moran looked up at the others. "That's it," he said.

Hornwell scoffed. "Does anyone in this room claim that the President is unable to discharge his duties?" He sat back, arms crossed over the rainbow of campaign ribbons blazing on the left side of his chest.

Daniels got to his feet slowly. "What Secretary Moran just read to us is the law, Admiral. And that law protects the President by providing legal means by which the President can once again resume his office if no inability exists."

"With the convention so close, if he wants to run, to challenge him would seem to be an unlikely event," Moran said softly, as though speaking to himself.

Daniels burrowed in. Looking closely at each man, he said, "If I may suggest a resolution—one not necessarily to be acted upon tonight, but kept in reserve, to be used only should circumstances arise that permit no other course—I would recommend that Admiral Hornwell, as the nation's number-one military leader, together with Secretary Jaggers, as the senior civil officer, be authorized to lay before the President the facts that could result in his stepping down." Daniels looked across the table at Hornwell. "Admiral?"

"You really think that, with a convention practically on top of us, and knowing the President intends to run, this group, with two key Cabinet officers in it, is going to do anything to precipitate a political crisis on the basis of one medical report?" Hornwell shook his head in disbelief. "We better think realistically."

"And what happens if he refuses to listen to any of us?" Clauson asked Daniels.

"If we are convinced of his inability to discharge his duties, we would have to call upon the Vice President and the Cabinet, all in strict accordance with section four of the Twenty-fifth Amendment, to initiate the action required of them under the Constitution. That, gentlemen, is *our* joint duty."

"In that event I can only say, God help our country." Hornwell picked up his cap and started out.

"Amen," Daniels said quietly as he shuffled his papers.

4

Chief Justice Everett Whitney stood before the dark stone fireplace, his handsome well-lined face solemn with internal strain. "I want to discuss Gloria with you, Lane."

"Okay." Lane Whitney swung his right leg over the side of a formal blue and gold tapestried wing chair in the Whitney drawing room.

"I want it stopped, Lane. Stopped! You understand?"

"Sure, I understand, but try telling that to Gloria."

"She's your sister."

"Sure. And she's your daughter."

"I know what she thinks of me, some stuffy old windbag who's spent his life splitting hairs in courtrooms. 'Old Marble Bust' she calls me. Well, she can mock me behind my back if she insists, but this drug business simply has to stop!"

Lane shrugged. "Look, I've talked to her. Jeff talked to her before he sailed."

The Chief Justice paced before the fireplace, then turned to his son. "Why? Why does she do it?"

"Maybe to get attention. Who knows?"

"She's beautiful. She's bright. I'm told she does an excellent job at the Smithsonian. What more does she need? She comes from a fine family. Why, her mother was—"

"She knows all that. Maybe it's him," Lane said, pointing to a photo of Harry Thompson and Gloria with the President. "She's never sure she has him."

"Is there another woman? Someone else? You ought to know, you work with him, you see him every day. Is that it?"

"No, I don't think so. In fact, I don't think I've ever seen him spend much time with anyone else—man *or* woman. Harry's a born loner. He can take it or leave it. Look, he likes her, I know that, but if he decides he's not going to be available, that's it. There's no persuading him. I think it bugs her, you want to know the truth. They're two strong-willed people. I'm afraid Gloria simply has to have her way. And so does Harry. That's not exactly a prescription for mutual anything."

"How old is he?"

"Same as me, twenty-eight. Maybe too preoccupied with one cause or another to get married. That's how I'd figure him."

"You know, he's never seemed like a *young* man to me," the older Whitney remarked.

Lane thought for a moment. "If you mean he doesn't care too much for small talk, you're right. Not unlike Jeff. All *he* wants to talk about is the Navy, Trident subs, accuracy of missiles. Now with Harry, you won't hear him talking about our new ball team, or about the NFL, or the new movies or TV shows, and you sure won't hear him talking about the hottest new group or singer—none of that for him. He's into the gold standard, Indian affairs, the FCC, the Federal Reserve system, veterans' rights—causes. Takes after his mother, from everything I've heard. Causes. You name it, he's in it."

The Chief Justice frowned. "Then what *do* the two of them talk about?"

"Fucking." The voice was a mocking drawl.

The two men gaped at each other, their eyes turning toward the other end of the room. They could see a small hand waving at them above the back of a brown leather chair. Gloria.

Everett Whitney drew himself up, half in shock and half in anger. "Your sitting there eavesdropping is highly improper, to say the least."

"And your talking about me behind my back is highly proper?" She jumped up and turned around to face them.

"Oh, come off it, Gloria," Lane said. "You know we're concerned about you."

"For my own good, right? I was asleep, if you want to know

the truth. I came in here to read, got tired, turned off the desk lamp, and just fell asleep, only to wake up and hear the two of you psychoanalyzing me and Harry. If you really want to know about us, just ask me." She started to walk toward them. "Who would know better?"

The Chief Justice put out a hand to stop her. "It worries me to see you unhappy, Gloria. That's all it is, nothing more. I want to help you."

"Really?" she said, pulling away. "You want to help me? Aren't you a little late? We hardly know each other, Daddy. We really ought to be introduced. All my life I've been away at school. If it wasn't Knox it was Foxcroft, if it wasn't Foxcroft it was Bryn Mawr. And where were you while I was camping out? In some law office, that's where, being a district attorney. Being an attorney general—was it New Jersey? Ohio? I forget. In court. Then on *the* court. We've never been together, not really." She began to laugh. "You know? I don't talk like you, I don't think like you, I don't even look like you. I *know* I'm my mother's daughter. But are *you* really my father?"

Once again the old man put out a hand to restrain her. "Gloria, I won't let you provoke me, no matter what you say. You not only know I'm your father, but you also know my concern is very real. So is Lane's. And Jeff's. There are important matters to talk over—"

"Oh? About how many pills I take? And when? What color? You mean big things like that?"

"Gloria, 'ridicule dishonors more than dishonor.'"

"Oh, Daddy, you and your quotations. Don't you ever have an original idea? Don't you get tired living your whole life on other men's ideas and all those damned precedents?" She turned and walked quickly to the door. "Oh, yes, in case you're curious, I'm going to the White House as Harry's guest to watch the press conference at eight o'clock. And afterward?" She smiled and rattled on. "You know how Harry's always complaining about headaches? No, Daddy, you wouldn't. Anyway Lane knows. So, if I can get Harry to take me upstairs into the Lincoln Room, I plan to push him down on the bed, grab his you-know-what, and wait for the ghost to appear and applaud Harry's cure from his headache. If you get the picture? No, you wouldn't." And with that she was gone.

The Chief Justice began to pace again across the room. He stopped momentarily and pointed to the doorway through which Gloria had just vanished. "That's her response. While I've tried to give her the best advice I'm capable of."

"Maybe what she really needs is something else, Dad."

"Like what?"

Lane sat silent for a few moments. "Well?" his father persisted.

"I'm not sure."

The Chief Justice pressed him. "Say it. Say whatever's on your mind."

"You won't like it."

"Try me."

"Love, maybe?"

The older man slumped into a chair. "Love?" he whispered.

"Love," Lane repeated. "Not advice, just plain old-fashioned fatherly love."

☆ ☆ ☆

Only four days had passed since the President's dinner with Hornwell, and only two since he'd studied the medical report. He had yet to discuss with his doctors and staff how and when the report would be made public. Now, as he willed himself to stride briskly along the main corridor toward the press corps gathered in the East Room, he concentrated on the image he wanted to project—a President up on the issues, alert, in complete control. Kathy had selected the suit he was wearing, a charcoal gray with a soft pinstripe, and a deep maroon tie. He had allowed her to dab some very light makeup on his cheeks, just enough to conceal his pallor. Every President had allowed himself to be made up for TV since Nixon's disaster with his famous five o'clock shadow in the debates of 1960. Nobody questioned makeup anymore. And Reagan had established image to be as much a part of governing as substance.

As he reached the podium, he took in a deep breath, straightened his shoulders, looked about the imposing room, smiled, and acknowledged the reporters standing before him. He waved them down and took a folded sheet of paper from his inner pocket. "I have a statement to read. If it catches anyone here off guard, I'll be the one surprised." A murmur rose throughout the room. Thompson took his time. "Any reason not to create a little suspense?" he asked with a chuckle.

Thompson looked straight ahead, prepared to direct his remarks to the television camera. He'd become a pro at the game of communicating; he knew where the real audience was: the people of America, tuned in. This was prime time, his audience in the millions, and he would make each and every one of them aware that they were conversing, person to person, with the President of the United States. He knew, from observation and practice, how to make intimate eyeball-to-eyeball contact. And he had discovered that, like Reagan, he had a quality in his voice that cast a spell upon his listeners and viewers.

"Good evening," he said. "I'm talking to each one of you, you in this room, of course, but also to you seated before your TV sets, my friends in Philadelphia, in Boston, Anniston, in the privacy of your own homes, on your farms in Iowa and Kansas, elsewhere, and to some working late—in your offices in New York, Chicago, Dallas—or about to work late in Los Angeles or Seattle.

"The reporters in this room will give you their impressions and their opinions—but through the magic of television you can form your *own* opinion, and your *own* impression. Right now, at this very moment, I stand before you, very much alive as you can see, and despite some impressions given by the opposition, very much aware of what you and I have accomplished during this first term. We need more time, you and I, to complete the job. I'm thinking of all we're going to do together—during the *next* years." He waited as the announcement sank in on the assembled reporters.

"Well, there it is—the worst-kept secret of the past month or so—but we have to let it out, so the reporters here can do their job of letting you know what you already now know straight from the horse's mouth."

The President smiled as the reporters jostled for attention. "I'll take your questions. Mr. Kelly?"

The ascetic Associated Press reporter stood up and asked, "Mr. President, will it be the same ticket, you and Vice President Hawley?"

Hawley, his jaws suddenly tightening as he sat in his home, alone, before a television set, waited for Thompson's reply.

The President smiled, remembering that Henry Kraus, his Chief of Staff, during the rehearsal and briefing for the press conference, had predicted that this would be the very first question thrown at him. "It could very well be," he said in measured tones. "The Vice President and I haven't discussed the matter." He turned to take another question, but Kelly went on. "Does that mean that if the Vice President decides he wants to run again—let me put it this way, Mr. President: aren't you the one who'll decide on your running mate? And if not Mr. Hawley, then who?"

Thompson smiled easily. "It's a mutual matter, Mr. Kelly. The vice presidency may not be the only challenge Mr. Hawley wants to meet."

Hawley tensed as he leaned in closer to study the President's face on his television screen.

Kelly persisted with his questioning, pointing a finger toward Thompson. "That sounds like a negative blessing to me. Are you hinting, maybe, that those off-the-record remarks Mr. Hawley reportedly made a couple months back—after that interview with the four major networks when he seemed to stray from the Administration line on the Soviets—is that giving you second thoughts?"

Thompson smiled again, well prepared for the question. "Not at all. The Vice President has many official avenues through which he can offer advice and counsel to the Administration—Cabinet meetings, occasional luncheons with the President, and so forth. He has many interests, many opinions. The vice presidency is only one option open to Mr. Hawley. As you know, there are other important areas with policy-making functions that might be interesting, too—in the Cabinet, for example. All of that will be under careful review within the party."

"But you'll make the final decision."

Thompson nodded. "Yes, I'll make the final decision." He turned to the matronly reporter from U.P.I. "Cynthia?"

Hawley felt a flush of anger and disappointment. Thompson's statement was now out, the first real intimation that he might very well *not* be on the ticket.

Cynthia Rodriguez, the oldest female member of the White House press corps, spoke. "Mr. President, I'd like to follow up on Mr. Kelly's questions. There's a story going around that while you may meet officially, at Cabinet meetings and so on, you've banned the Vice President from the Oval Office, that you wrote a specific memo on the subject. Is that true?"

Thompson shook his head. "I'll be glad to put that rumor to rest," he said. "No, the Vice President has not been banned. Not at all. That would be absurd and improper, for I have a very high regard for him. No, I simply had to insist that the practice of casually walking in on the President be terminated. This applies to everyone. To Mr. Kraus, for example, to the

Counsel to the President, to members of the Cabinet. There's just one exception." He took off his reading glasses. "Mrs. Thompson. I wouldn't ban her if I wanted to. I couldn't ban her if I tried. You see, I recognize real power." There was a ripple of amusement from the press corps.

Thompson turned to another reporter, and glancing down at a chart on the lectern he reminded himself of the name—Rob Kottner, White House correspondent of ABC Television. "Yes, Rob?"

"We understand that you went to Bethesda this past week. I have two questions. First, are you satisfied with your physical exam? And second, when will the results be made public?"

Thompson stretched out his arms. "The doctors at Bethesda will release their findings soon, I'm sure. But judge for yourself, Rob. I feel fine, fit as a fiddle."

☆ ☆ ☆

Hawley flipped off his television set and walked out to the broad porch of the vice presidential home, feeling the need for fresh air.

The memory of the interview to which Kelly had referred was painful for him. One of the four major network anchors had violated his pledge and passed on Hawley's off-the-record remarks to Henry Kraus, the President's Chief of Staff. Kraus had made a call to his office the very next morning leaving a message suggesting that when it was convenient he would like a moment or two of his time.

Hawley had made it a point to go to the White House to visit Kraus at once. Kraus, framed in his doorway entrance, rubbing his hands together in the oily manner familiar to all who knew him, obsequiously pointed to one of two large leather chairs facing a fireplace. "Please," he said as he waited for Hawley to be seated.

"Mr. Vice President," he began as he took his own seat, stroking his bald pate, "not every one of the four network anchors is your friend."

"Oh?" Hawley responded, trained for any surprise the political world might spring as he remained comfortably seated in a corner of his chair.

"Not your friend," Kraus repeated.

"I take it, though, he may be *your* friend?" Hawley shot back.

"I don't know that any of them is anyone's friend, really," Kraus countered smoothly. "They act like it, of course, but they're always after a story."

"But in this case, I take it, in giving one?" Hawley pressed on.

"Yes."

"Talking about some of the off-the-record remarks I indulged in, all the time thinking all four *were* my friends?"

Kraus shrugged. "I've had to advise the President."

Hawley remained quiet for a moment. "Because the press has it as well?"

"Yes. That left me no alternative," Kraus said. "Now mind you, it didn't come from any one of the four directly."

"How do you know that?" Hawley abruptly asked.

"I have my contacts," Kraus said with a stone face. Hawley concluded that Kraus, no Hawley fan, had himself planted the story.

"I'm sorry that I can't tell you just how it came to me. Frankly, I don't know which one is responsible and I really don't care—that's not to say *you* shouldn't—but to me they're all simply one thing, conduits." Kraus grinned. "But of course, naturally, we like them to be conduits for *our* viewpoint, the Administration's. Now, when they get a different view from, of all people, the Vice President, well. . ." Kraus stopped.

"I take it you're particularly referring to some remarks about the Soviet Union," Hawley volunteered.

"Yes, and how you wanted things to move more quickly, that if we don't, much of the good that's been part of the Gorbachev perestroika legacy will finally melt away. In short, that the President continues to deal from two positions—conciliatory to a degree, a modest degree, but that essentially he believes there's still a strong Stalinist core that might very well move in at the opportune moment. These are patient fellows, and time *may* be on their side."

Hawley looked across at the cold fireplace and then at Kraus. "It is, Henry. Time *is* on the side of the Stalinists, particularly if we don't do in economics what we've already been doing in this Administration and the previous ones, dating back to Reagan and Bush, mainly in the military and political spheres. What we've needed for some time is a new Marshall Plan, not only for Eastern Europe and the Baltic states, but, even more important, for the Soviet Union itself. We need it, Henry, to create and protect a new stability in Europe. Remember, Khrushchev promised to bury *us*. The Stalinists talk of burying Turgenev. I keep asking, how long will we play games while the greatest opportunity the West has had in generations finally slips away?"

"Don't you think the President—our party—don't you think that they—and you're part of it as well—have a clear-cut policy on how best to develop the right relationship with the Soviets? And don't you think President Thompson understands that while we continue to probe Soviet intentions we never forget their military capabilities?"

"Henry, I thought when I spoke off the cuff, to four seasoned responsible newsmen, that I was indulging in a few quiet moments of enjoying something called the First Amendment."

"Freedom of speech?" Kraus murmured, a thin smile crossing his face. "That's something you surrendered when you became Vice President."

The story had broken and Hawley had had to issue a statement that affirmed his support of the President's policies. Everything had been done to contain the damage.

"That's if it *is* damage," wily Richard Daniels confided to Hawley a few days later on a late-evening visit to the Vice President's home. "What this does is set you apart from some of your predecessors. It shows the public that you're not one of those smiling zombies who simply parrots what another man says and never has an idea of his own. Mr. Vice President, to the average guy on the street, this shows that you've got guts. You saw the letters to the editor in the *Post*, the *Times*. They're all complimentary. Hell's bells, it isn't so much what you said, it's just that you had the gumption to say something, and the network hotshot who spilled the beans of what was supposed to be confidential—this has hurt all of *them*. And Kraus? He's never been out front as one of your supporters. You wait and see: it's going to be a lot easier for you to deal with him and them in the future."

"If I have a future," Hawley said glumly.

"You have a future, Mr. Vice President," Daniels replied as he lit a cigarette. "You've been making it by listening a lot, doing your homework, having some of the top think-tank boys counsel you on the big issues—arms control, the environment, trading policies, you name it. Everyone knows you're not just attending funerals and going to South American inaugurals like other Vice Presidents. The future?" Daniels exhaled a smoke ring. "You're in it, today."

☆ ☆ ☆

Hornwell entered the White House at ground level under the South Portico, a military aide escorting him to an elevator that brought him to the President's private quarters. He stood at the entrance to the President's study, pausing for a moment. It had been three weeks since he'd dined with the President and only one week since the last meeting of the Committee.

As Hornwell entered the Yellow Oval Room, he observed Thompson seated behind the ornate oaken desk built from old timbers taken from a British ship and presented to the White House over a hundred years before by Queen Victoria. He was conscious of the determined glare Thompson fixed upon him, the gauntness of his face, even the rigidity of his posture as he sat at the desk. The President greeted Hornwell by simply waving him to a chair. Then, fixing his cold blue eyes on him, their color intensified by the oyster-white pallor of his skin, Thompson broke the silence. "The Twenty-fifth Amendment," he said.

Hornwell felt his heart leap as Thompson repeated the phrase, a twisted smile breaking on Thompson's face. His eyes were rheumy but alert, his voice firm and sonorous. "You know, as a student I loved physiology. I studied the brain, how it's constructed, how it functions, so I should know something of human nature."

The Admiral had no idea how to reply beyond a cursory sign of agreement. "Of course," he said.

The President's voice fell to a confidential level. "The Committee would be derelict if it didn't review the subject of the President's health from time to time." There was a sly twinkle in the President's eyes. "But I don't think anyone has to worry about my brain, Admiral."

As the President leaned back in his chair, Hornwell wondered once again whether any member of the Committee, or a member of the staff, could have broken its seal of silence. "You're aware," Thompson said, interrupting Hornwell's reverie, "that we'll soon be in an election. Things keep crowding in on us. No respite for any of us. So I've decided to take an occasional trip out of the capital. After I visit our missile control center, I think a speech in Omaha might be in order. Perhaps a visit to the National Weapons Lab as well. I plan to talk on the balance of power."

"Very good, sir," Hornwell replied. He watched the President place his hands on his desk top and raise himself. His movements were slow, deliberate.

When he was standing erect, Thompson threw back his shoulders. "I was with Nitze many years ago," he continued, "at the initial dialogue with the Soviets, the Strategic Arms Talks. Helsinki, not exactly the worst place in the world, despite the peculiar sound of its name." The President chuckled as he went on.

"The Soviets took nothing for granted. They never do, of course. Listening devices popped up everywhere. Of course we found them. I think they wanted us to find them so that we might get careless and ignore the more sophisticated equipment that had been built right into the rooms we occupied. I described all of this to Ambassador Curtis before she left for Geneva. She's got all the right stuff for her mission."

"Plus the patience to match theirs *and* the richest experience needed for the job," Hornwell said.

"You know, it was my late wife who introduced her to me, more than twenty years ago. Alice Curtis was already working on arms control for one of those brainy institutes, this one with some university, I think. Maybe Harvard. Anyway, Margaret thought we should know each other. Very astute, both of them. Mrs. Curtis is a good listener. Before taking the assignment in Geneva, she first insisted on meeting with all of her predecessors, going back to Max Kampelman, Reagan's man."

"And being fluent in their language, a very special asset," Hornwell volunteered.

"Enormous. The Soviets. Clever people. Wily. I remember I was impressed by their skill in using the vaguest of language to make limits on their side rather imprecise, while they demanded very sharp definitions, very specific terms to set limits on our side. As you point out, Mrs. Curtis's command of their language helps our whole team." Abruptly the President stopped speaking and slumped back into his chair. "I get a bit run down, something like a clock—" he smiled up at his visitor, "but a clock can be rewound. I'm in the process of doing that, rewinding. The trip to Nebraska will do me good. I'd like you to accompany me. Can you?"

"Of course, Mr. President." Hornwell hesitated for a moment, then added, as diplomatically as he could, "That kind of trip could be strenuous, Mr. President."

"I've no concern about that, Admiral. 'It's a young man's world,' some people are fond of saying, but together we'll show them, won't we?" With some effort the President stood up again, smiling, and extended his hand toward Hornwell.

"We will, sir," the Admiral said, admiring the presidential show of grit. "We need you, sir."

The President nodded. "Thank you, Admiral."

As Hornwell passed through the doorway, impressed by the President's mental acumen, he was for the first time more than concerned about his physical capacity to lead the nation for another four years. But there was hope. If Thompson could be held together for just another seven or eight months—until the election was over—there could be an alternative to Hawley, a new Vice President standing in the wings.

☆ ☆ ☆

Kathy Thompson pulled her burgundy velvet robe tightly about her. She stood at the bedroom window looking over the White House grounds toward the Washington Monument, most of which was enshrouded in fog. She stepped out of a new side door that led to the South Portico balcony, indifferent to the dampness of the night air, the sonorous breathing of the President following her and tormenting her.

She leaned against the wall, caught between conflicting emotions—her loyalty to the man she'd married, and her reluctant recognition that that loyalty was all but devoid of the affection she'd once felt. She was frequently unsettled now by frustration, self-pity, sometimes anger. Thompson's occasional references to Margaret especially nettled her.

It had been different at the start. She'd met Thompson when he was a candidate for his party's nomination, and she'd married him after a whirlwind courtship just before he assumed the presidency.

Having listened carefully to the press conference, she wondered now about his real attitude toward Hawley. Her thoughts went back to that first time she'd met Hawley at the Hay-Adams—long before Stephen Thompson had appeared on the scene.

She had actually sought the first favor when she'd learned of an opening for an interviewer at the Washington outlet of the Federal Broadcasting Company. She'd remembered Hawley's remark about Joseph Gratton, head of the network.

Hawley had taken her call in his House office, delighted to

hear from the pretty young journalist. "Do I remember our meeting, Miss Bryson—Kathy? Are you serious?"

"I'm always serious."

"I remember that, too. I know you're not calling about dinner—are you?" he asked, stretching his legs under his desk.

"I'm calling about Joe Gratton."

"Oh," Hawley said, sounding disappointed.

"You said you knew him."

"Yes, I do, I know him very well. As a matter of fact," Hawley added, "he's in town."

"Yes, I know. I'd like to meet him."

"Consider it done."

"Just like that?"

"Meeting him is easy. Do I get to know the rest?" he asked.

"The TV station here is looking for an interviewer."

"And you want the job?"

"Yes, I'd love it."

"I'll call him. You free tonight? Cocktails? Dinner?"

After a brief pause she said, "If you'd like, I can do cocktails."

"That's all I get for this service? A cocktail date?"

"And a rain check, if you want it?"

"That's a deal. Gratton has a weakness for a pretty face—" He sensed her reaction by the long pause. "Hello? You there?"

"Cliff," she said in a measured tone, "I want him to know that I can do the job. I know everyone—"

"Save the pitch for him, Kathy. I'm already sold. Let's say Aux Beauchamps at five unless you hear from me. Where can I reach you?"

"I'm doing an assignment at the *Post* this afternoon."

She remembered the meeting, finding the two men seated in a quiet corner, almost hidden by the greenery, some distance from the room's piano player. Even as she shook hands she hadn't liked Gratton—his puffy face, the dampness of his pudgy fingers. And she was annoyed by the insinuation that if he hired her (as he was obviously inclined to), they'd be seeing each other often. The interview had gone too smoothly for comfort.

"Don't you want to give me a test or something, Mr. Gratton?"

Gratton smiled as he jabbed a finger into Hawley's side and winked at her. "Cliff Hawley vouches for you, that's all the test you need."

"I don't want the job as any special favor," she said coolly. "I want to know that it's my professional qualifications that entitle me to consideration—"

"Hold it!" Gratton said, bristling, his smile vanishing. "You've *been* evaluated. The moment Mr. Hawley asked me to this meeting and mentioned your name, I had our people do a quick check on you around this town. We know the publishers, the bureau chiefs, the editors of the papers and magazines. We know the Hill, both sides of the aisle. No one goes on our Washington station without being persona grata. Very. I run the company, lady. I got there, first, by running the news operation, and second, by having a sixth sense about talent. Our top people, our on-the-air people, are every bit as good as the Diane Sawyers the other fellows have. Better, in fact. I've studied your face all this time. Your lips are straight. That's good because any little twist gets distorted on camera. You have good teeth. I look at everything, see? Hair, hands, fingers, nails. I hear your *pro*-nunciation and your *e*-nunciation. You have journalistic qualifications. I know my business, Miss Bryson. I don't do special favors for my very best friends. What I do is give 'em a chance to do *me* a favor. You've been tested—right here. That's why you got the job. Clear?"

"Clear," she said, "and thank you. Thank you both."

Nevertheless, her initial impression of Joe Gratton had been right. She didn't like him. Fortunately, she rarely saw him because he was in New York for the most part, turning up occasionally in the capital to testify at a congressional hearing or to attend a White House reception with his counterparts from the three senior networks. He knew the city well, having been a political columnist years before he'd entered the television field.

If Gratton was recognized by his peers for his political astuteness, he was also famous for his ability to consume inordinate amounts of gin and vodka—and that consumption began the moment he entered his office in the morning. At one of the White House press conferences she'd been asked to cover because of the absence of the regular network correspondent, Kathy had been surprised to find herself accosted by him. "Just in town for the day, Kathy," Gratton said. "Busman's holiday," he added, the aroma of gin on him as he took her arm. "My car's outside."

"Thank you, but I really like to walk when I get the chance."

"Today you ride," he said as his grip tightened and he led

her out through the crowded White House corridors. "Dropped in to see you at work; heard you were pinch-hitting for Costigan." He reached across the seat of the limousine and squeezed her hand. "You're better than she is. Okay?"

"Thank you Mr. Gratton."

She felt the firm squeeze again, caught the appraising look in his eyes as he released his hold. They rode along in silence, north on Connecticut Avenue, until the car swung into the driveway of Federal's new Washington office. "Giving you a reward for a job well done. Trip to the Coast. Vacation really. We're doing a special on the new Hollywood. All you have to do is interview a couple of upcoming stars. Keep up the good work." He pushed open the door of the limousine. As she stepped in front of him, putting her right foot out of the car, he patted her buttocks in a familiar manner. "Go see Matt Waters. He'll brief you and take care of your ticket, hotel, the rest. Good flight." Kathy stood on the sidewalk uncertain of herself. Gratton reached out to close the door. "Nice knowing you're real, Kathy." He slammed it shut and the car pulled out. She was angry at herself, but it had all happened so quickly and so matter-of-factly that she decided her ignoring his advance was the most appropriate response.

Two days later she discovered how wrong she had been when she was summoned to a fourth-floor suite in the Beverly Hills Hotel, where Joe Gratton was entertaining a handful of Hollywood celebrities. "That's television, Kathy, at the top. One week you're asking the President of the United States a question on war and peace, and the next week you're trying to find out which of the pretty little starlets the new Romeo over there"—he pointed to a well-known Hollywood star—"is sleeping with." He glanced about. "Knowing that son of a bitch's talent, I'd say he's probably made the room." Gratton squeezed her arm and winked, then added, "The bastard does have equipment, that I gotta admit. Saw him once after golf, in the showers at the Bel-Air Country Club." Gratton gave her a sly, sidelong look and tapped his glass against hers.

Kathy stepped back. "Mr. Gratton, if you don't mind, I'd much prefer—"

"But I do mind," he said, cutting in sharply. "Look here, Miss—"

"I think I'd like to leave," she said, turning away.

Gratton seized her arm. "You're staying, Miss Bryson, okay? You may not know it, but you're something like the hostess for this little party. For starters, I want you to mix with those two in the corner. Fags. But two of our top producers. And you get your chance to interview Romeo tomorrow for the show and what you do with him after is your business. Tonight, though, tonight, you're *my* business. Understand?"

"No, I'm afraid I don't," she said icily.

A waitress stopped by with a platter of hors d'oeuvres. Gratton fingered half a dozen, then took up two of them. "Let me spell it out. You got some silly idea you're going to be raped four flights up in the Beverly Hills Hotel, forget it. You must be the kind that thinks every man taking a quick feel means he's gonna try and push all the way up between your legs, right? Forget it. I like to drink. I like to know I'm with a woman. That's it, period. I'm not stupid, Miss Bryson."

"You're trying to take advantage of your position, Mr. Gratton. I'm an employee—"

"Fuck off, Miss Bryson. I know all about women's rights and sexual harassment. When you're harassed—by me—you'll know it. Consider your drawers a chastity belt." He flipped a hand across her shoulder. "You always act like someone out there's got the special key to your belt." Kathy felt herself flush. "I don't put my key into another man's safe, if you don't mind my mixing my metaphors. Okay?" He tightened his grip. "Now, let's you and I circulate among the guests."

5

From the first night of her marriage Kathy realized there was something missing in the equation, something she didn't want to acknowledge.

Kathy was thirty-three, less than half Thompson's age, when she'd slipped into the marriage. She had to admit an intense satisfaction in being the object of a President's ardent pursuit. What she did not admit, at first, was that the man who had most interested her had simply let her drift away. Clifford Hawley had introduced her to Stephen Thompson, and then, for reasons of his own, had stepped aside. Each had gotten something extraordinary out of that one television interview. She was First Lady; he, Vice President.

Overall, she had made the transition into working in television with ease, her skill at interviewing for magazines successfully transposed into conducting television interviews of Washington personalities, from members of the Cabinet to congressmen, from ambassadors to military leaders, men and women from the various federal agencies, visitors from overseas. She had first met H. Stephen Thompson while conducting such an interview.

"A small favor," Hawley had asked as they sat in a dark corner of an out-of-the-way little restaurant in Alexandria.

"There's a man could be important. To me, to you, maybe to America."

"Sounds very big-league," she had said, sipping her Tom Collins. "Is he the reason I haven't been seeing you so much, plus your sudden breaking off our dates in favor of college seminars, public-affairs symposia, your endless researching on this issue and that? Are you cutting down on *me* to keep up with *him*?"

"He's a challenge, that's for sure. Not a household name, yet. But he could be another Wendell Willkie—you remember from your history books, the businessman who tried to block FDR from a third term? Ever hear of Universal Corporate Investments?"

"Everyone's heard of H. Stephen Thompson, Cliff. Richer than Midas, isn't he?"

"Let's say very rich."

"I know he lives in one of the few private homes in Kalorama that haven't been transformed into an embassy. Very private. Top pedigree."

"He could be another Willkie. I'd like you to go out there, interview him. I cleared this with Joe Gratton."

"What's in it for you?"

"A piece of his coattail. Three or four of us think he's got big potential, including our mutual friend, Ed Jaggers." He raised a hand and began ticking off his fingers. "Industrialist. Financier. Lawyer. Public service. Worked for two Presidents. The U.N. Also for Congress. This man has all the right credentials. If it all fits, I could be tagging along. That's because I was in there second, thanks to Ed. Right behind him. He gave me the scent."

"What's in it for me? Besides an interview and a personal visit to one of those mysterious old mansions?"

"You never know. He could be Lochinvar."

"Meaning?"

"He's a widower—no youngster, but still a very attractive man. I've told him about you. He doesn't watch much television, so he hasn't the foggiest notion about how you talk and look. He's all alone, with one child, a son about twenty-five. And in that great stone bastion he says was built to last five hundred years, he begins to tell me how lonely he is—"

"With all his millions."

"It's the truth."

"You were saying something about Lochinvar?"

Hawley smiled. "That could be Thompson."

"All this from an interview for Federal Broadcasting? That's quite a scenario, Cliff."

"I have my instincts, Kathy. The man has formidable assets, not just money."

"Cliff, you want me to interview H. Stephen Thompson, I interview H. Stephen Thompson. I never forget a favor."

"I knew I could count on you, Kathy. I remember you once said—I believe it was at our first meeting—you wanted the feeling of power, maybe something in the foreign service, a career where you could travel. Am I right?"

"Until I was ready to settle down, yes."

"Thompson's got as much clout as anyone. He's done a fair number of confidential missions for the last two Administrations. Handle him right, Kathy, and you ought to be able to name your own embassy, wherever you'd like to work—Europe, the Orient, South America, wherever."

"And while I'm doing all of this travelling, where will you be?" she replied, appraising him.

Hawley reached over and took her hand. "I don't know. Part of his campaign staff, for sure, but the rest. . ." he shrugged, uncertain as to whether he should voice his real goal. Kathy's quick acquiescence made it unnecessary.

"If I can help, Cliff. . ."

"You are helping. This interview can be very important—to Thompson, to me, to you. I know it, Kathy."

"We'll find out," she said, withdrawing her hand, "and we'll leave everything else to kismet."

"Kismet," Hawley repeated, frowning. He sat quietly for a moment. "Something tells me I may be doing Mr. Thompson a favor—at my expense."

The following week Kathy drove up to Thompson's mansion, a turn-of-the-century French château, set on a bright green lawn bounded by high retaining walls and sealed off from the street by an imposing iron gate with black stanchions topped by gilt ornaments. Having gained admittance, she walked across the Belgian-cobblestone driveway.

She was led into a dim drawing room, with French windows overlooking a small formal garden with a charming green and white latticed gazebo at the end, set against a backdrop of oak trees.

Thompson, wearing a well-tailored blue business suit, walked in briskly, apologizing for not having answered the door himself, courtly and attentive to everything Kathy said, apparently interested in her authoritative handling of the camera crew, and her recital of the ground rules for the interview.

"Are there any areas of the house that are off-limits? Any kinds of questions you'd rather not answer?" she asked in her crisp manner. She lifted a notebook from her oversize bag. "I've done my homework on you, Mr. Thompson. With some background help from our mutual friend, Cliff Hawley."

"Well, I'm impressed. No, the house is open to you, any part of it. And no, there are no restrictions on the interview. And I'm grateful for Mr. Hawley's interest. Bright young man."

Thus began their first meeting, and two hours later, the camera crew having been dismissed, Kathy was on a first-name basis with H. Stephen Thompson. It was his suggestion. "Not really my first name, Kathy. No one wants to be called Hilary. Stephen. Steve."

"You look more like a Stephen to me," she said.

"Do I now?" was his pleased rejoinder. "I rather like that, though my late wife used to call me Steve."

"I've kept you far too long." She started to assemble her notes.

"Not at all, not at all. To tell you the truth, I'm sorry it's over. I've enjoyed it. Please thank Mr. Hawley if you see him before I do."

Kathy glanced at him, sensing his honesty and his genuine shyness, certain he was trying to find a way to prolong this first meeting.

"I don't suppose," he began, hesitantly, "no, that would be presumptuous. I've already taken up a great deal of your time—"

Touched by his old-fashioned gallantry, she had moved easily through the large house. Thompson had been attentive to her comfort—the right chair in the right light for her note taking, pointing out a prized painting or an antique table that might interest her. His courtesy and the unobtrusive sense he gave of being in command pleased her. "You're not presumptuous, Stephen. I doubt that you could be. . ."

"Dinner," he said, quickly, "tonight. If you're free." His raised eyebrows suggested anxiety, surprising in a man of such influence.

"I'd love it and I *am* free." She would have to call Hawley to postpone the hour of their meeting, but she was sure he'd be pleased at the success of the interview. And, she had to admit, she wanted to see Thompson away from the security of his Kalorama setting. "But I must go home to change," she said.

"You know the Cosmos Club? Would that be all right?"

She smiled inwardly at being invited to that staid old landmark whose members had once so vocally opposed the membership of women. "I'll meet you there, shall we say, at eight?"

"Perfect," Thompson replied. "I could come for you—send a car for you—"

"No, thank you. Let's meet there."

When she arrived, wearing a black velvet Chanel suit, he was standing in the spacious foyer and she noticed that he, too, had changed clothes. In the dining room, they picked up their conversation as though there had been no interruption, and she was surprised to hear him explain how he'd placed the bulk of his fortune in a foundation he had established, a fact to which he'd made no reference in the interview. "I don't really know why I'm telling you this, Kathy, but there I've done it. I wanted to see what benefits might flow from one man to science and the arts. And I'm happy to say my son, Harry, was all for it. Quite a mature young man to understand that. Of course I'm by no means destitute."

"What a wonderful idea—to watch one's money doing such wonderful things," she said.

"And my wife was behind it, too, a remarkable woman. We lost her some ten years ago." He paused for a moment, then went on. "Of course, I miss her still; she left an indelible mark on Harry. That you'll see when you meet him." Thompson paused again, toying with his salad as Kathy waited quietly for him to go on, fully aware that in his own oblique way he'd indicated that he wanted to continue this new relationship.

She had heard stories about the late Mrs. Thompson. It was said that Stephen Thompson had sainted a difficult, dictatorial woman who had frequently blamed him, even in public, for blighting any chance she might have had of making a name for herself in business.

"Will you have dinner with me again?" Thompson suddenly said, lifting his wineglass and interrupting her reflections.

"I'd like that, Stephen," she said, touching her glass to his.

The broad smile that swept his face gave way to a look of concern. "You don't mind the fact—" he toyed with his fork as he searched for the right words. "It's just that . . . well . . . Face facts—I've always said that in business—the plain, simple unvarnished fact. I'm really old enough—"

"Mr. Thompson," she cut in, "are you deterred by age when you're dealing with your opposite number in the business world or in a foreign government?"

"No, of course not. I deal with people of all ages."

"Then you can deal with me," she said simply.

Thompson's face lit up. "That's a challenge I gladly accept," he said with assurance.

☆ ☆ ☆

And so had begun a presidential campaign—sparked by the political skills and drive of Ed Jaggers and Clifford Hawley—that was to project H. Stephen Thompson onto the national stage. With it came the gradual blossoming, springing from a casual television interview initiated by Hawley, that was to propel Thompson out of his cocoon as a resigned widower and into the role of a man in pursuit of a vibrant young woman.

The demands on Thompson's time escalated rapidly as he relinquished his business and financial activities and threw himself into the world of politics, moving about the country in order to establish an identity, working tirelessly under the direction of Hawley and a key group he'd recruited, old political pros such as Jaggers and new, energetic team workers like Thompson's son, Harry, and the Whitney brothers. As the pace quickened with the preparation for the traditional battles in Iowa and New Hampshire, where it was mandatory for Thompson to score among the contenders for the party nomination, Thompson's absence from Washington and Kathy had to be endured by each of them.

Thompson, though, managed to meet Kathy from time to time while he weighed all of his political options and conferred with Hawley and Jaggers on his moves. They went riding in Rock Creek Park, attended an occasional concert at the Kennedy Center, frequented, when time permitted, restaurants still favored by the elite and powerful, such as La Maison Blanche and Lion d'Or.

As the political pace quickened, Hawley and Thompson developed a relationship that kept them in constant communication: Thompson on the road with a battery of aides to handle communications—the press, speech writing, television—and all of the elements of a sprawling on-the-move campaign; Jaggers and Hawley holding the reins of organization at Washington headquarters.

For Kathy there were equally difficult and hectic challenges. What had begun as a new friendship that might benefit her career was now emerging as something else. Thompson found her mesmerizing; Kathy, in turn, was attracted to Thompson's integrity and forthright manner. As Thompson's attentions began increasingly to manifest themselves, she discovered herself in an uncharacteristic position, unsure of herself.

The reason for the uncertainty was simple: Clifford Hawley.

Hawley had introduced her to Thompson, and now with Thompson's obvious indications of something more than casual interest, Kathy wanted to end the perplexing uncertainties that were crowding in on her. She called Hawley, and they agreed to meet—as they so often had in the past—in a quiet offbeat restaurant in Alexandria, where the patrons were ordinary local people. She lost no time in coming to the point.

"I have to ask you, Cliff, when you first met Stephen, I remember your telling me you told him about me." She sipped her cocktail and looked over the edge of her glass. "Did you tell him about *us*?"

"No."

"Why not?"

"Something told me to leave some things unsaid. You might say I was doing an impromptu juggling act. I didn't want to give him anything to think about, except an interview by a respected television reporter."

"With a secret life," she said softly.

Hawley smiled. "It may have been for the best." He reached over and took hold of Kathy's hands. "You know how I feel about you, Kathy, ever since that first night—" he smiled. "Now, if you were the marrying kind—"

"If *you* were the marrying kind, you mean," she replied.

"Let's just say we're just two of a kind then, the watchful, waiting, evaluating kind, with, maybe, some preconceived agendas—"

"Not including marriage, right?"

"Kathy, there are things happening," he said earnestly. "Do I have to spell them out? The convention? The election? The things I keep reading about you and Thompson?"

"Do those things disturb you?" she asked. Before he could reply, she said, "You don't have to answer. Our being here, almost invisible, says it all."

"You want Mr. Thompson to know about us? Now?"

Kathy withdrew her hands. "I'm not sure I know anything,"

she murmured. She sat thinking of the beginning of the affair, her initial emphasis on parallel lines. Hawley's efforts to cross them. The curious way in which they seemed both unconsciously and deliberately to seek those ultimate goals they'd talked about from their very first meeting at the Hay-Adams.

As Kathy sipped her drink, Hawley, too, reflected. Only a few weeks before, at a reception for the new ambassador from France, he had run into Kathy and she had chided him, with just a hint of jealousy, that she'd read a small item in a social column that linked him with the Hollywood actress Vivien Lessing. Then he remembered with satisfaction her final submission one evening as they said good night in the high-ceilinged vestibule of her small red brick townhouse. "I don't want you to talk anymore, Kathy," he said that night, gripping her firmly and kissing her passionately. And then, quite suddenly, she responded, shedding all past restraint. He remembered seizing her and lifting her off her feet as he started up the staircase. "Are you trying to be a Rhett Butler?" she managed to whisper. He didn't reply, and she made no effort to protest. It was something each had wanted from the first meeting. And now, he was forced to acknowledge, so much had changed, it almost might as well not have happened.

Neither one wanted to dissect their relationship and their motives any further. Hawley drove her home in silence. When he attempted to follow her out of the car she simply placed a hand on his arm and softly said, "I understand, Cliff. I think we both understand."

"Kathy," he began to protest.

"We'll do nothing, Cliff. These kinds of things have a way of working themselves out. We'll let it alone." She touched his cheek tenderly, and let herself out of the car.

☆ ☆ ☆

Even now, as she huddled against the dampness on the White House balcony, Kathy could see in her mind's eye the spent figure of her husband and hear his apologetic murmurings, his frustration at his true physical condition. Before the marriage she had learned of his dependence on heavy doses of Inderal and other drugs, and she knew the side effects they produced, though neither she nor Thompson had ever uttered the word *impotence*. The actual impotence, however, grew like an evil genie, never to retreat. She'd dismissed it before the wedding night, certain that the growing affection between them would be adequate compensation for a sexual consummation denied. But in the three years of her marriage that denial, and their silence about it, had become a full-blown nightmare.

She had yielded to the President's wishes that the traditional First Lady's bedroom be transformed into a sitting room. He had wanted his wife near his upstairs study. Regretting the change because her privacy had to be sacrificed to it, she nonetheless complied.

Long ago she'd admitted to herself, ruefully, that she wanted an important marriage. The taste of life at the very top of Washington society had only heightened her appetite. Being seen with Thompson at Washington's most exclusive parties, being even more visible as his constant companion, and being catapulted to the world stage as a President's wife—all this had been intoxicating.

She'd even managed to share with Clifford Hawley some of the excitement and tension she felt, making hurried phone calls to his office and meeting him once at Jaggers' country place near Leesburg immediately before the election. She'd insisted on a final meeting with Hawley so she could be absolutely sure of her decision. Jaggers had sent his housekeeper on a three-hour errand into town, and after bringing them tea and making sure a fire was blazing in the library fireplace, he went out to examine some fences being repaired on the far edge of his property. For all his flamboyance they knew they could trust him.

Kathy remembered Hawley's response when she told him she thought Thompson would ask her to marry him. "Parallel lines, Kathy, isn't that what we talked about at our first meeting? I remember I was the one who raised the possibility of intersecting lines. We had that, too. And it was beautiful. But, Kathy," he whispered softly, reaching a hand across the tea service, "you can't reverse your course, and even if you could, would you? You're going to be the First Lady."

She'd fought back a rush of tears. "Is that what I want?" she asked. "Is that what *you* want?" She watched him shake his head.

"Kathy, let's put it right out front. You know where I stand with you. I love you. Plain and simple. You know that."

"Wouldn't it work?" She dabbed her eyes with her handkerchief.

He spoke softly. "Kathy, it's too late. Thompson and I are

going to win. I'm going to be Vice President. There's no turning back for any of us."

They sat in silence on a small sofa before the fireplace, watching the glowing embers. Kathy was uncomfortable, acknowledging to herself that Cliff Hawley had practiced his political moves with great skill, and equally chagrined at her own acquiescence in all of his moves. It had been, she had to admit, reluctantly, a mutual operation; each, perhaps, had manipulated the other.

At last, she rose and spoke. "Maybe we made it happen too fast. Or maybe you didn't want to change anything." She raised her hand as he moved toward her. "Let me finish, Cliff. I gave myself—you know how I love you. You brought us together—Stephen and me—and then it was you who let go, Cliff. You let it all go."

"Kathy, everything's happened just as you predicted, without any deliberate planning. It just happened," he insisted, "and what's more," he added, "you're going to do everything you ever wanted to do. You won't have to interview anyone anymore. Instead, you're already the subject of endless interviews. You'll travel everywhere—you'll be the best-known woman in the world. And—you're going to be happy, Kathy." He placed his hands on her shoulders. "I'm proud of you, don't you understand?"

"And I lose you?"

"No," he said, reaching down to take her hands, "you never lose me. You'll see. Never." And with that he embraced her, but she sensed something missing. Perhaps Hawley was being kind, sympathetic but fatalistic. Perhaps that first Thompson contact was simply the result of his clever machination to win a place on the ticket. After his winning she'd become expendable.

She hated to acknowledge it, but she could never quite believe that Clifford Hawley hadn't really used her. She knew that, had Thompson known she and Hawley had had an affair that had never really ended with the cessation of their sexual relationship, she would never have become the President's wife, nor could Hawley ever have become the President's running mate.

The President's rasping cough broke Kathy's reverie. She had gone inside and slipped under the covers, thinking of Clifford Hawley, of his gentleness and fierceness in their trysts, and bitter, too, at rumors of his affairs with other women. Those stories had tortured her even before her marriage, despite her certainty that Hawley cared little for those women; there was some small comfort in believing his actions were only those of a vigorous man who wouldn't pass up a night or two with an ambitious and available woman. She wondered about Felicia Courtney, the growing frequency with which her picture was turning up with Hawley as her escort. And was it only coincidence that Vivien Lessing was in Palm Springs when Hawley was on vacation there?

As the President's stertorous breathing became more irregular, Kathy lay quietly, her frustration, she confessed to herself, piqued by jealousy. Clifford Hawley was always circumspect whenever they met at a social or political function, but there were moments when he seemed to want her to remember that his attachment for her had never wavered—the way his hand tightened over hers when they greeted each other, the concern with which he asked about her health and activities, the way his magnetic eyes blazed into hers.

The thought of Clifford Hawley continued to gnaw at her through a restless night—that and the awareness that she was seeing less of him at official functions. And now the President was making matters more difficult by not including Hawley in informal gatherings; the gossip in the newspapers even suggested that her husband was deliberately shunning the Vice President's company. After watching the press conference, she couldn't help speculating on the impact it might have on Hawley's future. One day he'd want to succeed the President; with the convention only a few months away, was it really possible the President could drop him from the ticket? The man who'd masterminded the President's first nomination? She looked across at the sleeping figure of her husband. Then tears filled her eyes, concern and unhappiness for his helplessness mixed with vexation at herself and Hawley. She had traded some of the best years of her life for the privilege of lying next to an important man who would never be capable of fulfilling her natural needs or desires. Confused by conflicting tides of emotions, she wrapped a blanket more tightly about herself, feeling a faint chill of repulsion as she saw the President's hand reach out toward her side of the bed.

6

Commander Jeffrey Whitney had just concluded a vigorous exercise drill with a detachment of the crew. For over thirty days the USS *Colorado* had held its position circling just above the floor of the ocean less than a hundred miles off the Spanish coast.

Since it was as important to organize the crew's leisure time as it was to go through the endless drills, the ship carried a large assortment of periodicals and books as well as films, tapes, and video games. His executive officer—an old friend, Lieutenant Commander Arthur Morgan, tall, balding, with deep-set piercing eyes—had dropped by his quarters carrying a copy of *Playboy*. Whitney lowered the book he was reading. "Charles Dickens? *The Old Curiosity Shop?*" Morgan said, shaking his head dolefully.

"Perfect author for a man whose mission is to help blow up part of the world," Whitney replied. "Very soothing fellow." He laid the copy of the book on his small desk. "You know how Dickens liked to think of himself? A creator of 'harmless cheerfulness.' Well, he was right—we have his complete works on board. You ought to try him instead of that crap."

Morgan sat down on the edge of Whitney's bed, stretching his long legs and riffling the well-worn pages of the picture magazine on his lap. "I'll think on that. On the other hand maybe we should put a suggestion box on this ship. And my first suggestion? The Navy forgets the books and the girlie magazines and just stocks the ship with a few live ones. Time our branch let them in: not only be a real incentive to keep submariners in the service, but good medicine to keep us all from getting fuzzy in the head." He opened the magazine and held it up for Whitney. "Good idea?"

Whitney scowled at his friend's impertinence. Staring from the page was a nude Vivien Lessing. "Everybody on board know we had a date?"

"Only me, Romeo. And you were the one who told me." Art looked at the cover. "Old issue, relax. Probably made this shot long before she was a star."

"Just to get started."

"So I hear. No big deal, they all do it. Then they stop until they begin to fade out. Then they do it again. Last gasp to stay on top, I guess. Want it?"

Whitney reached over to take the magazine and casually closed it. "Any other morale boosters for your captain?" he asked, tossing it onto his desk.

Morgan stood up. "Nope," he said, his eyes twinkling, "just figured private property shouldn't be so publicly available. I get an 'A' for special service?"

"Try *David Copperfield*; he'll calm your nerve endings."

"Maybe they'll be calm when we all know what the hell this mission's all about."

Whitney glanced up. "Patience," he said. "We've done our first thirty days here."

"We stay here, just circling?"

Whitney nodded. "We stay here."

"Well, thank you for the tip," Morgan replied as he raised a finger to his brow as a parting salute.

When Morgan had gone, Jeff picked up the magazine and searched for Vivien's picture. For a few moments he smiled, recalling his adventure with her the night Kathy Thompson had brought them together at the White House, a move on her part to blunt Hawley's interest. He remembered the drive, both of them drinking cognac, together sinking into a conspiratorial euphoria. She began to reminisce about what it took to become a star; he frequently thought of one story she'd told so beguilingly, almost innocently despite its wantonness, of the famous jockey she'd met, the jockey's attempt to seduce her with his charm, then venting his hostility and anger by suddenly seizing her with surprising strength and agility, pretending she was a filly he'd break into a champion racehorse, and tearing at her with power she'd never met in another man. What she didn't tell him was that the jockey had forced her to her knees, and mounted her, whipping her buttocks with the flat of his hand, ramming her with his knees, heels, and penis until she'd carried him across the room begging him never to stop.

When they reached Whitney's place he asked her if she'd come in, and she replied, "Why not?"

She smiled up at him as he led her into his modest condominium on Connecticut Avenue.

"This old place is full of history," he told her. "Truman lived in this building before he moved into the White House."

"To which you've been contributing?" she said pointedly.

"Maybe we can both contribute," he replied.

"Honey, don't believe everything you read about me in the papers. Sex goddess and all that jazz. I'm really not very good."

"Why don't I be the judge of that?" Whitney said.

Now seated in his ocean quarters, he slowly tore the picture from the magazine and shredded it into an ashtray. Then he set the paper afire. "You were very good," he murmured, remembering how roughly he'd treated her. In the midst of his passion he'd blurted out, "Okay, baby, now what about Mr. Hawley? How's he measure up to your goddamn jockey? And—how does he compare to me?" he'd added, looking down at her.

She had turned her head aside. "He treats me gently—like a lady." Her accent had imitated Liza Doolittle, but the words had struck him like a cold shower, and he had released her.

As flames consumed Vivien's picture, Whitney chuckled as he switched gears and returned to Dickens. But then the image of his sister, Gloria, hovered before him. He thought that once he was back in Washington he'd go to work to get her straightened out. Maybe it was time he and his brother put the right amount of pressure on Harry Thompson. Harry simply had to be persuaded to do the honorable thing. He was sure that would solve her drug problem. It was also long overdue.

☆ ☆ ☆

Dawn was breaking as Hawley stood on a secluded balcony of the Four Seasons Biltmore Hotel in Santa Barbara, watching a reddening sky pierce the black shield of night. He'd flown into Los Angeles to address a business group on America's place on the Pacific Rim and arranged to join Vivien Lessing for a quick rendezvous. When he turned to look through the panelled doorway, he gazed at her shapely body under the thin pink sheet. Her pouting lips, tousled blond hair, and creamy skin could bedevil any man as they had already captured the fantasies of male moviegoers and VCR owners. But the excitement of the chase was diminishing for Hawley. Vivien had become another predictability in a long line of females, in her words, her demands, her moods, even her orgasms. He acknowledged he was using her, but then he knew, too, that she'd been using him. And there was the danger of exposure. Despite the security he felt in being a bachelor himself, the demise of Gary Hart could still rise to haunt anyone in an official position.

Only one woman had ever mattered to Hawley, and she was in Washington, and now the President's wife. How, he had asked himself a hundred times, might he have openly competed with the President for her, and been able to survive politically? Kathy had complained more than once that he had simply let her go, but he believed that her own ambition had been the major contributing factor. It was a simple choice in the end; to marry and become the First Lady, or to marry and become the wife of a member of the House, an act that might even then have resulted in Hawley's eventually being purged by an angry President. Hawley sometimes thought Kathy had only pretended to feel rejected when she'd actually been following the course of action she had sought for herself.

Kathy had to know that were he to move toward the pinnacle, it wouldn't be on the arm of a Hollywood sex symbol; his marriage would have to have the kind of substance the American public could endorse. Someone like Gloria. Gloria Whitney had all the qualities Washington liked and the public would accept, but there was still an unsolvable difficulty—it would be foolhardy to court her as long as the President's son considered her his private property. He smiled ruefully, aware that the Thompsons had foreclosed his best options.

A soft tap at the door, the one he'd been waiting for, broke Hawley's reverie. He admitted one of the faceless men of the Secret Service, whispering, "If you'll just close that bedroom door and get her back to Hollywood—"

"Don't worry about it, sir," the agent said, "we'll take care of it."

Hawley nodded, picking up his jacket and overnight case and striding out into the hall. There, another aide saluted him, raising a finger to the brim of his hat, relieving him of the case, then leading him down through the opulent wood-beamed lobby. As the aide swung open the heavy doors, Hawley walked across the red paving blocks and stepped into a waiting car. This would be his last fling, he decided. No one had seen him and no one would know he had spent the night in Santa Barbara.

Except, no doubt, Richard Daniels.

☆ ☆ ☆

The plane swiftly ascended, crossing the green and yellow patches of the Santa Ynez Mountains as Hawley settled into his seat on the flight back to Washington. He wondered if he should talk over such personal matters as his relationship with Vivien with Daniels, the conduit through which he might achieve almost anything. But that raised another thought—was he getting too close to Daniels? The time, he decided, was not ripe and might never be. Why? He was troubled that Daniels might already be acquiring the quiet inside political power of a J. Edgar Hoover of another era.

At that moment Daniels was in his office, an office impressive for its size and barrenness. It was the way he liked it, as though its occupant could move out without leaving a clue to his identity, no paintings or photographs on the walls or tables, no personal objects on the steel desk. The room spoke eloquently for his detachment, his remoteness.

Two weeks had passed since the President's press conference, and Daniels still didn't know the next players in the arena of power. He didn't like that, but he felt he could learn the President's real motives. He prided himself on never losing key contacts, never cutting vital connections. A President, even an ill one, was vital.

But of more immediate importance, Daniels thought he might have to bring pressure on several influential party figures to help Hawley retain his position on the ticket, assuming the President actually could endure the strain of the impending campaign. As a starter, one or two good interviews in the right magazine or paper, or by the right network's news personality— he immediately thought of the Gratton connection—could help position Hawley properly in the public mind.

☆ ☆ ☆

A week after Hawley's return from Santa Barbara, he and Daniels met in Hawley's EOB office. "No need for you to appear to go quietly, as other Vice Presidents before you—like Burr and Wallace, for example," Daniels said, reporting on Memorial Day activities he had arranged with the Vice President's staff. "Your people have worked out a whole series of picture events. All quite good on television. Nice, patriotic pictures. Mike Deaver couldn't have done better for Reagan. Can't hurt. And you'll be in Arlington very early in the morning, so as not to interfere with the President's own wreath-laying in the afternoon." Daniels looked at his watch. "Fellows from *Time* should be waiting at your home for you just about now."

"How'd you do it so quickly, Richard?"

"No big problem. You had a firm handling your campaign, your polls, research—"

"Johnson and Royal. They did a good job."

Daniels shrugged. "They couldn't lose. You're not forgetting they handled your opposition as well, are you? Either way they had it made. No such thing as loyalty in their business, if you want to call it that. Town's full of them of course, ex-congressmen, ex-regulators, ex-staffers, you name them, all scratching for bucks. Big bucks. They have a fancy name for their services, but, Mr. Vice President," Daniels' voice suddenly turned hard, "they're all a pack of leeches! Parasites! Blood suckers! The whole rotten pack of them!"

"Part of the jungle we live in, Richard," Hawley calmly replied. "Maybe, these days, part of the new political process as well."

Daniels frowned. "Agreed. We use them. Bury our own people in them, if you want to know the truth. Including the networks and the top publishers." A cold smile crossed his face as he stretched out a hand, grasping Hawley's in a firm grip. "You'll have no problems with the *Time* crowd. They owe Johnson and Royal. Just do your stuff."

Hawley mixed drinks for his two guests in the small, comfortably furnished library that opened into the more formal drawing room of the Vice President's official residence. Chet Gaynor, national affairs editor, tall, Groton and Harvard educated, who spoke with a peculiar lisp, was a potential chairman of the giant communications-entertainment company. Jerry Burke, older, tousled, his face crisscrossed with deep lines, was a specialist in domestic politics.

Gaynor took the initiative after the amenities. "Jerry and I are very glad to have this chance to get you on the record, Mr. Vice President."

"Okay, Chet, let's have a go at it," Hawley said. Chet nodded to Burke.

"The President's either playing games with you, sir—or with the press. Want to talk to that?" Burke asked, staring at Hawley over his tinted glasses.

The Vice President steepled his hands together and nodded politely. "A good question, but really one that only the President can answer."

"You want to stay on the ticket?" Burke shot back.

"That's an easy one to answer. First, I've enjoyed my service as Vice President. Second, I wanted to be Vice President. Third, I *am* Vice President. Fourth, I would hope to continue as Vice President. That's it pure and simple."

"Well said, but then why doesn't the President make it just as pure and simple and just say the same thing—he hopes you'll continue as Vice President?"

"The President has already honored me by selecting me to be his Vice President *once*," Hawley said smoothly. "And, Jerry, I can't criticize him for keeping his political options open. I could imagine myself doing the same if conditions were reversed. In point of fact, you'll recall that President Eisenhower did precisely that a long way back with respect to Vice President Nixon before the election of '56. And then, of course, the President correctly stated matters at his press conference when he said he hadn't discussed the subject. At least not yet," he added.

Jerry said, "Look, *he* knows where to reach you. *You* know where to reach him. So why don't one of you just pick up a phone? Have a meeting?"

Hawley sipped his drink, pleased that the moment had come for him to send a message to the President by way of the pages of *Time*. He knew that Kraus's aides routinely scrutinized all political commentary in the national magazines and newspapers. "Oh, I'm sure that will happen. I've every confidence that when the President determines that the moment is right, he'll do just that and invite me in for a meeting," he said, choosing his words with care, "and for the express purpose of determining just where I might contribute to the Administration's success during his second term."

Gaynor picked up the thread. "State, Defense—he mentioned the Cabinet in his press conference. Let's presume that rather than put you on the ticket, the President could really be thinking of you in one of those capacities. You've done a lot of travelling for him, meeting the world's leaders and so on."

"That's always possible, Chet, but as you well know, Secretary Jaggers and Secretary Clauson are men of exceptional ability."

"Yeah, and everybody knows you don't go from the Cabinet to the White House," Burke interjected, "not these days. Last one to do that was Hoover. Of course Kissinger might have done it if he'd been born in the U.S."

Hawley felt that the basic question had been answered. He would wait for a meeting with the President. He had affirmed his desire to continue on the ticket. He had put aside a Cabinet post. Since the big cards were still held by the President, he would play the President's game and repeat his position. "Let's just say I stand ready to serve on the President's team. Meanwhile . . ." he flung out an open hand indicating that there were other areas to pursue. He knew that nothing else he would say in the interview would really matter—the rehashing of his position on Eastern Europe, the space program, hemispheric issues, the economy—even as they honed in on defense.

Burke ran a hand through his tousled locks. "Okay, what about space, what about underwater? Do we have to go nuclear in all of our antimissile defense systems?"

"We haven't, Jerry," Hawley replied. "You're both aware that none of the defensive weapons systems being examined by the Pentagon would be armed with nuclear capability—none, that is, that deal with space."

"Are you saying that space would be free of nuclear warheads?" Burke asked.

"Except for those coming in from a potential adversary, yes."

"But before being completely installed, wouldn't our defense systems be a destabilizing factor that might persuade some men in the Kremlin, with a dubious view of perestroika, that a first strike might finally be in their national interest?"

"A defense strategy such as the Administration has supported is designed to minimize any first strike—and without using nuclear weapons to do so." Hawley paused for a moment. "Now you both know that I'm not going to publicize our defense plans, or our defense systems—"

Jerry Burke cut in. "Look, everyone knows about the so-called swarm systems to defend our silos—with space showers of everything from rocks to lasers. What's to tell?"

Hawley stared at him impassively. "I'm not here to enlighten the Soviets, Jerry, or to affirm or deny your speculation. What I am saying plain and simple, just as the President has said it, just as Mrs. Curtis is saying it in Geneva, is this: all we want is for the Soviets to know that a first-launch strike is not an attractive alternative for them—or for that matter for us—to consider as a national policy."

Gaynor leaned forward. "But isn't it true that our submarine force, with its enormous nuclear strike capability, is the real deterrent?"

"Agreed," Hawley replied, "but along with the two other elements of our triad—our own land-based missiles and our nuclear carrying planes. In short, there's no such thing as crippling America's retaliatory-strike capability."

"If they don't decapitate our central command centers first, and as long as our submarines are invulnerable. How long can that status quo go on, Mr. Vice President?"

"No one knows for certain, Chet."

"Aren't the Soviets working at means to detect underwater weapons, and once they have it—or once we have it—wouldn't that destabilize matters even more, to an alarming extent?"

Hawley smiled, fully aware of the Navy's plans and of Jeff Whitney's secret mission somewhere in the Atlantic. "Nothing is invincible—and nothing is invulnerable forever," he said quietly.

"Well, let's just hope forever really is a long time," Gaynor said.

"I'll settle for that," Hawley replied.

"You and the President on the same party line vis-à-vis the Soviets?" Burke asked.

Hawley smiled, certain he detected Daniels' hand. The question was an opportunity to deflect the damage, if it had been damage, that Kraus had called attention to following the President's recent press conference. "Of course, Jerry. We've lived through the turmoil of a good deal of ethnic conflict in Eastern Europe as well as the settling of the Baltic issue—a different matter, as you know. But Hungary, Poland, Romania, even Bulgaria—there the ethnic problems are far less ominous than in Yugoslavia or even Czechoslovakia. Those ancient problems are always bubbling beneath the surface—"

"And in the Soviets' own western and southern republics?" Burke cut in.

"Right. There the Russians are truly a minority people except, perhaps, for Kazakhstan. You have to remember that Azerbaijan is only eight percent Russian and Armenia is less than half of that. These disparities always harbinger potential difficulties."

"And the Soviets' handling of them?"

Hawley cupped his chin in his hand and shrugged. "Gorbachev did his best—that's history. President Turgenev has followed with a program of some moderation."

"And Germany?" Gaynor inquired. "What of the Germans?"

"Who can say?" Hawley replied with a disarming smile. "We always favored reunification, as you well know, Chet. But there are dynamics there that, curiously enough, may be leading us from the old Cold War status to a truly warmer relationship with the Soviets."

"Are you suggesting we could become allies?" Burke interjected.

Hawley shrugged his shoulders again. "The President reminded us only recently in a Cabinet meeting that we *were* once allies. If that new relationship deepens, who's to say? A new reality might develop."

"A new reality," Gaynor repeated. "I like that phrase. It could identify an era."

As the questions continued Hawley deduced that the grilling he was undergoing was merely their way of assessing his own intimacy with defense matters and foreign affairs.

"Ever think you might take a run at the presidency?" Burke asked.

"That's a question that's really totally irrelevant at this time, with the convention beginning to press down on all of us and an election only a few months further off after that—"

"I agree," Gaynor cut in as he waved Burke aside. "But tell me, do you feel you're fully prepared to step into the presidency if anything were to happen to the President himself?"

"That's not very likely," Hawley said.

"Well, hypothetically—and it's why you were elected to the vice presidency, why we elect a Vice President," Gaynor said, pressing the issue.

"Well, of course," Hawley beamed, again secretly pleased with the question and certain, too, that once more he detected the hand of Richard Daniels in setting it up. "I think all Vice Presidents have been well prepared in recent years with the possible exception of Harry Truman. He was kept in the dark on too many things."

"Like the atom bomb."

"For one," Hawley acknowledged. "But these days, and particularly since the days of Eisenhower and Kennedy, all the Presidents have seen to it that their Vice Presidents are kept abreast of key matters."

"Secret matters as well?"

"Secret matters, too," Hawley confirmed. "Yes," he added as he thought of the scope of the Navy's secret project, Red Dye Day. "A Vice President has his regular meetings with the President, his briefings with State and Defense, and daily contact with the National Security Adviser or his deputy. There's no end to the personal contacts from the CIA, the FBI, you name it. And then the working papers that float in from every area of government. It's endless."

"We understand that you maintain additional contacts with special think tanks," Gaynor said.

"I do, as well with some university specialists. It's all part of the job these days. Which is why the President asked me to coordinate the executive departments on speeding up the repairs to our infrastructure of roads, bridges, and so on."

"How does the job compare, in reality, with your views about it when you hit the campaign trail last time?"

"You simply can't compare it once you've had the responsibility of the office, even if the Constitution spells out no vital duties. The office has simply grown."

"A training ground, maybe?" Gaynor countered.

"You could say that," Hawley responded. "It's an office that simply washes away pure ambition—which, I'll admit, is an affliction with which most of us politicians must contend—and really transforms that drive into an awareness of the substantial responsibilities of the office. That's the growth factor in a nutshell."

"Well said," Gaynor nodded with an approving smile.

Hawley had gotten his main points over, and now he signalled the end of the interview by pushing his chair away from his desk.

Chet Gaynor stood up. "One more question, Mr. Vice President."

"Shoot," Hawley said amiably. "Just one more."

Gaynor stroked his chin as he spoke. "One of our more dedicated reporters sent in an interesting note, something he's been looking into—" Gaynor hesitated momentarily, looking toward Burke. "Something of a personal—maybe a delicate nature as these things go—" He smiled and let the subject hang in the air for a moment.

Burke picked it up. "What the boss is getting at is one of our favorite subjects—women."

Hawley smoothed down the back of his hair. "One of mine, too, Jerry," he said casually, but immediately on guard. "What's up?"

After a moment Gaynor cleared his throat. "It's about the First Lady, Mr. Vice President," he said quietly.

"Yes?" Hawley said politely.

Burke broke the ice. "You're always good copy for the press on these matters, and we don't ordinarily have too much interest in this area. But of course, if it's upper echelon—the First Lady, not some ordinary gossip about you, a bachelor, and say some movie star, well that's for other parts of the press—" He stopped and looked directly at Hawley. "Any connection, way back in the past—"

"Connection?" Hawley repeated.

"Yeah—you and Mrs. Thompson. Connection. Any comment?"

Hawley leaned back in his chair and laughed. "Somebody's trying to invent something, gentlemen. I met the First Lady— let me see—sometime just before she became a television reporter for Federal Broadcasting. You'll remember I was among the first supporters of the President—of course he wasn't even a candidate at the time, but once I was assured of his possible interest I wanted him to get a lot of visibility, and I suggested to her—and others— that H. Stephen Thompson would be a good subject to interview. I arranged for them to meet—and you know what eventually came out of that meeting."

"They got married," Burke said. "Okay. But it's *before* that, not after, we're interested in."

"There's nothing before *or* after," Hawley replied affably. "Of course, during the Thompson campaign I set up a lot of interviews— with male as well as female reporters, all over the country, but he courted only one. Kathy Bryson then."

"But *you* and Miss Bryson?" Burke persisted.

Hawley looked Burke in the eye. "I've read a lot about myself and my lady friends and I've seen my picture with them in your magazines," he replied. Then turning his attention to

Gaynor, he added, "Chet, your enterprising reporters would probably find more pay dirt if they followed up *those* stories, but I'm not a Gary Hart. Not challenging you," he said, as they all laughed. "Anyway, I *am* a friend of the First Lady, glad to admit it, proud of it, but that's all there is to it." He stood up and put out his hand to Burke. "I don't mind your bringing up the subject of women. Everybody's trying to get me married—and one day I will."

"It would help if you want to be President," Burke said, as he stuffed his notes into his pocket.

Hawley good-naturedly slapped Burke on the shoulder as he walked his guests to the door. "Tell our reporter poodle to stop sniffing, that it, Mr. Vice President?" Burke asked.

"Let's say that when I have a real story in that department, you'll be the first to know."

☆ ☆ ☆

An early mist swirled about Clifford Hawley the next morning as he stood bareheaded before the Tomb of the Unknowns, reading the inscription: "Here rests in honored glory an American Soldier known but to God." He glanced straight ahead, over the cemetery and the Potomac, the image of a faceless sentinel in his peripheral vision until the soldier walked the prescribed line across the black rubber mat laid over marble paving blocks. Only the sounds of crisp orders given at the precise time of the changing of the guard and carried out daily round the clock disturbed the silence of Arlington—plus the cadenced tramp of feet, the click of heels, and the crack of rifles slapped hard against hands in the rituals of the guard.

At that early hour one might have thought the place deserted, except for the movement of a small group of men and women at a little distance to the side, focusing their television cameras on Hawley. Hawley paid no attention to them. He allowed himself to be drawn into the solemnity of the event, feeling an unusual awareness of the sacrifice so many others had paid so that he and every other American could, in turn, feel secure.

When Hawley left the white marble Amphitheater, he crossed the road, the camera crews racing before him. He stood for a moment at the mast of the ill-fated *Maine* which marked the burial site of scores of veterans of the Spanish-American War. Then he turned, got into his car, and told his driver to proceed to the rear entrance of the Lee Mansion. Once there,

Hawley emerged to step along a brick walk, slipping through a narrow passage cut from the hedge that circled a drab gray monument honoring the Civil War unknown dead. He read its inscription, now showing deep signs of erosion from the elements: "Beneath this stone rests the bones of 2,111 Unknown Soldiers gathered after the war from the fields of Bull Run and the route to the Rappahanock River."

It was his first visit to the site, and the thought of so many soldiers lying together in a single grave marked by a gray stone both oppressed and stirred him. He continued to ignore the questions of reporters eager to press him on political issues, but he was distressed more by the conflicting thoughts racing through his own mind: the high purpose of his visit as well as the cold political gains to be scored through his pilgrimage to some of America's most sacred shrines.

From this point he was driven to the airport where his helicopter took off for the short trip to the Gettysburg battlefield. There Harry Thompson and Hawley's advance team were laying the groundwork for his visit. He'd agreed that Harry's activities this day would be limited to Gettysburg, since Thompson had pleaded an important prior commitment, a personal one, and had flown in to Gettysburg in his own plane.

Hawley stood before the bust of Lincoln at the historic spot where the President had given his famous address, a soft wind blowing his hair, as he delivered his own brief speech. When he finished he pocketed his notes and started to move toward his car, but suddenly spotting Thompson in a small group, he veered over to shake hands with him. "Good job, Harry, and my thanks for all you did here."

Harry Thompson nodded politely, with scarcely a comment, and Hawley sensed his mind was elsewhere. He suspected it had something to do with Gloria Whitney. Hawley's other aides led him to a cordoned area where he boarded his helicopter for the quick flight to his next stop: Philadelphia. Hawley had wanted this Memorial Day to focus only on those he'd come to honor, and so immediately upon his arrival in Philadelphia he headed to Washington Square, home of the Unknown Soldier of the Revolutionary War, a shrine seldom visited by the emissaries of the White House.

He entered the Square from the northeast corner, acknowledging a few flag-waving youngsters who lined the old walks, and took his place before the stained bronze statue of George Washington. A black military officer preceded him, laying a modest wreath upon the weathered gray stone that covered the modest tomb. Hawley bowed his head and read the words carved on this Unknown's grave: "Beneath this stone rests a soldier of Washington's Army who died to give you liberty." The words moved him, and he reached down to touch the cold stone, acknowledging a deeper emotion that the moment instilled in him.

After a few remarks, inspired by the contact, Hawley slipped into his waiting car on Locust Street. A motorcycle escort led the way along the western edge of Society Hill, heading toward the landmark Bellevue Stratford where his parents were waiting in the presidential suite for a brief rendezvous with him before his return to Washington. A few reporters who had gathered in the lobby were politely refused admittance to the upstairs meeting.

Once they were seated together in the elegantly furnished suite, Hawley's lean, white-haired father, still teaching history, confronted him in his direct style. "I watched the President's last press conference and I didn't like it, Clifford. You're not on the ticket."

Hawley smiled, well aware of his father's command of history as well as his prescient knowledge of hardball politics. "He didn't say I wasn't."

"As good as," was his father's instant rejoinder. "When a politician wants you, he says it loud and clear; when he doesn't, he offers polite ambiguities all over the place. Why the rift?"

"There's no rift," Hawley countered. "It's the President's way."

"Son, you study as many political campaigns as I have, you learn that politicians don't fool the people in the long run, but they keep on fooling *other* politicians all the time."

"Oh, Herbert, hush. Pay no attention." Marian Hawley stretched out a hand to touch her son's arm. "Your father's never been able to say anything diplomatically, son. Don't mind him." Then, unaware of her own inconsistency, she asked, "Does he really intend to drop you?"

"That certainly is an option. Whether he exercises it—"

The old professor shook his head. "Consider it exercised."

"Exactly. I have to," Hawley agreed. "It explains why I've gone public, you might say, on Memorial Day—when I can't be accused of upstaging the President. He has Arlington. I was there early—when no one else was there—"

"Except a gaggle of television cameras, I'll bet," his father said, pointing his pipe at him.

"Yes, but I concentrated on some of the lesser-known shrines—Civil War ones, this one in Philadelphia, and then—"

"Not too many veterans of those wars around," his father said dryly, "but I can see some good television pictures. All that sort of thing. And keeping the two of us under wraps what with Mother's Day and Father's Day coming up and the other fellow not having a mother or a father around anymore. I guess you seem to have what they call a feel for television, son."

"He does have a lovely wife, though, doesn't he, Clifford? The President?" His mother turned her attention to a favorite topic. "What about you, son? A wife certainly hasn't hurt the President."

"And your mother's getting pretty impatient about grandchildren, Clifford," his father added as he fingered a decorative clock on the mantel. "Genuine ormolu, and here I thought everything in a hotel presidential suite would be expensive but still fake." He turned back to his son. "Well?" he asked, "what about your mother's fantasy?"

His mother's fine brows drew together as she whispered, "Not that Hollywood actress, I hope."

"Vivien Lessing," Hawley said.

"Yes, that one."

"She's quite respectable, Mother," Hawley said. An image of Vivien's voluptuous body at their last rendezvous floated across his mind and he heard her moans of ecstasy and her husky voice entreating him, "Oh Cliff, do it, do it! Please! Please! Now! Now! Oh, God!" Hawley observed his mother's concern and her glance toward his father. "Don't worry, Mother, she's just a friend, nothing more," he said.

Marian Hawley relaxed. "I know we can't really tell you what to do or who to see, but in your position, Clifford . . ."

"Marian," her husband said, reprovingly.

"Herbert, you were the one who spoke about grandchildren." She turned to Hawley again. "Now that Gloria Whitney, such a pretty little thing, and we saw your picture with her at some party there in Washington . . ."

"I'm afraid she's spoken for," Hawley volunteered.

"The daughter of the Chief Justice," his mother rattled on, "now she brings something. And as the Vice President . . . well you, *you* bring something, too . . ."

"Really, Marian," Herbert Hawley said, clenching his pipe. Then he chuckled. "Still, she may have something, Cliff. A romance—the right kind, naturally—now that would be the way to use television right up to the convention. Every woman in America will follow that a lot more closely than the trial balloons of this candidate or that."

"It's worth thinking about," Hawley said, reaching over to pat his mother's hands.

She looked up smiling. "Son, what about that magazine publisher—I can never remember her name . . ."

"Felicia Courtney."

"Yes, that one. What I'm trying to say, Son . . ."

"We know what you're trying to say, Marian," the senior Hawley said testily.

"How did you like the *Time* story?" Hawley said, wanting to change the subject and turning toward his father.

"Well said, well done," his father replied. "Only one thing, Son, and that's this: it's not easy to run for *your* office when the presidential office is already occupied. Pictures, publicity, television—it all adds up. But what counts is that one man's vote. The President's."

"And if it isn't handed to you?"

His father puffed rapidly for a moment or two. "Why then, if you want it, you go after it, come hell or high water."

"You may have hit on the right prescription," Hawley said.

7

Gloria Whitney held the white phone in one hand, ran a tortoise-shell brush through her ash-blond layered hair with the other, and stood before a full-length triple-paneled mirror in her white and blue bedroom, admiring her body. She stretched both hands above her head, tightening the muscles supporting her shapely breasts.

"Hey, where'd you go?" a male voice sounding far away echoed through the telephone.

"I'm exercising my pectoral muscles," she called out, keeping her hands pointed to the high blue ceiling.

"Your what?" was the distant reply.

"Pectoral muscles. Strengthens the bust line."

"You can stand it," her caller said.

She brought the phone to her lips. "Look, Junior," she said, using her favorite diminutive to put Harry Thompson down, "if you want to start talking about muscles and size, you've got one that *nothing's* ever going to help." She slammed down the phone, carrying it with her as she walked over to peek through the lace curtains. The phone rang and she spoke into it as though she'd never stopped the conversation. "My little rich Oriental neighbor is standing in his tiny little teahouse looking right this way. Like he's waiting for the show to begin."

She flashed the curtains apart for an instant, then started laughing. "Oh, Harry," she said, words and giggles pouring out together, "you should see him. You wouldn't believe it! He actually whipped out a camera, thinking I was just going to stand there while he got everything in focus. I can just make him out—no, no, no, the curtain's drawn, but I can see him through it and he's angry angry. If you know what that means. No, you wouldn't."

"Okay. No, I don't."

"Frustrated, stupid."

"Like you," Harry said.

"Yes, like me if you want to know the truth!" She carried the phone to her bed and lay down, pulling a sheet over her. "If all you ever think of is sticking Lane with a foil instead of sticking me with your—"

"Hey, hold it, your phone might be tapped."

"So? I don't mind the world knowing that at your age you're as limp as a wet noodle half the time—"

"I've got things on my mind, Gloria."

"And I've got things on mine. Like I want you to fuck me if you understand what *that* means."

"Is that the language of a daughter of a justice of the Supreme Court?"

"Balls."

"Yours or mine?"

Gloria slammed down the phone again.

Harry Thompson sat in a third-floor room he sometimes used at the White House, dialing her number once more, and again she came back on the phone talking. "And one more thing, Junior. If you don't care to satisfy my needs, there's someone else just waiting his chance. I danced with him the other night and I can tell you *his* sword was not hanging down in its scabbard, if you get the picture."

"Look, Gloria," Harry said curtly, "I just flew back from Gettysburg to be with you."

"With our honorable Vice President, weren't you?"

Harry flinched.

"He's a very eligible bachelor," Gloria went on.

"Sure, for a Hollywood tramp like Vivien Lessing or any other woman with money or a name or a body. I know Clifford Hawley better than you, better than most people. This Gettysburg business—if you want to talk about what's sticking out, it's his ambition, *that's* what's beginning to stick out."

"I know," she whispered softly. "I felt it."

Harry felt a surge of exasperation. "Good-bye, Gloria," he said, ready to slam down the phone.

"Don't hang up with a pout, Junior," she said blithely. "I want you, Harry. Tonight. Early. And if you don't come, you know what I'll do."

Hearing the click of the phone, he sat forward, cupping his head in both hands, his elbows resting on the walnut telephone table. He had loved Gloria in his fashion and she'd loved him in hers. Perhaps their relationship could still be called love, but he wondered about it, wondered if he'd been wrong in denying her what she'd wanted so long, marriage. He'd told her more than once to be patient, and she had been, even to waiting for him to graduate from law school. They might have lived together had their parents' prominence not restricted them. He had to admit that he was the one who'd temporized, been indecisive, uncertain about his own goals. Until those indecisions were resolved, it was clear he couldn't settle the issue of marriage.

He also knew that if he didn't accommodate Gloria Whitney she'd start popping pills. Mad as it was, that was one of her ways of ridding herself of her anxieties. Then there was her other alternative, turning to another man. She'd done it before and he knew he'd been forewarned: she wouldn't hesitate to call Clifford Hawley. He sighed deeply as he stood up. He wouldn't risk that.

After making his way through the barriers set up years before alongside the White House, Harry crossed into Lafayette Park facing the North Portico, his ever-present Secret Service contingent hovering nearby. Few tourists roaming the small square ever recognized him. He'd discovered, after the demonstrators and their placards had long since been compelled to set up their protest area in a confined part of the Ellipse, the broad grounds south of the White House, that he could sit on a bench in the park, his back to the White House, and take in a few minutes of fresh air to indulge himself in private contemplation.

Today, his peaceful reverie was marred as he remembered his confrontation only minutes before. After Gloria hung up, Harry had hurried down the long corridor into the West Wing and found himself face-to-face with Henry Kraus, the President's Chief of Staff. The older man, rubbing his hands together, stepped aside to let the younger man pass. "Some show you and Lane put together. Very nice of *you*, especially," Kraus added, his sneer reminding Harry of Uriah Heep.

Harry stopped and turned. "Anything wrong?"

Kraus waved a hand airily as he continued down the hall. "Not at all. But I doubt your father will appreciate the contribution you made to upstaging him today. Just that, Harry. Nothing at all." He walked away, a sarcastic grin on his face.

"Wait a minute, Henry," young Thompson said, following him. "I work for the Vice President. I take my assignments from him. If you didn't want him to go to Gettysburg, all you had to say—"

Kraus cut in coldly. "Look, Mr. Thompson. I didn't know the Vice President was going to Gettysburg. The *President* didn't know he was going to Gettysburg. *You* knew he was going to Gettysburg because you went with him. You have a different script?"

Harry Thompson leaned against a wall displaying some White House cartoons. "If I heard correctly, the trip was cleared through Lane Whitney—by you. Isn't that part of the script?"

An icy smile broke across Kraus's face. "Sure, he briefed me all right. Made sure he saw me when I was extremely busy. Just to tell me Mr. Hawley was meeting some old college friends—in Philadelphia. Not an American Legion ceremony. Maybe include someplace nearby—that was his word—nearby." Kraus took a step closer to Thompson. "Nearby? Gettysburg? Over a hundred miles west? That your idea of a briefing?"

Harry shrugged and started off. "I wasn't present, Mr. Kraus. I didn't talk to Lane. I didn't ask the Vice President if he had your permission . . ."

"He doesn't need my permission, Harry," Kraus cut in sharply.

"Well, then," Harry replied, "why all the fuss?"

Kraus took a few steps down the hall again, then stopped and retraced them. "Look, Harry, you can defend Mr. Hawley. It's part of your job. I admire you for doing it." He dropped his voice and moved in closer. "My advice to you?" Kraus squeezed Harry's arm. "Remember who you are, your very special position. Loyalty." Kraus smiled in his unctuous fashion, turned and moved off. Harry suspected that the last hadn't been heard of Hawley's Memorial Day trip.

Since he wanted to think about Gloria, Harry put Kraus in the back of his head. He wondered whether her real interest in him was declining, whether pills and sexual freedom were eating away at what had once been a steady affection. Perhaps too much time had elapsed since their first meeting, just after his father's election, in the spacious top-floor apartment of a Philadelphia financier friend of his father's. He'd been looking down through the towering floor-to-ceiling windows that stretched the entire length of the room when he heard a soft female voice behind him. "Beautiful view isn't it?"

He remembered the immediate impact she had on him as he turned to face her, the tight-fitting emerald green silk dress, her ash-blond layered hair, her open smile and beguiling eyes, a touch of innocent mischief in them. "It is now," he replied, immediately sorry that his effort to be charming sounded so sophomoric. She continued to smile at him, sipping white wine from a Baccarat glass, her wide green eyes still fixed on his. He shrugged his shoulders. "Sometimes you find yourself saying the dumbest, most obvious remarks. Things I'm sure you've heard about a million times." She continued smiling at him. "Okay, so I agree, it's beautiful. Very." He studied her in those first few seconds, hoping to keep her there so that he could know her better. He imagined that if he dared to voice his first impressions she'd laugh at him and walk back into the adjoining room where other guests crowded. She remained with him, though, still silent. "Look," he said, "you started this conversation, remember?"

"Are you happy here?" she whispered.

He remembered looking away from her for a moment, down at the street and the square green park below, before he responded. "Now, what's that supposed to mean?"

Her light laughter had a clear bell-like sound to it. "I'm an alien here," she said softly. "I have to go back, you see, in five years and two months to the day. Well, not really go back—like voluntary. What I mean is, they'll be coming for me. Do you understand?" she asked, a trace of a smile still on her lips. "No, you don't."

Harry picked up his own glass of wine, which he'd placed on a marble pedestal beside the bust of some ancient Roman—his host was an eclectic collector of art, from Mediterranean classical to Matisse and Picasso, both of whom were represented by large canvases at either end of the imposing drawing room. "Well, I'd hate to lose you so soon after meeting you," he said.

"You won't. I'm taking you with me," she said cheerfully.

"It's all ordained, that it?"

"You don't believe me, but you'll see."

"Okay, I'll believe you."

"You're just saying that to appease me, but it's true," she persisted. "You see," she added, placing a hand on his arm. "They said my mission was to bring back Harry Thompson and to let you know there's no escape."

"Just like that."

She leaned closer, glanced over her shoulder, and whispered, "It's best not to argue. They don't like a fuss once they've made a decision."

"Oh?" he'd replied. "And just when was this decision made?"

She put a finger to her lips. "Secret," she whispered. "When we know each other better, maybe I can tell you."

"Okay, you know my name. And you—you have a name down here?" he asked.

She slipped her hand into his. "Here, I'm called Gloria. Out there," she said, pointing her wine glass toward the sky, "I'm an apprentice angel. I'm not allowed to do very much. I can only give you three wishes."

"Three," he mused. "Well, let's see. Dinner tonight. Dinner tomorrow—here or in Washington, which is where I live."

"I know where you live."

"Yes, but of course," he said, sipping his wine, "and then the third wish. Two dinners later. Well, how about a week or two in Venice?" He noted her frown. "Paris? St. Moritz?"

"Harry—three wishes and not one of them to go to bed with me?" He felt the pressure of her hand as she looked at him, still smiling.

"I allowed for two dinner dates first," he said, "and *then* a week—in Venice. Wherever."

"You're forgetting the pressure I'm under. They're coming for me, remember?"

"Not for five years two months," he replied.

"I forgot you're studying to be a lawyer. You need a lot of time to make decisions. Right? That it?"

"Tonight's all right with me," he said cheerfully.

A tall man with white hair, looking both austere and affable, approached them. "Oh, Harry, I want you to meet my father, Chief Justice Whitney."

Harry recalled the sudden feeling of cold water spilling over him. He offered his right hand to the Chief Justice while his eyes watched Gloria Whitney. "Sir," was all he could say.

"This is Harry Thompson, Daddy. I think he wants to marry me," Gloria said.

The Chief Justice smiled. "My daughter likes to manipulate lives. My advice is, take care. Watch your step."

Gloria stepped beside Harry and slipped an arm through his. "They won't be coming for *him*, Harry. Just for us. He's jealous."

Everett Whitney nodded. "Her alien masters, of course. Caesar and his ides, Mr. Thompson. Remember, you've been warned. The aliens." With a gracious bow he left them.

"Are you ready for a big adventure?" Gloria said.

"Try me," Harry replied.

But the years had slipped by, and yet all of his early reservations about Gloria were still present—her dependence on drugs, her flirtatious ways, her fanning his feelings of jealousy. She had, eventually, pressed him about marriage. At first he talked about their being too young, then about his need to finish law school, then about the concentration required for his father's next campaign, then the demands of his job on Hawley's staff, the strain on his energies and time. But in the end he had to admit he'd been stalling.

It bothered him most of all that Gloria had a way of using every man she could, from congressmen to emerging bureaucrats. And Hawley could be just another victim. Maybe. Maybe in Hawley she would meet her match, but Harry didn't want to think of that. Perhaps, he thought, he was being unfair in holding on to her; perhaps he wasn't really in love with her anymore. But in any event he would never surrender her to Hawley, and Hawley wouldn't move against the President's son no matter how enticing the bait and no matter how honorable his intentions. Tired in body and spirit, he left the bench angry at his continuing irresolution and sickened by his admission of jealousy.

☆ ☆ ☆

When Hawley returned from Philadelphia to Washington that evening, Joe Gratton was at the airport to meet him, his hands in his pockets, his suitcoat buttoned over his paunch. Hawley's last stop had been the Vietnam Memorial, and Federal Broadcasting had been the only network to go the last mile: a mobile truck back on the street, its coils of cable snaking along the wall, sent pictures of Hawley back to the studio as he walked down the path, his image reflected in the polished surface of the black granite wall.

A few minutes later he was in Federal's television studio. He met the director in the control room and glanced at the bank of video monitors, each carrying a portion of the day's events. The Vietnam Wall footage was first on the screen as a backdrop for the anchorman's opening remarks: "And so ends a long day, the Vice President of the United States paying a unique tribute to all those who gave their lives through virtually all of our conflicts." Charles Cullen, Federal's senior newsman, a former Marine himself, distinguished by his famous jutting jaw and his blue eyes, conducted an interview with Hawley interspersed with brief segments of Hawley's entire day, from Arlington to the closing moments at the Vietnam Memorial.

And then the final exchange, neatly orchestrated by Gratton in his own private meeting with Cullen. "And Mr. Vice President, one final question—after so stirring a day, what about the future, *your* future?"

Hawley took his time in responding. "Mr. Cullen, this is a day we set aside to reflect on the sacrifices of others, not on our own ambitions." He spoke softly. "Each of us must serve our country in his own way. Not all of us are called upon to meet the supreme test, of giving up life itself." He paused, carefully stressing each word. "I want to do whatever I can, in the days—yes, in the years—that lie ahead, to keep my own faith with those we've remembered today."

Later, seated in his favorite corner of the Hay-Adams cocktail lounge, facing its baronial fireplace, Hawley thanked Gratton for the special program. "Glad to do it," Joe said, "and you sure as hell know how to use the medium. Considering all the speculative gossip, rumors, and talk in this town, your close was very effective."

"I appreciate the favor, Joe. I want you to know that." Hawley reached across the table to tap Gratton's arm.

"Do a favor . . ." Joe Gratton let the thought hang in the air as the waiter appeared with their drinks, Gratton stirring his with a pudgy finger. "Sitting this close to the White House makes you wonder how things go between the President and the First Lady. Know what I mean?" Hawley looked into his companion's rheumy eyes. He had no desire to exchange views about the Thompsons' private life with Gratton. "The lady practically cuts me the few times I've seen her since she resigned from Federal to take on her present job. Not exactly a grateful dame."

"That's not an especially gallant way of describing Kathy Thompson or her role."

"I wasn't trying to be gallant," Gratton answered bluntly. "You asked me to meet her. I hired her. Pushed her . . ." then he added, looking directly at Hawley through the thick lenses of his glasses, "gave her a lot of visibility and in turn she gives me and Federal the finger. She forgets she owes me." He gulped down half of his drink. "I hope she didn't forget the favor you did."

"I never thought of it that way, Joe."

"Clifford, my boy, if you weren't paid any favors for what you did—you are *owed*."

"I don't see it quite that way, Joe."

"Hey, Cliff, what gives?" Gratton leaned forward in his chair. "I gave her a job because of you. You introduced her to a man who becomes President. What do you mean she doesn't owe? She owes now, unless, of course, she obliged before she got married." Gratton immediately sensed Hawley's irritation. "Okay, you don't wanta talk, you don't talk."

The two men, as if by common agreement, relaxed and settled back. "All I did was wonder out loud, like lots of people wonder, how things go between a young woman and a not too young gent. I didn't figure you to be so touchy on the subject. If you didn't get a piece of the action, hell's bells, that's your problem." Gratton lit a cigarette. He wondered whether Kathy had ever talked about him to Hawley. "Never could figure why she's so goddamn cold to me. Ices me everytime. She ever complain about Federal? Me?"

"Never," Hawley said. Then changing the subject, he pointedly added, "Joe, I've had a strenuous day. I've got to turn in. But I do want to thank you again for all you did today and tonight."

"Nothing to it," Gratton said, tossing some bills on the table. Noticing a Secret Service agent at the entrance to the room, he added with a sly wink, "I hope you're not chaperoned all the time."

"Some complexities go with the job, Joe," Hawley said, smiling, "and you learn to endure them."

"And build up a collection of nice due bills in the process, I hope," Joe countered.

"Like this broadcast?"

"That one's on the house."

"I won't forget it, Joe," Hawley replied.

As they started out of the room, Gratton decided to backpedal a bit. "If there's anything I said about the lady you take exception to, consider it unsaid." Hawley walked ahead without responding. Gratton was now certain Hawley's reluctance to speak was proof of something more vital than any words they'd exchanged, and he found himself even more curious about Kathy and the Vice President. In all the time he'd known Hawley, they'd talked easily about women, but tonight he'd detected a note of restraint in Hawley's remarks. Hawley may have once made a pass or two at Kathy, and why not? As they came to Hawley's car, Gratton edged in closer. "Mr. Vice President, one thing you can be sure of. From here to the outer edge of the Beltway they'll be studying your words for the next week. What you've done is called tossing down the gauntlet."

Hawley turned as his driver held the car door open. "Joe, if someone wants to consider it a challenge, that'll be his interpretation. For me the whole day was basically an honest reiteration of my commitment to the President's policy on peace."

"Sure. But don't be surprised if some of your not too good friends see it more as your private declaration of war."

"Then they'll have to remember their Bible, Joe. 'Eyes have they, but they see not. They have ears, but they hear not.'"

☆ ☆ ☆

Daniels had listened impassively to Hawley as they talked over a late dinner at the vice presidential residence and Hawley reviewed the details of the interview with *Time*. As Hawley spoke, Daniels had been studying a large Hassam painting of a handsome, reflective woman set above an antique sideboard, and when he glanced across at Hawley, his first comment was surprising for its perception.

"This house could use a woman," he said, nodding toward the painting.

"The right one, yes," Hawley replied.

Daniels' heavy-lidded gray eyes focused on Hawley. "No one knows everything," he added. "No one ever finds out everything, including us." Daniels flipped open a new pack of cigarettes. "We can handle their reporter." He looked up at Hawley. "They called him a poodle?"

"Because, as they put it, he was sniffing around." Hawley

shook his head, "Reporters have built-in sanctuaries, don't they?"

"Impregnable, it's been said—against everyone, FBI, Mafia, CIA, you name it," Daniels replied as he struck a match, lighted his cigarette, inhaling a long draft. "But that's a fairy tale. Everyone's reachable—kings, popes, presidents, nuns, starlets. There are no sanctuaries."

"What are you suggesting, Richard?"

"The poodle?" Daniels shrugged. "We neutralize him."

Hawley frowned. "I'm afraid to ask what that means today, remembering what it once meant."

Daniels' face remained inscrutable. "Not assassination. There are many ways to neutralize people and you choose a method to fit the target. Now with a poodle, well, you might want to eliminate, or distract, or confuse its olfactory sense—get it barking up the wrong tree, so to speak. It's easy."

"I won't ask what *that* means, either."

"In this kind of matter it's better not to ask—and you don't give advice, no offense meant." He paused for a moment, leaning in toward Hawley. "Never forget: every man has his Judas." Daniels carefully dropped some ashes into an ashtray. "I have a fellow, name of Taggart. He'll make it all work."

"Honest reporters don't sell out, Richard."

"I don't doubt it. They're bought out. And I'm not being cynical, but everyone has a price. Ultimately. I include dedicated reporters, beautiful ladies, great researchers and scientists, even congressmen, yes, even Vice Presidents. You remember Agnew? If you'll study some history—and I know you have—they all simply get around to accepting the price, and sometimes—very often, in fact—despite their objection to selling, they accept because they're given no satisfactory alternative."

"An offer they can't refuse?"

"That's movie chatter," Daniels said, "but it'll do."

Hawley felt some concern about the anonymous reporter. "This reporter, he's not going to find out anything," he asserted, "it's just the nosing around, that's the problem. I certainly wouldn't want anything . . ."

"Hold it, Mr. Vice President," Daniels said politely, raising both hands as though to block Hawley. "Like I said, no advice, please. We'll take a look at the situation. I won't be interested in his motives, career, or integrity. I'm interested in only one thing: silencing the story. And note, I said story, not reporter.

We'll give him something to sniff about that simply removes him from your scent. It's that simple."

"All I have to do is forget it, that it?"

"Well said, sir."

Hawley reached across the table and proffered his hand. "Richard, I always value your good advice."

8

Hawley lay in bed, finally giving way to the exhaustion he felt from the hectic schedule of the day's events. Suddenly the ringing of his private line jarred him. He glanced at his watch. Few people had his special number, and fewer still would call after midnight. He knew it wouldn't be Daniels or anyone at the National Security Council; they'd use his official line. He knew instantly, however, that he didn't want to speak with Vivien Lessing should she be the caller. The truth was he'd been giving thought to changing the number simply because her calls had become more frequent and more demanding. He'd decided, since his rendezvous with her in Santa Barbara, to discourage her, gradually.

He let it ring, certain that if he did not answer and if it were Vivien she would finally conclude that he'd turned his phone off and would reluctantly give up for the night. He'd been doing that from time to time. In the end the ringing forced him to reach over and pick up the receiver.

To his astonishment it was Kathy Thompson. He immediately sat up, switching on the lamp next to the bed, all of his senses alert.

"I know it's late," she began, "but I thought I'd take the chance. I saw you on television," she said, letting the sentence hang there momentarily. "The interview with Cullen," she added.

"This is a surprise, and no it's not too late. How are you?" he asked, ignoring her explanation of the call.

"I'm fine. I just thought I had to tell you I'd seen you. Your visit to all of those historical places. It was very impressive, Cliff."

He was still not quite adjusted to the fact of her calling. "Well, I thank you. You didn't think maybe it was sacrilegious? Maybe too obvious? I mean mixing politics, speeches, that windup on Gratton's network?"

"It was all in good taste," Kathy insisted, "which is why I simply felt compelled—I think—yes, that's the right word, compelled, to make this call. I've had this number—"

"You never used it before."

"Yes, I know. I could have waited until morning, called your office—"

"I'm glad you didn't. I'm still up . . ."

"Well, yes. It's just that you're so seldom moved by anything on television these days . . ."

There was a brief pause, and Hawley began to wonder what had *really* prompted the call, wondering where she was in the White House, in what room. Kathy, at the other end of the line, held the phone tightly in her hand, wanting to speak out, hoping, perhaps, that Hawley might make some kind of inquiry, give some hint as to his own state of mind about the upcoming convention, but she felt constraint on showing more of an initiative than she'd already taken. "I simply wanted you to know, Cliff, that—how shall I put it? Yes—that one of your constituents thought you accomplished something quite memorable this day."

"I do thank you, Kathy."

"And I didn't wake you up? I see it's past midnight," she said.

"No, no," he said, "I'm very grateful you took the time." Then cautiously he added, "I hope you know you can do it—whenever . . ."

"Have another day like this," she said laughingly, "and you'll get calls galore and loads of fan mail."

"Maybe, but I especially appreciate *your* calling, Kathy. It's helped make the whole thing very much worthwhile."

"Thank you, Cliff." Then after a long pause, she said softly, "Good night, Cliff." He heard the click of the phone, then sat in his bed staring at the instrument, certain that behind the call there was a purpose. She had never called him on his private line. That in itself sent a signal. His thoughts were abruptly interrupted by the phone ringing again. Quickly he picked it up, thinking for a split second that she might have similar thoughts and had decided to be more direct. But this time it was Vivien.

"Your phone's been busy, honey," she said.

"Oh. Hello," he replied, trying to conceal his let-down feelings.

"Disappointed?" she asked. "Expecting someone else?"

"No, no," he replied. "Not at this hour," he said pointedly.

"Too late?"

"No, I'm up. But it's been a busy day."

"Out of the usual?" she asked, and Hawley knew she hadn't seen him on television.

"Watch the evening news, if you're in California. You are in California, aren't you?"

"I never watch the news. It's always so depressing. And I'm depressed enough. Yes, I'm here. At the house. The picture's not doing as well as they'd expected. Least, that's what they're telling me."

"The reviews have been excellent. That screening Jack Valenti set up last week—everyone there loved it."

"You think so?"

"I go by what I read and what everyone was saying."

"Jack Valenti's a dear little man. He likes everybody's picture."

"Don't you believe it," Hawley said, knowing exactly what had to be said to a Hollywood star. "Jack may be the greatest ambassador the movies ever had, but he doesn't gush about everything he sees. And he likes you."

"And you?"

"Are you in need of compliments, Vivien?"

"A woman never gets enough."

"You were sensational," he said, without enthusiasm.

"I don't believe you believe that," she replied.

Hawley smiled to himself, aware of Vivien's instant ability to go behind words, to dissect unspoken meanings.

"You were," he said with more conviction this time. "Believe it."

"Like those words last week at the Kirkland place in Chevy Chase?"

It was right after the screening, when a select group had been invited to the stately Kirkland mansion for a nightcap. Retired and elusive oil magnate P. J. Kirkland, who loved to bankroll movies in partnership with major production companies, had made his spacious home available to Vivien on her whirlwind promotion tour covering half a dozen major theatrical markets. Vivien had told the other guests that their reclusive host wanted everyone to have a good time, but he especially wanted a private meeting with the Vice President. And so, waving to the others, Vivien had led Hawley up the circular staircase, telling him that Kirkland, fast becoming a successor to the manners and eccentricities of a Howard Hughes, was waiting for him in his upstairs library.

Instead, she'd led him into a spacious bedroom. "P.J.'s not here," she said laughing. "He's in Borneo or Saudi Arabia or who the hell knows where, but the place is mine for the night. Nobody ever really knows where he is. I think I've seen him twice in my life, but he's always on my phone, flowers by the dozen every couple of weeks, beautiful gifts," she added, pulling at an emerald-encrusted bracelet, "and promises, promises that one day he'll be visiting, but you know that's all lies because he likes teenagers and is supposed to have a couple of harems filled with them and he can't get away with that in the states, no matter the millions or billions or whatever he has. The place is ours, darling," she said, throwing her arms around him.

Hawley listened patiently, annoyed that his private pledge to himself to cool the romance had been abruptly dissolved. When he kissed her perfunctorily, she crossed the room and dipped into her purse to take out a cigarette. "You don't like the arrangement?" she asked from across the room.

"Perfect," he replied. "But I can't stay, Vivien. I have a briefing first thing in the morning. Can't be put off."

"I'll be in Boston in the morning."

"Well, there you are," he said politely.

"I could just not show up," she said, sitting on the edge of the bed. Hawley knew from personal knowledge that Vivien Lessing had been the source of frequent confrontations between herself and Hollywood's production companies. She had, in fact, become increasingly unpredictable, and his concern had been sharpened by the fact that his name had been, on more than one occasion, linked to hers as a possible cause for her failure to show up on the set in the middle of production. Her defiance of studios and directors had become legendary, and was tolerated only because of the huge successes her pictures had scored.

Hawley looked across the room at her as she lay back against the elaborate headboard, scanning him. "If the picture isn't doing well, do you want to risk breaking your schedule?"

"Fuck the schedule," she replied airily.

"Won't that alienate them?"

"So?"

"You'd risk that?"

"I've risked that, Mr. Hawley, more than once. Just for you," she said, blowing out a smoke ring.

"I'm aware of that," Hawley said, "but—"

"So what if you're late for *your* briefing? What if you're just tired? Who can fire *you?*"

"Touché," he said, "but if this picture's in trouble, if it's not doing business, do you really want—"

"Cliff," she said, snuffing out her cigarette, "if the picture flops, you flop. Yes, the star gets all the credit if she's a big enough star. And all the blame. I can be the biggest pain in the ass to the director, the producer, the cast, even to moneybags, but as long as the customers are paying, they'll tolerate it. If the picture flops, that's a different story. I hate the whole business if you want to know the truth."

"Your fans love you."

"They're fickle." She took out another cigarette and lit it. "You're fickle, too."

"What brings that on?"

Suddenly she leaped from the bed, crossed the room, and threw her arms around him. "Because you're trying to tell me something but you can't or you won't and I know it. I hear it in your voice. I see it in the way you behave. You have me and then you leave in the middle of the night which is when I want you, when I need you. Don't you understand, Cliff, how a woman needs a man and wants him especially after he's used her? Sneaking away like you did in Santa Barbara? When I woke up alone—"

"Vivien," Hawley said, "you knew I was going to leave. I'd told you."

She leaned against him. "I know, I know you did. But I didn't show up that whole day, the studio was furious. And tonight . . . I'm here. Cliff, I'm not certain anymore about anything, about Hollywood, about pictures—"

"Hold still. You have a career, a great one. You have commitments, you've told me, in Hollywood, London, Italy—"

"It may not be the commitment I really need," she said, looking up at him.

"You can't throw all of that away, not yet."

"I don't know," she said, moving away. "I don't know about anything anymore. About us. Do you?"

Hawley shrugged. He didn't want to get into any sort of heart-to-heart conversation. He reached out and pulled her toward him as a gesture of understanding.

"How much time do we have, Cliff?" she asked. "Do *you* have?" she asked, pouting.

"Time enough," he said, taking her in his arms.

☆ ☆ ☆

Harry Thompson was uncomfortable in the presence of his father as they sat together in the Oval Office.

"You might have thought a little more about going up to Gettysburg yourself, Harry," the President said. "Mr. Kraus put it bluntly. Your being there gave the whole business my blessing."

"I didn't know it was all tied into Arlington and Philadelphia and the Vietnam Memorial."

"Mr. Hawley seems to have pulled off a nice little stunt."

Harry pointed toward the ceiling. "That's what Kathy said."

"Kathy?" Thompson seemed puzzled.

"Called to congratulate him."

"Called? Him? You know that?"

Harry Thompson pulled out a small cassette from his pocket and placed it on the President's desk.

The President stared at his son, icy anger in his eyes. "I thought this had all ended," he said pointing to the cassette.

"It *had* ended," his son insisted, "except for what Jeb picked up." Noting his father's irritation, he added, "Jeb. Lieutenant Rossmore. I mentioned him last time. Chap who's in charge of the Signal Corps unit that handles communications—"

"Tapes," his father said sarcastically.

"Tapes," Harry repeated.

"It's to end, Harry. Period." He shoved the tape toward Harry. "I want this destroyed. This and all of the others."

Harry Thompson raised a hand of protest. "You don't want to listen? To just one small section?"

"Don't you understand, Harry, how loathsome all of this is? Am I to sit here and believe that you actually want me to do that? Do you know what you're asking me to do?"

"It seems to me that it's all for the best," Harry said glumly.

"The best." The elder Thompson shook his head in disbelief. "To tape private conversations, here in the White House. To eavesdrop. Worse. To preserve the evidence. And for what purpose?"

Harry seized the opening, the words rushing out. "To protect the presidency, that's the purpose," he argued. "To make sure you know what's going on, yes, right here, right under your very nose, here, at the White House."

"To catch somebody when they're totally unaware—"

"She has Hawley's private number—"

"Stop it!" Thompson shouted.

"She used it! The tape proves it—"

"I don't want any proof of that call or any other call! Am I making myself clear? I will not be a party to this, Harry!" He picked up the tape and flung it to his son. "You're to destroy it and the whole shabby system. Do I make myself clear?"

"Yes," Harry muttered. "We just thought—"

"You tell young Rossmore it's over! And make sure none of these tapes exists! No copies! They are *all* to be destroyed!" He sat back shaking his head. "This is evil, Harry, evil!"

Harry fumbled with the tape. "I'm sorry you feel that way. What this tape proves—"

"I don't care *what* it proves!"

"—is that they knew each other—"

"Of course they knew each other! You seem to forget that I met Kathy *through* Mr. Hawley!"

"Before. They knew each other *before.* That's what's implicit—"

The President stood up, the veins throbbing in his temples. "I refused to listen to your tapes before, Harry. I refuse to hear you tell me what's on *that* tape and what inferences you care to draw. The matter is closed, Harry. Closed!"

Harry Thompson stood quietly before his father. The President sat down and turned his attention to papers on his desk.

"You don't even want to think about it?"

"I don't want to think about it at all. No." Without looking up, he added, "I'm busy, Harry."

Harry Thompson pocketed the tape and stood for a moment in silence before his father, watching him scan some papers on his desk. There was, he knew, nothing more to be said. And it didn't matter. He had completed his objective; he had left no doubt of a key element that the tape proved and that his father had to know: Kathy Thompson and Clifford Hawley had a prior relationship. It wasn't necessary for his father to hear the tape. The essential fact was now known. The President would have to deal with it. Harry was satisfied that he had marked Hawley.

☆ ☆ ☆

Commander Jeff Whitney had summoned his executive officer to his quarters. He handed a sheaf of papers across to him. "We've passed the first part of our mission, Art," he said, "and now the hard part as you can note from special orders."

Morgan pulled over a chair and started reading. Suddenly he looked up. "Ninety more days underwater?" Morgan asked, a look of surprise on his face as he read on. "And no contact from this ship? We just continue to listen?"

Whitney nodded. "We listen. And scan all low frequencies as usual. Coded, naturally. That's what came in an hour ago."

"Now I finally know why Doc's aboard."

"Not hard to guess."

"We told the crew it was training for *him*."

"Now they'll know. It's training for *them*. He's aboard just in case we have an unexpected major medical problem."

"What if it's a problem he can't handle?"

"He's a surgeon."

"Okay, but what if it's something he's never handled before?" Morgan persisted.

Whitney shook his head. "He'll *have* to handle it. Period."

"No outside above, that it? No emergency outs?"

Whitney nodded.

"Crew's liable to get a little edgy."

"That's something else we'll find out, among other things. Let's spell it out to them." Whitney stood up and started out down the long pale-green narrow passageway, Morgan following.

As they came to a closed watertight door the sailor on duty swung it open.

"How you doing, Porter?" Jeff asked.

"Fine, Captain."

"Good. Any problems?"

"No, sir."

"That's good," Whitney replied.

"Aye, aye, sir."

Whitney and Morgan continued on the upper-level passageway, one of three levels of the sub, and entered the command center, a large open area of some forty by fifty feet crammed with gauges, piping, control equipment, a chart table, and banks of electronic devices. Whitney nodded to the men nearest him and went to the ship's loudspeaker. "All hands, this is the captain speaking," he said.

"With the large number of movie films and videotapes we have on board and the jammed freezers and with every nook and cranny full of food and other consumables, I know you're all geared up for our usual patrol of seventy days plus or minus a day or so." He paused for a moment. "This mission will last for at least twice that. Minimum."

Whitney heard one sailor whistle softly and glanced about the command center noting another sailor's lips pursed with a look of great surprise on his face. "Minimum," he repeated. "This is, first of all, a challenge for the other side to figure out what we're up to; second, it's an endurance test for each and every one of us aboard. We will continue as heretofore to maintain as much quiet as possible within the ship. Any unnecessary noise will result in disciplinary action for the offender. No exceptions. For your information a sister sub is out on patrol undergoing the same endurance test in the Pacific. These boats can go to great depths. We'll be changing our depth shortly, headed down to test a depth that's deeper than many of you have ever experienced. The ship can take it. We will also be heading south and west for a deep-sea mount in the area. Once there we'll remain on patrol until further orders. That's all."

Jeff moved to the navigator's desk and gave him the new coordinates. He nodded to the two planesmen and headed back to his own quarters, once again passing the same sailor on duty at his watertight door. "Any problems for you now, Porter?"

"No sir, you answered them," he replied with a smile.

Morgan and Whitney returned to Whitney's quarters. "Captain," Morgan said, "I think most of them knew. They saw all that canned stuff stored everywhere. And the smart ones were guessing. And even old Chief Walker, while at first he was surprised at the number of movies we had, finally said to me one day, 'There has to be a reason.' He'd never seen so many. Got him to thinking. He figured somebody upstairs is cooking something for somebody downstairs. Us."

"Hornwell," Whitney replied. "He's the cook. Now I can tell you that I met with him. This is something he wants. I'll tell you the rest another time. But first he wanted us to get the ship away from Soviet surveillance—he figured we'd lose them for sure when we camped under that high-speed tanker without leaving a trace on the surface. Second, he figures a routine seventy-day patrol is no substitute for this kind of assignment—to test the full capabilities and limitations of this boat and her crew. They think they're seasoned, but we're going to make sure."

"We can handle it," Morgan said. "This boat and its crew are the best in the Navy."

"Agreed. But be ready for surprises," Whitney countered, "because that's why we're here."

☆ ☆ ☆

The President chatted amiably with the special guests he'd invited to the Oval Office to attend the television interview he'd granted NBC. Pleased at the compliments he had received on his statements and appearance, he glanced at Kathy, who smiled her encouragement from the opposite side of the room.

In the past years he had become such a television pro that he knew the modest makeup he was wearing concealed the evidence of his failing health. Kathy had helped him in the privacy of their bedroom. When he entered the office, the network's young makeup man, sable brush in hand, had approached and quietly told him, "You don't need any makeup, Mr. President. You look just fine."

The President had walked over to Kathy. "Young man, I want you to meet the President's special makeup artist."

"I remember her very well on camera, Mr. President. We miss her."

"Well, who knows? Someday maybe she'll want to do some television again." The makeup man smiled politely. "And in the meantime," Thompson added, an enigmatic smile on his face, "I get the benefits of her expertise."

Kathy looked sharply at her husband, a quizzical expression in her eyes. She turned to the makeup man and said, with a laugh, "It's my way of keeping my hand in the business. The President really needs very little help from me."

After the crew removed its equipment from the office following the interview, the guests felt free to move about and chat. Henry Kraus, like Kathy out of range of the cameras, had given the President little nods of encouragement throughout the session. Robert Mountain, once a leading man in Hollywood and now a television adviser to the President, Cabinet, and White House staff, picked up the few cue cards he'd personally held for the President's opening remarks. Kraus considered the former actor a nuisance, but it amused him and other staff members to see Mountain arrive, still lean and always tanned, dressed in striped trousers and black formal jacket whenever his services were required.

Thompson moved easily from one guest to another, letting the staff photographer shoot pictures as he moved about. He shared a brandy with the diminutive Minority Leader, Harvey Jordan, listening courteously to the latter's complaints, especially determined to give him a glowing impression of his own vitality. When Robert Olsen, a former Cabinet officer, raised his own camera to catch the two of them, Thompson playfully said, "Hold it, Mr. Olsen. Only with the express permission of the Minority Leader." There was polite laughter in the vicinity and Jordan, in a broad southern accent, said, "Permission granted, provided the President signs two copies, one for each grandchild."

"Done," said Thompson as Olsen clicked away.

The President moved over to greet Dr. E. Wilson Nichols, a renowned Jeffersonian scholar. "I want to thank you for sending me the note about Jefferson's tombstone, professor. I'd quite forgotten there was no reference on it to his being Secretary of State, Vice President, and President, that he much preferred being remembered as the author of the Declaration and the father of your university."

"You paraphrased it very well tonight, Mr. President—his wanting to be remembered not for what his country did for him, but for what he did for his country. Nicely put," Nichols said, touching the President's glass with his.

Thompson smiled. "A bit of a switch on Kennedy's famous words," he said.

After a few minutes more of social conviviality, Kraus went to the door leading out of the Oval Office, whereupon each guest, recognizing the signal, took his leave of the President and First Lady. But the President touched the arm of Frederick K. Vance, Chairman of the Senate Armed Services Committee, and said softly, "Kathy and I would like to visit with you, Senator, if your time permits?"

A surprised Vance took a place in the corner of a sofa to which the President pointed. Thompson, relaxing in a comfortable wing chair nearby, asked, "How did the TV interview go in your opinion, Senator?"

Vance nodded his head approvingly. "Perfect, Mr. President. Just perfect." He pulled out a long Havana cigar. "Do you object, Mr. President? Mrs. Thompson?" The President waved his approval, and Kathy smiled politely.

"You didn't mind—you don't think the public would mind the couple of times when I seemed to stammer?" the President asked.

"Certainly not," Vance said. "That only makes you seem all the more natural. Who speaks in precise dictionary language anyway? I don't know anyone, except maybe the Vice President. And that's not meant to criticize him."

At the reference to Hawley, Thompson's eyes narrowed. Kathy, wearing a brown linen suit, was annoyed by the senator's critical comment about Hawley, but she remained silent, self-composed, smiling in a way familiar in news photos.

Vance decided not to light his cigar, not in the Oval Office, not in the presence of the First Lady. He was pleased, though, as he leaned back on the comfortable sofa, conscious of the singular attention Thompson had accorded him. The word would go out, along with a seed of further doubt about Clifford Hawley's future.

Vance fingered the old gold watch chain suspended from a tiny gold bar in his lapel buttonhole. The watch, a family heirloom, was tucked neatly in his pocket behind a carefully placed white handkerchief. He patted the errant brown hair that fell across his forehead and stroked one knee covered by the worn brown tweed of his favorite suit. Vance imagined that the President liked his own unpretentious style, and more important, the way he'd supported the President's bills on the floor of the Senate. His having been asked to attend the interview was no capricious act; the President was not a capricious man—he had to have a purpose. Vance shrewdly concluded that the purpose would be good news for the senator from Kansas.

The President broke into Vance's reverie. "I'm going to take an occasional trip out of Washington," Thompson announced, "and I wondered if your schedule would permit you to accompany me." Vance felt his pulse quicken.

Kathy was fully aware of the significance of the invitation and wondered whether anyone else would be invited on the proposed trip. The President confirmed her suspicions. "I don't want to make anything big out of this, you understand, Senator, even though it would just be the two of us. Oh, and one more." He looked at Kathy, their eyes meeting briefly before he returned his attention to Vance. "Hornwell. Promised him. Since he's Chairman of the Joint Chiefs and you're Chairman of the Senate Armed Services Committee, we'll—" For a moment he paused to search for the right words. "—We'll just let it sit like that. That all right with you?"

The senator found it difficult to conceal his own satisfaction. He would sit back and let Thompson call the shots. "I'm sure I can make the necessary arrangements, sir. My pleasure. My pleasure," he repeated.

☆ ☆ ☆

The clash of foils echoed through the White House gymnasium. Lane Whitney found himself giving ground, doing his best to parry the slashing advance of Clifford Hawley. The latter kept pushing his attack, thrusting and lunging, pressing his opponent, forcing him off the marked area until finally, in a series of brilliant feints, parries, and ripostes, Hawley, with a twist of his foil, suddenly disarmed Whitney. Hawley removed his protective mask and offered his hand.

"You could have run me through a dozen times," Whitney said, taking the proffered hand.

"And miss the whole point of the exercise?" Hawley replied good-naturedly. He passed his foil to the Secret Service agent who had escorted him to the gym. "Where you miss, Lane, is in your finger play."

"I know, I know. I hold the damn thing too tight."

"Right. It's the action of the fingers, right there," he pointed to the hilt of Whitney's foil, which he'd picked up. "Thumb and forefinger, not the wrist. You can direct the blade quicker and more precisely to the target. Watch Harry next time he drops in. He sticks to the fundamental principles. Practices all the time, which is another reason you're vulnerable."

"He's been developing a new style, too."

The two men began to walk to the locker room. "I've noticed that," Hawley said. "Keeps his blade from striking yours."

"Sure, so you do all the work, feinting, moving—"

"That forces you to show your own hand a bit. You have to draw him out, find out his plans." Hawley paused a moment. "Something like politics, wouldn't you say?"

"Could be. Yeah," Lane added. "And speaking of politics—see that note on the President's trip to Nebraska? With Senator Vance and Admiral Hornwell? I can understand Hornwell, but Vance?" Lance scratched his red hair.

"The senator is Chairman of the Armed Services Committee," Hawley said noncommittally.

"I know. But they're not just going to Nebraska to have a look at the missile control center. I'm talking about the L.A. trip."

Hawley frowned. "Los Angeles? Vance?"

"What's that all mean, Mr. Veep?"

Hawley shook his head. "I don't know."

"When the press gets word, you're going to be questioned."

"For sure."

The two men stripped down and headed for the shower. "This isn't the first time Vance has gotten special attention," Lane shouted as Hawley stepped under the cold water.

Hawley raised a warning finger to his lips. "The Senator's worthy of it. A big vote getter," he said, a half smile on his face.

There was no need, Hawley thought, to risk any further discussion within the White House itself, or to examine the various inferences that might be drawn from the spotlighting of Vance. The question was whether President Thompson, in separating himself more and more from his Vice President, was indulging in preconvention feints to throw the opposition off guard, or whether the move was designed for something else. In this game Hawley knew that the President held most of the cards.

But Hawley also knew there was one card in his own hands. The Committee had just begun its work.

9

Alice Curtis was on the last leg of her daily walk around the park across from her hotel and along the lake, enjoying the sights and sounds of Geneva, now almost a second home to her. She loved its old mansard roofs, the wrought-iron balustrades of the hotel balconies, its fountains, and the splash of color of its seasonal flowers that together gave the city its distinctive visual charm.

She looked at her watch, aware that Ralph Saunders, her senior arms-control adviser, always prompt, would be waiting for her in the fashionable suite set aside for her in Le Richmond, first among the great hotels of the city.

Hurrying back through the park, nodding politely to an elderly couple who obviously recognized her, she walked through the elegant lobby, filled with international visitors chatting in little clusters amidst the lavish furnishings and the valuable etchings that adorned the walls.

Now seated at her baroque desk she let her eyes rest on the papers that lay on it. Saunders had risen courteously upon her entrance and resumed his chair across from her, pulling out a folder from his attaché case containing papers identical to those Mrs. Curtis was reviewing.

Alice Curtis had tried to respond to Thompson's request that she draft a personal letter to the President of the Soviet Union, but she knew the letter she'd prepared was too long and too full of technical details. She glanced at Saunders, a former congressman who'd wound up serving as Chairman of the House Armed Services Committee, one of a handful of legislators who had mastered the arcane world of nuclear armament and of the complex theories that dictated tactical and strategic use of nuclear weapons. He was a key part of the American team, elements of which had been meeting with their Soviet counterparts for a dozen years.

"Well?" she said, as she pushed the papers aside.

"If your letter's to be sent by Mr. Thompson, its thoroughness will impress the Soviet President—of that you can be sure," Saunders said, his eyes directed at the papers.

"You said 'if.'"

"I believe Turgenev knows all, or most, of what's in it. Who was first with the atom bomb, the hydrogen bomb, with intercontinental missiles, missile-firing subs, multiple warheads. He knows how lethal every weapons system is. He doesn't want the Soviet Union incinerated. He knows *we* don't want to be incinerated. He understands the dilemma."

"So?"

"I don't think this letter should be sent."

"Why not?"

Saunders removed his glasses and began to wipe them with his blue silk breast handkerchief. "I don't believe in one-on-one private correspondence between an American President and a Soviet President, even if they were capable of sitting down and talking the same language. I'll admit, Alice, that *you* could do it with Turgenev, as you did with Gorbachev, because you speak their language, you understand idiomatic phrases and nuances and subtleties—still, nothing can come of it."

"That's a pessimistic attitude, Ralph."

"Realistic." He carefully adjusted his glasses. "I'm afraid just saying how dreadful the situation is and how it ought to be resolved for the sake of one's own family does nothing to settle the issues. Alice, no one can really personalize nuclear power."

"If people back home heard you, they'd say you think the situation is hopeless."

"I'd never admit it, but even after all that Gorbachev precipitated, I often have to fight off that very feeling."

Alice Curtis lit a cigarette. "One of my two for the day,"

she said, inhaling. She fixed her green eyes upon him. "It goes deeper than the President sending a letter, doesn't it, Ralph?"

"Like I said, I've never believed in intimacy between an American President and a Soviet President. They can never be true friends. Remember Carter embracing Brezhnev? Nixon sharing the same footrest with him? Eisenhower jollying it up with Khrushchev at Camp David? Johnson with Kosygin? Reagan with an arm around Gorbachev? It was always like oil and water. They simply don't mix. And Thompson and Turgenev are even farther apart."

"Why do you say that?"

"Because Turgenev is clever, more clever even than Gorbachev. Don't forget he was a top lawyer, too. He knows details about research, about weapons systems. Put them in a room together and Thompson must come out bested."

"All from a letter?"

"Yes. Because it has the danger of leading to personal meetings. Meetings that are something less than formal summits. Like the first Bush-Gorbachev meeting in the Mediterranean back in '89."

"You think the President would give away the store?"

"This President might. Not deliberately, of course. I just don't like to see us start something from which there'd be no turning back."

Alice Curtis snuffed out her cigarette. "Ralph, you said *this* President. Meaning?"

Saunders rocked back and forth in his chair. "I'm only echoing something you said to me after your last visit to Washington."

Alice Curtis remembered the concern she'd expressed about her evaluation of the President's health and state of mind.

"If we were talking about someone else—Mr. Hawley, for instance . . . his retentive power, his specific knowledge of the technical details on both sides. Maybe it's because he's younger, maybe it's what you told me, the way he's grown in office, the way he does his homework—so, if this were a matter between him and Turgenev—but it isn't," Ralph said, letting the matter hang.

"I understand, Ralph," she said. "A formal summit has built-in protection for both sides." Alice put the papers aside. "Perhaps," she said, "it's time we had dinner."

"Good idea. Shall we try the Amphitryon? I promised Edna I'd bring you. Amphitryon okay?"

"Le Pavillon. Just as good, less expensive," Alice replied. "I'm very glad she's joined you, Ralph. I hope she stays for the duration."

"Six more weeks, she says. Then I have to fend for myself."

"You'll manage, you always do." She suddenly smiled. "Ralph, I think I know how to handle the President's request. It's a matter of timing. The election's coming on, fast. The President shouldn't do anything to encourage Turgenev to push him for a summit when it might not work to the President's advantage—politically, that is. After the election, well, that's a different matter."

Saunders picked up his attaché case and glanced up at Alice. "Will he take Hawley?"

Alice passed her papers across to Saunders. "Will you handle these, and I'll meet you in the lobby in ten minutes?" Saunders placed the papers in his case. "Hawley? I don't know. You've heard the rumors? Vance?"

"A good man. Well informed."

"Yes. Senator Vance knows more details about arms and arms control than anyone else in Congress, that's for sure. But Hawley has the edge. For me," she added. "He has knowledge, too, plus that indispensable ingredient that marks a potential leader."

"Judgment?" Saunders suggested.

"That's it," she said. She wondered as Saunders left the room whether she should let the President know her views. Probably not. She wasn't a politician. Perhaps this was a matter she should discuss with the Secretary of State. She had confidence in Jaggers and he had always supported her. She liked him, and even more important, she knew Jaggers was close to the Vice President.

☆ ☆ ☆

The President had steeled himself from thinking about the tapes and their secret messages. He had characterized the whole system as evil, and he knew that even to think of the matter was also evil and self-destructive. He didn't want to think of Kathy calling Hawley to congratulate him on his obvious political sideshow. He didn't want to think about private phone numbers, or Hawley's past relationship to Kathy. And so he immersed himself in his work.

Thompson sat at his desk in his upstairs office wading through an assortment of official bills and departmental reports, and dictating correspondence to Betsy King. Kathy entered with a white-haired black butler carrying a tray. She shook her head, her short auburn hair gently touching her cheeks. "I know, I know, Kathy," the President said, pointing her to a chair, "but going from one place to another just to eat, that's a waste of time. Am I right, Betsy?" he asked, looking at his secretary.

Betsy King began to reassemble the papers on the President's desk so that the tray could be placed before him. "I don't make the decisions for you, sir," was her quiet reply. Kathy smiled at the older woman; she knew that Betsy had left out the word *anymore.* Thompson had more than once told Kathy that after the death of his first wife, Betsy had simply taken over and made life bearable for him. Now, of course, things were different; with Kathy on the scene, Betsy had been forced to retreat to her own cul-de-sac, a place that still brought her, occasionally, rewards of its own. When Thompson talked of economics, Betsy was able to communicate in an idiom foreign to Kathy. Having been Thompson's secretary through the years of his rise in the financial world, Betsy had a special kinship with Thompson that was for Kathy a goading reminder that Thompson and Betsy still had much in common. The trouble for Betsy was that she had not expected Thompson to be so foolish as to marry a woman half his age.

Kathy sat at one end of the desk as the butler set the two modest lunches in place, Thompson watching Betsy hurry away. "You don't like her very much, do you?"

"I don't like her is correct, Mr. President, especially when you ask her for *her* opinion on something *you* decided was already best for you—a break for lunch until you regain some of your old strength." Kathy rose and went around the desk to pick up the President's napkin, which had fallen to the floor.

"You're pouting," he said chuckling. "I'll admit Betsy has her own curious way of letting you know of her disapproval by a look, or by the way she snaps up her papers, but seldom in words."

"She's snide," Kathy commented.

Thompson sat back in his big chair. "Snide," he repeated. "That's not a nice word."

"She must once have dreamed of marrying you," Kathy replied.

The President burst out laughing. "Betsy? Betsy King marry me?"

"Why not? She'd worked side by side with you for years. She knew all of your foibles and whims. She was five or six years younger—"

"I always thought she was a hundred and ten, even when she first came to work for me, and at that time she must have been about twenty-eight. Old, proper, detached even then."

"But a female. And if you hadn't been married then she would have spun her own little web. Given time," Kathy said with emphasis, "*she* would have married *you*."

"You've analyzed it that much?" Thompson said, picking at his salad.

"I wish you'd eat more, Stephen, really. The doctor says you have to put on some weight."

The President leaned forward, his penetrating blue eyes looking out over his rimless glasses. "And did *you* marry *me*?"

Kathy smiled mischievously. "George Bernard Shaw said it in his plays: women marry men."

"And you women let us believe that it's we who win you, that it?"

"It's the pretty words that finally tip the woman over, not the masculine physical supremacy. And you, Mr. President, have a gift with words."

"Knocked out all those young Lancelots."

"You did just that," she said in her crisp, positive manner.

There was a momentary pause before he spoke. "You've never told me about them, these—these Lancelots." His voice fell almost to a whisper. "Tell me, Kathy, are they still around flexing their muscles? Someone in particular? Waiting perhaps?"

As he observed Kathy's eyes grow moist he couldn't suppress the sudden vision of Hawley standing beside her, the knowledge that there was more to that relationship than he'd ever been told. And as Kathy searched her husband's face it pained her to realize that Thompson was suffering a sense of personal inadequacy. She went around the desk for a moment to place a reassuring arm around the President's shoulder. "Stephen, you're never to say that again. Never, never!"

He stood up, walking her to the window, looking out toward the iridescent fountain and the green lawn. "There are times when I wake up and hear you—do you know you toss and grind your teeth?"

"And you don't stop me?" Kathy said with mock disapproval.

"Well, now you'll be getting some real rest because of the trip I'm taking with Senator . . . Senator . . . *damn!*" he stopped abruptly, his right fist slapping into the palm of his left hand.

"Vance," Kathy said, softly.

"Yes, of course. Vance and I and—and Hornwell—we're going off on an inspection trip. Command center is top security, but I'd like you to join me in Los Angeles. Will you?"

"Of course, Stephen. You think I wouldn't?"

"Well, it's all wrapped up with politics—which, as you know, leaves me very cold—and with the convention . . ." He moved back to his desk and picked up his teacup and saucer. "Convention'll soon be on top of us. Plus some very important decisions," he said as he sipped his tea and turned to study her.

She wondered if he was trying to encourage her to ask the one question that was on her mind at the moment: Is Clifford Hawley to be your running mate? She simply said, "I'm sure you'll make the right decisions, Stephen."

"Yes, yes," he said, as he returned the cup and saucer to the tray on his desk. "We'll be there together. It'll be sunny. We'll tour the city, probably in an open car. It's all hogwash, of course, but I'm told that sort of thing will assuage a lot of doubts. About my—let's say—indisposition. People just don't know that there aren't enough hours for any President to do the job he sets out to do. The damned entrenched bureaucracy and the little cabals that think their secrets aren't known!" His face clouded with anger. Then, with a sidelong glance at Kathy, his voice becoming intimate, he said, "And others who may think *their* little secrets are protected. They'll have to make an accounting! All of them, all in due time! We're going to change some things that need changing." He began to chuckle, the thick veins that a moment before had stood out along his temples now pale blue tracings on the surface of his skin.

"You will rest for an hour, won't you?" Kathy asked solicitously.

He stood in the doorway leading to their bedroom. "Senator Vance. Good man, Kathy, good man. Honest. Loyal." He waited a moment for her reaction.

"I'm sure he is," she replied.

"Loyalty. Faithfulness. Rare qualities today. Rare." With that he was gone. Kathy wrapped her arms about herself. She felt cold and drained. For a passing moment she wondered whether any of his diatribe had been directed at her. She brushed aside any such feelings. Her concern was about the trip to Los Angeles, whether her husband could cope with the strain of a campaign. And she worried about the future of a man whose name had remained unspoken but whose presence she felt. She had wanted to say something to Hawley during her midnight call of the day before, to give him some warning, but her instincts told her that he must already know.

☆ ☆ ☆

Since there had been no Cabinet meeting for some weeks, Thompson had acceded to Kraus' suggestion that he call one, if only to demonstrate that he was on top of his job and that his recent remoteness had no particular significance. As the President entered the cream-colored room, the members of the Cabinet rose from the long oval table, in use since the presidency of Richard Nixon. Thompson walked briskly to his oxblood leather chair (identical to all the others) and indicated to the Cabinet that they be seated. A full complement of staff aides, plus other officials of Cabinet rank, resumed their seats set against the inside wall. The President placed his large gnarled hands upon the polished mahogany surface of the table and, smiling at his colleagues, turned to exchange a few cursory remarks with Edward Jaggers.

Thompson's eyes rested momentarily on the face of Clifford Hawley, directly across from him. He heard his son's voice. "She has Hawley's private number." Now he wondered how often she used it, and why. He gripped the arms of his chair to gain his self-control. He made no effort to acknowledge Hawley's presence, but looked past him to the Rose Garden, then glanced momentarily at the portrait of Ronald Reagan hanging over the fireplace to his left. Opening the meeting in a brisk manner, he called on the ascetic-looking Secretary of the Treasury, John Mantley, to review the nation's economy.

Thompson tried to listen with care, fully aware that he, not Mantley, was the center of interest and that the others were surreptitiously examining him. He slipped his hands from the table and placed them on his lap, so that their occasional tremor might be less noticeable.

The President made a polite inquiry of Mantley. Struggling to keep his private thoughts suppressed, he was embarrassed to learn that Mantley thought he'd covered the matter inadequately a few moments before. "Your field, Mr. Secretary, sometimes is so filled with esoteric—some would even say—" floundering for the right word, he looked from one adviser to another for support.

Hawley moved in adroitly. "The President is absolutely correct, Mr. Secretary. Your expertise—and his," he added, deferentially, "especially in a field that seems to the rest of us to border not only on the esoteric but more on the occult—" here there was polite laughter "—is something that can bear not only a little repetition, but a bit more explanation."

As Hawley spoke he'd hoped to find a touch of appreciation in the President's attitude; there was none, leaving Hawley increasingly baffled at the President's continued indifference to him.

After hearing several more reports, the President straightened up and summarized the key matters brought before the Cabinet. "Well," he said, "I think this has been a fine session. Now, I have one bit of news to report myself." With a show of enthusiasm he outlined his pending trip to Nebraska and Los Angeles.

When the President concluded his remarks, Jaggers, on his right, addressed him. "All of us wish you a fine trip, Mr. President, and incidentally, we're all of us very glad to see you looking so well." Then with a glance toward Hawley, he added, "And each and every one of us is available to you, if need be, out on the road, if we can be of service."

Thompson stood up. "Thank you, Mr. Secretary, I appreciate your words and your offer. But I'll be counting on all of you to do your part right here while I do mine out there among the people." He looked again from one Cabinet member to another, as he said, softly, "It's time they had a look at their President, too, wouldn't you all agree?" Smiling, he took the extended hands of those nearest him. Then waving farewell with both hands raised above him, he strode out of the room.

Jaggers glanced over at Hawley, eyebrows arching, shoulders shrugging, his movements indicating that the President had chaired the meeting very well. No matter that he'd apparently gone blank once or twice, asking people to repeat themselves. Jaggers knew—they all knew—that some members of the Cabinet had the gift of rendering any room somnolent. He'd even gone blank himself on more than one occasion.

Hawley hesitated for a moment, and then, on impulse, made a decision to overtake the President to wish him well, but he was too late. Thompson was moving down the corridor accompanied by a military attaché, the aide's gold-braided fourragère sparkling with reflected light from an overhead chandelier. Hawley watched the President and the aide march off; although unaware of Hawley, Thompson was determined to demonstrate his vigor to any viewer by setting a lively pace.

☆ ☆ ☆

Hawley's visitor was waiting impatiently in his White House outer office. Chunky Joe Gratton was cracking his knuckles when Hawley entered the room. "Come on in, Joe, sorry to be late. Cabinet meetings sometimes stretch." He waved his visitor to one of the two blue and white striped love seats that complemented a square marble-topped coffee table. Hawley picked up a decanter; he was well acquainted with Gratton's appetite for gin and vodka. Glancing at his watch, he said, "A bit early, but if you'd like?"

"It can wait," Joe growled. "I hate your lousy Washington weather. It's either too hot or too cold and it's always humid. Stinks."

Hawley returned the decanter to a sideboard. "From the message you left, I take it this isn't one of your courtesy calls," Hawley said, as he settled into a corner of the seat opposite Gratton.

"No, it isn't. I don't like runarounds. I especially don't like them from ex-employees." He stared hard at Hawley through his thick lenses.

"Meaning?"

"The First Lady is what I'm meaning."

"Oh?" Hawley remarked. "I didn't realize we'd be talking about her so soon again."

"She's predictable as far as I'm concerned. I didn't mention this the other night, just in case I was wrong about her." Gratton's eyes hardened as he looked at Hawley. "I'm not going to be so polite about her anymore. She is getting to be just another little fucking—"

"Joe, hold it!" Hawley snapped, raising both hands in protest. "Let's just calm down . . ."

"That's how I feel," Joe grumbled. "I don't like the feeling of being had. On second thought . . ." he pointed to Hawley's decanter.

Hawley got up and brought over vodka and a glass. "Ice?"

"Skip the ice. Just a touch more," he said as Hawley poured.

Gratton raised the glass to his lips. "We were talking about her working for Federal. Of the favors I did, you did. Like I said, I hired her because of you. *You*," he repeated. "Put it another way, I did *you* a favor."

"If I remember correctly, Joe, you specifically told the lady that it was the other way around—I was doing you the favor by bringing her to *your* attention."

"Bullshit."

"Those were your words, Joe."

"What I said was I let people like you—you were in the House then—do me a favor. That was a nice way of putting it. But the point is she wound up getting a job. The main point. Right?"

"I'm listening, Joe."

Gratton rolled his tightly cleaned fists against each other. "I sent her a letter. Very polite letter. Not a word about our former association. Nothing like a quid pro quo, not a hint, not a trace. Just an invitation, to do what other First Ladies have done. Jacqueline Kennedy. Nancy Reagan. Mrs. Bush. A visit through the White House, all America watching. An hour of prime time. If not the White House, then Camp David, the Smithsonian—she names it."

"And she said?"

"She said nothing! Zip! That's what she said!" He reached into an inner pocket and flung a letter across the table. "She's so goddamn busy, so committed to this and that, she hasn't got the time to answer her own mail. A spokeswoman answered for her. That's Kathy Bryson, ex-interviewer. Too fucking busy to write a letter to the man who happens to be the one who okayed her going out to meet the man who was not only to become the President of the United States, but her fucking husband as well, that's what!" Gratton sipped his drink, then put his glass on the table. "You remember calling me with your suggestion she do it?"

"I do, Joe. And we talked about it at the Hay-Adams." Hawley picked up the letter and deliberately took his time reading it, wanting Gratton to cool down. "I can understand, Joe," he said, looking up, "reading this, your irritation, etcetera. I think she was just trying to be conservative—"

"Conservative!"

"She hasn't said no, flat out—"

"Well, she sure as hell hasn't said yes!"

"I think she's being diplomatic. Doesn't want the other networks to think she had an obligation to—"

"Fuck the other networks!"

Hawley ignored the outburst. "—to do something special for you just because she once worked at Federal. That's all this is. She'll get around to doing it. She hasn't closed any doors."

"I don't play games, Cliff. She owes me. Look, you don't forget the past ever, okay? People are very interested in her now. First Lady's a big jump from some little television interviewer. She's what you call emerging. It happens to First Ladies, to all of them. They come onstage as little Mrs. So-and-So, wife of Mr. Big Wheel, and then it dawns on them that maybe they're *Mrs.* Big Wheel and—presto!—out of their cocoons! Only trouble is some of these pretty little butterflies get to be like fucking bees: they suck you dry, then they sting you!"

"Not a flattering portrait of our First Ladies."

"Not meant to be. People have to get to know the President first. Then they get to be curious about the First Lady."

Hawley simply nodded.

"Not too much is known of her past," Gratton went on. "*Time* reporter was in to see me a week or so ago—little bastard I never liked. Ferret. Snooping. I couldn't tell him anything. Except how she got to be on our payroll." Gratton's eyes narrowed as he studied Hawley's face. "Didn't mention your connection. Something told me not to."

Hawley returned Gratton's stare. "You could have, Joe," he said easily.

"I figured I'd just let little Sammy Wellman sniff somebody else's manure. If there'd been something in it for Federal . . . but he was just fishing. I don't know what for." Gratton pulled out a cigarette, and as he lit it he asked, "You?"

"Not a clue. The lady was a reporter, that's public knowledge."

"Sure. But getting from there to somewhere else to *here,*" his eyes swept the room, "could be a story if Sammy can find the spoor."

Hawley wanted to end the interview. "What can I do for you, Joe?"

"It's not the biggest story of the year putting the First Lady on television. I just don't want someone else to get the deal. That's it."

Hawley glanced at the letter and the signature as he passed it back to Gratton. "I know Anne Koyce, her assistant. I'll talk to her."

"Can't you talk to the lady herself?"

"Sure, if I have to."

Gratton stood up and put out his hand. "However you want to handle it. I knew I could count on you—" He shook his head. "This whole fucking, dirty place with its clean white marble and its columns and its monuments, and its handsome, well-dressed men and women, is a goddamn lousy jungle. That's what I've always called it and that's what it is."

"Joe, if it's important enough for you to drop by to see me, you know you can count on me." He patted Gratton's chunky right shoulder as he led him through the reception area.

When he returned to his office, he wondered how he should go about delivering on his offer. He decided, too, to pass along Sammy Wellman's name to Richard Daniels.

☆ ☆ ☆

Harry Thompson bent his body over the old-fashioned porcelain washbasin and studied his image in the oval-shaped bathroom mirror as he ran his hand across his shaven face.

"Smooth *now*, you bastard," Gloria Whitney said from the bedroom, her pretty face reflected in the mirror as she held a light cover to her throat. "I begged you all night—" She snapped open a dainty cloisonné-finished compact to examine her own face. "My God, look at my chin! All scraped. *Red*, Harry, flaming red! How do I explain *that* to my father?"

"Very simple, angel," he said, combing his hair in place. "You just tell him that instead of visiting your girlfriend's as you'd originally planned, you decided to seduce the President's son and spent the night with him at his place. Your father's a judge, sees all sides. He'll understand."

"Very funny." Gloria fingered a tender spot under her lips. "I look like a half-dead bird dragged in from a cockfight."

"You *would* call it that," Harry said, chuckling. "But I didn't hear you complain last night."

"Last night was last night. Harry," she pouted, "you know how tender my skin is." She sat up.

He pulled through the underside of his tie and knotted it in place, walked over to the old Victorian bureau, and began to pick up his change, his keys, his credit cards. "If I recall any of the events of last night, I distinctly remember hearing a plaintive little voice begging, 'Please, Harry. Bruise me! Hurt me! Beat me!'"

"But not my face, Harry." She slipped a leg out from under

the covers and examined her thigh. "I'm black and blue," she said, "all the way to my hip."

"It won't show," he replied, amiably.

She leaped out of bed and stood beside him at the bureau, turning around to examine her buttocks in the full-length mirror beside it. "All over, damn you!"

Harry patted her affectionately. "Unless you take showers with your other dates, no one will notice."

"I'm not thinking of them." She put her hand on the zipper of his slacks and smiled up at him. "I'm thinking of you. You were very good, Harry." She moved in closer to him and he put his arms around her. "And about time." She shut her eyes and moved her lips toward his as she started to slide the zipper down. "You're growing, Harry."

"I'm a growing boy," he murmured, as he felt her lips part. "But I have a luncheon date."

"I know," she said.

"With the President. The President's going away."

"I know," she repeated, her hand slipping between his shirt ends.

"You trying to make me late?"

"Very late," Gloria whispered as her hand tightened. She half opened her eyes. "You're like the Washington Monument now, Harry. You're not going to waste it, are you?" She gripped him hard and led him back toward the bed.

☆ ☆ ☆

Harry lifted his eyes to the balcony of his apartment as he gunned his black Mercedes convertible and headed to the White House, observing a bit of white waving in the breeze. He could see it was Gloria, and she wasn't waving a face towel or one of his handkerchiefs; it was her bikini.

The smile that had crossed his face vanished as a montage of the night's events cascaded in his mind's eye. There was no doubt that Gloria continued to exert a strong hold on his appetites and his affections—that he had to admit. But of increasing concern to him was her insatiable desire for sexual intimacies that bordered on the sadomasochistic. Her pleadings with him to hurt her, and his accommodating her demands to a greater and greater extent, were not only maximizing the sexual impact on his own body and mind, but at the same time they were threatening to loosen the emotional and intellectual ties that first bound him to her.

Some of that he was sure came as a by-product of her dependence on pills. He criticized her for removing the prescription labels from the bottles she carried in her purse, but trying to talk with her was futile. Not since the afternoon he'd brooded about Gloria while sitting in Lafayette Park had he faced up to the reality of his dilemma and hers. Marriage might solve *her* problems, but would it not also generate a host of new ones that lay beneath the surface? As he drove through the White House gate, he wasn't sure he could handle them.

Once in the White House Harry headed to the family dining room on the second floor. As an usher held the door for him, the President and Kathy looked up from the table. "I'm sorry," Harry began to explain, "and I'm glad you didn't wait."

"We waited almost an hour," the President said, making no effort to conceal his annoyance.

"I'm sure Harry can explain," Kathy said, reaching a hand across the table to touch the President's.

Harry took a seat facing both of them, wondering if the vexation he sensed in his father's manner and words was directed more toward Kathy than toward him. He lifted a napkin and placed it across his lap. Then he looked across at Kathy; he never found it easy to accept Kathy for what she was, his father's wife. "First, I couldn't phone . . . not under the circumstances . . . To start at the beginning, Kathy," he began, chuckling to himself, "I was with Gloria Whitney, and if you'd like to hear a personal confession in private—"

The President cut him short. "Please. Just have your lunch, Harry. Skip the witticisms."

"I'm really not hungry, sir," Harry said, glancing again at Kathy and adding, "let's just say I was detained by circumstances which were only partially under my control. All right?"

"I was only thinking of your father, Harry," Kathy replied politely, "his time, what he has to do. What you do with yours, Harry, is not really my concern."

"Can you both drop the subject?" the President said irritably.

Harry nodded. "You have to make this trip I've heard about?"

"No, I don't have to. But I *want* to. If you'd like to join—"

Harry shook his head. "I'd rather stay here," he said. But on noting his father's disappointment, he added, "If you really needed me—"

"It's all right, Harry." Then staring at his son, he added pointedly, "Kathy will be with me in Los Angeles."

The three sat in silence as a butler quietly removed the luncheon plates. "Stephen," Kathy said, touching her husband's shoulders. "I know you'd like a few minutes alone with Harry. I'll have coffee waiting in the sitting room. That all right?"

"Fine," he replied as she headed to the door, "fine. We won't be long."

Harry glanced to watch her leave, then turned to his father. "Doctors okay this trip, Dad?"

"You're the only one not afraid to ask."

"You've got a few appointments—important ones—waiting to be filled. I read in a column today—"

The President interrupted. "They'll be filled. I'm giving them considerable thought."

"Okay. Just thought I'd tell you what I read. And you haven't answered my first question."

"No, I haven't because I didn't ask anyone's permission, doctors included. What are they going to say? 'You have some hardening of the arteries?' I already know that." He lowered his voice. "I'm not one hundred percent, Harry, but I'm no Franklin Roosevelt, either. He never knew what his true state of health was, never inquired, didn't really want to. Simply took his own inner soundings. Did his job as he saw it."

"Killed himself, from what I've read."

"Might have died a lot sooner if he'd let himself slip." He reached out and grasped his son's arm. "I'm in a lot better shape, and *I* happen to know. The care I take, the medicines, Commander Jensen—Jensen, you know him?"

"Of course I know him. What makes you think I don't?" Harry replied irritably. "Your doctor. Practically lives here. Of course I know him."

"Okay, okay, so I forgot for the moment. Well, Jensen's always within call, and if he's not, why then I have the buzzer here that I can press to summon help, and if I can't reach it, there are others set in my desks, into this table, all over the White House, so even my knees can strike an emergency signal."

"What about the plane?"

Thompson smiled. "Jensen'll be there with me. In L.A., when we tour the city, he'll be in the car behind me." He started rubbing his hands together. "Familiar with the Twenty-fifth Amendment?"

"Sure. Not word for word, but I know the essence of it."

"Good. Thought you would. You know I haven't been in Los Angeles for it must be, let me think, two, maybe three years. Always like the weather there. I *always* liked the sunshine. Your mother and I, we'd take a cruise every so often, just lazing about on deck, reading books, good talk. She was a good researcher when I met her." He slouched back in his chair, his voice trailing off. "That was a long, long time ago . . ."

Harry listened, aware that his father was talking in non sequiturs, but he didn't want to let the earlier allusion pass by. "You mentioned the Twenty-fifth Amendment."

The President's eyebrows shot up. "Oh?"

"You asked me if I was familiar with it. And I am."

"Never been used except in the matter of Nixon appointing Ford and Ford appointing Rockefeller. Maybe Reagan's letting Bush be Acting President for eight hours during that operation of his. Can't say I think much of its philosophy in theory or in practice. The law of succession—1886 it was—had its virtues. If the Vice President's office was vacant, why then the Secretary of State was next in line, then Treasury. St. Wapni's Law it was called, an acronym for State, Treasury, War, Attorney General, Postmaster, Navy, Interior. In that order, seniority of the establishment of the departments." He sat back studying the look of surprise on his son's face, and he felt pleased with himself. "Didn't know that one, I bet."

"No, I didn't—very impressive history lesson, Dad."

The President rose from his chair and began to move about the room. "Some of our well-meaning patriotic zealots aren't as impressed with memory as you are. Which is what made me bring up the subject. I've gotten wind of their concern. Don't ask me how, accept it. There used to be an old television commercial that warned against fooling around with Mother Nature." He let a hand pound the top of a chair. "It doesn't pay to fool around with the President, either. A President has enemies, of course. He wouldn't be a good President if he didn't. And he has friends. He couldn't function without them. And then there are the sycophants, the do-gooders, the army of would-be Presidents—all of them always anxious to tell you how to do your job. They all forget one thing. A President gets a lot of information just by opening his door." The elder Thompson resumed his seat and rubbed his big hands together. "You get your best information from the press. People always talk to them—on the record, off the record, talk, talk, talk! Everyone wants to look good. Maybe it's in somebody's column, maybe it's something labelled for history. Jaggers is the kind of man who thinks of his place in history. Talker."

"The Secretary of State?"

"Which is why the law of succession wouldn't be ideal today."

"I'm not following you," Harry said.

"Well, if it were in force, and *if*, mind you I said if, the office of the Vice Presidency were vacant—Jaggers would be next in line for the Presidency. Of course *now* it's the Speaker, next the President pro tem of the Senate." The President shook his head sadly. "Jaggers is one of my mistakes."

"You said if—"

The muscles of the President's face tightened and the veins of his temples could be seen suddenly throbbing. "Take that fellow Daniels. Cold. Cunning. Like a hyena lurking in the underbrush, waiting for the kill. Their little hush-hush meetings. They sometimes seem to forget one important fact: the Committee reports to the National Security Council and the Council reports to the President!" With that he slumped back in his chair, his facial muscles sagging.

Harry had risen halfway from his chair.

The President waved him down, noting the look of concern on his son's face. "Sit down, sit down. I'm fine, fine. Lot on my mind. Lot to do." He smiled warmly at Harry. "Time is short. Admitted. But there's nothing ominous intended in that, Harry. Man gets to be sixty plus, he knows he's far past half his life. You still have a lifetime ahead. Kathy, too."

"You can outlive us all."

"What was it Lincoln said? 'I do the very best I know how—the very best I can; and I mean to keep doing so until the end." The President struggled to draw himself erect. "You've never really liked her much." He saw a sullen look cross his son's face. "But she's been good for me, son. Oh I know you're thinking of those tapes. But," he emphasized, "if I can put them out of my mind, you can do the same, understand?"

"I hear you."

"While I'm gone—" The President suddenly frowned. "What I was talking about earlier—" He paused. "—about Daniels I mean. My unkindness . . ."

"Don't worry about it. Forgotten."

"He's first and foremost an able man . . ." his eyes shut momentarily, his voice barely audible. He leaned across the table, a curious smile on his face. "Able," he repeated.

"I don't want to hold you, Dad," Harry said. "She's waiting for you."

"Yes, I know. While I'm gone, Harry, it would be nice if you were to stay here." He noticed his son squirm in his chair. "I know the third floor of the White House doesn't give you the freedom the old family place does, or that apartment of yours, but it does have one advantage. You can keep an eye on Kathy for the short time I'm in Nebraska. Not for checking up on her—nothing like that," he hastily added, "it's just that I'd like her to feel that she has someone—" He stopped speaking.

Harry sat waiting, curious.

The President turned to face Harry. "Don't make anything more out of it. I'm not getting suspicious. I can't allow myself . . . She's all alone, you know, no brothers, sisters, parents killed in that terrible automobile accident some years ago. She's remarkable. But she's been worrying needlessly about me. Feels I've gotten a bit gaunt on Jensen's diet. Strain on her, I see it. That's why I'd like you to pay some attention—show some concern—"

"I'll do whatever I can."

The President pushed himself up from the table. "She's got coffee waiting for me—" He took a few steps toward the door and stopped for a moment as though he were about to add something else, but then had decided against it. He shook his head. "We'll let it stay just like that."

"I'll keep an eye on things," Harry said as he, too, rose from the table.

The President abruptly turned back toward Harry. "Let me be frank with you, son. Mr. Hawley has disappointed me." He saw the impact of his words. "I know you worked with him last election, Harry, and that you liked him—you still work with him. But you should know—I won't go into details—" he paused, studying his son. Then the President suddenly lashed out. "Hamilton once said it of Burr—'despicable'—that's the word." He emphasized each syllable: "'de-spi-ca-ble.' From what I know . . . I'll say no more, but the cut of the coat fits Mr. Hawley."

Harry stood still as the elder Thompson stalked from the room. He went back to the table and sipped a glass of water, remembering the enthusiasm with which he and Lane and others had so eagerly sought to be members of Hawley's team, and the turn of events that had catapulted Hawley into being his father's running mate. His eyes turned toward the chair so recently vacated by Kathy Thompson. She'd been part of that team, too. It was Hawley who'd brought her into the Thompson orbit. He wondered about his father's request that he keep an eye on her, about Hawley's parting shot in the gymnasium a few days back that if he, Harry, could clue him in on what was on the President's mind he'd appreciate it. Now he knew. Hawley was going to be dropped.

10

The ringing of the phone awakened Hawley. He flipped on a lamp and looked at the small Cartier clock on his nightstand as his private phone kept ringing away. He was angry at himself for having forgotten to turn it off. He was certain it was Vivien Lessing.

With a sigh he picked it up and immediately heard her voice. The words came rushing out. "I'm sorry, Cliff, and I apologize, I'm really sorry, but I had to speak to someone, someone who cares, someone I can trust." A moment later he heard her trying to stifle her sobbing.

"What is it, Vivien? What's wrong?" He was suddenly wide awake.

For a moment there was only the sound of her efforts to regain some degree of self-control. "Everything," she finally said. "Everything. I just wish you were here. I know it's wrong. And I know it's very late. I'm just so alone." He could sense her still struggling to contain herself.

"You have friends, hundreds of them," he said reassuringly.

"Not really. Not when I need them. And I need one. That's why I called. Like I say, I know it's late, but you see—" her voice dropping into a whisper "—they're not picking me up . . . the next picture," she said softly, "the contract. They're not picking it up. The new picture's not making it."

"Every picture can't be a big hit, everybody knows that," he said, still trying to comfort her.

"Yes, everybody knows that. But just the same, everybody runs for cover the moment your string runs out. That's what's happening. I see it coming."

"That's because you've chosen to look on the dark side, and that's one of your weaknesses, Vivien," Hawley added. "Besides, you've told me you had contracts in London—"

"They all have outs written in them. When the word gets around, and it gets around fast out here, they'll begin to *think*. And I have no one I can speak to, no one, Cliff—" She paused for moment. "That's why I called you. Could you come out, Cliff?" she asked plaintively.

"That's not possible, Vivien—"

"I knew you'd say no."

"I have an NSC in the morning. National Security Council. In the afternoon—"

"Meetings," she said flatly.

"Meetings," he repeated.

"Maybe I could hop a plane . . ."

Hawley shook his head as his fist tightened around the phone. "Where to?" he asked, fully aware of her intent.

"When you put it that way, I know it's not to Washington. Right?"

"Well, it wouldn't be the best timing, not with my present schedule. The President's going to be out of the city—"

"It's all right, Mr. Hawley—"

"My time's just not my own, Vivien," he said defensively, waiting for her response. "Vivien?"

"I'm here. I'll manage," she sighed, "for now."

"Of course you will," he said, reassuringly again. "In the morning things will look different. You've got to think of who you are, your career, all of the things you've accomplished. All of the things you're *still* going to accomplish. Think of all that tomorrow."

"You remember what I said last time when we were together in Chevy Chase? About my not being certain anymore about anything? Do you remember?"

"Yes," he said reluctantly. It was a topic he had no desire to pursue.

"I'm doing a lot of thinking about that," she said. Then after a brief pause, she added, "Will you do some?"

"Yes, of course," he said in a noncommittal tone.

"Promise?"

"Promise."

"Thank you, Cliff," she said, and a moment later he heard the phone click. He put down his own receiver and stroked his chin. He had allowed the relationship to last much too long, and the stakes were far too great to invite any unnecessary complications. Vivien had become an unnecessary complication. He knew the time had finally come to alter the status quo.

☆ ☆ ☆

When Thompson stepped into the glare of the television cameras set up in a spacious new hotel banquet room in Omaha and took the first questions, he felt confident and at ease. His voice was firm and forceful. Yes, he was satisfied with his visit to the Strategic Air Command's central control headquarters. Yes, he felt that America's strength was unsurpassed. No, he did not feel that there was any change in the military balance of power, but it was proper for the President, as Commander in Chief of the Armed Forces, to make his own personal observations from time to time. Yes, he was pleased to have Hornwell and Vance with him.

"Mr. President," Carl Eastman, a young network reporter, asked, "are you satisfied that if a nuclear attack occurred, there'd be anything left of that installation? If it came now, wouldn't we all be among the first to go?"

"Well, Carl, that would be one way to terminate a press conference," the President said as laughter filled the room. Then he added, "Yes, of course, this place is a top priority for any adversary. So, I might add, is *their* central command headquarters."

"We know where that is?" Eastman continued.

"I think it's fair to assume we can find it," Thompson said with confidence.

"The central communications systems. They're the prime targets, right, sir, for both sides?" Eastman didn't wait for a response. "Now if they know that and we know that, isn't that incentive enough for one side or the other to seek superiority?"

"All we want is parity. To go beyond that—to be able to attack, for example, in the boost phase, to narrow the time between launch and interception—that could be especially dangerous."

"Why so?"

"Because it could precipitate a launch-on-warning, thereby setting off exactly what deterrence seeks to avoid—encouraging a first strike." The President spotted an older bearded man from the *New York Times*. "Mr. Stallings?"

Vince Stallings stood up. "Mr. President, you're the only person authorized to give the signal that launches our missiles. What happens if you're not able to do that—if you were taken out first?"

Thompson said, "The President isn't going to be standing on the White House lawn saying, 'Here I am.'"

Again there was a good-natured response to the President's sally, but Stallings, pointing his pencil toward the President, persisted. "But suppose, for the sake of argument, that a President—not you, sir," he said, "but a future President—just wasn't as, let's say, as psychiatrically well prepared as the controllers who sit at the switches waiting for a presidential decision. Let's assume the human machinery of a President doesn't function. What happens then?"

The President looked directly at the reporter, pleased at the opportunity to end speculation about his health. But the *Times* man cut in. "Does the Vice President take over?"

"No, the Vice President does not take over," Thompson snapped. "Not necessarily," he quickly added.

"But there are constitutional provisions," the reporter persisted.

"Yes, and I'm very familiar with the Twenty-fifth Amendment," Thompson replied. "I'm also familiar with the exchange of notes between President Eisenhower and his Vice President when Eisenhower was ill. The transfer could be formal or informal, if a transfer were deemed necessary or desirable—*by the President.*" Thompson pulled himself erect. "Time for one more question," he announced, pointing to a pretty female reporter. "Yes, Roberta."

"The convention will be along in a few more weeks—"

"Do you really want to talk politics in this setting?"

Diminutive Roberta Chase smiled at the President. "Maybe my question will have as much dynamite in it as one of the missiles you could order up from here."

"Try me," the President said, preparing himself.

"You've brought Senator Vance along with you—"

"Yes. He's Chairman of the Senate Armed Services Committee."

"Yes, but he has his counterpart in the House, and Mr. Roberts isn't here, and the Secretary of Defense isn't here, and the Vice President isn't here—"

"I understand your question, Miss Chase."

"I haven't asked it yet, Mr. President," she said as the press and the President joined in laughter. "It just struck me that Senator Vance *might* be under consideration as a possible new running mate for you, Mr. President."

"What is your question, Miss Chase?" Again the room burst into good-humored laughter.

"Is there a chance that Senator Vance might be your next running mate?"

Thompson looked down at Vance. The Senator simply shook his head in mock disbelief as the room waited.

The President removed his glasses and smiled. "Miss Chase, I don't think a missile site is the best place to talk politics. Or to launch the next campaign. All I can say to that is what any of you could say, and that is that the Senator, like Mr. Hawley, is as well qualified as any man to be any presidential candidate's running mate. His knowledge suggests he's one of those very few capable of assuming a heavier responsibility. Then his service record in the Navy in Vietman . . . we'll just let the matter stand there. After all, the decision will be made by the Committee—"

"Did you say the *Committee*, Mr. President?"

Thompson's smile vanished as he wiped his glasses and slowly replaced them. "The convention," he said softly, "the convention."

"What about the appointments you haven't made, sir?" a reporter shouted from the rear of the room. "The seat on the Supreme Court—"

"We don't rush that kind of appointment. Just be patient."

"But it's been over four months, sir . . ."

The President felt a sudden compulsion to end the press conference. He stepped away from the rostrum, starting off under the combined escort of his aides and the Secret Service, leaving the question unanswered.

Another reporter farther back in the room shouted, "Mr. President, Mr. Hawley says he wants to be on the ticket! What do you say?"

Thompson, waving to the group, called back, "We'll know everything at the convention."

☆ ☆ ☆

Hornwell sat quietly in the hotel's newly decorated presidential suite as the President chatted about the success of the press conference. Except for the final momentary confusion caused by the President's reference to the Committee and his quick correction, he'd been impressed with the virtuosity of the President's performance.

The President's doctor stood smiling at the doorway.

"Time for my nap, right, Commander?"

Jensen, short and flabby, nodded deferentially, his cherubic face cast in a perpetual sympathetic smile. The President pointed at him. "Robert, you're always at me about my weight, my diet, my rest—and look at you, twenty pounds overweight if you're a pound, right?"

"My heritage, Mr. President. Have to blame it on my mother's genes. She could never lose weight."

"Maybe," the President began, his eyes twinkling with mischief, "maybe we could persuade Admiral Hornwell to have you stationed in the Persian Gulf, or the Indian Ocean—someplace where you could sweat it off."

At that moment the phone rang. The President picked it up and smiled as he swung the red leather chair back and forth on its swivel, listening to his wife. "Everything went well, Kathy. I've the Admiral's word for it . . . And the Senator's . . . No, no, I'm not overdoing anything. Jensen's standing right in this room ready to tuck me in." The President chuckled at the thought, but as he listened to Kathy, his face began to cloud over. "You're not going to be too tired for L.A. doing that, are you? . . . Who's escorting you there? . . . Oh, Harry. Fine, fine. Who else did you say will be there? . . . Secretary Clauson? Good. Yes, yes . . . Who else? . . . Mr. Hawley?" For a moment he felt a sting of resentment, and let the phone rest in his lap. Then picking it up he said, "I'm still here, Kathy . . . All right, I understand it's not *your* party . . . All right, let it be, let it be." He changed his tone from vexation to accommodation. "You have a good time . . . I'll be resting in Beverly Hills . . . Jensen's nodding his head. Approves . . . Good dreams, little girl . . . " He listened to the mild protest. "No one's here but Jensen and the Admiral. They'll keep our secret. Good night."

He cradled the receiver. "Kathy. Wanted to go out tonight. Can't blame her, being cooped up in the White House isn't exciting. She's young—" He turned to stare out of the window. "That's all, Robert," he said, as he sent Jensen out of the room.

"We've both gone through some hard times together, Admiral.

Your lovely wife. Mine. Margaret," Thompson said, his voice almost a whisper. He turned to look into the Admiral's eyes. "You remember Margaret?"

Hornwell nodded sympathetically. "Fine woman. A brilliant woman." But, as always, he remembered with distaste the halo of smoke that circled her head when he drew her as a dinner companion.

"Yes," the President said, rubbing a big hand across his chin. "Margaret was someone to talk to about issues. I'd hoped she might be here . . . Kathy," he murmured, as he turned his eyes away from Hornwell. The thought of Kathy at the same party as Hawley forced a recollection of the tapes to surface in his mind, to remind him of the few provocative words he'd heard. He hunched forward in an effort to shake off his tensions as he continued speaking to Hornwell.

Hornwell was uncomfortable. He'd always bottled up his private feelings; he didn't know how to cope with another's personal dilemmas. Thompson's simple pronouncement of his second wife's name was something he'd no desire to probe.

The President hunched forward in an effort to shake off his inner tensions. "Multinationals. Big problem there," he said. "Remember when Angola was a puppet state controlled by the Soviets and how multinational corporations controlled by Americans and the British made *us*, not the Soviets, their biggest trading partners? Ironic but true. When I practiced law I used to represent their interests. Key problem with them: their customers come ahead of their country. No patriotism in multinationals."

Hornwell nodded again, pleased at the change of subject even as he adjusted to the suddenness with which the President shifted his thoughts from a personal dilemma to a public issue. "What do we do about them, Admiral?" Thompson repeated the question. Then, not waiting for an answer from Hornwell, he said, "They could suborn our national security. Damned near did during the oil crises of the eighties. What do we do about them?"

"Closer regulations? Some kind of sanctions?" Hornwell ventured.

Thompson frowned. "They're so well organized—with an international committee sitting on top dividing up the whole world." He waited for Hornwell to respond, then added, "The Committee—*our* Committee, Admiral, with all of its power and vigilance, how does it cope with *their* committee?"

"We have the real power, sir," the Admiral said.

"No, we can't win that way. We just might have to do something, let's say, clever." Thompson winked as he added, "We have to find a way to infiltrate them, to capture them from within, to put our own people on *their* committee."

"How do we do that?"

"This is a job for Mr. Daniels. Matter of fact, a very good way to divert his attention from something too much on his mind." The President slowly stood up, stretched his large frame, and peered down at Hornwell. "The Twenty-fifth Amendment, Admiral."

Hornwell was stunned. He wondered whether Thompson had facts. And if so, where were they coming from?

The President turned to Hornwell, and then abruptly murmured, "Senator Vance. You like him, Admiral?"

Hornwell sat up, his face again revealing his surprise at Thompson's rapid changing of subject matter.

"Vance." Thompson, not waiting for Hornwell's response, went on, "Good man. Ambitious, of course. But a good man. Straight. Good record. Mr. Hawley has a good mind, too. Curious, too. Likes the wisdom in Loren Eiseley's books. Know that?"

"No, sir," Hornwell replied.

"Discovered he'd read him quite extensively—without his knowing that Eiseley, next to Thoreau, is a favorite of mine, too. One of the things I liked about Hawley. Maybe the thing I liked best. I remember once telling him I was lonely . . . before I married. I—I have thoughts now about Hawley." He sat quietly tapping his forehead. "Kathy has every right to enjoy herself," he said abruptly, hands clenched together. "Harry's there . . . what were we talking about?"

"Eiseley?" Hornwell volunteered.

"Yes . . . Eiseley . . . Kathy likes to dance . . . and Margaret did, too. Met her . . . just a slip of a girl. Brown eyes, soft hair. Very natural. She had her own ambitions. Sometimes a bit too forceful. Died too soon." Slowly he began to drum his fingers across the arm of this chair. "Too soon," he murmured, "too soon. She had potential, like her friend Mrs. Curtis. I was very lonely, Admiral . . . after her leaving . . . "

A long silence followed. Hornwell, distressed by the rambling talk, finally decided to break into the President's thoughts. "Perhaps, sir . . . Commander Jensen wants you to take your nap, sir." As Hornwell spoke the President's head slumped to his chest, his hands relaxing. Hornwell sat upright in his chair, listening to Thompson's stertorous breathing. He rose and started across the room, and as he reached for the doorknob the door swung inward slowly. Commander Jensen entered, nodding politely to Hornwell on his way out.

☆ ☆ ☆

Jeff Whitney headed down a narrow passageway, flexing his shoulders to get a little exercise after poring over charts of their patrol areas for the past two hours. He was surprised to find his executive officer standing outside his cabin waiting for him. "Thought you were sleeping or watching a movie with the crew," he said, as he continued moving his arms and shoulders.

"I've seen it, Captain."

"Not worth another look?" Jeff asked as he entered his cabin.

"No. Saw it in Washington somewhere, couple months back. Saw it aboard two weeks ago. Not worth a third look."

"Sit down. Art, you didn't come to talk about movies. What's up?"

"While you were looking over the charts I had to get the Chief of the Boat to pull two of our men off each other."

"Oh?" Whitney began doing a few easy calisthenics.

"The Chief had to handcuff one of them—Benson, a little fellow, but feisty. Lost his temper. Other chap, Corman—he lost a tooth. Doc is working on him right now."

"Think Corman will want to get back at him?"

Morgan shook his head.

"You want to bring charges against Benson?"

"Don't think it's a good idea. May well be the whole crew's getting a little edgy with the extended patrol. Hundred and ten days? More than any of them has ever experienced."

"What was the fight about?"

"Nothing really. Once we found out what was behind it you could see it coming."

"Like what?"

"Like Benson didn't like the calendar Corman was keeping posted on the side of his bunk. Seems Corman, who's a very stable husky fellow, likes to check each day off, one by one, like he was in some kind of cell. Like a Count of Monte Cristo. Thing got annoying as hell to Benson. Finally, it built up until he just tore it down and ripped it to pieces. When he did that

Corman hauled off and decked him. Nobody else said anything or did anything, they just let the two of them go and suddenly there they were using each other as punching bags."

"Nobody tried to stop them?"

"Only me and the Chief of the Boat."

"And the others?"

Morgan pulled on his right ear lobe. "Damndest thing. Here they were pounding each other and the compartment quiet as a tomb. Nobody saying a word, nobody making a move, just letting the two of them get it all out of their systems."

Whitney sat down at his desk doing some isometrics. "We've been a long time down here, so if just a couple of our younger crew members get carried away but the rest stay nice and calm, I'd say things are going pretty well. Now, if it was one of the chiefs, somebody with lots of patrols under their belts and carrying a lot of responsibility on board, like say with our missiles, then I'd be concerned. Very," he emphasized. "But I still don't honestly understand why it happened. These men are all handpicked. They've all been psychologically tested. They've all been through sub school and they've all had at least a couple of submarine tours, at least I thought they did. How did we slip up on Benson?"

"I just reviewed his service record and found out that all of his sea duty has been in the boats used for training sub-school students. I doubt that he's ever been at sea before for more than four weeks at a time."

"Christ," Whitney muttered. "I sure hope we don't have any more amateurs on board."

"No, sir, we don't," Morgan responded. "I've rechecked the records of all the other men who reported on board just before we sailed, and all hands had at least one long patrol under their belt. But I do have one suggestion, skipper."

"Shoot."

"When Doc's through with Corman's jaw, cuff Corman to one side of a table, Benson on the opposite. Just enough to keep them apart. Let the two of them see each other. Let everybody else see them. Give them an hour to work it out between them. Pass the word they're on their own. What do you think?"

"Okay. But maybe you start with the COB sitting down with them for a couple minutes. He can talk to them at their level and try to help settle them down. If he can't do it no one can."

"Good idea, Captain," Morgan said with a smile.

"Something funny?" Whitney asked.

"No, like I said, it's just a good idea: putting two fellows together and letting them work out their differences in their own way. Maybe the United Nations should get the American and the Soviet Presidents together the same way with just interpreters between them. Release them only after they've come to a recognition that every problem's got to be solved."

Whitney looked up from doing knee bends. "They do that they'll put most of us out of work."

"That'll be okay. After all, a lot of this military hardware will have to be floating around for a long time even after the superpowers have made some kind of final accommodation."

"Yeah, that's a possibility. Maybe they'll even have some of their fellows aboard our ships and we'll be aboard theirs. We'll all be policemen ready to handle the crazies who'll always be in charge somewhere, maybe threatening to go out of control."

"Why not?" Morgan said, joining Whitney in some stretching exercises. "I only wish they'd send through a little bit more news than we've been getting, skipper. Gotta be some personal messages backed up somewhere in the system."

Whitney stood up, did a few final slow twists, raising his arms over his head. "A little more of my tapering off business." He paused a moment. "This is the way the top boy probably wants it," he said, repeating the routine.

"Hornwell?"

Whitney nodded. "Great believer in training, being on guard, at the ready. I already told you I had some time with him just before I pulled the assignment."

Morgan was still impressed. "Can you talk more about it?"

"Sure. Who you gonna pass it on to?" Both men chuckled. "He made one thing very clear. We have only one mission if the big showdown ever comes. Everything we've been doing all these years, everything we do from here on out, our one single mission is to knock out the enemy's Central Command Center when and if. Take no chances. If we're to be knocked out we have to stay alive just long enough to finish our mission. That's it."

"He still doesn't buy the end of the Cold War?" Morgan asked.

"No way," Whitney said.

"Not with all the things that have happened with the Soviets?

The reforms, the recognition of ethnic feelings, the shift from making more arms to increasing consumer goods? He doesn't see the great progress, the changes these past ten years?"

"He knows all that, but in a world of uncertainty, of power grabs by other men, he keeps his mind focused on the possibility that someday, somewhere, there could be a backlash."

"And we're sitting down here on the front line, right?" Morgan waited for Whitney's response.

"That's *his* position. It may not be the President's—he has to think of politics, and sometimes national security gets shoved aside. But it *is* Hornwell's. National security, first, last, always."

Morgan reached across Whitney's desk and ran his fingers over a calendar. "You forget things down here. But politics, captain, you're right. There's a convention coming up. A few weeks away. Politics. That's bound to consume a lot of the President's time, put a lot of pressure on him."

"While Hornwell and the rest of the Joint Chiefs tend to their business. Keep our strategic forces in position to deliver a knockout punch if needed. Us, in particular . . . "

"It's amazing that we can remain undetected with all that's out there, the sensors on the floor—"

"Mostly ours," Whitney interjected.

"Agreed. But *they're* looking—"

"But their reach isn't as good as ours. A few hundred miles at most compared to our thousand or more. If they'd tagged us—but they can't at this depth. We can slip past *them* and they know they can't slip past *us*. Not anywhere." Whitney pointed to a map on his wall. "Six of us on station here, the Pacific, maybe the Indian Ocean—that's a deterrent force they can't risk. This exercise will be an eye-opener when we do our best to let them know we're returning to port—that'll be a cruncher." Whitney glanced down at his watch. "You'd better get back to Corman and Benson. Have the COB settle them down as soon as he can. We can't afford to let anyone get distracted by personal animosity of any kind. Okay?"

Morgan stood up. "Aye, aye, sir," he said. "I'll bet you in a couple of hours they'll be swapping jokes and apologizing to each other."

☆ ☆ ☆

Seated in his office, Daniels looked up at the young agent handing him the papers. "Thank you, Mr. Taggart," he said, as he appraised Taggart's manner, clothes, and attitude. Very proper young fellow, he concluded, a good representative of the CIA. Taggart had been tested by specific assignments and had proved himself capable of setting up a drug bust in the car of someone marked for constant surveillance and testing by the agency, or supervising the training of attractive young women who wanted to serve their country, no questions asked, or taking out an enemy agent when the necessity arose. Taggart was a man upon whom one could depend.

As he stood at a careful midway balance between ease and attention, Taggart never let his eyes drift from Daniels'. Like all the others privileged to have personal contact with the Director, he was aware that Daniels would always address them with a curious formality. No one in the department, he knew, would ever be able to boast that he was on a first-name basis with Mr. Daniels.

"What does the Navy call that radar system they use for detection?"

"SAR—synthetic aperture radar, sir," Taggart replied.

"The Soviets are pretty deep into it."

"Yes, sir. In the report, you'll see that the Navy was doing it pretty well way back in '78, capable even then of mapping the floor of the ocean to depths of about five hundred feet."

"And doing much better now."

"Yes, sir. Like the Soviets." Taggart pointed to the sheaf of papers in Daniels' hands. "You'll find that in section four. Things are going very well on our side."

"What about the other side?"

Taggart nodded. "They've done some good work on spotting thermal activity."

"Nothing stays invincible." Daniels glanced over at Taggart. "What's going on with that little snoop Wellman, from Gaynor's rag?"

Taggart welcomed the abrupt change of subject. "We've opened the doors to his studying some inside stealth operations— letting him get the hang of special coatings and some electronics. Nothing vital."

"Nothing that the Soviets don't already know, that it?" Daniels said, this time the glint in his eyes indicating a vote of satisfaction.

"Correct, sir."

"Take him out of the capital?"

"Right through the election."

"Perfect. Feed everything out slowly."

"Yes, sir."

"Thank you, Mr. Taggart."

As Taggart's hand touched the doorknob, Daniels said, "One more thing, Mr. Taggart. When you've fed out just about all we intend to give him—give the final piece of information to the fellow from *Newsweek*. You understand?"

Taggart nodded once. He understood completely. He'd lead *Time*'s Sammy Wellman on, week after week. Then, quietly, he'd hand the climax to those many weeks, those months of effort, to his chief rival. Ruin his story, break his morale, set him up for dismissal. All in a day's work.

11

As she stood under the gleaming Waterford chandelier, Kathy Thompson's eyes swept the crowded embassy drawing room. She smiled at Edward Jaggers, a few feet away, busily dispensing amenities to the ambassador's wife as he stuffed himself with caviar canapés, washing them down with large gulps of Dom Pérignon. Dressed in a striking gold silk lamé gown, Kathy was happy to be out of the White House, free to enjoy herself, though she was aware of the constant scrutiny of her escort, Harry Thompson.

She'd arrived late, hoping that Clifford Hawley would already be there searching for her, but when he did arrive, she was vexed to see him escorting Felicia Courtney. She'd caught sight of them moving easily together in the company of Chief Justice Whitney and his daughter. Ashamed to admit her pleasure in noting Gloria's pouting, she assumed that Gloria was also annoyed that Harry had had to bring his stepmother to the party. Kathy had ambivalent views toward Gloria, but it was Felicia Courtney, poised and statuesque in a forest green sheath, who gave her even more concern. The little group headed straight toward her. Then, after their routine greetings, Gloria bluntly seized Harry's hand and led him away. The ambassador's overweight wife deserted Jaggers and captured the attention of the Chief Justice.

"I love your dress, Felicia," Kathy said after greeting Hawley. "Green is your color."

"Not too conspicuous?" Felicia replied. "I was going to wear black."

Kathy smiled. "*That* would have been conspicuous."

"But more appropriate?"

"Felicia, you're the style arbiter in Washington. And what's more, you'd be conspicuous no matter what you wore. No matter when."

"Compliment?"

At that moment there was a flash of light. "A photographer from the magazine," Felicia said, easily. "With your permission, of course. The three of us?" She turned to the photographer. "You did get all three of us, Randy?"

"Yes, Mrs. Courtney," he said as he started away.

"One moment," Kathy said to the photographer. "You should get Mr. Hawley and Mrs. Courtney together, without me."

"No, no," Felicia replied archly, "we'll do that tomorrow at the Kennedy. But perhaps one of *you* and the Vice President?"

Listening to the feline exchange, Hawley was aware that behind the smiles and courtesies was more than ordinary badinage. And his political sensors alerted him to an acceptable photo of the First Lady with the two of them and the quite opposite reception that could be accorded at the White House to a photo of just himself and the First Lady. It would be awkward, but as he was about to make a mild protest, Kathy interrupted.

"I'm sure Mr. Hawley would prefer the photo that's been taken," she said, as she dismissed the photographer. She glanced at Hawley, certain he understood.

At that moment, dabbing at his moustache, Jaggers turned and spotted the new arrivals. "Mr. Vice President, Mrs. Courtney," he said, beaming. "Felicia, I need your advice, about my gardens." Suddenly there was a sound of music. "Could I steal her for just one dance, Mr. Vice President?"

Felicia smiled as she said, "On one condition, Mr. Secretary."

"Name it," he said.

"A bit of news, and if not news, at least a hint. Agreed?"

"Agreed," he said, crooking his arm.

Felicia passed her beaded handbag to Hawley. "I'll be back to claim it," she said, as she walked off with Jaggers.

"And *you*," Kathy added, watching them turn into the ballroom.

"Not quite," Hawley said, as he now stood alone beside Kathy.

"We could pretend to be admiring the Beauvais tapestry," he said.

"You're late," Kathy said.

"I know," he said, eyes twinkling. "Planned it. Wanted you to wonder what detained me, whether I was coming . . ."

"Sometimes, you can be such a charming scoundrel," Kathy said with a smile, "if I can use such an old-fashioned word."

"I know—guilty as charged," he admitted. "But the truth is we had early cocktails with the Chief Justice, and when we arrived here I wanted to make certain that Miss Gloria spotted Harry, so I steered her directly to him. I knew that would free you for a few minutes at least. So?" he bowed slightly. "Am I acquitted?"

"I appreciate that," Kathy replied. Then as Hawley began to relax she added, "And Felicia?"

"Felicia is Felicia. She's at all these affairs. Escorting her is something no one particularly notices."

"*I* notice."

"Then all the more reason for me to invite her," Hawley replied laughingly as he led Kathy to a corner of the long drawing room and invited her to sit in a handsome Louis XV chair. Hawley's mood suddenly changed. "Seriously, I want to thank you for that call the other night," he said. "After that hard, long day it buoyed my spirits no end. I'll confess something else, too." He leaned down for a moment. "I've missed seeing you," he whispered.

As Kathy looked up she eyed him questioningly.

"You know that," he insisted.

"A woman likes to hear it. *Wants* to. We talk so seldom," she said. "Maybe at parties, embassy affairs, official committees, but they don't count . . ." She pointed to a chair, indicating that she wanted him to sit beside her.

"Part of the price," Hawley said as he pulled it over and sat beside her.

"But just to talk? You could come visit, find a pretext . . ."

"At the White House, Kathy? No, no, that's impractical. Just think—"

"Am I some kind of prisoner, Cliff?"

"In one sense, yes—and with over two hundred fifty million wardens, all watching."

They continued to sit in silence for a few moments, each searching the other's eyes. "We shouldn't be too obvious," she said. "*He's* always watching."

Hawley glanced at Harry across the room.

"He doesn't like me much, Cliff."

"These days he doesn't seem to like me too much, either."

Hawley saw the look of surprise in her eyes. "It's something recent. I don't know what it is; I just *know*," he said. "My political antennae at work."

"That worries me."

Hawley moved his chair closer, welcoming an opportunity to probe. "Why?" he asked, "why would you say that?"

"I don't know how to say it, or how to put it, and I'm not even sure I've a right to discuss it. It's just that I'm worried."

"Something to do with our friend Frederick K. Vance?" Hawley ventured.

Kathy wondered whether she should tell him what she now feared was taking shape. "I'm not absolutely sure. The President said—" she started to speak, but abruptly stopped.

Hawley cut in and placed a hand momentarily on hers. "I never want you to feel any pressure, Kathy. Anything about me and the President that makes you . . . "

"Oh, Cliff, be still. I'm not a child. You know how he calls me 'little girl,' and the last thing I want is for you treating me like one, too."

"You surely know I'd never think of you that way, Kathy."

"I'm dying, dying!" she suddenly blurted out. "Cliff," she said, turning toward him, "I have to say it . . . because it's the truth . . . I've missed you, too."

A waiter offered them champagne. "Have a glass, Mrs. Thompson," Hawley replied, as he lifted two glasses from the tray. "This way we won't be bothered again," he added softly. "Just sip it."

"Cliff, what if he changes things?"

"Like?"

She put the glass down on a small Sheraton table and ran her fingers over the smooth inlay. "Like putting that man on the ticket."

Hawley sipped his drink and laughed. Kathy's face showed puzzlement at his laughter. "I want young Harry to have the feeling that you've just told me something very amusing," he said. Then, his mood changing, he asked, "Did the President come right out and say that?"

"No. And he made a point of saying that he didn't want to make anything big out of taking Vance. But how else are people to take it—his inviting the Senator on the trip?"

"I don't know. All I know is that when he was in Omaha

and was asked if the Senator might be his next running mate, he fielded the question very skillfully."

"He should have denied it."

"He didn't, though." Hawley looking at Kathy, struggled with the question of how much he should tell her, whether even to refer to the Twenty-fifth Amendment, but the figure of Richard Daniels loomed in his mind's eye. He must say nothing. Nor should he allow his inner feelings to fantasize any future personal relationship: Thompson could live for years.

Kathy broke into his reverie. "Is he playing some kind of game with you, Cliff?"

Seeing the ambassador moving toward them, Hawley rose. "I don't know for sure, but I think so. I just don't know why, I don't know his motives."

"You like Felicia?" she asked abruptly.

"Everyone likes Felicia."

"Don't be clever, Mr. Hawley."

Cliff smiled. "I wish I were," he said. "I think I'm obvious."

"You'll be careful?"

"Obvious *and* careful."

"And clever," she added, "maybe too clever."

Hawley turned to greet their gray-haired, dark-visaged host. "Mr. Ambassador, I suspect that smile isn't for me."

"Mr. Vice President, I'm afraid I have to steal the First Lady from you. It's time we went in to dinner. We don't want to delay the Secretary of State anymore, do we?" he said, chuckling as they looked over at Jaggers standing with Felicia and reaching for an hors d'oeuvre.

Across the room, Harry Thompson watched the scene with amusement. "She probably passed on some White House secrets," he said to Gloria.

"You're spiteful. And I'll prove it," she said as Hawley headed in their direction.

"Gloria," Harry said, lowering his voice, "please, no fooling around."

She laughed. "Oh, Harry, you can be such a jealous little fool!" His fingers pressed into her upper arm as he started to lead her away. "You're hurting me, Harry," she said, her voice a little too loud.

"That's just for starters if you decide to show off."

She smiled up at him. "I love it when you get angry, Harry. And I'm going to make you very angry tonight."

She wrenched herself away, letting her evening bag slip to

the floor. Hawley had seen the brief contretemps. Picking up the silver bag, he hurried after them. "Gloria," he called.

She turned with feigned surprise. "How silly of me, Mr. Vice President," she said as she retrieved her small pocketbook. "You *are* going to dance with me tonight, aren't you?"

"Wouldn't think of not dancing with you, Gloria."

She turned to look at Harry. "Do you mind, darling, giving up one dance? Or two, if the Vice President insists?"

"Don't give it a thought, Harry," Hawley said. "One dance with me and Gloria will have had it." Thompson remained impassive as Hawley smiled and headed toward the Secretary of State and Felicia.

The latter reached for her own bag and, turning to Hawley, said, "I have to freshen up. I'll return in a minute or two."

Jaggers was washing down another canapé as he watched her go. "Quite a lady," he said. "Marvelous how nature can turn one body of 115 pounds into a work of art." Then nodding in the direction of the ambassador's wife, he added, "And another, maybe at 160 pounds, maybe 170, into a lump of repulsive flesh." Then he added, as he brushed his moustache, "Best table in town. These people know how to spend money. On food. Excellent."

"Part of our foreign-aid dollars, I'll bet."

Jaggers jabbed a playful finger into Hawley's chest. "Know of a better use for it? All spent here, except for the caviar and wine they bring with them. Look in there at that table. Splendid, isn't it?"

Hawley looked through the door at the long table with its delicate china and silverware, three crystal chandeliers flashing iridescently on the table settings, elaborate floral displays running the length of the table. "Pure opulence for those who govern, while the poor governed count their food stamps," Jaggers whispered, sipping at his drink while his eyes studied Hawley across the top of his glass. "What do you think of the trip?"

Hawley knew Jaggers' technique of chattering away on inconsequential subjects followed by a non sequitur of significance. He smiled inwardly at Jaggers' abrupt switch. "The President's handling it very well."

"Must be a bit of a surprise to friend Daniels, wouldn't you say?"

Hawley also knew that his own words had to be discreet whenever he dealt with any member of the Committee. Friendly as he and Jaggers were, he'd say nothing that might bring trigger doubt in Jaggers' mind as to his own purposes or ambitions.

"I'm sure Daniels is relieved. The President, obviously, has his own inner strength, and it shows."

"Courage, also."

"Yes, that, too."

"Section four, Twenty-fifth Amendment." Jaggers focused his owlish eyes, already heavy from the champagne he'd consumed, on Hawley. "If Hornwell and I failed—even if he abstained and *I* struck out persuading the President, assuming we reached that turning point—the burden would be enormous. All yours." The eyes took on a solemn look. "Ready for dinner?" Jaggers asked amiably as Felicia reappeared.

The two men made their way to their seats. Hawley knew that Jaggers had given him a message: that if the Daniels resolution were to be acted on by the Committee, and if Hornwell abstained, Jaggers was prepared to follow through. He'd made it clear, in his own way, that in a crisis he was Hawley's man. The exchange reinforced Hawley's belief that a one-minute chat at a social gathering could bring greater results than weeks of carefully planned conferences, interviews, and meetings.

Throughout dinner Hawley made pleasant conversation with two women seated on either side of him, one the widow of a senator long dead, whose millions still gave her entrée to choice embassy functions, the other an even older relic of status, dowager empress of the capital's corps of leading hostesses, an aging disciple of Elizabeth Arden, and still wearing ageless Mainbocher gowns.

At times his eyes caught a view of Kathy's profile at the other end of the table. As he listened to the ramblings of his two dinner companions about a Washington now vanished, troubling images of Kathy, the Kathy who'd once been his, surfaced in his mind's eye.

Music from the ballroom signalled the end of dinner. Felicia was a popular target of the younger guests and was whisked off to the dance floor. Hawley was grateful for the time her absence gave him to stroll about, chatting with men who had no interest in dancing, preferring a brief meeting with the Vice President of the United States, a meeting that could (like his with Edward Jaggers) make the evening worthwhile. Halfway around the room, he was buttonholed by a heavily bemedaled Argentine general who maneuvered him against an elaborate French sideboard to make his several points. There he smiled gratefully at the sight of Gloria Whitney, reflected in the ornately framed mirror that hung above it, edging her way through clusters of guests with a definite purpose of her own.

"I'm sorry to interrupt you, General," she said, taking Hawley's arm. Then, noting the trace of irritation on the General's face, she added, "On second thought, I'm not. That's because *you* don't have the next dance and I do." With a light laugh, she led Hawley to the floor.

"You don't mind, do you?" she asked, as she placed a hand on his shoulder. As his arm circled her waist, she said, "I can tell you don't."

A good dancer, Hawley was on guard when he felt her leg brushing against his. He'd learned from past experience that Gloria Whitney made no effort to conceal her provocative nature. "You still like me, don't you?" she said, with an impish smile.

"Everyone likes you," he replied, smiling down at her.

"I don't like everyone."

They danced in silence for a few moments. Then once again he felt her leg brush against his. She smiled up at him. "I like dancing with you, Cliff. You *can* tell, can't you?"

"You're very good."

"I'm good at everything," she said boldly.

"I wouldn't doubt it," he replied. He was amused at her bluntness. "You're as good with dialogue as Harry is with a foil."

"I don't think Harry's that good. Besides, he's always so damned preoccupied with his crusades on this or that, that they take all of the—shall we say—starch, out of his—shall we say—sword? I tell Harry, so it's no big deal," she rattled on, "and it's no big secret, not with me. Meetings, research, phoning, going to hearings—all that comes first with him. Then comes fucking."

Hawley shook his head in mock admonition.

"If I tell Harry that you and I were talking about fucking, it'll blow his mind—which, if you don't mind my getting to the point, is often about all that he wants to do."

"Gloria, *we* weren't," Hawley said, the smile disappearing from his face. "*You* were. Let's not go around inventing trouble. I happen to like Harry—"

"He's very jealous of you."

"I don't believe that. He has no reason to be."

Her fingertips brushed against the back of his head. "He knows I like you—"

"Everyone knows you love him," Hawley said, "and everyone knows he loves you."

"Really? Then how is it I don't know? He's always so full

of excuses. Meetings. Speeches to write—I'd like to go home with him."

"Well, maybe you're about to get your wish," Hawley whispered as he glanced over her shoulder, eager to shorten his time with her. "We're about to bump right into Harry and his partner, so if you want to ask him, the timing couldn't be better."

As Hawley led her closer to Harry, Gloria turned and said, "Harry, would you like to take me home?"

Thompson smiled pleasantly. "Sure, but I didn't bring you, tonight."

Gloria appealed to Harry's partner. "Kathy won't mind, will you?"

"Harry knows he's perfectly free to do whatever he likes," Kathy replied.

"I brought you and I'll take you back," Harry said quietly, staring directly at Kathy.

The two couples circled each other. "The Secret Service brought me, Harry," Kathy said. Then as she turned, she added, "You escorted me. The Secret Service will make sure I go straight back to the White House, whether I'm with you or not."

"I promised my father—"

"He'd understand, Harry." Kathy's voice was so emphatic and determined it made Hawley uncomfortable.

As Thompson paused, the music stopped. He stood, rubbing his chin, a bit uncertain as to how to respond when Felicia's partner, a handsome young embassy aide, escorted her back to Hawley's side.

Kathy suddenly clapped her hands. "I have a better idea for everybody. Instead of just Harry taking me, why don't we all go back to the White House for after-dinner drinks?" She turned to Gloria. "Once Harry's done that little duty he'll be absolutely free of any further obligations." Then touching Felicia's arm, she said, "And Felicia's always said she wanted to see something of the White House living quarters. Am I right?"

"I'd love it, Kathy," Felicia said, glancing at Hawley. "Is it all right with you?"

Hawley wanted to say no, it wasn't all right with him. It was, in fact, moving into an area laced with mines and unforeseen dangers. He'd been caught off guard, and he'd innocently triggered the incident by his own desire to extricate himself from Gloria's machinations.

Hawley heard Harry, still protesting. "Look, like I said, I promised my father—"

Kathy cut him short. "Harry, you *are* taking me home as you promised. Now, I insist."

"Kathy's right," Gloria said. "Stop being such a stickler. We're *all* seeing her home."

Fifteen minutes later Kathy led the group to the wide expanse of the Center Hall of the White House's second floor, an usher taking their orders for drinks. In the meantime Kathy began answering Felicia's questions about the furnishings and the decor. "It was Mrs. Kennedy's idea to have the color scheme the same as in the Yellow Oval Room—that's the entrance just over there," she added as she pointed to the doorway.

"I love those bookcases," Felicia said as she fingered the magazines resting on a drum table. "No copies of *Insider's Washington?*" she asked mischievously.

"They're in my room," Kathy said.

"Really? I'm very pleased. The settee over there . . . Sheraton? Genuine?"

"Genuine," Kathy said, "same as the four matching chairs. And that drum table. Well, not the table; it's Sheraton-style, I think you'd say. The bookcases were put in during Mr. Truman's presidency."

"And the Chinese coromandel screens at the end? They go back very far?"

"*They* do," Kathy said, "seventeenth century, I believe, but they're relatively new in the White House, a gift back in the sixties. I don't know the source, but we can get it if you're interested."

"I am interested, and I'd love to photograph the things you've brought in. Is that possible?"

"I'm sure I can arrange it with the press secretary."

At Gloria's insistence Harry and she had moved into the East Sitting Hall, away from the others. "Boring, listening to all that folderol. Who'd want that old crap anyway—Sheraton, Pembroke, Chippendale? None of it's comfortable."

"You wanted to come," Harry said, a touch of surliness in his voice as he peered back toward the Center Hall.

"You afraid your stepmother's going to give you the slip, Harry? She's here in the White House, with the rest of the antiquities, all nicely catalogued and accounted for. Now can we go up to your room?"

"No, we can't go to my room."

"Your place, then?"

Harry accepted his drink from the usher. "In a minute or two."

Back in the Center Hall, Hawley stood admiring a painting hanging to the left of the bookcase. "Kathy, haven't I seen this before, but not here?"

Kathy took a step from Felicia, who was studying two paintings by William Glackens hanging on either side of the north doorway. "Yes, it used to hang in the Oval Study. A Thomas Moran."

"Moran, one of my favorite Americans," he said.

"Really?" Kathy replied. "Then you'll like the new one the President personally selected just a few months ago. Let me show it to you." She pointed to the doorway. "Felicia, will you excuse us a moment?"

"Yes, of course. Besides, I loathe those western scenes. Especially Albert Bierstadt's work. Give me Glackens any day, the city, especially old New York." Kathy smiled and led Hawley into the Yellow Oval Room.

"That's it," she said, directing Hawley to the right of the fireplace. "I'm not sure such an American scene really goes with the Louis XV furnishings," she added, with a laugh. Then, smiling at Hawley, she whispered, "How did you like little Gloria's talons stroking the back of your neck while you were dancing? You don't have to answer. Besides, I think I should worry much more about *her*," she said, glancing back toward Felicia in the Center Hall.

"You don't really mean that, Kathy, and besides, shouldn't you be mingling with all of your other guests?" Hawley replied, as the usher entered to offer them their drinks.

"But I *am* mingling," Kathy retorted. "And why should we waste these few moments? Please?" she said, lifting her glass to touch his.

"That needlepoint," he said, singling out a cushion on a settee, its back to a window overlooking the South Lawn and its fountain and the Washington Monument visible in the light of the full moon. "Your work, right?"

"You remember that?" she said, pleased.

"I should. I watched you make it," he said. "Before all this," he added, his arm sweeping the room.

"Yes," she said softly, "before all this. Being First Lady has its advantages. But, Cliff, the disadvantages. You may not believe it, but I'm beginning to weary of it." She turned her back to

Hawley and murmured, with a note of petulance in her voice, "Oh Cliff, what am I doing with my life, my days? My nights?"

Hawley took a few steps toward her and stood close enough to inhale the scent of her hair, resisting the impulse to move closer and let her body rest back against his. Suddenly, both were aware of a small sound . . . a faint laugh of amusement. Framed within the doorway was Harry Thompson.

"Come in, come in," Kathy said, moving slowly from her proximity to Hawley. "Where did you leave Gloria?"

"I'm not disturbing anything?" Harry said, smoothly ignoring her question, his tone overly polite.

"Of course not. Cliff and I were looking at the Moran. We were—" she stopped, momentarily flustered, aware that the Moran was hung at the other end of the room.

At that moment Felicia and Gloria entered the room.

"I just wanted to tell you that I'm taking Gloria back home," Harry said, a supercilious smile on his face.

"So soon?" Kathy replied, quickly recovering her poise as she turned to Gloria.

Hawley took the opportunity to move toward Felicia. "That's the Moran," he said, pointing to it.

"Hate it," Felicia said, "hate all those scenes of mountains and rainbows and endless panoramas. Like *her*, though," she said, directing her gaze toward the portrait above the mantel.

"Frances Folsom Cleveland," Hawley said.

"Ah, the young woman who married the last bachelor President. We ran an article on that, let's see, some four issues ago," she said, studying the portrait. "I've been telling Cliff, Kathy, that they don't elect bachelor Presidents anymore. Wasn't it Adlai Stevenson who tried it last?"

"He'd been divorced," Kathy said. "Am I right, Cliff?"

"Yes, and Eisenhower would have clobbered him even if he *had* been married."

Harry raised a hand. "We'll say good night."

Hawley glanced at his watch, determined not to let Harry leave while he himself remained in the White House. "Perhaps it's time for all of us to go," he said, turning to Kathy.

Felicia put a hand on his shoulder. "Cliff, do we really have to hurry off? I love being upstairs here . . . it's really quite fascinating."

"Then stay. Both of you," Kathy urged them, smiling. "There's absolutely no need to rush off. Please, sit down, and let's have some coffee."

But Hawley ended the visist to the White House with Felicia moments after Harry's departure. He knew his departure time would be logged, and he wanted it to be apparent that he had not lingered behind.

"I'm sorry to have cut your first visit to the upstairs White House so short," he said as he stopped his car in front of Felicia's home.

"It wasn't my first visit, Cliff," she said with a laugh. "It was my first visit since Kathy became First Lady."

"Oh?" he said, a note of surprise in his voice. "I thought you said . . . " He stopped and smiled at her.

"I was just curious to see what *she'd* done."

"Oh?" he repeated. "And were you . . . satisfied?"

"Well, the truth is I liked the coromandel screens better when they were opposite the bookcase. Now they're too conspicuous; they darken and narrow the entranceway to the East Sitting Hall. But I do think she made the Yellow Oval Room more inviting, grouping the chairs in front of the mantel." She turned to face him, "You *are* coming in, this time, for a nightcap?"

"I am?" he replied easily.

"They won't object?" she said, glancing back at the Secret Service car parked inconspicuously behind them as she let herself out of Hawley's car, confident that he'd follow.

She led him to a small, comfortable room filled with etchings of scenes from Shakespeare's plays and an assortment of the Bard's likenesses made from marble, bronze, wood, and plaster of Paris. "Ted's hobby, if you remember," she said, going behind the bar. "What can I get you?"

"Cointreau, water on the side. Want me to help?"

"No, you sit right there on that stool. I'll do the honors." She reached up and picked two Baccarat cordial glasses, and then poured out the liqueur. "How many of your predecessor Vice Presidents were bachelors when they took office?" she abruptly said.

"That's an interesting question, and I don't really know. I'll have to research that," he said, coming around the bar for some ice.

Felicia put up her hands to stop him. "It's too crowded back here for two," she said. "You want something, just ask. Now you go back to your stool."

"Well?" she asked, as he remained standing close to her.

"I'm thinking, Felicia, of what it is I want," he answered with a smile.

"Ice?" she volunteered, as they eyed each other warily. "Yes," she said, her hazel eyes twinkling, "lots of ice, and it's in the bucket over there right in front of your seat."

"I wasn't exactly thinking of ice," he chuckled as he made his way back to his stool.

Felicia liked Clifford Hawley, and she was familiar with his social life and his taste in women. She had seen him over the years at various parties long before he was Vice President; and as a longtime friend of her husband's he'd escorted various women to her own dinner parties. There had been congresswomen, university consultants attached to his committees, even a legislative staff assistant on occasions. But the two who had had the most impact on her had been Vivien Lessing and Kathy. She'd met Vivien only once, when the actress performed at the Kennedy, but she recalled having seen Hawley on more than one occasion with Kathy before Kathy's marriage.

"You like Kathy Thompson, don't you?" she asked abruptly.

"Of course. I always liked Kathy Thompson."

"I don't mean *that* kind of liking," Felicia said.

"You *can* be direct," he said.

"Yes," she said, sipping her drink.

"Kathy's married. Kathy's the First Lady."

"I know," Felicia said.

"Kathy and I were friends. Still are. Always will be. That should close the subject," Hawley replied.

"There are a lot of Clifford Hawley students these days, Cliff."

"I'm aware of that. Goes with the job."

"Especially when you're single. Young. Good looking. And as I said, I don't think anyone around can remember when we last had a single Vice President. But when we did, the vice presidency probably didn't matter the way it does now. You're the biggest catch in town," she said, sitting down directly across from him on a stool on her side of the bar.

"There you go again," he said, shaking his head.

"That was a line Reagan used, or something like it. Helped torpedo Mr. Carter way back in 1980."

"You remember your history," Hawley said.

"I'm a student. And I'm a reporter. And I think I know how to watch out for torpedoes."

They sat together enjoying their mutual banter. Hawley found her amusing as well as enticing, and as he studied her, he was even more aware of her beauty and her candor. All of these winning factors made him determined to make no move that might complicate, alter, or even possibly derail a relationship he thought worth exploring. He placed his glass on the bar. "Time," he said, glancing at his watch, "and I don't want to give my keepers . . ." he lifted both hands toward her.

"Are you thinking of my reputation or yours?"

"Ours," he said, reaching over to cup her chin in his hands.

"I'm enjoying the process," she said.

"The process?"

"Of getting to know you." She leaned against the back of the stool, appraising him. "I'd rather not rush it." She set her glass on the bar and took his hand. "I'll see you to the door."

☆ ☆ ☆

The routine aboard the USS *Colorado* proceeded on its regular schedule. There were fire drills, the checking of flooding procedures, the call to battle stations, the controlled rush to missile stations with a full rehearsal of all key steps preparatory for launch, the daily test of the nuclear power plant as well as of torpedos and missiles.

The sighting of a small oily rag, the drowsiness of a sailor standing watch, brought swift punishment—assignment to extra duty, withdrawal of the privilege of seeing favorite movies, longer stints at polishing brightwork. As the milk and vegetable supply began to run out, and the crew became more dependent on canned and dehydrated goods, the crew's stamina and mental state were further tested.

Jeff Whitney continued to spend his spare time in physical activity, frequenting the rowing machine in the small gym. One day, while pulling vigorously on the oars, secretly looking forward to the time when he could take a scull down the Potomac, he was interrupted by Benson, the messenger of the watch. "Excuse me, Captain. Sorry to bother you. Commander Baker and the XO would like you to meet them in the after crew's quarters."

Whitney was irritated by the failure of the executive officer to report himself and by the interruption of the regularity of his workout, which was important to him. "What's the problem?" he asked, glancing at his watch as he strained to increase his tempo.

"It's Corman," Benson said, standing ill at ease.

"Corman? Again? You two have another fight?" Whitney glanced up at the sailor as he continued to pull at the oars.

"It's not that, sir."

"Okay, then what is it?" Whitney demanded, a tone of annoyance in his voice.

"He's dead, sir."

Whitney fell forward as the oars dropped from his hands. "What?"

"Corman's dead, sir," Benson repeated.

"Dead?" Whitney began to struggle to his feet. "How? What happened? Did you—"

"No, sir," Benson cut in, "I didn't do anything. It was Chief Denoff, came looking for him. Corman didn't show up for his watch. I was on duty in the control room at the time. Chief found him in his bunk. Curtains closed. Dead. Me and him had that fight all right, that's true, sir," Benson said, talking rapidly as he and Whitney hurried along the passageways heading toward the after crew's quarters as quickly as they could. "But we were friends. Not the closest, but friendly, except for that calendar business. I think the long patrol was getting to him."

In a few seconds, the ship's doctor, Commander Baker, filled in Whitney. The two of them, along with Morgan, stood quietly together, while Benson stood off to one side, Corman's body lying in his bunk, a fresh blanket covering it.

"There's nothing you could do?" Whitney asked.

"Nothing," Baker replied. "Rigor mortis had set in. He probably died a few minutes after he hit the sack. Heart attack. Eight hours ago, maybe. Nobody paid any attention, figured he was sleeping."

"That was his way, Captain, begging your pardon," Benson said softly. "He'd just flop on the bed and be out, asleep, just like that. Typical."

Commander Baker glanced back toward Benson. "When the Chief came to get him he found him curled up, called to him, then went to shake him. That's when he found out."

"Christ," Whitney whispered. "This is a first."

At that moment a seaman passed a file to Baker. "Thanks," he said to the sailor as he looked across at Whitney. "His medical record. Let's see . . . blood chemistry . . . " He paused a moment to read and once again turned his attention to Whitney. "Cholesterol a little high—taken a week before we sailed. Nothing though to alarm anyone, maybe ten points or so above average for his age. Puzzling."

Whitney said, "What do you need to do?"

"We'll have to have at least a preliminary autopsy. Notify his family."

"Can't be done, Commander. You know our orders," Whitney said.

"I know we're on radio silence. But, Captain, in an emergency?" Baker studied Whitney's face. "I understand, Captain." He pointed down toward the galley. "We'll have to empty one of the freezers."

The two men stared uncomfortably at each other. Whitney said, "I'd better let the crew know. I expect some of them know anyway. How soon can you complete the autopsy?"

"Maybe an hour. Two, no more. I'll need a couple of men to help move him."

"Let me know," Jeff said. "We'll have a service . . ." he glanced at his watch. "At 0800."

Whitney reached down and placed a hand on the blanket. He took a step toward Benson, touched him gently on the shoulder, then headed to his quarters. En route he thought of Hornwell. The President. He thought of Corman's parents, Corman's wife. One less man on his ship, but it made a world of difference.

12

The President paced the balcony of his elegant suite at the Beverly Hills Hotel, pausing momentarily to gaze across the tops of the stately palms, their fronds waving and fluttering in the surprise rainstorm that had gripped southern California. There had been no record of such a heavy May rain for almost a hundred years.

His staff had recommended that he cancel the scheduled drive through Los Angeles, but he'd stubbornly rejected their advice. Jensen had expressed his opinion, and now Kathy, who'd kept her promise to join him in Los Angeles, added her voice to those who opposed him. He listened patiently and then walked out on the balcony, but in the end nothing anyone could say would deter him.

He strode in to give his final decision to Jensen and Kathy. "We're going to make the tour. We're going to do it in an open car. You'll have to bear with me on this, Kathy." He pointed a finger at Donald Gibbs, the trim chief of the Secret Service detail that had made the advance trip some days before, along with the Signal Corps coterie headed by Jeb Rossmore, and the advance team from the President's staff. "Gibbs," he said, with a smile, "you have the route. You and Jensen work out the stops where Kathy and I can change our clothes to dry ones."

Jensen advanced toward the President. "Sir, as your doctor—"

"I know, I know," Thompson said with a touch of asperity, "it's not good for me, etcetera, etcetera. But what you don't take into account is that if I fail to appear, or hide within the bubble on a warm spring day, the press will slaughter me. The people'll say, 'You see, the rumors are correct, the old man cancelled the ball game because of rain—probably thanked God there was rain in the first place—that way he wouldn't have to show.' *That's* what they'll be saying. The rain may not be good for me, but my not showing is even worse."

"Mr. President, no one will criticize you for using the bubble top on the car—"

"Ordinarily no. But this is not an ordinary time. There's a convention coming up and an election. Everyone's feeling the pressure those events create. Politicians, to be sure. And the people. What's more, the people have the right to know that their President can function any time of day in any kind of weather, and if a little springtime shower happens to fall, well, they'll think all the more of him for having the guts to ignore it. The American people want to be shown, and by God, I'm going to show them!"

"But Stephen, while I know you wouldn't be doing this just for the people here, the people of Los Angeles—"

The President cut in, "You're right, Kathy, I'm not. Take a look outside down the street at that flotilla of TV trucks and equipment. You know as well as I that what happens here will be on every news program in America." He began to chuckle. "I remember reading about the time Franklin Roosevelt had the same problem in New York. Only *he* was ill. Really ill. And it rained. It rained for four hours and he made that whole trip with the top down, with water running down his fedora, dropping on his pince-nez. He got wet, but that rain helped win him the election."

"And it may have cost him his life," Jensen interposed.

"Nonsense! If anything, it gave him a tremendous lift. He proved to Dewey and all of the others—who always liked to hint about his health and worse, suggesting he was even non compos mentis—he proved they were whistling in the dark. And we're only scheduled for two hours. And one more thing. Remember, out here on the coast it rains in one part of the city while out in the valleys the sun can be shining."

"Thank God for that," Kathy said.

"Don't worry, we'll have rain gear to cover your hair, Kathy."

Thompson glanced at his watch. "It's time." Then he turned to his press secretary. "You've told them the speech would be short."

"Yes, sir."

"Good! Now, someone take this suitcoat and give me that special water-repellent pea jacket the Admiral sent over."

Jensen helped the President into the heavy woolen coat. "If this doesn't keep the dampness from my bones—"

"We should have carried those special undergarments the astronauts use," Jensen said. "From now on we will."

"Kathy, suit up!" She shook her head as she slipped into a fashionable raincoat brought over from Fred Hayman's, one of Beverly Hills' most famous boutiques.

"Now, let's get this show on the road," the President said, smiling.

And so they toured parts of Los Angeles, waving to clusters of people gathered on Wilshire Boulevard; to larger groups in the Fairfax section, with its delicatessens and retirement homes of elderly Jewish citizens; into the elegance of the continually developing Bunker Hill section, with its luxury apartments and renovated hotels; through the heart of downtown Los Angeles, where small crowds of Mexican-Americans and blacks gave the Thompsons an enthusiastic welcome despite the showers. Then the presidential caravan, with its entourage of newspaper people, television camera crews, and the Secret Service, all escorted by the famed Van Nuys Task Force motorcycle corps, raced along the freeway into the San Fernando Valley, where thousands greeted the President along Ventura Boulevard. Then a dash back down the San Diego Freeway and a speedy journey on Wilshire through Santa Monica all the way to the ocean and back to Beverly Hills.

At three points, the President's car swung off the route to a spot where he could replace his pea jacket with a fresh one. It was plain that the tour was an exhilarating experience for him. At each stop he gulped down hot coffee the Secret Service had ready for him. Even Jensen, who checked him quickly, was pleased with his famous patient's exuberance and his ability to stand up against the elements.

Finally, the caravan pulled up on the cobblestone driveway before the opulent main entrance of the Regent Beverly Wilshire Hotel, a small band of people applauding the President. At the hotel, Thompson would make the first address ever by an incumbent President before the Hollywood Radio-TV Society. The

Society, representing the top brass of the communications field, was meeting for the occasion with the Caucus for Producers, Writers, and Directors, who represented the leadership of television's creative community.

He walked arm in arm with Kathy and whispered, "I'm glad you were able to make it out here, Kathy. I was afraid you might not."

"What on earth made you think that?" she asked as she smiled at the reception committee.

"Harry called me this morning," he replied, searching her face. "You had a good time, I take it, at the embassy."

"Both of us had a very good time," she said.

The President nodded. "That's what Harry told me." He turned to greet the chairman of the welcoming committee, who led him through a side passage onto the stage. The audience rose to its feet, giving him a noisy welcome. In a few minutes he was standing at the rostrum addressing the group.

"The heavens overlooking your beautiful city gave me a special welcome—" he began, at which his audience laughed. "And now you have topped the heavens. I told the First Lady that we were going to be here even if we had to swim. And believe me, today we've been doing some swimming!"

He paused for a moment and listened to the appreciative audience. "I've come here to talk about television and motion pictures," he said, reading from his prepared text, "and I won't be long. If Lincoln could say something memorable in 271 words, perhaps I can try to say something at least as stimulating to you folks, even if I wind up using a few more. My son, Harry, is deeply involved with a lot of causes; he's something of a crusader, and sometimes he's in an adversary role when it comes to television and motion pictures.

"You mustn't abandon your traditional standards of quality and excellence. You have an obligation to provide that kind of entertainment. But you mustn't forget the role of television: to stimulate debate on public issues, plus its enormous power to educate and inspire.

"I share some of those views, but I also recognize many of the great accomplishments that you ladies and gentlemen have already achieved."

Kathy watched him as he talked—confident, forceful, commanding. She was pleased that the events of the motorcade had bolstered his old self. As she reflected on the President's comments, she felt certain that Harry Thompson had said very little—certainly nothing of the brief encounter he'd observed between herself and Hawley.

A prolonged burst of applause and the ensuing ovation by the audience as the speech ended startled Kathy from her reverie. The President was beaming. Holding out one hand to her, he waved graciously to the crowd with the other.

"It was a good speech, Stephen," she said.

"Something Harry's been at me to say. He wrote most of it."

"Then you both deserve the credit."

"He says things quite to the point—*succinct* is the word." The President stopped to shake hands with a few of the guests of honor on the dais.

"You've given us something to think about, Mr. President," the chairman said.

"Stop the thinking and start the doing," the President replied with a smile.

They threaded their way through the crowd to their car, its bubble top now installed. Settling back into the rear seat, the President said, "If I say so myself, I'm rather proud today, Kathy. Proud."

"You should be. Like I said, the speech was really very good. You can be proud of Harry, too."

He nodded to her, then shut his eyes. After a few minutes he looked up. His eyes were rheumy, and he stared at Kathy with such intensity she was uncomfortable. Slowly the words came out, "Now you can tell me about that night—in the White House."

Kathy's heart jumped, and she felt herself flush.

"What went on at the window?" the President asked, his voice edgy.

"Window?"

"Yes."

"I don't know what you're referring to, Stephen."

The President continued to glare at her. "Harry *said* you wouldn't tell me. It seems Mr. Hawley was a visitor?"

"Nothing went on!"

"You two were alone?"

"There's nothing to tell, Stephen," she said hotly. "Am I being spied upon?"

"If you won't tell me—"

"I'm surprised at Harry creating such a shameful innuendo and—"

"I put his remarks way back in my head right after he called this morning, until now."

"I can't imagine him telling you something he had to know could disrupt your whole day—"

The President raised a hand as though to shield himself. "I wouldn't *let* it, not with the stakes so high. Now, let me make an announcement. Mr. Hawley is not to have the privilege of the family quarters of the White House. You understand?"

"I hear you, Stephen, and I don't accept your judgment. Besides," she went on, "we were a group, Felicia Courtney—"

"I know who was there," Thompson said, cutting in. "And now let me emphasize that soon—very soon—" He rubbed his eyes as though to blot out an image.

"Nothing happened, Stephen! Nothing!"

"Harry said you wouldn't tell me," he repeated.

"If either you or Harry knows something that I don't know—then I think one of you should be man enough to say it!"

Thompson shook his head, his face burdened with anxiety. "Don't force us, Kathy."

"But to punish Clifford Hawley, to humiliate him—"

"I want to believe you, Kathy, *in* you. Perhaps," he said, as he closed his eyes, "I don't want to hear. If I don't hear, then I don't know. If I don't know, then I can't be troubled. And I need my peace." He glanced over at her. "Yes, peace. Peace at almost any price."

"I know nothing," Kathy said, looking straight at him. But as she looked at him, and as he stared coolly back at her, what she wanted to say was, "If you need peace, then believe me, I need my peace, too, Stephen. Yes, you've been kind, good to me. Very good. I don't want to hurt you, Stephen. I never want to hurt you, but the truth is—and it's hard to say but it has to be said—you're burned out, you can't love me. And it's no fault of yours. It's simply that I've discovered you can't really do anything for me. Perhaps it's time we both face the facts—the reality of our lives. You look upon me as your 'little girl'—but I'm a woman with a woman's needs and desires. Yes, I'll admit it—Clifford Hawley does mean something to me. I can't say what it is, but this I know: you and I—we wound up together making a bargain: you got me, my youth, my desire to taste life at the top; I got you, a man who was already *at* the top, who could give it to me all at once. But it hasn't worked ... Now we have to face something no one in the White House ever faced before ... Maybe it's time to think of it, if only for the peace you say you need. The peace *I* want and need, too. Maybe we have to consider it. It's all very simple ... It's called divorce."

She wanted to say it all, but she couldn't.

They sat apart, in silence, as they returned to the hotel.

13

Alice Curtis rested on a French gilt-edged chaise lounge in a small area adjoining her bedroom in her quarters in Geneva. She frowned as she pondered the Washington phone call just ended. The President had clearly shown his irritation when he raised the subject of her dispatch counselling against sending a personal message to Turgenev. She was puzzled at the abrupt way in which he'd come on the phone, brushing aside all of the usual amenities, determined, so it appeared, to get directly to the point. Despite her efforts, nothing would convince him that such a contact could be counterproductive at the present stage of arms-control negotiations.

She summoned her executive assistant, Carolyn Hemsley, a Georgetown graduate enrolled in the foreign service after a stint working as a political analyst for Federal Broadcasting in Washington.

"I have to go to the capital—the President's asked me—as soon as arrangements can be made." Carolyn's brown eyes widened in disbelief. "I know it's not an ideal time," Alice Curtis said, as she began to straighten papers on her desk, "but I think

I should be able to settle everything in twenty-four hours, and meantime Mr. Saunders can handle the schedule here."

"Won't the Soviets think something's up?" Carolyn asked.

"They may, but our story will be that I returned to get clarification on my instructions from the Secretary of State and the Secretary of Defense. And my returning within a day or two will minimize any speculation."

"He's never broken into your schedule before."

"There's always a first time for everything," Mrs. Curtis said, going across the room to a closet to select some clothes. "I'll travel lightly," she added, pulling out a business suit. "There were several firsts, as a matter of fact. The summons. The flat-out rejection of my recommendation. The peremptory manner—almost impolite from him."

"Perhaps," Carolyn ventured, "something else triggered his attitude."

"It's possible."

As Alice Curtis examined her clothes, Carolyn rambled on. "There're lots of pressures on him. The convention's coming," she said, "and all the rumors about his replacing the Vice President. Then the *Time* piece on the health of senior government officials, the hint that the President's memory may not be too sharp—the reference to 'creeping senility,' as they call it—the pointed remarks about stress . . . "

"Yes, there *is* the stress of marriage—" Mrs. Curtis interjected.

"To Kathy Thompson?" Carolyn asked in some surprise.

"No, no, the first Mrs. Thompson. Margaret was no pussycat, and I knew her before I'd even met him. Very positive—brash, dogmatic. Not the most appealing qualities for a woman. Life with her, that all had to create stress."

"I'm glad you've given the first Mrs. Thompson all the credit, and not Kathy Thompson."

"I'm not a hundred percent sure there, either."

"But she's the easiest-going—"

"Carolyn, I was thinking of her age. And the President's. That's a prescription for creating its own kind of stress. We won't ever know, of course, but we could be the innocent, unfortunate beneficiaries, if you want to call us that," Mrs. Curtis said, "of that very difference. You and I. And Mr. Turgenev, too. It wouldn't be the first political or military event that had its real origin in a bedroom," she added, with a sigh.

☆ ☆ ☆

The grinding monotony had begun to show on the faces of some of Commander Whitney's crew, but there was no letdown in their response to the routine of drills and duty.

The death of Corman initially had produced a sudden drop in attendance at the showings of the movies, but gradually the old habit returned. Both Whitney and Morgan also sensed a deeper spirit of camaraderie; gin rummy and poker games became more frequent; the exercise gear in the gym was more in demand. A regulation blanket had been placed over the door of the freezer that held Corman's body. On occasion Whitney noticed members of the crew reaching out to touch it as they passed by in the cramped quarters. Nobody said anything, but everybody was aware.

Meanwhile, the ship continued its monotonous routine, maintaining bare headway while circling endlessly inside the coordinates established by the navigator, and at a depth far below that normally used by ballistic-missile submarines.

Reports by the conning officer were given to Whitney of ships picked up on sonar, their signatures identified by the sonar men, most often merchant ships as far away as 150 miles, but occasionally a silent-running Soviet submarine only a few miles off. Whitney and his crew felt the tangy thrill of invisibility coupled with invincibility.

As the days and weeks stretched into months, Whitney and Morgan had resumed their chess games whenever time permitted. And there was much debate about politics, about the changing international stituation precipitated by the years of Gorbachev and his original policies of glasnost and perestroika right up to and through the Turgenev period.

"If we ever come to the conclusion that the Soviets can become part of the economic system of Western Europe, that's when we'll become obsolete, Art," Whitney said as he picked up one of Morgan's knights.

"That won't happen until they decide to put the ruble on the gold standard," Morgan replied, "and that's still a long time off."

"They've got the gold," Jeff replied. He moved his queen. "Check," he said.

"Yeah, and they've always been smart enough to keep it. Because once they let it go, before it makes economic sense for them to go on the gold standard, they'll be in the soup without ever getting really started." Morgan stopped to stare at his pieces, then looked up as Whitney chuckled.

"I think it's mate, chum. *You're* in the soup," Jeff said.

Morgan pushed away from the table. "You got my mind off the game with all the talk about global money business."

"Distracted you," Whitney said.

"Deliberately, too."

"That's what we have to look for in dealing with the Soviets," Whitney went on. "These fellows—the ones in power—they try to take the long view. Same as the ones who're sitting waiting, very quietly, to make a move the first time there's a real sign that the masses have finally been so indoctrinated with the great disease of the West—freedom—that they suddenly want everything all at once, no more patience. And let's not forget they've had a few generations of being passive hordes, just like their forefathers, the serfs. *That's* when we might see the backlash of repression. Old Henry Kissinger's preached that theory for years, and he's smart.

"And that's why Hornwell's been the right man for us right now. No pushover for a couple of vodka toasts and a bear hug by whoever's top dog in the Supreme Soviet at any given moment. That's why we needed a political leader with that same kind of quiet reservation who says, 'Hey, we've spent billions and billions to win the war—the Cold War—let the damn Soviets sink, let them disintegrate, that's what this war's been all about . . . let them spend a generation or two to work it out.'"

"That may be the President's position, Captain, I wouldn't know," Morgan said. "But what about the Vice President? I heard him give a talk—it was at Annapolis—where he sort of raised a question that these past few years might turn out to be one of the great turning points in world history, that we can be the leaders restructuring the whole works, that NATO and the Warsaw Pact are anachronisms, at least the Warsaw Pact—"

"That died the day the Berlin Wall was breached. Matter of fact, Art, I heard him, I was there," Jeff interrupted. "Didn't know you were. The President's son, Harry Thompson, he was the key advance man for Hawley, friend of my brother, Lane, too. And I also remember him saying he thought Hawley was getting too far out front from his old man. You hear that?"

"No, but I keep reading how Mr. Hawley's transformed himself over the years from just being a cagey politician who once served in the House to someone who's grown intellectually with his role as the Veep. This man never was a Quayle. People take him seriously because he's begun to take himself seriously. Even when he had something of a playboy image. Know about that?"

Jeff thought for a moment of Vivien Lessing, her confession about Hawley. "Not much. He's taken my sister out a couple times—but more as an escort I think," Jeff said. "It's well known that Gloria and Harry Thompson have been a number for some years now."

Morgan laughed. "Not bad to wind up with a Vice President or a President's son as a brother-in-law," Morgan said as he stood up. "Got a preference?"

"Nope. That'll be Gloria's decision."

Morgan was at the door. "If she wants my advice I'll pick Hawley. Man with a future."

"I'll tell her."

"Good night, skipper."

Whitney waved to him and then boxed the chess pieces. Glancing at the family photograph of the Whitneys that perched on the edge of his desk, he pulled out a pad of paper. He looked over his last entry. He'd been writing a letter to Gloria, expressing his views about the very subject Morgan had raised, the merits of the men in her life. He liked Harry Thompson, but he'd also come to resent the long delay in Harry's decision as to his and Gloria's future. He picked up his pen, and as he touched it to paper a sudden, unnerving muffled sound reverberated throughout the ship. He sat immobilized by the shock of the sound and then was jolted by a second wave of reverberations that originated from the other side of the ship.

In an instant he was rushing down the passageways, heading straight to the control room. As he raced along, Morgan leaped out from his room and followed a few steps behind, calling to him. "What the hell do you think, skipper?"

"I don't know," Jeff shot back, still racing ahead. Both men were suddenly stopped in their tracks as the heavy sound resonated again throughout the ship. "Something's out there—that's for sure!" he said as he lunged forward and heard the conning officer pass the word on the intercom. "Man battle stations torpedo! Man battle stations torpedo!"

In the control room both men found everyone glued to their monitors and earphones. In that split second Whitney felt pride in his team. There they were, thousands of feet below the surface of the ocean, eyes wide, to be sure, but not one sign of panic. Concern, yes. Puzzlement, yes, astonishment. But no panic and no fear.

He looked forward to one of the sonar men, eyes fastened on his monitor. "Judson?"

The young sailor, no more than twenty-two years old, glanced up. "Don't know. Can't read it yet. Could've been a small submarine or a mine. Something bounced off of us."

"At this depth?" Morgan interjected in disbelief. "A mini-sub?"

Judson nodded. "Yes, sir. I understand some of them can operate much deeper."

"But if its a mini-sub it would have to have a mother ship around somewhere," Morgan persisted.

Judson shrugged. "Nothing's been around for a couple hours, except a freighter."

"That could be where it came from," Morgan said.

"Could be," Judson replied. "But we would have picked it up, sir. There's been nothing."

For twenty minutes the submarine glided at its stately pace, arcing in a great circle as every man stood riveted to his post. There was no sound. No one spoke until Morgan turned to Whitney. "Do we go up to take a look?"

Whitney shook his head. "Negative. We increase our speed." He turned to the conning officer. "Make turns for ten knots."

"Turns for ten knots. Aye, aye, sir," the conning officer repeated.

Minutes later a different sound began, at first on the port side, a series of heavy metallic taps, designed, Whitney thought, to command everyone's instant attention. And then came the word, tapped out in Morse code: "Welcome." Followed by silence for a few moments.

Morgan muttered, "Guy out there, whoever . . . has a sense of humor." A moment later another series of tapping began on the starboard side of the ship.

"Two of them," Whitney said softly.

Then came the words: "Soviet SSN."

Whitney stroked his chin and called once again to Judson. "Hear anything else out there?"

"Not a thing, sir," he said, sitting at rigid attention and straining to hear something.

"And nothing else unusual during your whole watch?"

"That one freighter. Made her out about an hour ago. Went right over us."

"They *had* to come off her," Whitney said, looking toward Morgan.

"Divers? Impossible. At this depth? What do you think, skipper?"

"I don't know. But we surface. Have to break our silence. Washington has to know. Immediately!" He looked about the cramped room, turned to the conning officer, and barked out his order. "Bring her up to periscope depth!"

☆ ☆ ☆

Sitting back in his brown leather chair, Clifford Hawley gazed at his two dozen colleagues scattered in the Senate chamber. They were listening to a dull salute to President Thompson's new Asian policy delivered by the senior Senator from Kansas, Frederick K. Vance, in a voice as flat and monotonous as the plains from which he came. While he had his own respect for Vance's ability, he wondered if it could really be true that the President would select Vance over himself as a running mate.

And now, even as he thought of the convention only eight weeks away, and almost as soon as he felt the tension within, a page slipped a note on his desk. The message said that Richard Daniels would appreciate his calling at his first opportunity.

Hawley pocketed the note and sought the eye of the Senator from Montana, President pro tem, summoning him with a nod of his head to assume the chair. He got up and moved by two sergeants at arms who'd thrown open the double doors leading to the Senators' Lobby. He strode past the leather sofas and desks that filled the private corridor, heading toward the office reserved for the Vice President in the East Front corner. Once there, he sat behind the polished mahogany desk, studying in its glass top his own image reflected back by surrealistic snips and fragments reflected from the cluster of prisms hanging from the crystal chandelier above him. The desk was bare save for a phone. Hawley reached over and picked it up to call Daniels.

Less than an hour later, they were sitting together in the Vice President's library, sipping drinks. The news that Daniels brought was disquieting. The USS *Colorado* was returning thirty days ahead of schedule.

"That's Jeff Whitney's command," Hawley said.

"Correct."

"Any reason?"

"None given so far." Daniels removed an envelope from an inside pocket. "But I think we know. Hornwell said, some two months or so back, if you recall, that our technical breakthrough would enable us to spot any Soviet submarine above or below the surface, day or night. We're at that very point now or just about."

"Good."

"Not so good," Daniels said, exhaling a stream of smoke and snuffing out his cigarette. "The Soviets are already there."

"Are you certain?" Hawley was surprised.

Daniels passed the papers to Hawley. "This report spells it out." Then his hands mechanically rolled another cigarette between his nicotine-stained fingers. "Things are getting to the critical stage, Mr. Vice President," he said, looking up at Hawley. "The convention's coming. The President's health is no better—"

"No worse, either," Hawley interjected.

"Could be, but the demands of a campaign, the continuing pressure of this silent underseas war with the Soviets, the world looking for something from Mrs. Curtis's mission—all these matters could wind up being just too much." Daniels waited for Hawley's response.

Hawley chose to be noncommittal. "You could be right, Richard. But then again, you could be wrong."

"I think I'm right," Daniels said firmly. "That's why the Committee has to meet on this. We know we can't count on Hornwell, and that, of course, means the military establishment will stand with him—maybe not all of them, but clearly a majority. Hornwell's still their man. And Secretary Clauson will tend to lean toward Hornwell. Agreed?"

"Yes," Hawley said.

"On the other side, you know Jaggers is yes. Moran, too. And with me added in, that's a majority—excluding you, of course. But you do have a vote. Now, if you were to go with the other side, Hornwell and Clauson—" Daniels shrugged. "You get the picture?"

Hawley got up from his corner of the sofa and looked out across the broad curving veranda to the well-tended gardens, his back to Daniels.

Daniels continued puffing on his cigarette. "We do nothing ... you do nothing, the door could open up for Vance. You want to see the country in his hands?"

"No, of course not, but it's not because he isn't qualified.

He is," Hawley said, turning to face Daniels. "But to answer your question . . . No. The real question is one of time. And if there is a *right* time."

Daniels picked up his hat. "I'll buy that," he said. As they walked together through the spacious reception hall Daniels stopped at the front door, adding, "The matter of Red Dye Day is upon us. To delay a decision there . . ." Daniels shook his head. "Not to mention the number of federal appointments *still* awaiting the President's decision. A Supreme Court Justice, a vacancy on the FCC, the Circuit Court of Appeals, you name them. This time you'd better study the Twenty-fifth for real. This time it's not likely to be only an academic exercise, Mr. Vice President, for either of us."

☆ ☆ ☆

Harry Thompson stretched out on the black leather couch in the living room of his private apartment; across from him was Lane Whitney.

"He send you?" Harry asked, referring to Hawley.

"No, he didn't send me. I work for the man and I've got obligations. You want a prick like Vance to wind up on the ticket?"

"Is there that much of a difference?"

"Come on, Harry."

"Fits both, if you want my honest opinion."

Lane pulled his chair closer. "Look, buddy, you were one of Mr. Hawley's chief lieutenants in the last campaign. What's eating you?"

Harry stretched his hands behind his head. "You really don't know?"

"No, I really don't know," Lane repeated.

"Look, the little bastard's conniving every day to stay on the ticket. He's got you. He's got his personal Rasputin, Daniels. He's got half the Cabinet, he's got a line into Kathy—"

"Oh? You know that, for a fact?" Lane asked.

"Just figure I know," Harry said, looking smugly at Lane with a knowing wink.

"So? What else is new? I see the man close up, Harry, and I still like what I see. Most of Washington does. So he's ambitious. He's also on top of all the issues. Anything wrong in that? All I came over for was to get a line on where *you* stand. I want to put the team back together."

"Very noble of you, Lane, old boy. Let's say I haven't quite decided."

"Harry, this is the man who more than anyone else put *your* old man in the White House. Can all the noble shit. You're either working *for* him—or you're working *against* him. Which is it?"

A light tapping stopped Harry's reply. "Do you mind?" Harry said, nodding to Lane to open the door. There, smiling cheerfully, the bright lights of the entrance hall reflected in the large, pale green tinted glasses she wore, stood Gloria Whitney.

"Well, surprise! Am I interrupting something very hush-hush?" she asked, entering the room and patting Lane's face. "What do you want with Harry?"

Lane pushed his sister's hand away and looked over at Harry. "I'm waiting for your answer, Harry."

Gloria pouted and said, "I'm waiting for yours, Lane. Money? Girls? Sex?"

"Shut up!" Lane snapped.

Gloria curled up in a corner of the sofa and pulled Harry's loafers off. She glanced over at her brother. "Good-bye, Lane."

"Well, Harry?" Whitney said impatiently.

"Lane, can't you tell you struck out?" Gloria said. "You haven't heard, I guess, how Daddy just issued a statement that he wasn't going to hear poor Harry's appeal about all those greedy little Indians of his who claim they own a couple of states by virtue of some crazy treaty written about 1840? I went all the way down to that old marble cemetery, sat in that dark, musty room he likes to call his chambers, listened to him pontificate in front of his old black marble fireplace, and I asked Daddy, 'Please, hear Harry's case, please, just for me?' But no go. So that's two of us Whitneys down. I don't know what you're here for, but I'm here to make it up to Harry in the best way I can."

She began to pull one of Harry's socks off. "Cut it out, Gloria," Harry said. "Your father pays a hell of a lot less attention to the rights of ordinary people than the Burger court did, and someday, maybe, if he wakes up one morning without a scalp, maybe then he'll remember there *are* Indians in this country."

"You leading the scalping party?" she said, holding onto his leg.

"Come on, Gloria, it's still daylight," Harry said, pushing her hand away. "And yes, if there ever is a scalping party, I could be leading it."

She reached up to his belt. "It's past seven and night is coming on fast. And Dracula's little milkmaid is thirsty—"

"Hey, slow down," Harry said, a smile crossing his face, "can't you see your brother's still here."

She began to pull at his belt. "I don't mind his being here."

"Well, I do," Harry said, nudging Gloria aside and standing up, placing a hand on Lane's shoulders. "Let's just put it this way. I'll think on it, okay?"

"That'll disappoint him."

"It's all I'm going to offer tonight." Harry started to work his feet back into his loafers.

"We need your help. We need it fast."

"Lane, I've given you my answer."

Gloria stretched out on the sofa. "You're always talking politics, you two, as if I didn't know. Lane doing his little ole pitch for Cliff Hawley. Whom Harry suddenly detests. Absolutely detests. Did you know that the big green-eyed monster took a big bite out of Harry? That he's jealous of Cliff Hawley? Did you know that, Lane? No, you wouldn't."

"All right, Gloria, stay out of it," Harry said.

Lane picked up his briefcase. "Think about it, Harry." He turned to look across the room at his sister. "And it's obvious you've been not only popping off, but popping too many. And you know what I mean."

Gloria only laughed. "Good-bye, Lane."

Lane slammed the door behind him. Harry sat down on the edge of a mahogany coffee table. "Your brother's right, Gloria."

"I'm not here for sermons, Harry." She reached over to flip open her pocketbook. A variety of pills of different shapes and colors rolled about the surface of the table. "Take your pick. Uppers. Downers. Something there that's guaranteed to wipe that hostility off your face. I hope," she added. She reached down, picking up two of the pills, quickly swallowing them.

"Jesus!" Harry said as he swept the rest up in his hand and started across the room to his bathroom.

Gloria leaped up from the sofa, racing over to him. "Harry! Give them back to me! Do you hear me?!" She grabbed at his arm as he brushed her aside. "Harry! Harry! Listen to me!"

He held her off with one hand as he flushed the pills down the toilet. "If you were stopped for going through a stop sign—for speeding—Christ! What do you think this would do to your father?"

"You bastard," she said softly as she slumped against him.

"You keep me waiting three whole days while you play Galahad to some of your creepy clients—"

He led her back to the sofa. "Look, those people you call creeps need help, they have no money, they really need me—"

"*I* need you."

"You *have* me."

"Not when I want you. Last week it was the same. Two months ago it was the same. Two months from now it'll be the same. Won't it?"

"Gloria, I've told you a thousand times, I have my work, my interests—besides, you know damn well how I feel about you."

"You don't show it."

Harry rubbed his forehead. "Look, I'm no machine—"

"You're telling me."

He looked at her coldly. "Then go buy yourself a vibrator."

She leaped to her feet. "I can do better than that, Mr. Thompson. You're not the only man in town!"

"You should know!"

"And what does that mean?"

Harry shook his head in mock disbelief. "You pretend not to know? You? The belle of all the Washington balls? All those bright Pentagon assholes cutting in and sniffing around? Your embassy aides? You stand there pretending you don't know? Measuring the size of every cock you lean in against? Sure, I'll just bet you don't!"

Gloria's face paled at the assault. Tears came to her eyes as she picked up her pocketbook. "I'm sorry, Harry, just plain sorry that you never, never could understand. Yes, I flirt. Yes, I've led men on. But I've been faithful to you even when I was dying to have a man take me in his arms. So I let out some of my desires in dancing—big deal . . . dancing . . ." She took out a handkerchief.

"All the time pushing in your legs. I've seen you at work—dancing."

"I'll pretend I didn't hear that, Harry. I'll pretend we never really knew each other. I'll pretend I never received those beautiful letters from you—"

"Pretend or not. What it boils down to is that maybe it doesn't really *matter* anymore, Gloria. I don't know. Maybe we had the best of each other a year ago, maybe two years—"

"I've been waiting for you, Harry. Oh, how I've waited. Years . . ."

"Okay, you waited. You want me to feel guilty."

"I loved you, Harry." Her eyes had lost their sparkle. "From the time I first told you I was an alien and had come here to take you away. Remember? We really had something, Harry. We were going to get married. You always said we were."

"Well, maybe I did." He sat brooding for a moment, elbows on knees, head resting on the palms of his hands. He spoke as though she were no longer there. "Maybe I should have known—I think I did some time ago—that maybe we wouldn't make it. *You* can't help yourself with your drives; *I* can't help myself with my own needs, my work. We have to face it," he said, glancing at her. "The way we live, we actually live quite apart."

Gloria rummaged through her handbag and found a small cloisonné pillbox. A smile crossed her lips as she opened it, extracting three pills. "You missed these, Harry," she said, swallowing them before he could reach her. "I really needed them, Harry," she pleaded. "I came here to make love to you, to have you make love to me, to help you forget my father—the decision—and you've just told me the truth. You don't really want me, you don't even need me. You haven't for a very long time."

"Look, you're tired, I'm tired. I'n not going to put anything into concrete tonight—"

"But you have darling, you have. 'We wouldn't make it.' Plain and simple, you just said it."

"Please, Gloria, please," he said as he got up and moved toward her. "Don't hang on every word I say in the middle of an argument. It has nothing to do with you. Like your father's decision today. Or your brother coming in here trying to save Hawley—"

"Mr. Hawley." She nodded her head and smiled. "Mr. Hawley," she repeated.

He stopped and searched her face. "So? Mr. Hawley, so?"

"I'll go to him. He's the one man who's always wanted me, but he's just been too decent, too honest to try, knowing I was promised."

Harry's face flushed with anger. "Look, I've been trying to explain. But, goddamn! You wear me down with your threats. If it's so easy for you to jump from one man's bed into another's—good luck and good fuck!"

She opened the door. She stood looking at Harry, a soft smile on her face. "Remember. I loved you very much, Harry." And then she was gone.

Harry started toward the closed door. In a sudden burst of

anger he kicked off a loafer and sent it flying against the window. Then, crossing the room, he pulled the drapes apart so that he could look down to the street below, watching Gloria as she stooped to open the door of her small silver Chrysler convertible. As he saw her stop for a moment to glance up at his window, he quickly retreated from his position.

He poured himself a small glass of brandy. He'd grown accustomed to her bluffing. He was certain she wouldn't go to Hawley.

☆ ☆ ☆

The Vice President rubbed his face as he lowered his shaver. He had accepted an invitation from Oliver Moran's wife, Valerie, to attend a concert at the Kennedy Center. Hawley liked Moran; he had always been impressed that Moran had managed to serve the government in high posts for twenty-five years, and before that had been a Pulitzer Prize historian. Oliver Moran rose as Hawley, still putting the finishing touches to his black tie, entered the vice presidential library. "Sorry to keep you waiting, Oliver," he said.

"We have time," Moran said. "No rush, except for the rain we're having. Besides, Valerie and Felicia both told me as I left that they'd hold the curtain as long as they could 'til we arrived."

"Nice to have two ladies of influence in our corner," Hawley said amiably. "Time for a sherry?"

Moran glanced again at his watch. "That would be fine. Very nice."

Hawley summoned a butler and ordered the drinks. "Your next book, when it comes out—"

"Yes, *when* it comes out," Moran chuckled. "Been planning it for at least ten years and here I am still in the planning stage."

They'd had a good relationship for a long time. "My father's always felt that politicians should keep on the good side of historians," Hawley said, "because, as he says, historians make the choices that place some men in the center of events and leave others out on the fringe."

"He gives us historians too much credit." Moran glanced at the bookcases. "Nice collection of books on past Vice Presidents," he said.

"A legacy started by Walter Mondale. I've been reading them. Studying what motivated them—" A sudden crack of thunder followed by a flash of lightning interrupted them and a heavy rain swept in across the porch, striking the windows of the library. A moment or two later, the butler returned and whispered to Hawley. "Here? She's here?" Hawley asked, a note of perplexity in his voice.

"Yes sir, in the reception hall, sir."

"Well, show her in, show her in." He turned to Moran. "We have a surprise visitor, the Chief Justice's daughter." Hawley rubbed his chin, uneasy. "Can't imagine why . . ."

Moran glanced at his watch. "Maybe we won't have as much time as I thought now that I look, and this rain, that could slow down traffic—"

Gloria entered the room, her hair and face gleaming from the rain. "Do you arrange this kind of reception for visitors, Mr. Vice President?" She turned to Moran. "Good evening, Mr. Secretary."

Moran rose from his chair and greeted her warmly. Then he looked at her clothes. "My dear girl, you're soaked through!"

She shrugged and laughed. "Just coming from my car, it was like walking through a swimming pool. I made the mistake of not parking right under the porte-cochere. Unfortunately for me, there was another car there and I didn't wait."

Hawley sensed instantly that her appearance, unheralded, represented an act of defiance against Harry Thompson. He didn't like surprises, especially when they carried potential time bombs. Her easy smile and her relaxed manner brought an edge to his voice. "What brings you here, Gloria?" he asked.

Moran spoke before she could reply to Hawley's question, "Miss Whitney, aren't you supposed to be going to the concert with your father?"

As she shook her hair, a thin spray of water shot out around her. "I'll answer the Vice President first. My car broke down." She dangled the keys before her. "Wasn't I lucky that it happened right outside your house? The guards were so polite." She laughed as she said, "I think all the rain must have been locked up in one cloud right over my head."

At that moment a maid, alerted by the butler, entered the room with a large terry towel, which she brought over to Gloria. When Gloria tossed it over her shoulders, the maid wrapped it around her.

"Thank you. And to answer you, Mr. Secretary. I *was* going home. But not now. I couldn't possibly get home, get changed, and get there on time."

Hawley turned to the maid. "Mary, you'd better take Miss

Whitney upstairs to a guest room and find her a robe. I'll take the car keys," he said to Gloria.

"Thank you, Mr. Vice President," Gloria replied, cocking her head with a mischievous look as she handed them to him. "And could I please have something, maybe a drink to take the chill off? Scotch?"

Moran clapped his hands. "Well, I think I'd better be going if I want to keep up my standing with Mrs. Moran. That's all I'd have to do, fail to show, rain or no rain."

"I'll see you to your car, Oliver, and you be sure to tell Valerie and Felicia that I'll be *right* along," Hawley emphasized. Then glancing back to Gloria he said, "I'll call the Chief Justice and explain matters. Mary will look after you."

Gloria shrugged her shoulders. "Lead the way, Mary," she said nonchalantly.

Having escorted Moran to his limousine, Hawley passed Gloria's keys to a security guard, asking him to check her car. He returned to the library to phone Chief Justice Whitney, explaining Gloria's delay and apologizing for being unable to escort her home because of his own commitment to attend the concert. He was precise in all he said, anxious to leave no loopholes for Gloria to exploit, anxious not to do anything that might later provoke Harry.

By the time his brief conversation with Everett Whitney was finished, Mary was standing in the doorway holding Gloria's wet garments. "Miss Whitney would like to see you, sir," she said.

He looked at his watch. "I'll just make the concert," he said, turning and striding into the hall. As he started up the stairs, the security guard returned and handed him Gloria's keys. "Car's okay," the man said.

Gloria was refilling a tumbler with scotch as he entered the guest room. "I'm so cold," she said, "all the way through." She clutched the collar of the robe tightly. "It's nice seeing you, Clifford."

"Now will you kindly explain what you're doing here, Gloria?" he demanded.

His abruptness startled her, but she sipped her drink without revealing it. "That doesn't sound hospitable to me."

"Your car didn't break down," he said, flipping the keys over to her.

"Really? What a quick recovery." She plucked a red rose from a vase, inhaling its scent. Then she sniffed the robe. "Smells nice. I feel like I'm right next to you in this." She fingered the initials on the robe. "C.R.H. What's the R for, Cliff?"

"All right, I'll ask you again, Gloria—"

"I came to get laid!" she said, her tongue licking her lips. Hawley stood looking down at her with an impassive face. Gloria began to giggle. "You should see your face, Cliff. Glowering. Stern. Mad. Very mad." She lifted her glass to her lips, trying to focus her eyes on him.

Hawley reached down and took it from her, placing it on a side table. "What's more, you know drugs and drinks don't go together. I'll see that you get home."

"I'm not going home," she said, stretching her arms to the back of the sofa.

"You can't stay here."

She let the robe slowly part. "And why not?"

Hawley decided that it might be better to take a different tack. "Look, Gloria, it's all messed up. Another time, who could say?" She stood up, letting the robe slip to the rug. "That's not going to help either of us right now," he said, hastening to pick it up and draping it around her.

"I want you, Cliff, and you want me. You've always wanted me," she said, moving in toward him.

"Okay," he said, humoring her, "and I'd like to have you, but you picked a bad night. Felicia Courtney's waiting and the Secretary—"

"Fuck him. And fuck Felicia Courtney!"

"Sure, just like that. But you heard me tell him that I'd be joining him—"

"He's a man or was, whatever's left of him. He isn't going to mind. He probably—"

"He expects me. Mrs. Moran expects me. Felicia expects me."

She threw her arms around Hawley's neck and as he reached up to release them she said, "Goddamn you! I picked you! You've always wanted me and I'm here! I'm wet, Cliff, and not just from the rain! I want you to hold me, Cliff, to hold me tight, to touch me, to take me!"

Hawley held her hands before her. "Look, Gloria, you're going home. I'm going to that concert. I have to go! Moran was here! He saw you. I can't stay. And you can't stay, either." He saw the anger in her eyes and decided to be a bit more conciliatory. "Not tonight. Just put it down to bad timing, poor luck."

She fought loose and placed one of his hands against her breasts. "You want me, Cliff, you *know* you want me." She reached up to kiss him.

"I'm not saying I don't," he said, restraining her. "I don't think you quite understand what you're doing—the circumstances—"

"Oh, Mr. Vice President!" Gloria put her fingers to her lips to suppress her laughter. "You think I'm compromising you. And your career!" She laughed loudly. "Your career! Like maybe you still have one! Oh, Cliff, you can be such a fool!"

"All right, Gloria, pull yourself together," he said, ringing for the maid.

"You haven't got a career, don't you understand?" she whispered, her words beginning to slur.

"Gloria, you're a little bit drunk, and mixing alcohol with those pills—"

"So what? You're afraid to face the truth, like all the rest of us. Isn't that it?"

"I have to go, Gloria. Mary will bring your clothes back up when they're dry. And then you'll be taken home."

She slumped down onto the sofa, reached for the drink, her head resting on the back. "Face the truth, that's what we don't do, face the truth . . . Harry . . . with his commitments. You . . . with all your schemes . . . where does all that leave me?" Her eyes shut as Hawley started out of the room. "Good-bye, Cliff. Remember . . . later . . . you could have had me. You and your stupid—fucking—protocol." She sat up, her eyes wide and her vision distorted. "Shove it!" She pointed a finger at him. "Go! Go on and sit next to Felicia Courtney and her—her ice-cold, refrigerated vagina! Good night, Mr. Whatever-You-Are bastard!"

☆ ☆ ☆

Three men were thinking of Gloria Whitney as she stretched out on the sofa in the Vice President's guest room waiting for her clothes to dry out. Harry Thompson sat in the darkened atmosphere of his apartment, wondering whether he should call her, apologize for his callousness. He decided he'd been rash and inconsiderate, especially in telling her that they wouldn't make it together. Maybe, in fact, in spite of all the time they'd shared together, more time was, in truth, needed. And if more was needed, one thing was certain—he didn't want Gloria Whitney offering herself to Clifford Hawley. Not yet. Not ever.

He began to think of Hawley, his occasional role as an escort, but always, he had to admit, when he was himself unavailable or indisposed. He decided to call her as soon as she'd returned from the concert, maybe even see her. Better yet, he decided to intercept her before she left.

That phone call left him with a sense of dissatisfaction. The Chief Justice had sounded strangely aloof and ambiguous in his response to Harry's direct inquiries. "I'm sorry, Harry," he had said. "I repeat, Gloria's not available at this moment."

"But, sir," Harry asked, "the concert—"

"We won't be going to the concert tonight, Harry."

"Well, then," Harry persisted, "could I speak with her, just for a moment?"

The Chief Justice did not reply immediately. He could not bring himself to discuss her whereabouts. When he did reply, Harry heard the long sigh and detected a sound of concern in his voice. "Harry, she's not available—"

"But, sir," Harry interjected.

"I've already answered you, twice," Whitney said, cutting him off, a note of asperity now in his voice. "She's simply not available."

"May I leave a message, sir?" Harry countered, rushing ahead. "I apologize for my persistence, it's just that we met earlier . . . Gloria and I . . . I want her to know that I apologize for—" he broke off for a moment. "She'll understand, sir."

"I have the message, Harry."

"It's important," Harry insisted.

"I have the message. You apologize. Good night, Harry."

Harry glanced across at the phone, waiting for Gloria's call.

In the meantime, Hawley sat in the semidarkness of the concert hall in the Kennedy Center, mesmerized by the extraordinary speed, power, and dexterity of the great Russian-born virtuoso Alexander Yeremenko as he pounded the keyboard of the Steinway with incredible force. The eruption of the striking dissonant chords of Prokofiev's Seventh Sonata broke his reverie and reminded him that he had once been in another group, which had included Gloria, and that they'd been listening to the same Yeremenko in a concert devoted to Stravinsky. Gloria's comment about the artist during the intermission had been another of his exposures to her directness.

"Are you enjoying the concert, Miss Whitney?" he had asked politely.

"I am, but not so much because of the music. It's his playing. Dazzling. And I'm enjoying a private fantasy. His fingers are amazing. They're like a crazy ballet," she'd replied as she smiled up at him, observing his puzzled look. "It's just that I *feel* his fingers," she said, a gleam in her eyes. "I feel them up and down my spine. What a masseur! What a massage! What music *that* would make! Can you imagine?" She laughed. "No, you wouldn't. Too proper, Mr. Vice President."

"That would be a virtuoso performance, indeed," Hawley had said with a smile. "I'm sorry I don't have his talent," he'd added.

"Mr. Vice President, don't be so lacking in self-confidence," she'd replied as Harry Thompson came by to claim her.

As the concert continued, Hawley glanced at his watch, certain that Gloria was being driven back to her home by one of the Secret Service agents on duty. He was glad he had arrived before the concert began, and had enough time to chat with Oliver Moran, expressing his surprise again at Gloria's sudden appearance at his home.

"She was lucky her car broke down near the home of someone she knew," Moran said. "It's not the safest kind of predicament for a young woman in any part of the city."

Hawley decided to be candid with the Secretary. "That's part of a tiny puzzle, Oliver. I had the security guard check her car. Just before I left, he told me it didn't break down."

Moran raised his eyebrows. "The young lady does have a reputation for doing the surprising."

"I'm sure she's home by now. I called the Chief Justice to tell him to expect her, and to explain that I couldn't escort her because I wanted to be here with you, Valerie, and Felicia. He was very understanding."

"And by now experienced," Moran said knowingly.

As the concert began, Hawley resolved to discuss the matter directly with Harry Thompson. He didn't want to face Gloria's unpredictability, particularly in a period of high political tension, and he wanted Harry's friendship a good deal more than he might ever desire Gloria's body.

The third man, Chief Justice Whitney, removed his tuxedo jacket and his cummerbund. He had been doing considerable soul-searching ever since the time Gloria had suddenly made known her presence the day he and Lane had been discussing her problems in this very room. Gloria, he had concluded, required psychiatric therapy, maybe even a stay in some private retreat. He wasn't sure exactly what it was that was consuming her, but he sensed that some part of it had to be a deep frustration that centered on her relationship with him, her father, and even more important, with Harry Thompson. He detested her use of drugs; it repelled him, and now it had finally begun to alarm him.

Gloria's inexplicable appearance at the Vice President's home was a different matter, just another example of some of Gloria's errant ways. He was glad that his son Jeff had returned from submarine duty, ordered to return to Washington shortly after the *Colorado* had sent its first report on the Soviets' discovery of the sub's secret mission. Perhaps Jeff could do what neither he nor Lane had been able to do, set Gloria on a better course. She needed stricter supervision, more precise direction. He would begin the process this very night. He would do it out of love, he told himself, not out of duty alone.

14

Upon leaving the Vice President's home, Gloria Whitney decided that she needed time to think and that all of that thinking encompassed three men—her father, Hawley, and especially Harry Thompson. She drove aimlessly through Washington and into the Virginia countryside, returning to the city toward midnight. She began to thread her way through a heavy fog down Constitution Avenue, past the Washington Monument and toward the Jefferson Memorial and the Tidal Basin.

She smiled as she drove past the cluster of buildings that housed the Treasury's Bureau of Engraving and Printing, the fog now so thick that it made driving even more hazardous. A few minutes later she glanced at her watch and noted that it was past midnight, that officially the Jefferson Memorial was closed and that most of the lights in the area were already turned off.

Opening the glove compartment of the car, she extracted a bottle of scotch and began to drink from it. She then wiped the interior of the windshield with her hand, thinking to improve her vision, but the night had become even murkier as the heavy mist obscured the shapes of buildings, trees, and the distant Memorial itself.

She slumped down in her seat, pleased at being at this particular spot, for the Memorial was an area where she and Harry had frequently taken quiet walks around the Basin and under the Japanese cherry trees that edged its borders. She rummaged through the glove compartment, found what she was searching for, and began to take a variety of pills, swallowing them with quick drafts of scotch.

A pleasant lassitude began to envelop her, but it gave way to a tearful interlude as she thought of Harry and heard his words again: "We wouldn't make it." When she began to feel drowsy, she drew herself up in her seat, mumbling, "Have to go for a walk, clear my head." She chuckled as she drew Hawley's robe around her, wondering how Harry would react if he could see her now.

Another glance at her watch told her it was past one; she was certain that on a foggy night like this the park guards would be staying close to quarters. No one in his right mind would be taking a walk around the Basin, fogged in as it was—so thick the park lights, still turned on, were only dimly visible through the hazy atmosphere.

Gloria Whitney began to walk, stumbling some. Her instinct kept her in the darkest parts of the Basin—as did the moonless sky. She skirted the area where the public rented paddleboats, then stopped to try to pierce the fog and make out the bronze figure of Jefferson through the white columns of the Memorial some distance across the Basin, but monument, columns, and figure all blurred into the darkness.

She searched for the right spot along the edge of the Basin, climbed through the rail, removed her shoes, sat down, and let her feet dangle in the water, pleased to find it warm and comforting. As she sat there, taking more pills and longer draughts from the bottle she'd carried along with her, she began to feel more and more languorous. She remembered how often she had challenged Harry about swimming in the Basin, and suddenly she felt that she could do it with no one around to stop her.

She slipped off Hawley's robe and folded it neatly beside her, fingering Hawley's initials again, surprised to find that she had shoved the rose she'd held in his upstairs room into one of the pockets. She placed it on top of the robe, then slipped out of her bikini, placing it neatly under the rose. She raised her arms above her head, wondering what Harry Thompson and Clifford Hawley would think of her now, totally exposed in a public place, oblivious to all the dangers of the city at night.

She took the last of the pills and a long swallow from the bottle, turning it up to see if it was truly empty, amazed and amused that she had consumed all of it by herself. Then she closed her eyes and ran her hands through her hair, suddenly feeling tired and, worse, unwanted. She cupped her breasts in her hands and began to weep. Hawley had rejected her. Harry had used her. She thought she ought to write a message, but then on reflection she was glad, glad that she hadn't brought her pocketbook with its pen and notebook but only a small makeup bag. No, she thought, she could see them bewildered, even grief stricken, wondering what could possibly have induced her to go to a public place and surrender to the unknown. She smiled as she let herself slip into the embrace of the water. They'd rejected her and they knew it. The water felt warm and soothing. Drowsiness was overcoming her. She knew she shouldn't have mixed pills and scotch. But she was happy; she'd always wanted to swim in the Basin and now she was floating. In the distance she saw a paddleboat that had broken away from its moorings. It would be fun to reach it and drift about the Basin. She felt good; she would enjoy their embarrassment if she were found. Better, she really was happy for the first time in hours. And why? Because she knew they would all be feeling the burden of guilt. Guilt. Theirs.

☆ ☆ ☆

A park police officer spotted the body at dawn and summoned the Medical Examiner. While the body was being examined at the scene, the contents of a small makeup bag were unceremoniously dumped on the concrete walk.

Officer Malone, a seasoned veteran, stood by the side of the Examiner. "Another case of 'circumstances undetermined pending police investigation,' Doc?" he said smugly.

The Medical Examiner, bald and unshaven, resented his having been summoned so early in the morning. "You insisted she looked familiar. You get me to rush down here. I'm goddamn tired and goddamn cold. Now you're asking me if this is a CUPI case. You have any idea who she is?"

Malone pulled at his nose. "Just looks familiar."

"You could have had her picked up and taken down to the morgue."

"Hold it," a voice called out. A young officer called them over to the stack of personal belongings. He held up a small bottle. "Seconal. Bottle's empty." He displayed an empty bottle of liquor. "Scotch. Nothing in it."

Dr. Lehman asked, "Name on the bottle? The pill bottle?"

The young officer said, "Yes. Gloria Whitney."

Malone whistled. "Holy shit. No wonder she looked familiar."

"Know her?" Lehman asked.

"Christ, Doc. Whitney. Whitney! Doesn't that tell you? For Christ sake!"

"Whitney?" Lehman repeated. Suddenly he was wide awake. He raised the tarp covering Gloria's face, studying it for a moment. "I'll be damned." He looked toward the ambulance and summoned two aides. "Let's get this body back to the shop. We got our work cut out for us."

As they walked back to Lehman's car, Malone asked how long he thought she'd been dead.

"Seven, eight hours."

"Find anything?"

"No marks."

"Couldn't have been dead before she hit the water?"

Lehman shook his head. "Autopsy'll tell us. Looks like—" He shook his head again. "You better get the chief to make the call." He turned to watch the attendants carry the body to the ambulance. "Funny world, when you see a thing like this happen. Goes to prove that nobody knows anything about nobody."

The death of Gloria Whitney shocked the city. Her body had been found floating facedown in the Tidal Basin. The Vice President's robe, neatly folded, with a wilted rose on top, had been picked up on the stone wall that circled the basin.

Out of respect to the Chief Justice, the investigation had been brief. The testimony of the Morans and of Hawley's staff had absolved the Vice President. It was established that he had arrived at the Kennedy Center only minutes after Deputy Secretary Moran. The security guard on duty had observed Gloria leave the Vice President's home; he thought she was wearing a coat—which turned out to be Hawley's dark blue robe. He had told her to wait until he found someone to drive her, but she had said she was fine. According to his statement, she had behaved normally, driving off as if in control of herself as well as the car.

The only puzzling note in the testimony was the fact that

she told Hawley, in Moran's presence, that her car had broken down. A guard had checked it at the Vice President's request, finding it in good operating condition. Why then, Washington asked, had Gloria Whitney gone to Vice President Hawley's official residence?

No one had an answer that satisfied those most deeply interested. Medical opinion confirmed that she had ingested large amounts of Seconal and alcohol, in excess of twenty tablets and as much as half a bottle of scotch. The careful placement of her bikini, the neat folding of the robe, and the positioning of the wilted rose indicated that her actions, up to that point, had been deliberate and planned. Death, according to the report of the Medical Examiner, was the result of suicide.

The impact on Washington was a mixture of shock, curiosity, and malicious gossip.

Harry Thompson retreated into the White House. His behavior concerned Lane, for Harry spent hours practicing his fencing, sometimes dueling with a fury that made Lane glad their foils were rubber-tipped. Harry resented the occasional probing of the Whitney brothers and what he perceived as their intent to lay blame on him. He avoided the press, but in the privacy of his room he wept, accusing himself of being the trigger that had sent Gloria to her doom. Worst of all was the personal pain Gloria had inflicted on him by her going to visit Hawley. He began to wonder how often the two might have met secretly. But in his heart he was tormented by the thought that she had made the visit chiefly to taunt him and to play on his jealousy.

Hawley had been both stunned and angered. He knew that he'd exercised great care in his relationship with Gloria out of deference to Harry, but her decision to visit him on the fateful evening, her wearing his robe to the place of her death—all this, he sensed, had been her retort to his rejection of her advances. But those advances, he also reasoned, were the weapons she used in order to bring herself more into focus in Harry Thompson's eyes. More than one columnist had written the story in a fashion that dramatized the actions of a woman scorned. In most of them Harry Thompson bore much of the responsibility, but other stories carried the nagging question of why Gloria had chosen to drop in unannounced that fateful night on Clifford Hawley. No matter how many explanations were given—by Hawley, by Oliver Moran, by Mary—there was always left a tantalizing innuendo that reflected unfavorably on him.

☆ ☆ ☆

After Gloria's funeral, the President was driven to the Chief Justice's home to pay his personal respects. Lane and Jeffrey Whitney escorted him inside. The two men sat quietly in the old white frame Georgetown house that had been built after the administration of Thomas Jefferson; legend had it that the original part had been designed by Jefferson himself much in the fashion of Monroe's Ashlawn.

The President found the Chief Justice seated in the dimly lit drawing room, staring at the gold-framed portrait of a laughing, impish Gloria Whitney. Whitney rose and proffered an old black horse-hair-covered rocking chair to his distinguished guest. For a time the two men sat opposite each other in silence.

It was the President who finally spoke. "Did the same thing, Mr. Chief Justice, when Margaret passed on. Sat before her portrait for three whole days. Couldn't believe it. Times when I still don't . . ."

The Chief Justice said, "I remember her. A splendid woman." Ironic, he thought, that Thompson, the most clear-sighted of men, should have canonized a woman others had scathingly called "meddlesome Maggie."

"Yes . . . she's a great comfort to me now."

"I beg your pardon?" Whitney said, momentarily confused, as he turned to observe his guest.

Thompson smiled. "She's with me—when I need her. I've only to close my eyes—"

"Ah . . . yes, yes, of course. Now I understand . . ." Whitney said, reassured.

"And she's *there*. You must remember that, Everett. You must remember . . . you can shut your eyes . . . Gloria, she'll be with you, too."

"It's a comforting thought, Mr. President."

"You'll find it's more than a thought. It has . . . its own reality. Its very own reality . . . a daughter is someone unique to a father—"

For a moment the Chief Justice placed a hand over his eyes.

"And remember, Everett," Thompson went on, his voice falling to a whisper, "Margaret is alive. That's because I *keep* her alive. Just so—Gloria is alive. *You* must keep her alive in your mind."

Whitney reached out and gripped Thompson's arm. "It's very good of you to come by; I know you have a lot on your mind."

"If you knew, if you only knew, Everett," Thompson said, sinking back in his chair. "No one can really help," he whispered.

"I will help you, Mr. President, all I can. You know that."

Lane Whitney entered the room. "The Vice President has called to pay his respects," his son said.

"Well, show him in, Lane, show him in." Whitney looked over to Thompson. "It's all right, isn't it?"

Thompson shifted in his chair. "Mr. Chief Justice, perhaps," he began, "we may talk again, later."

As Thompson stood up, the Chief Justice rose with him. "Mr. President, I'm always available to you." He saw Hawley standing just inside the entranceway. "Come in, Mr. Vice President," Whitney said. Hawley stepped across the room and took the outstretched hand of the Chief Justice, then turned to face the President. "Mr. President," he said politely.

Thompson, nodding curtly and with a terse, "Good evening, Mr. Chief Justice," strode out of the room.

"Please be seated, Mr. Vice President."

Hawley's eyes were still on the doorway through which the President had vanished. The Chief Justice studied his younger visitor, aware of the President's slight.

Hawley turned his attention to the Chief Justice. "I just wanted you to know how very, very saddened I was by all of this. I'm sorry that I couldn't have sensed whatever it was that troubled Gloria that night—"

"You couldn't have been expected to know, Mr. Vice President. Her instability. Even I was unaware of its depth. Our duties—" he shook his head sadly, "duties of office . . ."

"They take their toll."

"Toll, that's the right word. We see it in others and fail to recognize it in ourselves. I see it in the President." He paused and edged in closer to Hawley. "The President should take better care, be persuaded to delegate, to conserve his strength. I've watched you. You've grown on the job. Our system—it's most unfair to Presidents and Vice Presidents alike."

"What makes you say that?" Hawley asked politely.

Whitney eased back into his chair. "Something happens to men when they become Presidents."

Hawley waited for the Chief Justice to continue.

"They know they're elected by the people, they and their Vice Presidents. Just the two of them. Sometimes it's the Vice

President who puts across the ticket. Some say—" He stopped for a moment. "Maybe it's a kind of envy, even fear?"

"Fear?" Hawley repeated.

"Maybe." Whitney moved closer to Hawley. "Presidents, all leaders, think of their place in history. There's only one President. He carries all the burdens, even those he should place on others, but won't. And it shows on the President, it shows." The Chief Justice slumped back in his chair.

At that moment Lane Whitney stood in the doorway with a delegation from the British embassy. Seeing them and sensing fatigue in the older man, Hawley rose. "I appreciate your observations, particularly under these terribly sad circumstances," he said, extending a hand.

"Mr. Vice President, it was good of you to come," the Chief Justice said, wrapping his hands over Hawley's. "I appreciate it very, very much."

"I only wish I could have been of more help to you and your family," Hawley replied.

15

Daniels and Hawley were together in the Vice President's upstairs office—resplendent with its antique furnishings. "You don't want to let this Gloria Whitney matter fester so that rumor begins to take on the coloration of fact," Daniels was saying. "You're a reader of history, so you can remember how Ted Kennedy allowed the Chappaquiddick affair to spread into a stain he never really overcame. Had he acted more promptly, been more candid—"

"I understand, Richard. I agree with you. Let me sound out Joe Gratton. If he agrees—"

"He will."

"Then I'll do it. I have absolutely nothing to hide."

"And if he asked me I'd be advising Harry Thompson to do the same thing. Get it all out, quick, once and for all," Daniels volunteered. "But he won't be asking, not me."

Hawley agreed. "I saw him yesterday."

"And?"

"I knew Gloria had been with him before she dropped in on me—Lane filled me in on that—but I could see that nothing I said could persuade him that I had abolutely no clues or ideas to offer that could satisfactorily explain her visit to me."

"If you had, he didn't want to believe you anyway," Daniels said, lighting a cigarette.

"Right. And I'm afraid he also really doesn't want to spell out any of the details of the last conversation *he* had with Gloria." Then, thinking of his own confrontation with her, Hawley added, "I think I can understand his reluctance."

"In his case it doesn't really matter. He's not a candidate for anything."

☆ ☆ ☆

The broadcast was speedily arranged. Two of Federal's most respected reporters helmed what was billed as a conversation with the Vice President. Herbert Rush had been a Washington fixture for many years, had once been Federal's White House correspondent. His partner, Janet Lake, was a younger version of an aging Barbara Walters and an ideal counterpoint, a reporter with a tart tongue whose questions sometimes bordered on the malicious, even the tasteless.

Some brief perfunctory remarks established the broadcast's agenda—politics, the Gloria Whitney affair, and the arms talk in Geneva. Then Lake, her gray eyes narrowing behind her large glasses, asked about the presence of Alice Curtis in Washington. "Why is she here, Mr. Vice President? What do the Russians think about her sudden departure from the arms talks?"

"I don't think I could speak for them, Miss Lake."

"You're not being kept in the dark, are you?"

"Not at all," Hawley said easily. "Mrs. Curtis made a statement at the airport. She's here for instructions, conversations with the President, the Secretary of State." He was glad Jaggers had touched base with him on the subject, even though Jaggers himself was at a loss as to exactly *why* the President had summoned her home for consultations.

"Mr. Vice President, the city's been shocked by the tragic news of Gloria Whitney," Rush interjected. "But there are one or two areas that are still puzzling. The flower, for example, the wilted rose that was found at the Tidal Basin atop your robe." He paused and raised his eyebrows as he looked at Hawley. "What about the rose, its significance?"

"I don't know, Mr. Rush, beyond recalling her holding it when I went upstairs to let her know I was leaving. I believe she actually picked one while I was there. A few flowers were in a vase in that room, taken from the garden, and I remember seeing it in her hands."

"What did you two talk about?"

"I explained to her that I'd spoken with her father, that we were making arrangements for her to be driven home—"

"But she drove herself. How did that happen?"

"It *shouldn't* have happened," Hawley said emphatically, "but Hennessey, the agent on duty that night, explained how she persuaded him she was quite capable of driving herself home. When she got in the car, she seemed perfectly normal to him—"

"Had she been drinking?"

"She'd had a highball. Mary Hudson, the maid on duty, had prepared it. At her request."

"Was she under the influence when she arrived at your home?"

"Both Secretary Moran and I have already explained that she seemed quite normal when she arrived that night except for the fact that she was soaked to the skin. That sudden downpour."

Janet Lake cut in. "You could have offered her coffee."

"Yes, I could have, but I left that up to the staff. I had the Secretary as a guest, we were planning on going to the concert together—"

"—that all makes sense, Mr. Vice President. What doesn't make total sense is why. *Why* did Gloria Whitney simply pop in on *you*? Why did she lie and say her car broke down when we know it didn't? Why," she hammered, "did Gloria Whitney choose *you*?"

Hawley took his time. "Miss Lake, I wish I could answer that question." Then adroitly, he said with great earnestness, "It's the very question I've asked myself a hundred times. And I have no answer. I just don't know."

"Didn't you ask her?"

Hawley remembered every moment of that encounter with Gloria, but he knew he couldn't reveal her purpose, her offer to give herself. Most of all, he didn't want to contribute anything that would exacerbate his relationship with Harry Thompson.

"I took her at her word that her car had failed."

"But she took that flower with her, wearing your robe, Mr. Vice President. Was she trying to say something?"

"I don't know. I have no easy way of answering that. The staff thought she was borrowing the robe and would return it later. And it *was* quite cool after the rain that night."

"Had the two of you—?" Janet Lake smiled, the smile signalling a tough question on the way. "Did you and Gloria Whitney have any kind of understanding, some kind of past intimate relationship?"

"Not in any way, Miss Lake."

"You've been seen with her in public."

"Yes, of course, on a few occasions I escorted her to a concert, a White House function, when she required an escort. We were friends, nothing more."

"Never a private date? After all, she was quite beautiful, quite available—"

"Wrong." Hawley cut in. "I'm sure you know that Miss Whitney had a very close relationship with Harry Thompson. Very special. Everyone in Washington knows that—her brothers, her father—and I think it can safely be presumed that somewhere down the line, in a matter of time—" he shrugged.

"Marriage, is that what you're saying, Mr. Vice President?"

"I would think so."

"We know she was with Mr. Thompson before she rushed over to you—what made her decide to come to you?"

"I've already commented on that," Hawley said.

"Did you ever tell her, as one of Washington's most eligible bachelors, that if she ever broke off with Harry Thompson you'd be waiting in the wings?"

"Certainly not."

"Wouldn't she have been interesting to you, Mr. Vice President? Could it be—" and Hawley noted that sly smile again, "that maybe she was trying to send a message to Harry Thompson, or even make some kind of declaration to you? We know she was outspoken."

"Now you're speculating, Miss Lake. That's something I don't want to do. I can deal with facts. I can't deal with gossip or conjecture. Yours or anyone else's," he added sternly.

"What do *you* think went on with Mr. Thompson and Miss Whitney that night?"

"I've no idea," Hawley replied.

"You didn't ask her?"

"No, I didn't, I'm just not inquisitive about those kinds of matters . . ."

Janet Lake looked at her notes and then spoke again to Hawley. "What about Mr. Thompson's telephone call, asking the Chief Justice to tell Miss Whitney he apologized. Do you know why, what for?"

"No, I don't."

"Mr. Thompson claims he doesn't recall leaving that message. The Chief Justice says he did. That's in the testimony."

"I read that, but I still can't help you."

Janet Lake wiped her glasses. "Mr. Vice President, how do you think this whole affair will affect your political career?"

"I don't think it will affect it at all."

"Really? You think the President won't wonder—even a little bit—about the mysterious role you seemed to play in the life of his son's lady?"

Hawley raised a hand as she was talking. "*You're* characterizing all of this as mysterious. It isn't, Miss Lake. There is *no* mystery, and that's why I'm here: to end any speculation that silence on my part might possible convey. I'm here to present the facts as I know them, nothing else. And one more thing—your question. No, I don't believe for an instant that the President has given my role in this matter any thought. I know, of course, how very saddened he was to hear of Miss Whitney's tragic end; I was there when he extended his condolences to the Chief Justice and to Gloria's brothers. There is no politics in this tragedy. Only sorrow, genuine sorrow."

Rush took over the last minutes of the interview, concentrating on the outlook for the party and for Hawley's place on the ticket. "We'll never know, of course, what was in the mind of Gloria Whitney," he said as he wound up the program. "We'll never know and—as you yourself have said tonight—you'll never know what prompted her to pay you a visit. Miss Lake and I appreciate your visit, your willingness to answer all of our questions—"

Janet Lake cut in. "We hope that we'll be able to persuade Harry Thompson to do the same. He might be able to furnish some of the missing elements. It's just possible he can unravel the mystery . . ."

"We'll have to let matters rest there," Rush said, interrupting. "Thank you, Mr. Vice President."

Gratton met Hawley for a few minutes in his Washington office. "Good job," he said.

"I don't know," Hawley replied. "You sure?"

"I'm sure. For one thing your coming on, taking any question, answering them out front—all of that goes well with the public. If you did nothing, said nothing, people might think you were hiding something. That's what they're going to think if Harry

Thompson doesn't speak out the way you've done. They'll want to know what's he hiding."

"Truth is I don't think he's hiding anything, Joe," Hawley said. "Frankly, she was unpredictable. And her behavior? That was always something of a challenge."

"Well, one thing's certain—she made sure she'd be remembered. That little lady was also something of a sadist. She may have had it in for Harry all right, but she didn't mind sticking you in the process, and *that* she did. Sure, Harry Thompson can do a lot to clarify matters, maybe give us more of an idea about little Gloria Whitney's *motives*—if he *wants* to." Joe looked questioningly at Hawley.

But Hawley had his own misgivings; what concerned him most was that Harry could elect to do nothing. If that happened, the mystery Janet Lake had touched on could grow in intensity. He didn't like the power in Harry's hands.

Hawley had no way of knowing that Harry Thompson had watched the interview and had smiled with satisfaction at the cloud of suspicion Janet Lake had developed. All Harry had to do, to let gossip and rumor mushroom into speculation and doubt, was to say nothing.

☆ ☆ ☆

The following evening after dinner, Hawley and Felicia Courtney were seated together in Secretary of the Treasury John Mantley's gracious colonial drawing room in Alexandria. "Every stick of furniture, every single item—the clock, the candlesticks, the andirons, the paintings—everything is absolutely genuine. Including," Felicia added, with a little laugh, "the Mantleys themselves. He's got credentials going back to William Penn's original settlers, and she," Felicia nodded toward their petite hostess, "stretches back to the Adams line in New England. Did you know," she added, "that Angela Mantley was related to Gloria Whitney?"

"No, I didn't," Hawley said.

"They had a common Colonial ancestor. By the way, I thought your interview was excellent."

"I hope the country agrees with you."

"Poor little Gloria. We had her story, you know. Pills. Everyone on the inside knew about that. The ups and downs with Harry. Lots of details."

Hawley looked surprised.

"We just didn't print it. We're not one of those gossip sheets, Cliff. Ted and I talked it over, oh, two years ago, maybe more. Just decided not to run it. We get inside stories like that," she said, a provocative look in her eyes, "that are just *too* inside for anyone's good."

"That makes you a bit more responsible than even the *Post* or the *Times*," Hawley said.

"We don't want to hurt people. We don't want to embarrass people, either. We really know a *lot*," she emphasized. "Like some things about you," she added cheerfully.

"And if you printed them, would it hurt me, embarrass me . . . or others?" He smiled at her but remained very much on guard.

She sipped her cocktail. "It could complicate matters."

"You're being evasive."

"Discreet's a better word," she said.

"Am I supposed to continue this inquiry?"

Her hazel eyes focused on him as she delayed her response.

"We're in the real world," he said, "so there has to be a price. Right?" he asked.

"Shades of Oscar Wilde," she replied, "and spoken like a true-blood Washington cynic." She slowly ran the tip of her tongue across her lips. "I don't think you'd pay it," she finally said.

Hawley chuckled. "Well, now that I've established that there *is* a price—"

"As you said, everything has a price," she replied.

"And everyone?" he asked.

"Perhaps," she said.

"That sounds like the tough world of the CIA. When the chips are down, no rules, no angles, no dealing with such abstractions as justice, mercy, fairness."

"That's also the world of leaders, Cliff, life in the political jungle. Where there also *are* no morals and no ethics, either," she added.

"Speaking of the jungle and leaders," Hawley said, "I'll give you one of my favorite authors, Machiavelli. He said a leader 'must be a lion and must also know how to play the fox.'"

"True, and in Machiavelli's world—the way I remember his advice—a leader has to know when he's the hunter and when he's the hunted, right?" she asked, surprising him as she finished her drink.

"Right. But if he's to survive," Hawley said, "a great leader has to be both."

"And are *you* both?" she asked.

"Well, I think given a choice, a hunter follows two rules: he's always on guard *not* to be the hunted, and he always takes care to avoid traps."

"A good rule for the future," Felicia said. Then pointing to the adjoining room, she added, "Speaking of the future, Angela has two gypsy fortune tellers in there working with all of the guests. Feel like trying one?"

Hawley shook his head. "I'll take my chances with you."

"All right," she said, staring at him. "How about this one? I think you're going to be President." She stopped for a moment, amused at his sudden look of surprise. "There's only one thing I don't know."

"And what's that?" he ventured a moment later.

"Something that boils down to marriage and whether you'll be a Buchanan, who never married, or whether you'll be a Cleveland, who finally did."

Hawley chuckled.

"Something funny?" she asked.

"No. Just a curious coincidence—talking abaout Buchanan and Cleveland. I had a similar conversation with Kathy, and if I remember correctly it was at our very first meeting when I was in the House."

"And did she tell you you'd go further, politically, if you were married?"

"She may have. But I remember your saying a President *has* to be married these days to be elected," Hawley said. "It was in the White House, the night Kathy invited us over. Very recently."

"I did, didn't I?" Felicia passed him her empty glass. "Could you be a dear and get me another? Champagne?" Hawley stood up, and as he was about to start off, she said, "I didn't say you'd be elected."

For another moment Hawley stood transfixed, thinking instantly of the Twenty-fifth Amendment. Then, signalling a waiter, he resumed his seat. "Felicia," he said, turning to her in his most disarming way, "*you* could be a fortune teller. They inevitably get things wrong."

"We don't print rumors. And we don't write fortune cookies," she replied. "But if we ever received confirmation, that's a story we'd go with."

He glanced at his watch. "Maybe it's time I take stock," he said, with a chuckle, "and recognize that, perhaps, this is the moment it may be in my best interest to play the fox."

"Smell a trap?" she said, laughingly.

"Time I was getting you back to your place," he said quietly.

"If you're willing to pay the price . . ." she began. Then looking at him appraisingly, she said, "You *are* fearful there really *is* a trap, aren't you?"

"No, but to tell the truth, I'd be disappointed if one didn't exist. I like challenges." Hawley studied her cool looks, the intriguing lines of her body encased in a form-fitting black crepe silk gown. "That would be rushing things, letting you bargain on a hunch. It's been you who's always said we have time." He stood up and held out a hand. "We'll have to settle for that for now. At the risk of mixing metaphors—something my old friend Joe Gratton's often doing—I don't have enough chips for the game."

As she rose, she took his arm and said, "When you get them, why then we can bargain . . . and play."

"I'll settle for that," Hawley said with a smile.

☆ ☆ ☆

Later that same night Hawley's private line rang. "You haven't called me," Vivien said complainingly. Then, abruptly changing the subject, she added, "I caught your interview with Janet Lake. She was very soft on you, Cliff."

"She tried," he replied easily.

"Any fool has to know there was *something* that made that girl drop in on you. That was no accident. Her car was okay. So, what makes her pick you out of all those others that she just casually drops in on you with a cockamamie story? How do you answer that?"

"The way I answered Janet Lake."

"Bullshit, if you'll pardon my Radcliffe language. Her car knew exactly where to turn its little nose. Are you going to tell me she was never in your residence, Cliff, your very private residence?"

"She was here once or twice at official receptions, things like that, yes," Hawley said.

"Something you've never invited me to," she replied icily.

"Vivien," he said, anxious not to prolong the conversation, "your schedule has never fitted in with mine—"

"Except at bedtime. Cliff, did you have an affair with that girl?" Vivien said abruptly, then hurriedly added, "I shouldn't have asked that, I know. I'm sorry."

"It's all right," he said, again determined to end the conversation. "The answer is no."

"I'm jealous of her," Vivien said. Suddenly her words poured out. "Cliff, could I come to Washington? This week? I can always invent a tour for something, some charity—my publicity people are always fighting those people off. Maybe you make arrangements for me to take a tour of the city—see the White House, the Capitol, even your place? Could I?"

Hawley shook his head vehemently. "No, Vivien, that wouldn't be at all practical at this moment—" he began, as he was abruptly interrupted.

"I get the picture, Cliff. It's no. Not at this moment. No, not this week. No, not anytime in the near future—"

"I haven't said that," he insisted.

"I don't need a road map, Mr. Hawley. That little drug addict could pop in on you in the middle of the night! Unannounced! Walks out of your place wearing your robe over nothing! She didn't need directions! She'd been there before! Lucky for you, you had to go to some stupid concert. Unlucky for *her* you just weren't in the mood, or were stuck because some Cabinet official was expecting you! Thank you, Mr. Hawley, thank you for helping me when I needed some help. All I really wanted were some words, that's all . . . some words . . ." she began to sob.

"Vivien," he said, struggling to stem his rising anger. "Vivien?" But he felt relieved when he realized she had hung up.

☆ ☆ ☆

Jeff Whitney, tall and muscular, stood speaking to Admiral Hornwell aboard the Admiral's ship, the *Decatur*. Hornwell, his back to Whitney, stood peering out a porthole as he listened attentively.

"We underestimated them, Commander," Hornwell muttered softly. "Damn, damn, damn!"

"Yes, sir."

"They did it to us years ago with that first little sputnik of theirs while all the time we had the technology, just never believing that *they* had it, too. *If* they had it," Hornwell added scoffingly, as he turned to face Whitney. "We know they had it, but did they *invent* it or *acquire* it?" he asked rhetorically, rushing in with his own answer. "One thing we know they're very inventive at is *acquiring* technology. Why bother inventing it when they can squeeze it out of an open society?"

"They are good at that, sir," Jeff said accommodatingly, "looking at their record."

"Good? *Good?*" Hornwell replied sarcastically. "Sputnik?

That was an embarrassment. It didn't mean that much, but it sure made us look foolish and second-rate, that's what. But *this!*" Hornwell's head seemed to rise from his grizzled neck like an angry eagle's. "This is a challenge! And their way of advising us was insolent! 'Welcome'!" he said, spitting out the word.

"Getting men to that depth, two of them, that's plain incredible," Jeff said, thinking the remark might appear helpful.

"Incredible?" Hornwell said softly, taking a step toward Whitney.

"Sir, I only meant after all of those weeks and weeks we spent on a silent mission, thinking all of the time we'd been successful at isolating the ship when they had to know—"

"Know? Of course they knew! Don't you understand, Commander? Don't you understand what I'm telling you? Think! Think!" Hornwell moved in closer to Jeff, his eyes blazing. "Think!"

"Sir!" Jeff said, backing off a step.

"They wanted us to *know*, Commander. You understand that from their message, don't you, that they wanted us to know?" Hornwell repeated.

"I do, sir," Whitney said as he tried to cope with the Admiral's fierce gaze.

Hornwell finally broke off the tension and returned to his old oak swivel chair, stroking his lean, wrinkled face. "So they acquire what they can't invent," Hornwell said, looking up at Whitney. "They didn't invent that ability for their divers to go down to such great depths, Commander. We know that. Take my word for it. What we *didn't* know was that they knew what *we* know. Now do you understand?"

Jeff looked into Hornwell's probing eyes. "They acquired it, you said," Jeff replied. "You mean from us? Right?" he added hesitantly.

Hornwell nodded. "Now you understand, Commander. Naval Intelligence missed it. The CIA missed it. Says a lot about the glasnost and perestroika they've been preaching now for some years. All the time still practicing their *real* skills. And bettering us—quite a bit deeper than we've gone." His head rose again like an angry eagle's. "Ferrets!" he said scornfully.

Jeff remained silent.

The Admiral rose from his chair. "You know something now, Commander, that's been top secret. On our side. Now the mouse has turned into a cat, a mean one. And they think they have an edge." Hornwell shook his head in anger. "Just when we had them, just when we thought we *really* had them. It's all something of what we've been calling Red Dye Day. That's our way—that *was* our plan to let them know that *we* had *them.* Now . . ." He stared out of the porthole again. "We've missed out." Then turning back to Jeff he said, "Alice Curtis is in town. You know her?"

"Never met her, sir, but of course I know who she is, her mission."

"We'll have to let her know that the game's been, let's say, tied. You'll attend the meeting."

"Yes, sir."

"That'll be all, Commander."

As Whitney started out of Hornwell's cabin, Hornwell said, "Hard luck for that sailor, Commander. I understand he was a Washington lad."

"He was, sir."

"I'll be at the services."

Whitney stood at attention. "Thank you, sir." As he again turned to leave, Hornwell interrupted his departure once more. "Very sorry about your sister, too. Fine young woman. We met once or twice. Tragic, tragic."

Jeff bowed.

Hornwell returned to his desk and, glancing up, said, "You'll hear from my aide."

☆ ☆ ☆

It was almost twilight, and Secretary of State Edward Jaggers was giving Alice Curtis a tour of his country place just outside Washington; she had proven to be an admirer not only of his stable of horses but of his collection of ancient carriages, from an authentic Wells Fargo stagecoach to a four-in-hand claimed to have been used by George Washington on a trip from Mount Vernon to Philadelphia. "I knew you'd be interested in these," he said, as she stopped to admire a reconditioned landau.

"I see you used acrylic lacquer on the doors. I did the same on the one I keep."

"Did it chiefly to preserve it because this is the one I like to use. Problem is to find a driver willing to sit on the outside when it rains."

"And what becomes of all these beautiful coaches?"

"They're all heading for the Smithsonian, eventually, if they have the room. Sooner, of course, if Stella has her way," he chuckled. "Doesn't like things equestrian—anything connected with a hunt, and that includes everything from riding sticks and crops right down to my own jodhpurs."

They made their way back into the main house. "You're leaving late tonight, I understand?"

"Yes," Alice said as Jaggers went to the small built-in bar in a corner of the library.

"You'll have something?" he asked.

"One jigger of bourbon, ice, and a lot of water."

"Done," Jaggers said, preparing drinks. "You've been held up, I know. The President's schedule, the tragic incident—"

"I met Gloria Whitney only once. Vivacious, lovely little thing. Will there ever be a complete explanation?"

"I don't know. Perhaps. Provided everyone who knows anything comes forward and lays it all out," Jaggers said.

"The President's son?"

Jaggers nodded as he handed Alice her drink. "I understand he's taken it very hard, holed himself up in the White House."

"I watched the interview with Mr. Hawley."

"I caught it, too. I think the whole country did. I think he spoke with absolute candor. To his credit."

"I'm afraid, though," Alice said, "he's still in a tangle of unanswered, perhaps unanswerable, questions. That'll be a problem, with the convention breathing down everyone's neck. The President made a passing reference to it."

"Oh?" Jaggers looked up inquiringly.

"He simply said that, unjustified or not, a suicide that touches the occupants of the White House has to complicate a political campaign. He was weighing the impact of the involvement of all parties concerned."

"I see," Jaggers said, smoothing his moustache. "In that case, he almost certainly has to be thinking of himself first, then."

"Why do you say that, Mr. Secretary?"

Jaggers shrugged. "Well, I think this city expected that the President was likely to become the father-in-law of the young lady. At some point I suspect he'll ask his son some very specific questions, particularly about the last time Harry saw Gloria. He's the only one who can really pursue that. And the President's very strong on questioning. Part of his training as a lawyer."

"I'm aware of that skill," Mrs. Curtis said. "It was his questioning on some arms-control matters—you're familiar now with the reason the President wanted me to leave Geneva?"

"Yes, of course. Kraus ran the idea of the President's notion past me and Secretary Clauson some time ago, something about a letter to Turgenev. We were not very enthused."

"I'm glad to learn that, because I recommended against it, too, and that's why I was summoned home for a meeting. We finally had it today. It was partly his questions—" she paused a moment, looking down as she stirred the ice in her drink. "What I'm trying to say," she started, as she looked squarely at Jaggers, "is that the President's questions, together with some of his comments, made me . . . how shall I put it? . . . uneasy?"

Jaggers pulled over a small cane-backed chair and placed it near Mrs. Curtis, now seated in a corner of a large floral-decorated sofa. "Please, go on," he said as he sat down.

"Well, he presented all of his arguments in favor of a personal letter, quite cogently. He wanted us to move off of dead center, as he described our negotiations. He seemed to think that with satellite reconnaissance and with swarms of inspectors from their side and ours, all looking at everything being manufactured and deployed, we should pick up some of their old offers to eliminate, at the very least, not only all of the short-range missiles left on both sides but a respectable number of the ICBMs, starting immediately."

"And your response?"

"What we've always said privately. We really think we know what they've manufactured in recent years, and we really do know what they've deployed. What we don't know, what we may never know, is what they've actually manufactured going back fifty years or more, how many weapons, how many delivery vehicles they may have stashed away. He insists that both sides must eventually go to a zero status. And that's impossible. Not while other countries have them."

"Agreed," Jaggers replied.

"But what concerned me was some confusion—and I don't expect the President to have every weapons-system detail at his fingertips—but somehow, at one point he had our warheads confused with their SS-18s, and those, of course, have been disappearing very rapidly over the past couple of years. And we're way past the old SALT II balance on both sides, but the President started talking about our Minuteman 2 ICBMs as though he didn't know we've been putting three warheads on them for years, and that every single one of the Minuteman 3s already has triple warheads."

"And his response to that?"

"The President began to talk. Quietly. As though I weren't

in the room. It was all very mystifying." She took a few steps toward a window, looking out at the lighted gardens. "Very lovely the way you've handled your landscaping." She turned to face Jaggers. "It was about Margaret, the first Mrs. Thompson. He was talking about her . . . as though she was upstairs . . . he seemed almost not to be seeing me for a time. When he did become aware of my presence, he began to talk about the Midgetman, and he wanted to know my position as though it had never been resolved." Alice Curtis quietly resumed her seat. "A President may not know—but if he ever knew he must *never* forget." She stopped to sip her drink and then said, "The puzzling matter, and this was as I was about to leave, was the President's returning to his, shall I call it a fixation? His compulsion to write to Turgenev."

"Did you tell him that it might possibly complicate the negotiations you're conducting?"

"I did more. I reminded him that this was the policy of the National Security Council as well as the Committee." Mrs. Curtis set her glass on a table.

"And?" Jaggers asked expectantly.

"I've no idea as to whether he's going to write it or not. He simply got up and then thanked me for dropping in. Dropping in," she repeated. "He seemed to have forgotten that he *ordered* me home. I must confess he has me a bit confused. More than that, to tell you the truth. Let's just say I'm concerned."

"I understand," Jaggers said as their eyes met.

16

The Soviet flag lay upon the table before the Committee, a symbol of the silent war that raged day and night in space, under the seas, in the science laboratories of the two superpowers. The Committee sat listening attentively to Hornwell's report. "That's it, gentlemen. The ship's in drydock. There are obvious marks at the various areas where Commander Whitney and the crew heard the tapping."

Jaggers replied, "Could it have been a bit of luck? A knowledge of this particular ship's orders?"

"Mr. Secretary," Hornwell said quietly, "they had it right down to the exact longitude, latitude, and depth. This is not a matter of luck. Furthermore, we've had a similar report from a second submarine on the same kind of assignment. The *North Dakota*, stationed in the Pacific. The second incident was obviously designed to confirm the first."

"And our system?" Oliver Moran asked.

"It's operative," Hornwell replied. "The information will have to be passed to them," he said, "this Committee approving, of course. We can't allow the Soviets to believe they have an edge, a vital one."

Moran turned to Hornwell. "Can we demonstrate it, the way they've done?"

"We can't operate quite at their depths. Not yet. But, yes, there is *one* way we can demonstrate our capabilities, even better," Hornwell said, "and in a most positive way."

"What would that be?" Moran asked.

"If it were necessary, as proof of our system—taking one of their submarines *out*," Hornwell replied as he turned to the Secretary of Defense.

"The President would never permit that," Anthony Clauson exclaimed vehemently.

"Not this President," Daniels countered. "But the loss of one submarine, compared to a potential outbreak of full-scale war—wouldn't you say that's a small price? So, I think the Admiral is correct. The Soviets most likely believe they've achieved what they've been struggling to achieve for years, nuclear superiority. That's what all this adds up to. It's what we thought *we* would have with our own breakthrough. Am I right, Admiral?"

"Correct," Hornwell said tersely. "There is no way, regardless of treaties, summits, grand communiqués, you name it, that the United States of America can ever yield control of the seas. We must protect our commerce and support our allies all over the world. That control of the seas means we must also control the skies and space as well."

Daniels placed his hands on the back of Hawley's empty chair. "Gentlemen, what a potential Soviet superiority in nuclear warfare really means is that the threat of conventional warfare could even be intensified." He turned to Clauson. "Mr. Secretary?"

"No question about it," Clauson said. Daniels lit a cigarette as Clauson took over. "We don't know their real intentions, we never will. But in the last five years alone—after Gorbachev—they've added perhaps three hundred thousand men to their armed forces, half of them facing our old NATO lines—this in spite of all the unilateral cutbacks, the SALT agreements, and the public declarations of the old Warsaw Pact nations. While they talk about not increasing the number of their divisions, they're very silent about how each division has been expanded internally. One reason, of course, is that in reality there never was a true Warsaw Pact—those Eastern European countries were simply occupied by the Red Army. Their navy is no longer a coastal defense force. They have thirty-five missile-carrying cruisers where once they had none. When Ford was President they had forty-five nuclear submarines. Now they have over two hundred and fifty ballistic missile subs. Plus four carriers."

Daniels picked up the thread. "So, in the area of conventional warfare they've always had an edge. We all know what our strategy has always been, to maintain the kind of nuclear deterrence that combines a flexible reaction, uncertainty as to the type of response we'll exercise, the form, the weaponry, the place. We want the Soviets always to be concerned, to be unable to determine whether they should risk any forward movement that might trigger massive-force reaction. But here we come to our own special problem." He stopped to light a fresh cigarette. "A human problem," he said, taking a long drag. "One, gentlemen, that the Soviets know about and that creates an enormous problem vis-à-vis all of our alternatives. In short, it brings us to the President, the state of his health, the state of his mind, particularly the state of his mind under pressure. *This* kind of pressure."

Hornwell glanced at Daniels as he began to place his papers in his briefcase. "Mr. Daniels, I recently returned from a trip across the country with the President. He handled himself very well, very well indeed."

"All the time?" Daniels asked.

"The President is fully aware of what he's doing. The President has an able staff. He has his Cabinet. He has the National Security Council. And, may I remind you, he has *us.*"

Daniels leaned across the table. "And he had no lapses, he was in perfect control? All the time?" he repeated.

"Everyone in the country knows he's going to run for a second term, Mr. Daniels. Doesn't that answer your question?"

Daniels shook his head. "No, no, it doesn't. We've seen the complete medical reports. That means the question is: When action is required that only the Commander in Chief can authorize—and we all know that the minutes he would have in which to act are diminishing every year—will he be fully capable of making all the necessary decisions? *In time?*"

It was Jaggers who broke the silence. "What we must first determine is whether we have reached the actual crucial moment at which the civil and military authorities have an obligation to place this very question before the President."

Hornwell scoffed. "Mr. Daniels, if I can respond to you first, he'll accept your resignation and mine the instant you question his ability to make a decision. Of that much I'm certain. And as to Mr. Jaggers' comment, the staff of the Joint Chiefs is busy—tonight—analyzing Soviet ship and air deployment in order to determine if that crucial moment, as you characterize it, is at hand."

"That doesn't necessarily settle the issue," Daniels interjected.

"You're back to the Twenty-fifth Amendment, Mr. Daniels," Hornwell said coldly, "and if you think the Cabinet is going to join Mr. Hawley in declaring the President unable to carry on his duties, you're a thousand miles off course. Especially now with some unanswered questions revolving about Mr. Hawley's own character."

Daniels bristled. "You're referring to the tragic case of Miss Whitney?"

"I certainly am."

"The investigation absolved Mr. Hawley of any responsibility in her unfortunate death."

Hornwell got to his feet and looked down at his colleagues as he ticked off his charges. "Gentlemen, she lied about her car. Why didn't he have her escorted under Secret Service protection just to make certain she *did* get back home?" He paused a moment, then added, sarcastically, "Perhaps he hoped he'd find her at his place on his return from the concert. He saw her drinking. She could have slept it off waiting for him. There are plenty of people who say the Tidal Basin may become Mr. Hawley's Chappaquiddick."

Oliver Moran reached up to put his hand on the Admiral's arm. "I have to protest in the Vice President's defense. I was there when she arrived. It was quite obvious that he had no knowledge that she was coming to his home. He made it clear to her that he was going to attend the concert and, as a matter of fact, he arrived at the Kennedy Center just a few minutes— maybe five in all—after I did. It was embarrassing for him, but he handled it quite well."

"We're not here to debate whether Mr. Hawley acted fairly or irresponsibly," Daniels said sternly. "The issue is the question of the President's ability to discharge his duties, plain and simple. Mr. Hawley *has* that capacity, and no one in this room doubts it. It's the *President's* faculties that are under question. He's brilliant, incisive, informed. That we know. But the underlying question is the one I put to you a few minutes ago: namely, is he capable *all* of the time? Does he have mental lapses?" He tapped the papers before him. "The medical reports provide clues to the answers."

Hornwell strode to the door. "Gentlemen, the President of the United States is my Commander in Chief. And yours," he added as he stared across at Daniels. "I respect all of you, but I will take no part in a cabal that has even the most distant odor of—"

Jaggers suddenly spoke. "Hold it!" he said in a peremptory manner. Then more softly, he added, "Please, Admiral Hornwell. Please, sit down. I have something I must inform the Committee about." Jaggers waited as Hornwell slowly removed his hand from the door and resumed his seat. "Thank you, Admiral." Jaggers turned to the group. "A few moments ago I raised the question of whether we've reached a critical time in which those with the highest civil and military responsibilities may have to raise the question of executive capacity with the President. Last night I had difficulty sleeping, the result of a meeting I'd had with Mrs. Curtis. I believe Mrs. Curtis has had the most recent personal contact with the President, and her experience was *not* reassuring."

At this point Jaggers related the details of the Curtis meeting. "In short, the gist of her recollections was that his talk was full of—" he stopped for moment "I want to characterize this properly. Disquieting irrelevancies," he said as he turned to face Hornwell.

Hornwell once again rose from his seat, picking up his papers and striding to the door. "I hear you, Mr. Secretary. When I was with the President, his mind was first-rate. I hear your report on Mrs. Curtis. I respect her. I assure you that if you think we have any evidence of presidential incapacity, and if any one of you wishes to present such an issue to the President of the United States for *his* views, you'll find yourself in a tumbril of your own making. That's the reward he'll mete out—" He stood for a moment at the door, his face flushed with indignation. "Yes, I'll say it: for what borders on treachery!"

Moran and Clauson leaped from their chairs in protest, but the Admiral, flinging out an arm indicating his total disdain of their words, stalked out. Daniels urged his associates to be seated. "The Admiral has made his position clear," he said, "but the Constitution of the United States is also clear. And it says whenever the Vice President and a majority of the Cabinet present to the President pro tempore of the Senate and the Speaker of the House their written declaration that the President is incapable of discharging his duties, then the Vice

President shall immediately assume those powers as Acting President."

It was Moran who spoke first. "I wish it were that simple, Mr. Daniels. But you know, we all know, that if the President insists he *is* fit—and that's the Admiral's contention despite Secretary Jaggers' report—then the Constitution has a complicated set of rules designed to adjudicate the matter. That's a process that could take days, weeks." He mopped his face with his handkerchief. "I'm afraid this all isn't as clear as we'd like. No matter how certain we may be, the truth is that President Thompson would, in all probability, very well resist such a move. And if that happened, the welfare of the country might be in greater jeopardy than if we waited until the matter is so plainly visible that either he couldn't fight or he couldn't actually comprehend a crisis. We need more time, more facts, more—"

"Time is pressing on all of us," Daniels said. "I'd like to point out—"

"Excuse me, sir," Clauson interrupted as he turned to Moran. "What you're saying, Oliver, is that you see it as a question boiling down to three possibilities: one, do we depend on the President's own opinion of his fitness; two, if the Cabinet declares him unfit, do we carry him out over his protests; or three, do we do nothing except wait until he has a collapse?"

"God help us in any case," Jaggers said.

17

Senator Frederick Vance enjoyed the drive from his suburban home in Chevy Chase to the Capitol. He liked watching tourists posing before famous buildings and monuments, pleasured in watching hundreds of government workers scurrying to their offices. Despite the heat, things seemed to be moving faster; Washingtonians, otherwise conditioned to the routine of capital life and its mixture of bureaucratic bustle and apathy, sensed, along with him, the excitement that politics generates when played at the highest level—especially as a convention comes closer to a deadline. The Senator relished the fact that he was now a participant at that level.

Vance had become a sought-after guest for network interviews. He was well aware that the slightest miscue could be blown out of all proportion and might tip the scale for or against a candidate, and so he had decided that a low profile would best serve his interests. When questioned about the Vice President's relationship with Gloria Whitney, the Senator properly voiced his distress at the incident and deftly avoided any personal comment that might be misinterpreted. He had to admit, though, that he was not unhappy when the incident continued to surface.

It was, however, Harry Thompson's emergence, after ten days of isolation within the White House, that added new spice to the political stew. What made it intriguing was that young Thompson, although an occasional visitor to the Capitol as a witness testifying on one or another of his favorite causes before a Senate or House committee, was making a rare visit to the Russell Senate Office Building. And he was making that visit to see Vance.

The two men faced each other, indulging in casual pleasantries as they sat in oversize brown leather chairs in the Senator's spacious office.

"I don't want you think I'm being presumptuous in coming here, practically on a minute's notice—" Harry began. He was sure he could ask for Vance's help on virtually anything now that his father had dangled the Vice Presidency before the Senator's eyes. For a moment he enjoyed the scene, recognizing that he was dealing with a man who would promise almost anything to win his favor. "I was thinking—no, it's a group, we call ourselves the Washington Six—"

"I've heard of your group," the Senator said politely, keeping to himself his own lukewarm opinion of all do-gooders and moral crusaders.

"Jeb Rossmore, Jim Bird . . ."

"I know Bird. Works with Senator Crandall."

"Yes, and Lane Whitney, couple of others. We're interested in television. Network television primarily. We're interested in cleaning it up. We know your feeling about the lack of quality. Senator Crandall's told that to Bird."

That again, Vance thought, the familiar, old business, a futile business, too, attempting to place some kind of control over programming, when everyone knew that both sides would be wrapping themselves up in the protective embrace of the First Amendment. "The President was very compelling in his remarks in Los Angeles," Vance said, choosing his words carefully.

"What do we do about it, Senator?"

The Senator didn't want to do anything about it, not at this moment, not when he was anxious to have the goodwill of network managements, not when the convention was beginning to press in on him. He phrased his response defensively. "What would you have me do?"

The answer pleased Harry. He was well aware of the Senator's point of view, but he had his own objectives as well; one was actually to exercise some benign influence over the television medium, and the other, even more important at the moment, was to set in motion an action that just might involve Hawley at a time when Hawley might prefer to stay on the sidelines. "Coming out in favor of better television is an issue that won't hurt you, Senator," Harry said.

Vance was pleased at Harry's comment. What he really liked was Harry's tacit admission that politically Harry recognized Vance's growing ascendancy in the President's eyes. "I'm sure you're right," Vance said.

"Perhaps making a point, not by some sweeping indictment of everyone and everything, but by focusing on the weakest link in the chain. Federal Broadcasting isn't a CBS or an NBC."

Vance scratched his chin. "How will the other networks take an attack on Federal?"

"They'll react like they always react. If Federal's got a problem, let Federal solve it." Harry was pleased, too; he sensed Vance was aboard. "The focus goes on Federal—on its chief executive."

"That would be Joe Gratton?"

"Mr. Gratton," Harry nodded. "Gratton will react, of course. You can offer him an opportunity to place his remarks on the public record with your subcommittee on commerce, and by then the convention will be over and the focus will be on the campaign."

Vance pondered the proposal. "There's nothing here that would disturb the President?"

Harry smiled. "Senator, I know the President would welcome some congressional interest in his California speech. You can be sure of that."

Vance put out his hand. "Harry, we'll get the ball rolling." He escorted his visitor to the hall.

What pleased Vance most was Harry Thompson's final comment that others would be picking up the issue after the election. Not Vance. Not the Senator from Kansas. No, the Senator from Kansas could be the next Vice President of the United States.

☆ ☆ ☆

The President sat in his upstairs study signing letters, working through the small stack in a deliberate way, examining each paper, then slowly and carefully placing his signature on it. When he was halfway through, Kathy walked in, seated herself in a large armchair across the room, and watched him silently. At last he looked up at her over the rim of his glasses. "Was told years ago when you write you should concentrate on the writing, never rush the hand. The hand, you see, in a very real sense, is a part of the brain, an extension. Doctors—when they write prescriptions—they're the worst offenders." He leaned back in his chair examining her. "I like you in white," he finally said. "I haven't seen that suit before, have I?"

"No. I picked it up locally last week. Chanel. I'm pleased you noticed."

"I notice everything, Kathy, everything. It's a characteristic of all the Thompsons," he added, with an enigmatic smile.

"Are you feeling all right?"

Thompson compressed his lips to conceal his irritation. He'd begun to dislike inquiries about his health from anyone. "I'm fine, Kathy," he said tersely. "You just relax and let Jensen do his thing. He watches me like a hawk."

"Betsy said you wanted to see me."

"So I did, so I did. We're always kept so busy, both of us, and the pressures of this office don't allow me enough time to talk—"

"I agree, Stephen," she said, interrupting him, "there are just too many—" she stopped speaking, looking across toward the South Lawn. "It's just that there are too many pressures all at once," she said.

"Well," he said, "if I can stand them, with everybody clawing at me for a piece of my time, why then I think that you—"

"—I wanted to see you, too, Stephen," she said again, interrupting.

"Well go ahead. Speak up. What's on your mind?"

"It's just this: I've been doing a lot of thinking. Stephen, can you really stand all of that clawing plus all the crazy demands of your office? Can you really *take* four more years? And *should* you? That's what I've been thinking—the campaigning, all those public appearances, all those daily crises . . ."

The telltale signs of anger, the throbbing, quickly enlarged dark veins, were immediately visible along Thompson's temples. "Are you suggesting that I give up? Quit?" He suppressed his anger as he dabbed at beads of perspiration on his forehead.

"I'm concerned, that's all," she said, "and I didn't come in just to upset you."

He snorted. "Well now, that's very kind of you, Kathy," he said, "but what about the country?"

"The country?" she repeated. "Mr. President, I'll ask you something none of the others would dare." She paused a moment, taking a deep breath, and then said quietly, "Stephen, are you the only man in the whole country who can carry the burdens of the White House? Risking his own life in the process?"

"That's something a President's expected to do," he said. "That goes with the job."

"And what about the President's wife?" she went on as she leaned in closer toward him. "Is she supposed to sit idly by, day after day—watching—knowing what's happening? Yes, and night after night, listening . . . I don't care what Jensen says! I hear you! I lie there awake!"

"Kathy," he said, shaking his head, "a President has his duties!"

"Duties? But what about his wife, Stephen? What about his duties to *her*? His obligations to *her*? Or," she added, "perhaps you've forgotten those."

Thompson was stung by her words. "Kathy, you shouldn't try to measure personal obligations—and I don't like the word *obligation* in referring to us—and duties. In truth, a President has no choice . . ." As he poured himself a glass of water, he glanced up at Kathy's forlorn look. "I know I've failed you," he murmured, "I know that . . ."

"Please!" she said, feeling his distress. "I don't know what made me say that, Stephen. It was unfair."

"Perhaps. But I have to admit . . . there's truth in what you said, what you're thinking, what you leave unsaid."

"We can talk another time," she replied, beginning to rise from her chair.

"No, sit down, sit down. We'll talk now. I want to get everything into the open." He dabbed his forehead again.

"No, I really don't think it *is* the right time," she said as she stood before him. "It can all wait. So, please, let's do it later, another time, Stephen," she said, seating herself on the edge of the chair.

"It's just a spell, Kathy, just a little spell, means nothing. Sit down." He moved forward with his elbows on the desk, digging the fingers of both hands into his forehead. "Sometimes, I'll admit, the headaches . . . almost unbearable . . ."

"You can't go on like this, Stephen."

His hands spread out and his eyes looked at her from between his fingers as his flesh turned reddish from the pressure. He looked grotesquely like a superannuated child playing hide-and-seek. "I must, I have to," he said. "I've got to hold the party together—get the ticket through the convention, through the election."

Kathy hesitated a moment. "The ticket?" she asked. "Is there any doubt about the ticket?"

"I'll be nominated, there's no question there. It's a question of the Vice Presidency that concerns me," he said. He paused, letting Kathy absorb the impact of his words.

"I read all the political gossip," she replied. "If you've doubts, can't you let the party decide, Stephen?"

"Hawley," he said, scrutinizing her. "Keep Hawley, that it?"

"Whoever the party wants," she replied lamely, suppressing her agitation.

"That can't be risked and for a very simple reason. I will *not* have him as my successor." It was the first time that Thompson had flatly stated his opposition directly to Kathy. "That's the bottom line."

"But he *is* your Vice President, Stephen."

"Was. It's enough for you to hear this from me. It's why I wanted to get this in the open between us. Clifford Hawley is *not* going to be my successor. He is *not* going to be on the ticket. He is not going to be President. *Ever.*" They stared at each other for some moments, like boxers sparring for an opening.

"Why are you telling me this?" she said at last.

"Because you are my wife. You are the First Lady. *My* First Lady," he said, emphasizing each word. "No one else's."

Kathy flushed. She was angered by his distrust, and she despised herself for allowing him to make her feel guilty.

"I've been doing some research. Very interesting, too."

"Research, Stephen?" she said, her hands suddenly clenched.

"I know something about your past relationship with Mr. Hawley, that's what," he said bluntly.

"You know *what* about my past relationship with Mr. Hawley?" she answered angrily.

He patted a folder on his desk and said magisterially, "Oh, you can believe me. I won't have that man use you for his ambitions. I'm putting a stop to it!"

"Using *me* for *his* ambitions, Stephen? Clifford Hawley should be judged on his merits, not on some past phase of his personal life."

"I knew you would defend him. And Harry knew it! He could see it, the way the two of you look at each other."

She stood frozen, fearful. *That foolish moment in the White House*, she thought, *by the window. Thrown up again.* "Then you and Harry know something I don't," she said evenly.

He opened the folder. "Quite possibly. Apparently you don't know how Hawley uses people. Think of it, and you'll see the pattern. It's in here. He used me. He used you. He's trying to use you again. And he used that poor girl." He pulled out a couple of pages. "It's all here. You can read it."

"Stephen! Surely you're not going to be taken in by malicious gossip?"

"Harry knew Gloria Whitney better than anyone. He knew what she was capable of doing. And Mr. Hawley knew that, too." The President glared at her. "Now, I'll ask you, Kathy, what do you think would have happened at the Vice President's house if Oliver Moran *hadn't* been there?"

She stood up and went to the door, then turning, said, "I'm not going to speculate on what might have happened. And I'm not going to listen to whatever you or your spies have gathered on *me* in that folder."

He tapped the folder. "I didn't know you had Mr. Hawley's private phone number—that you use it."

"How do you know that?" she demanded, approaching his desk as she suppressed her anger.

Thompson looked up, flushed, regretting his words. "I'm sorry, but it's all in here, Kathy. We *know*."

"I don't want to believe what I'm thinking," she retorted, "and if you want to know the truth, ever since Los Angeles I've been praying for peace and harmony between us. Now all I can say is I'm ashamed of you, Stephen! Ashamed!"

The President placed his bony hands on top of the desk and slowly raised himself from the chair. "And what, then, am I supposed to think of you, Kathy?"

She faced him across the desk, looking at him coldly, fighting back a sense of newly felt revulsion. "Stephen, you may think whatever you wish."

"That's your answer?"

"Yes. And one more thing, Mr. President. You said you failed me. Well, maybe I've failed you. What it adds up to is that we seem to be failing each other. Because of that I won't be needing a sitting room any longer. I prefer a private bedroom."

"That kind of talk simply magnifies the problem. I have my duty, Kathy. None of this," he said pointing to the folder, "ever has to go public—"

"Duty," she repeated. "Well, you may have your duty, or whatever you want to call it, and I have mine. I don't think mine requires me to share your bedroom any longer, Stephen, not when you put spies on me. Clearly my being there or my not being there makes very little difference." She walked quickly to the door and closed it behind her.

Thompson started to the door, then sank back into his chair and shut his eyes, but he felt no peace. He wanted to rest, but he could not keep the image of Hawley from intruding on his thoughts. He recoiled from hearing Harry's words—"They knew each other *before*" . . . He felt sickened by the insidious pain of jealousy and found himself recoiling even more at the very thought that he could contemplate revenge.

☆ ☆ ☆

Kathy had immediately returned to her own suite of offices in the East Wing, surprising Anne Koyce, busy tidying up the day's work. "Never expected to see you back here," Anne said, glancing at the stately grandfather clock that stood beside the doorway leading to Kathy's private office. "Anything I can do?"

"No, Anne. You do whatever. I just wanted to be somewhere where I could think. Alone."

Anne shrugged as Kathy swept by her and went inside the office, settling into the large comfortable chair behind the desk. She picked up a pencil and began tapping it against her teeth, then put it down. "Anne," she called out.

Anne Koyce appeared at the doorway. "I don't want you to stay on my account. I just wanted to check on tomorrow's agenda," she said, flipping open her desk diary, "among other things." For a moment she debated about confiding her inner turmoil to someone, and she knew that Anne was the one person in the White House whom she could trust. But to talk about the President, to reveal the anxieties that were eating at her peace of mind, to admit to the cold fear of unknown forces surrounding her, to bring someone even as close as Anne into her innermost confidence—none of it was feasible.

Anne went to the door, pausing long enough to give Kathy Thompson an opportunity to open up on whatever it really was that had brought about her sudden appearance, but Kathy looked up and simply said, "See you in the morning. Good night, Anne."

The moment Anne closed the door, Kathy pushed the diary away from her. Over and over again she kept wondering about her husband's assertion that he knew Kathy had Hawley's private number. She searched her mind, wondering if the subject had ever come up between them, perhaps early in the Administration.

She wondered what Clifford Hawley would say if she were to call him. She hated leaving Hawley in the dark—assuming he hadn't deduced the President's intentions. In the political world every minute counted, and information, reliable information, was vital. She hated the predicament Stephen Thompson had created for her—but *that* she knew was cold-blooded and deliberate.

And then she began to wonder whether Stephen Thompson had actually heard her talking to Hawley—she reviewed the time and circumstances of the call, when she had phoned around midnight to congratulate Hawley on his television appearance. She struggled to remember the exact words Thompson used, the words that had shocked her—"I didn't know you had Mr. Hawley's private number—that you use it." How, she began to wonder, did he know that she used it? She was sure she had never used it before. And then it struck her. Perhaps what the President was revealing was that it wasn't that he had heard Kathy talking *to* Hawley, but rather talking *with* Hawley.

She frowned as her right hand instinctively shot to her lips as though to silence a gasp. Stephen, she remembered, was in bed, presumably asleep when she made the call. Her hand slowly touched the phone on her desk. Was it conceivable, she wondered, that there could be a taping system in the White House with which she was unfamiliar, but which was there by presidential order?

18

Seated in the cheerful upstairs sitting room of the vice presidential residence, looking down at the grounds landscaped in the manner of a stately English park, Hawley and Daniels were reviewing the Twenty-fifth Amendment and the complex political situation. "If the chips ever do really come down for the Twenty-fifth, shouldn't we have one final meeting, one in which all members of the Cabinet are present, so that all sides can be fairly heard?" Hawley asked.

"That would lead not only to confusion but quite possibly to even greater dissension," Daniels replied, "not to mention a leak. So far we've been lucky."

"If we got a seven-to-six vote in the Cabinet, I'd consider that disastrous," Hawley said.

Daniels shrugged. "The Supreme Court makes major decisions on a five-to-four vote."

"The President's a good man," Hawley said, "perhaps even a great man. I have to believe that when and if the time ever comes and the facts are set before him, quietly and impartially by those in whom he has the greatest faith, he would respond with intelligence and patriotism." Noting Daniels' frowning, he then said, "Yes, I say that knowing the word's out everywhere that he won't be putting me on the ticket. Kraus is orchestrating that, I'm sure."

"Yes, and the question still has to be, Why?"

"I've tried to figure it out," Hawley said, "but I haven't been able to. No one has." He got up and went over to a small side table and poured two glasses of sherry, handing one to Daniels.

"What about your role at the convention?" Daniels asked. "If the President hangs in, doesn't pick you . . .?"

"I've made that decision. It may all be thought of as an act of political bravado, but my name will be placed in nomination. It's a question of setting the right timing."

"Good."

"That, of course, would precipitate a real floor battle with the President supporting Senator Vance, and you can't take away Vance's impressive record. On the other hand, some members of the Cabinet would probably be supporting me as far as the nomination goes—of that I'm reasonably certain."

"They should, if gratitude means anything. You helped put most of them there."

Hawley shrugged, a wry smile on his face. "Richard, I've never counted on gratitude. But even so, I believe some'll favor an open contest for the number-two spot. Pat Bromley in Commerce may be the best one to leak this. At the right moment."

"Pat Bromley? You sure?"

"Bromley and I have always had a comfortable relationship. I know he's with me," Hawley insisted.

"Good. What about your staff? Those young tigers of yours? Are they pitching in? Lane Whitney?"

A look of concern crossed Hawley's face. "Lane's around, but hasn't been the same recently. Understandable, since the tragedy of his sister."

"May I make a suggestion?" Daniels asked, sipping his sherry.

"Of course."

"I never like lukewarm support. After the convention—I suggest you lose him. This is no time for you to have weak sisters around. And no time," he added, turning and lifting his glass toward Hawley, "to let yourself be vulnerable to any kind of outside surprises. You don't wait for them. You anticipate them and end them." As though handed a cue, Hawley decided this was the ideal moment to make known his concern about Vivien Lessing's instability.

Daniels listened imperturbably, exhaling rings of smoke from his cigarette. When Hawley finished, he said, "I don't think she'll be a problem."

"For me? Or for you and the CIA?" Hawley said smoothly.

"Hollywood," Daniels chuckled. "The place is so full of stories about the CIA when their own backyard is so damned chock-full of mysteries—people who disappear, get stabbed, murdered. The place reeks with double crosses, manic egos, broken promises, jealousy, under-the-table dealing—you name it." He snuffed out the cigarette. "I don't think we have to worry much about Miss Lessing. Hollywood likes to boast they take care of their own." He looked over at Hawley. "But I'm glad you told me."

☆ ☆ ☆

The summons came as a surprise to Hawley. The President's appointments secretary suggested that Hawley enter the White House grounds through a little-used entrance in order to avoid newspaper, television, and radio reporters customarily gathered in the West Wing, and to join Thompson in his study in the family quarters on the second floor. Hawley had taken the message in his office at the Capitol, and as he was leaving he gazed up for a moment at the stern features of Peale's portrait of Washington, cool and aloof. He suspected that he would find a similar attitude in Thompson. The President had given no indication of the subject matter he wanted to discuss, but Hawley concluded that the purpose of the meeting was to be an airing of political necessities now crowding in on both of them. Perhaps, he thought as he walked down the East Front steps of the Capitol, the time for decision was at hand, both Thompson's and his own.

It was a meeting he had hoped for; he even fantasized that a frank and open discussion might bring about a reconciliation between them. Then, thrusting wishful desires behind him, he decided the best approach would be to make a friendly, even a conciliatory opening statement, followed, perhaps, by a realistic appraisal of the current political scene. He would, however, let the President call the shots, although he was determined to meet every issue between them head-on.

Hawley saw the tension in the President's posture as he stood at the doorway leading into the President's upstairs study. He quickly dropped most of his preconceived ideas.

Thompson was seated behind the room's famous Victorian oak desk. Hawley noticed the way in which his large fingers were pressed tightly together, the bluish line of his thin lips, and the intransigent glare of his blue eyes. The atmosphere was clearly charged.

Hawley sat in the chair before the President's desk. "I'm very glad to see you, Mr. President," he began. "I've been hoping for some time that we might have a private meeting." Thompson remained silent as Hawley rambled on in a disarming way, complimenting him on his recent television appearances, resolved not to be the first to raise any issues.

"Mr. Vice President," Thompson finally began, "the convention will take place in six weeks' time."

"Yes, sir." Hawley was surprised more by the directness of the President's first words than by the absence of any cordiality.

Thompson, leaning forward, then said, "You are not going to be on the ticket."

Hawley felt the blow as though he and his supporters had never discussed the subject. His jaws tightened as the President continued to stare at him.

"Three weeks from today I shall expect your resignation as Vice President."

This thunderbolt had a stunning effect on Hawley. How had he and Daniels, Jaggers, and the others overlooked this menacing demand? *His* resignation? He foresaw at once the immediate destruction of all that he had carefully planned. The end of a dream, the beginning of a nightmare.

"I don't understand, Mr. President," he replied guardedly, struggling to maintain his composure in a whirl of instant sudden alarms.

The President's lips parted in a thin smile as he spoke with a faint hint of malice. "But I'm certain that you do."

"Your prerogative about the ticket . . . I can understand, with great and real regret, Mr. President. But my resignation? Why? On what grounds?"

"Three weeks from today," the President reiterated curtly as he sank back into his chair, waving Hawley off by way of dismissal and busying himself with some papers on his desk. But Hawley remained in his chair, recalculating his position, determined to force the President to discuss the matter.

"Mr. President," he began, as he controlled mixed emotions of shock, anger, and resentment, "your loss of confidence in me and your demand I resign come as a most unwelcome surprise."

"To be President," Thompson said, looking up, weariness evident in his voice, "means that one has to be capable of making vital decisions. I believe that you feel that I've lost *my* competence to act decisively." He gazed coldly at Hawley. "You're wrong. And your considering making the Twenty-fifth Amendment operative, your own hesitation to act, your deliberate concealment of this personal hostility toward me, all of these things—and others—have forced me to take this action."

Hawley gripped the arms of his chair. "I have no such hostility, sir. Quite to the contrary, I have enormous respect for you. I can say—"

"It no longer matters, Mr. Hawley, what you say. You have three weeks from today to make a gracious withdrawal. Now if you don't mind, I have some other matters—"

"I do mind, Mr. President," Hawley said sharply, a hand touching Thompson's desk, "and I have no intention of resigning."

Thompson looked at him icily. "You were elected, of course, and you can't be removed by any statement of mine. You played your part in my election. I know that. You still want a political career, possibly even the presidency. But you are not going to take the presidency from me. And no matter what you think, when the political chips are down, the Cabinet isn't going to support you."

Hawley realized that the President's reference to the Amendment showed that the discussions within the Committee had probably been known to him for weeks. The image of Hornwell flashed through Hawley's mind, but certain as he was of Hornwell's devotion to the President, he wanted to believe the leak had come from a disgruntled member of the Committee staff: clearly an assignment for Daniels.

"Oh, there are some in the Cabinet who share your views," Thompson was saying, "some who share mine, a few who are the swing vote. I can dismiss members of the Cabinet who oppose me, Mr. Hawley. I have that authority. But I have a campaign to lead, and I don't want to fire any member of the Cabinet unless I'm compelled to."

Hawley shook his head. "Mr. President," he said, still containing his shock, "of course your dismissal of members of the Cabinet would provide your opponents with so much ammunition you'd very likely risk losing the election altogether. It would open the doors to the very issue—the very crisis you want to avoid."

"The crisis," Thompson repeated. "My health, isn't that it?" Thompson said sneeringly. "You're very concerned about it,

I'm sure, but I don't think I need your advice on how to win this election, Mr. Hawley. I have a record that speaks for itself."

"I'm part of that record," Hawley said bluntly.

"Were," Thompson snapped. "Mr. Hawley," he said, rising from his chair, a tone of dismissal in his voice, "I think all's been said that has to be said."

Hawley felt the sharpness of the angry thrust as he, too, rose to face Thompson. "I repeat, Mr. President, I'm not resigning."

Hawley held on to the back of the chair, collecting his thoughts as the President spoke. "You won't be the first Vice President not to be renominated. Jefferson had two, so did Lincoln. Roosevelt had three. Even Eisenhower was tempted to drop Nixon. Should have. Now if you take my advice, you'll step down as well."

"Rejection as the nominee I can accept, Mr. President. From the delegates," Hawley emphasized as he noted the President's irritation. "*Your* rejection," he noted, "no." Without declaring his own candidacy Hawley added, "Senator Vance will at least know there's been a battle."

"*If* he's a candidate," Thompson said, observing Hawley's look of surprise. "Oh, I know what's in the papers and on television, but they don't know what's in my head," he said, tapping his temple. "It might be Vance, it might not be Vance. It won't be you." He pointed directly at Hawley. "You want to know why *you're* going to resign? It's because, among other matters, you're the subject of too much scandalous talk, and that makes you not only an undesirable running mate but also an undesirable sitting officer of this Administration."

"Scandal?" Hawley spat out the charge. "Scandal? So, it's come down to that!" He felt his control returning despite the President's accusation. "I've already answered to the public, but if you want to make it an open issue all over again, I'll answer to anyone! But let me give you some free advice. Beware of reckless charges, Mr. President! It's been proved beyond doubt that I had nothing to do with the death of Gloria Whitney—and *you* know it!" Then pointing a finger directly back at Thompson, he said, coldly, "And your *son* knows it!"

"I'm not reversing . . . re—" The President stopped speaking momentarily to regain his composure. "What I mean is, I'm not referring only to that," Thompson said, flushing with anger as he picked up the folder on his desk, almost tempted to break his silence about Hawley's past relationship with his wife, but resisting that impulse because he felt it might instead bring him knowledge he couldn't bear hearing, thereby only magnifying his own growing anguish. "It's all there . . . in here, Mr. Vice President, in here," he emphasized, passing the folder across to Hawley while continuing to speak.

Hawley, aware that the slurring of Thompson's words had become increasingly apparent, glanced at the papers, feeling a new surge of outrage. "These are simply allegations, Mr. President. Less! They're pure, simple lies! There's not a word of truth in any of this!" He flung the papers back on Thompson's desk. "I came here prepared to review the political scene, the problems of the campaign—"

"Which you're certain I won't have the strength to conduct!" Thompson said, lashing back.

"It *is* a matter for concern, Mr. President, but my coming here was, I had hoped, rather naively I'll admit, a step to begin building a new partnership in which I could be helpful to you—"

"That's over, Mr. Hawley. Now, if you compel me to go public—" Hawley noted the President's clenched fists as he stood his ground "—I won't hesitate. You'll not be on the ticket! And you'll not be in the wings! Do you understand? Now, sir, this meeting is over." Thompson sat down, and picked up another batch of papers. Then glancing up he lifted three fingers. "Three weeks. I've been open and candid, spoken to you face-to-face. *Three weeks.*"

Thompson abruptly turned his chair around. That simple movement, rude and conclusive, made clear that there could never be polite formalities between them again.

As Hawley turned to leave, he noted the two flags on either side of the doorway, the American flag and the presidential standard, always carried from this room as the President escorted state guests down the grand staircase to receptions and dinners. In his imagination, ruffles and flourishes mocked him as he departed. If he was to believe Thompson, he would never hear those sounds for his own entrance.

Walking out of the White House, he was overcome by a sense of defeat as he recognized the President's power to make or break an opponent, real or imaginary. He had gone into the meeting with a sense of hope but now recognized the hostility of a man who openly revealed his enmity toward him. A presidential public confrontation based on fact or even unsubstantiated charges would destroy him. Thompson's surprise ultimatum had jolted him so much that for the first time since the Twenty-fifth Amendment surfaced into open discussion with Daniels and Jaggers he felt himself losing his bearings.

He sank into a corner of his limousine, ordering his chauffeur to drive back to the Capitol. Even though it was nearly five o'clock, he wanted to be in a place that might restore his shaken self-confidence. He needed time to think.

Images collided in his mind as the car rolled along the Mall. At the east end the squat, bronze figure of Ulysses S. Grant huddled on its horse. As Hawley was driven past, he looked up at the artillery group, on Grant's south flank, its horses churning up the muddy road as caisson and soldier crew hurtled into battle, the whole action-filled tableau fixed in metallic motion for as long as the Republic should stand. He reviewed again the President's biting statements.

The car rolled slowly along the East Front, where the inaugural platform had stood some three and a half years before, an area now shimmering in the sun and humidity of Washington in July. But despite the heat outside and the comfortable air-conditioning in the car, he felt the stab of winter. That Inauguration Day had climaxed his own meteoric rise.

He saw himself walk to his seat in the stands, glimpsed once more the thousands of spectators stretched out across the Capitol plaza, heard the muffled roar of approval surge toward him, and measured it against the muted sound that floated down from those whose presence on the stand was determined by protocol and power. That was a polite echo, studied, perhaps even hypocritical, its tone of acceptance mixed with fear and envy.

As he moved through the Capitol, he recalled how, at the Inaugural ceremony, Kathy had congratulated him, offering her white-gloved hand, letting it rest in his own, withdrawing it slowly as she discreetly returned her attention to her husband.

In that moment, Hawley remembered, too, how he had caught the new President's son looking down on him. Had young Thompson noticed the byplay between him and his attractive stepmother? Hawley had marked down a warning postscript in his memory file on Harry Thompson; he would not forget the coldness in his eyes that somehow made it clear that young Thompson, in catching the new First Lady's congratulatory gesture, considered it curiously inappropriate.

In his Capitol office, Hawley pulled out a copy of the Constitution from a desk drawer; he had carefully studied every word of the Twenty-fifth Amendment, but now he read the words again. Presidential resignation, he knew, was not in the cards.

It was obvious to Hawley that Thompson, despite his own physical liabilities, would, like Wilson, FDR, and Eisenhower before him, decline to resign. In fact, this President had actually had the audacity to reverse matters by demanding that Hawley, in the very best of health, resign. In that event, Hawley knew that the first step Thompson would take would be to implement section two of the amendment and nominate a Vice President.

There was no question that energetic Frederick K. Vance could win the approval of Congress were he the nominee.

Finally, Hawley read section four, which only *he* could activate. He noted its language, its vagueness, realized that though its terms seemed logical and precise, to execute them could create the kind of turmoil that would threaten the very existence of the government.

If the Cabinet supported him and declared him Acting President, what was there to stop President Thompson from instantly responding that no inability existed, or even admitting that such incapacity that might be visible was not of such a character as to preclude his discharging his sworn duties?

The issue supposedly would then be resolved over a twenty-one-day period by the Congress, assuming the country could endure such a contest, one in which the nation, possibly for weeks, might as a result have two Presidents, each vying to exercise the powers of the office. To whom would the nation look in the event of an international crisis spawned by those very events? And where was the proof of presidential inability? The need to declare Red Dye Day operative was at hand. His briefing by Daniels and the National Security Adviser had alerted him to the growing urgency. The Soviets could not be allowed to believe for a moment that they had achieved nuclear superiority.

As he sat in his office thinking, Hawley had a premonition of danger to the nation so tangible that it chilled him. National survival was, finally, a matter of personal survival. If he resigned under Thompson's ultimatum, he knew he could never attain the presidency. If, on the other hand, he refused to resign, Thompson had already told him what the consequences would be; a denunciation by the President that not only would eliminate him as a running mate but would end his career.

He finally realized his role was being defined, even triggered by the President himself. The only path left open to him was to succeed to the presidency, at once, but in a lawful manner and with just cause. Red Dye Day could be the trigger to that cause.

It was now imperative that he take counsel with those whose first concern was the security of the nation—the Committee. He picked up the phone on his desk and asked to be connected with Richard Daniels.

A moment later he heard the soft voice of the CIA chief. "Yes, Mr. Vice President?"

"We should have dinner," Hawley said. "My place, in an hour?"

"I'll be there."

As Hawley cradled the phone, he thought of Grant, saw him as a young West Pointer, so dejected he'd left the Army only to be summoned back years later to duty that finally led him to the White House. Now he felt that Thompson had issued his own summons, actually a challenge, and he, Hawley, would take the first measured steps to meet it.

19

Through his years as Chairman of the Senate Armed Services Committee, Frederick Vance had become close to the defense establishment; Hornwell, from his years as Chief of Naval Operations, had learned long ago how to fight for the Navy's interests not only through cultivating the bureaucracy of the Pentagon, but in mastering the way through the labyrinth of the Hill. And Vance had played a major role in Hornwell's rise to the top spot in the hierarchy of the Joint Chiefs.

Their trip west with the President had underscored their relationship, and the projection of Vance as a likely successor to Hawley had drawn them closer. Hornwell's invitation to a private meeting at the end of the day aboard the *Decatur* was another welcome sign to Vance that his star was, indeed, rising. The amenities were brief but warm.

Hornwell found it easy to bring up the subject of the convention, now only a few weeks away, and with it to express his own pleasure at Vance's prospects. But with it he spoke of his concern about Thompson's health and the problems that it might create. And he emphasized that their meeting was taking place out of his lifelong commitment to duty to America. Now Hornwell stood peering out a porthole as Vance sat quietly at the Admiral's desk holding a book in his hand, reading a passage of the Constitution that Hornwell had underlined, the Twenty-fifth Amendment.

As the Senator sat reading, Hornwell pondered his next move. First, he wanted Vance in position, and then he would proceed with his resolve to check out the President's true state of mind. After hearing Ed Jaggers' reservations about Thompson, Hornwell was determined to test the President's ability to make a speedy and necessary decision. He felt confident that Thompson would not disappoint him, but he had to know from firsthand observation. He expected to see Thompson within hours.

"Interesting," Vance said, breaking into Hornwell's thoughts, "but also not good. Not good," he repeated, looking up at Hornwell.

"And the Senate and the Congress can do nothing," Hornwell said, containing his agitation. "Nothing! It's all spelled out clearly enough."

Vance held up a hand. "Unless the President resists. That's very important. It says so right here," he said, picking up the book. "'Thereafter'—meaning after the Vice President has assumed the office of President with the written approval of the majority of the Cabinet—'thereafter when the President transmits to the President pro tempore of the Senate and the Speaker of the House of Representatives his'—I emphasize the word *his*—'written declaration that no inability exists, he shall resume the powers and duties of his office *unless* the Vice President and a majority of either the principal officers of the executive department or of such other body as Congress may by law provide—'"

"Senator, you're an authority on the Constitution. Is there such another body?" Hornwell cut in.

"No, there isn't. There's nothing except the Cabinet." Vance fumbled with his glasses and then resumed, reading aloud, "'—transmit within four days to the President pro tempore of the Senate and the Speaker of the House of Representatives their written declaration that the President is unable to discharge the powers and duties of his office. Thereupon Congress shall decide the issue—'"

"Hold it, Senator. Let me ask you. Do you think matters would ever get that far?" Hornwell asked. "The country's in very serious danger, Senator. Very serious. It's the Vice President and the Cabinet who have the power here—the real power—because no other body has been created by the Congress to handle this kind of situation, and once they move—" Hornwell pulled a chair up close to Vance and sat down. "No ifs, it's *when*, Senator, *when*." Hornwell's agitation showed in the tautness of his lips. "I've been wrestling with this dilemma for days," he said, his voice dropping to a hoarse whisper. "The Cabinet is being lined up. At this very moment."

The two men sat in the dim light of the aft quarters. Vance sensed his political future drifting away. "You know that? For a fact?"

Hornwell leaned in closer. "I do," he said.

"But if it's constitutional, if it's legal—"

"Forget the ifs, Senator!" Hornwell exploded. "It's legal, Senator, of course! So what?" he snapped. "The Twenty-fifth is full of legalities, technical answers on how to handle conflicting testimony. But the writers forgot one thing!" he concluded, eyes narrowing as if gauging his target.

"And that is?"

"There's no *time* for debate, no *time* for conflicting testimony. There's only time for action. You, Senator, have to get your party and your friends from the opposition party—all of them—lined up, counted. Those other plans have to be shot down before they get started. Otherwise—"

"Taking a tally—Admiral, there's no way then of keeping the matter secret. There's bound to be a leak—" Vance stopped, suddenly aware of Hornwell's central point. "Are you saying that if the Vice President were to become Acting President and the President insists he's fit to do his duties," his voice fell to a whisper, "he wouldn't be able to?"

"Once that office and its powers are taken, under these kinds of circumstances—the President's health, the convention just around the corner—do you think they'd voluntarily relinquish them? They wouldn't risk a congressional vote, not with the President's personal popularity. It's just that simple, Senator. They'd take him over to Camp David on some pretext or other—maybe commit him to Bethesda with the help of Mr. Daniels and the CIA. And Senator," Hornwell said, stressing each word, "they'd be *right*."

"How can you say that?"

"Because we can't afford such an open squabble for power in the United States. Our adversaries would exploit it for all it's worth." He stopped for a moment. "There's no alternative, Senator. Either Hawley and his people win—by being bold and decisive, or—" he threw out his hands, appealing to Vance.

"What do you expect of me?"

"I don't know for certain, Senator. It's why I took the liberty of talking to you . . . It's clear the President is considering you on his ticket. We know that. That ticket can win the election, and the country would be safe then, no matter what happened after. That's because *you'd* be in place. Things would be orderly. The transition, whenever and however it came, would be acceptable.

"If the election were tomorrow there'd be no problem, but it's not tomorrow. *And* . . . if anything were to happen to the President between now and the convention, before any nominations have been made, we'd have a new President." Hornwell's eyes fixed on Vance. "You understand?" he said.

"Mr. Hawley," Vance said.

Hornwell leaned confidentially toward his guest. "Mr. Hawley's friends want President Thompson removed. I know that."

"And Hawley?"

"We know he's ambitious. But I can't say that I know—as a fact—just what he might do. I have to admit he's been circumspect in all of his words and actions. But," Hornwell emphasized as he paused for a moment, "if Mr. Hawley were *not* the legal successor, under that very same Twenty-fifth Amendment the President could name you as Vice President and you'd most certainly be approved by the Congress."

"But Mr. Hawley *is* the official next in line," Vance said.

"Yes, to be sure. But, Senator—" Hornwell again dropped his voice to a whisper "—there's a puzzling omission in the amendment. It talks about removing the President. It says *nothing* about removing the Vice President in the event the President, together with a majority of his Cabinet, find *him*—the Vice President—incapable of discharging *his* duties. Unless—"

"Yes?" Vance waited, tense, startled by the direction of the talk as Hornwell continued.

"Unless, in an emergency session, the Supreme Court would find that the power is implied within the framework of the amendment itself. Certainly if the Vice President could remove the President, the President should not have less of an option to act than the Vice President. You're a constitutional lawyer. What do you say to that?"

"I can't answer a question like that without some study," Vance said, his tongue licking the edges of his dry lips, "but it is a most intriguing idea."

"The key, of course, is the Cabinet."

"I understand what you're suggesting, Admiral—a Cabinet that would resist those championing the Vice President, one that would support the President, in fact, in *removing* the Vice President." Vance observed Hornwell's smile and added, "The President controls the Cabinet."

"Yes, yes," Hornwell said, softly. Then he added, in a confidential tone, "He does if he *wants* to exercise control."

The two men sat quietly, each studying the other. Vance broke the silence. "He can always discharge those whose loyalty he doubts," Vance volunteered.

"Precisely." Hornwell edged closer to Vance. *"There's* the key, Senator. The *real* key. And that's proper and legal."

"Then it's all a matter of timing—meeting with the President—convincing him—timing. You've given me much to think about." Vance clasped Hornwell's outstretched hand.

☆ ☆ ☆

At the same time Hornwell was meeting with Vance, Daniels was at Hawley's residence having cocktails. They stepped out on the broad white-railed veranda, Daniels rubbing himself, for even in the mildness of summer he sometimes felt a chill.

"The picture is clear to me, Mr. Vice President," Daniels began as a butler walked toward them with refills. He took a glass and waited until the butler left.

"Go on," Hawley said, sipping his drink and sitting in a white wicker chair.

"The President's decision or lack of decision may turn out to be a blessing one way or another. May even compel some of the straddlers in the Cabinet to take a position," Daniels said, leaning against the top railing.

"If he doesn't fire them first," Hawley said.

"He won't. Not unless he knows for sure that they've swung away from him. And *we* won't give him any such opportunity."

"Could be," Hawley said, "but I wouldn't make a move unless the Committee is unanimously committed."

"Fair enough. And the Cabinet?"

Hawley shook his head. "No, there I can accept a difference of opinion. In fact, I expect it. That's politics."

Daniels flicked some ashes over the railing. "What we really need now is absolutely reliable information. We need someone inside. We have to know what the man is thinking. What he's planning."

Hawley nodded. "Okay. And how do we do that?"

"*We* don't." Daniels replied. "*You* do."

The two men faced each other, Hawley at once certain that Daniels' plan was for him to involve Kathy. He didn't like it and what it implied. Daniels spoke again. "*Only* you can do it."

Hawley looked at him. "Kathy Thompson?"

"Why not? She owes you, Mr. Vice President," Daniels said coolly.

"That's putting things a bit baldly—"

"There are some who think she used *you*," Daniels said bluntly. He saw Hawley recoil in resentment.

Since Daniels knew he'd made his point, he spoke quickly, in a more conciliatory manner. "Mr. Vice President, I don't like it, either, but it's best if we keep all emotion out of this."

"Well, that's not so easy," Hawley said.

"I understand. We've looked into this matter a little bit, of necessity, of course—"

"What's that mean, 'of necessity, of course'?" Hawley said warily.

"We've followed Sammy Wellman, the *Time* reporter, fellow interested in your private life? You remember him?" Daniels replied easily.

"What about him?"

"We know what *he* knows," Daniels said, his gray eyes fixed on Hawley over the rim of his drink.

"And what does he know?" Hawley asked.

"Not too much. You introduced her to the President—"

"Everyone knows that."

"Okay. She looked you up when you were in the House—"

"That was her job, getting interviews."

Daniels took a deep drag on his cigarette. "He hasn't been able to fill much in between your interview and the President's."

"And you, your people?" Hawley persisted.

"You didn't leave many tracks," Daniels said with a touch of professional approbation. "We do know she was among those who suggested you as a possible running mate. That was her way of thanking you for having been the one to introduce her to the President?" he added, ending his comment in his usual questioning manner.

"Well, if it were, then she'd have every right to consider the favor I'd rendered—if you want to call it that—amply returned."

The two men stared at each other, each preoccupied with his own thoughts. Hawley broke the silence. "I don't know whether she'll be all that cooperative."

Daniels lit his cigarette, knowing with certainty now that Hawley would make the effort. He felt comfortable; he had just enough information in the Hawley dossier to know how eagerly he and Kathy had pursued each other. His knowledge of human behavior told him that the itch was still there; he'd seen it in Kathy Thompson's eyes whenever Hawley was present. He knew that the euphoria of being First Lady had to wear thin along with the President's health. Daniels had observed Kathy at parties dancing with diplomats, congressmen, and Cabinet members, and he had noted that she never moved quite as close to them as she did to Hawley.

"We handle this contact very discreetly," Daniels said, willing now to talk about Kathy candidly and dispassionately. "You and the First Lady are on a number of committees together, fine arts, handicap training. You just call a meeting. Get her aside—tell her what's happened. It may be news to her."

☆ ☆ ☆

It was in the Kennedy Center's South Opera Lounge, under its handsome, magnificently recessed Waterford chandelier, that Clifford Hawley, at a meeting of the Washington Fine Arts Committee, gave Kathy Thompson the news of the President's ultimatum. Kathy was stunned, impulsively placing a hand on Hawley's arm. "Your resignation! I can't believe it," she said. "Why would he ask a thing like that?"

"He claims to have reasons," Hawley said. Then noting an interested bystander a few feet away, he added, "and we're being watched again, Kathy."

"I don't care," she said, glancing at the saturnine face of Harry Thompson across the room, "especially him. He's always watching. Here. At the British Embassy last night. In the White House. Everywhere I go, he's there, glowering."

Hawley waved a greeting as he nodded and smiled at Harry. "No need to antagonize him, Kathy, and he is a member of this committee."

She turned back to face Hawley. "I don't understand Stephen. You've been his friend—"

"Was. Not any more. By choice, Kathy: his."

"But why?" she protested. "Why?"

"The President—let's just say he's been weighing all the various options open to an incumbent—and he wants me out."

"I'd like to do whatever I can, Cliff . . ."

"I may want to see the President again and I may need your help."

"You mean he won't see you if you ask for an appointment?"

"He may think I'm coming over just to submit my resignation."

"Well, if that's what he wants, why wouldn't he see you?"

"He'd want *that* done through channels, by letter, to the Secretary of State. He's not interested in another conversation. But if I were in the White House to visit you about some committee work . . ."

"Cliff, that could make him angry. Very. You've no idea . . . you really don't know." She wondered whether she should reveal her suspicions. Kathy glanced about the room for a moment, brow knitted in thought. "I worry about him all the time. I don't want anything to happen to him, Cliff—" Then remembering the shocking statements Thompson had hurled at her, she looked up at Hawley and spoke with sudden decisiveness. "Cliff, if you want a meeting—you'll have a meeting."

Hawley, speaking softly, said, "I was sure I could count on you. Whatever comes of this—I won't forget it, Kathy. But I don't want you spying, anything like that—"

She glanced over at the brooding figure of Harry Thompson. "Why not? The President has his spy."

"Harry?"

"More," she said enigmatically.

"What does that mean?"

Kathy took a step closer to Hawley. "My phone call to you. Someone heard it . . ."

Hawley flinched. "Are you certain?"

"*Someone* heard it while we were talking, or someone *taped* it." She saw Hawley's shock and then recounted the scene with the President.

"A week ago I'd have said, 'I can't believe it,'" Hawley said, "but after my own meeting with the President I'm almost ready to believe anything."

"I didn't want to believe it," Kathy said. "I still don't."

"Your guess may be just a shot in the dark," Hawley replied.

"You don't really believe that, Cliff. Those words are burned into my memory. 'I didn't know you had Mr. Hawley's private phone number—that you use it.' That means he *knows*—"

"Have you discussed it with him since then?"

Kathy smiled. "No. We're very civil. Neither one of us has mentioned it again. But it's *there*, Cliff. And it won't go away." She looked up at Hawley. "Am I really some kind of prisoner? Do you think I'm in some kind of danger?"

"No, no," he said, wanting to reassure her, but aware too, now, that it was their relationship that could be the core of the President's demand that he resign. "No, not in danger," he said, "but a man holding onto power, if he feels threatened—that man can be very unpredictable. Power does strange things. I don't have to tell you, I don't have to give you a history lesson."

She frowned, her large dark eyes narrowing. She focused her eyes on Hawley. "What about the men who *want* power?" she asked. "How dangerous are they?"

He hesitated for a few moments. "I don't know the answer to that," he finally said. "But I do know Harry's never let his eyes off of us. I don't want to give him any new ideas. I hate to go, but it's best I leave now." He bowed, and made his excuses to other committee members as he moved toward the door.

Harry Thompson came directly to Kathy as the Vice President left the meeting room. "So now you know," he said cheerfully, standing at Kathy's side.

"Know what, Harry?"

"Spare me the games," he laughed.

"Your supercilious manners really don't become you, Harry."

"Oh, really? Well, I was just thinking you're in a most enviable position as a First Lady. First Lady to the President." He smiled easily. "And . . . quite obviously, First Lady to the Vice President? No one in our history has been in exactly that position, have they?"

Kathy looked at him with distaste. "I don't like your ugly insinuations, Harry."

"Insinuations? On the contrary, I think of them as facts. The one thing I haven't been able to find out—in my research, that is—is who got to whom first?"

Kathy looked at him with open hostility. "Now I can understand the pressures you placed on Gloria Whitney," she said coldly. "You must have really tormented her, Harry, and all the while the poor girl thought she loved you. Driving her to pills, to hallucinations—right down to the Tidal Basin. Well, you're not driving me! This time you've gone too far—"

"You can leave Gloria out of this," Harry shot back, stepping in close to her. "Too far, Kathy?" he said, mimicking her. "We have enough of your history." As she turned to leave, he seized her arm. "We know you, Kathy, for what you *really* are."

☆ ☆ ☆

Admiral Hornwell sat quietly in his quarters aboard the *Decatur* thumbing through his official diary. He stopped to reread a passage entered a year before when the Joint Chiefs made their first presentation to the President on the subject of Red Dye Day, its importance and significance.

Then he noted the record of a meeting with the President attended only by Secretary Clauson and himself, held six months previously, when the secret mission of the *Colorado* and her sister ship in the Pacific were presented and approved. He recalled the President's inquiring as to its current status on their recent trip to Omaha. Senator Vance had heard their discussion; as Chairman of the Senate Armed Services Committee, Vance and his counterpart on the Joint Committee on Intelligence had already been privy to the scope of Red Dye Day.

As he returned the diary to his private safe, he knew that the time was now at hand when the decision to implement Red Dye Day had to be made. Only one man could do it— the President of the United States. Hornwell was certain that on *this* subject the President would respond with vigor because of his familiarity with the project and his awareness of all of its implications. He was certain the National Security Advisor had briefed the President. It was a daily routine. But he still could not, even as he made his way to the West Wing entrance of the White House, shake off his inner fears; duty would compel him to acknowledge any failure on his part to secure the presidential order.

Hornwell stood beside a Chippendale chair near the President's desk in the Oval Office. He hated the West Wing of the White House, not only because of the necessity of passing the gauntlet of White House reporters but also because he cared so little for most of the President's staff. In fact, something about all presidential staffs alienated him—the former advertising-agency executives around Nixon, the so-called Georgia Mafia of the Carter Administration, the ambitious clique surrounding Reagan.

He thought it providential that the timing of the Soviet advance in marine science had permitted him, at a very critical moment, to be able to judge for himself the alertness and capacity of the President. If it meant dealing with men he considered more hangers-on than policymakers, well then, so be it. He could play politics when necessary.

As he glanced about and took a seat next to Deputy Chief of Staff Tom Latham, Hornwell thought not even Thompson's men were immune. Academics were no less susceptible to the flood of power that flowed from the Oval Office directly into their own veins than the others. The pomposity and assumption of grandiose manners that had afflicted appointees from academia in past administrations should have served as a warning to the President when he canvassed the Ivy League to man his staff. While Hornwell could put up with Kraus, he found Latham, a onetime professor of classical languages, tall and athletic, whose black hair showed not a single strand of gray despite his fifty years, particularly irritating. Latham had an annoying habit of spiking his talk with quotations from ancient Greek and Roman writers just to puzzle his listeners, until he translated them as if he were bringing enlightenment to the ill-informed. The Deputy Chief was an unexpected participant in the meeting with the President; Hornwell had expected Kraus.

Thompson greeted Hornwell perfunctorily and signalled him to begin. Hornwell launched into the details of Commander Whitney's mission and its abrupt ending.

The President was seated in a rocking chair, that symbol of Everyman that Kennedy had introduced during his brief presidency. He had been staring down at the presidential seal emblazoned on the rug, rocking himself gently, from the moment Hornwell had advised him of the implicit dangers confronting the country since the return of the test submarines. The long delay in Thompson's response was disconcerting to Hornwell. He had wanted a quick, decisive reaction.

Seated in a corner of a small sofa, Latham leaned over the arm to speak softly to Hornwell. "You believe the Soviets think they've achieved some kind of invincibility?"

"I don't know *what* they think," Hornwell said crisply, eyes focused on the President.

"*Fere libenter homines id quod volunt credunt,*" Latham volunteered.

Hornwell turned to glance at Latham.

"'Men willingly believe what they wish.' Caesar," Latham said with a smug smile.

The Admiral nodded curtly by way of acknowledgment. Then turning his attention back to Thompson, he felt a further sting of alarm, seeing Thompson, eyes closed, unresponsive, as if unaware of the dangers he'd just outlined. What if Daniels were right, what if the President could not act swiftly, authoritatively, and wisely when face-to-face with a truly critical decision? Studying Thompson's face, he noted with growing concern a small amount of saliva edging from a corner of his lips. As the President continued his slow, rhythmic rocking, Hornwell felt his own pulse quickening.

It was Latham who broke the tension, clapping his hands together and doing his best to smile serenely at Hornwell. "Admiral," he said, "would you like some coffee, some tea, some other potable?"

"Thank you, no," Hornwell replied, his eyes still fixed on Thompson.

The President had slowly lifted his head on hearing the slap of Latham's hands, reaching into his breast pocket to pull out a handkerchief to dab at his lips. Then he turned his eyes on Hornwell. "And do we know the location of all of their ships?" he asked.

Hornwell was surprised at the question; those facts had been presented to the President in a series of meetings with the Joint Chiefs over a long period of time in this very office. "Red Dye Day?" Hornwell said in an effort to jog Thompson's memory.

"Red Dye Day," Thompson replied, his brow creasing as he looked toward Latham. Latham stared blankly at Hornwell. "Red?" the President repeated.

Hornwell, still wanting the President to make an instant recollection, courteously said, "Mr. Latham wasn't in those meetings, sir. You remember it was Henry Kraus—Kraus, Mr. President. And yes, red, because the compound we're using—it's phosphorescent."

"Yes, yes," Thompson said, nodding politely and waiting on Hornwell to proceed.

Hornwell glanced again at Latham and pulled himself erect in his chair. He was determined to do his best to bring the President into the discussion not only as an active participant but as *the* decisive voice. "The plan, Mr. President, the one you reviewed—recently with Secretary Clauson and me—was that at the site of every submerged Soviet submarine—" He waited, hoping the President would now take over.

Thompson merely nodded and said, "At every site, yes. Go on, Admiral."

In that same instant, Thompson, now finally alerted, brows more deeply furrowed, wrestled with all of the implications in Hornwell's statement, desperately trying to recall the details of the meeting.

Hornwell continued. "Of course, we were talking only about submarines submerged outside of their own territorial waters. Our aircraft, that of our allies where necessary, would cover the areas immediately above the submerged positions with a heavy red dye, perhaps a one-square-mile area over each submarine—"

"Red dye, yes, yes. That meeting . . . yes, I recall it, Admiral," the President said, shifting in his chair. "And you're here . . . ?" he asked expectantly, looking at Hornwell.

"We have to take action, Mr. President," Hornwell said sternly. "*Implement* Red Dye Day," he added with emphasis. A few moments passed. "Red Dye Day," Hornwell again repeated. "Sir, I suggest that we advise the Soviets—give them the details of Red Dye Day—and let Mr. Jaggers handle this at State with the Soviet foreign minister."

"I see," Thompson said wearily. "And shouldn't Secretary Clauson be filled in?" Thompson asked a moment later.

"The Secretary was *at* the meeting with you and me, Mr. President. You remember that, I'm sure," Hornwell said, more and more ill at ease.

"Of course. Clauson was present, of course. Now, what I have in mind is that we mark the site of every Soviet submarine—every submerged submarine not in their own waters—simultaneously, with red dye. Every single one of them, no exception, right?"

"Correct, sir," Hornwell said.

"This requires a good deal of thought," Thompson said. "You agree, don't you, Admiral?"

"Decision, sir," Hornwell insisted. "What is required is your decision."

Thompson looked over toward Latham. "You've made notes, Tom?"

Latham held up a small pad in which he'd been jotting down the substance of the meeting.

"Well then," Thompson said, "we'll review all of this." Then, as a sign that he was on top of the situation, he turned to

Hornwell and said, "It was good of you to come by ... to fill me in ..."

"And your decision, sir?" Hornwell demanded.

"We'll come to it, Admiral, we'll come to it," he said, as he extended his hand, "and my thanks for your coming by—"

Hornwell, no longer trying to conceal his exasperation, took the President's hand. "We *must* have your decision, Mr. President. "Today," he said firmly.

Thompson nodded. "I know, I know that's what you want. I appreciate your concern. And you'll have it, you'll have it." He shut his eyes and slumped down in his seat. "In due time, Admiral," he said, glancing up momentarily and adding, "Thank you, Admiral." Slowly he began to rock in the chair.

Latham rose and led Hornwell to the door. Hornwell glanced back at the President's head, now resting against the slowly moving chair. He'd failed to get what he'd come for, but what alarmed him even more was his realization that the directive might never come.

When he returned to his headquarters ship he sat in the half-lit cabin, aware that he had to make a decision himself. Delays on making official appointments, even to the Supreme Court, could be tolerated, but Red Dye Day had to be implemented by presidential action as soon as possible. He had done his best to get the order from Thompson, but no such order had come. The situation was unacceptable; the Soviets could not be permitted to assume for one instant longer than necessary that they had achieved their long-desired goal of underseas superiority. There were facts he could not in conscience deny. On this issue he had his duty. The Committee had to have the facts. Hawley had to be informed. National Security was at stake. A decision *had* to be taken.

☆ ☆ ☆

The three men met at Downey's, a quiet late-evening rendezvous near George Washington University. At Downey's, there was none of the obvious effort to establish a special atmosphere so characteristic of many of the night spots in Washington, no stained-glass windows, no Tiffany shades, no mid-Victorian artifacts, no attempt to duplicate the twenties or to re-create the honky-tonk atmosphere of an old-fashioned summer resort. Downey's was subdued, its walnut-panelled walls burnished with a patina of elegance. Its heavy carpeting muted the sounds of guests and help; its three chandeliers cast a warm glow over the high-ceilinged room. On a curved banquette, in the back of the room, Harry Thompson sat, flanked by the Whitney brothers, all three oblivious to the presence of others.

Harry Thompson had brought up a subject that was becoming the chief topic of Washington gossip. "Don't believe every word you hear. The old man's in good shape. Maybe not for a marathon run or for a hundred-yard sprint, but for his age, the demands on him—not to worry, he's plenty okay."

"Then why doesn't he make more appearances, hold more press conferences, get out and be seen more?" Lane Whitney asked.

"You already forgetting the trip to the coast? That drive in the rain? All the news photographers, the reporters by the dozens?"

"That was last month," Lane said.

Jeff stirred his drink. "We take your word, Harry, that it?"

"Why not, for Christ sake!" Harry replied defiantly. "And you two can spread it. The bastards that think the old man's going to crack are in for a rude awakening. When the time's right, he'll be all over television, popping up and down in Air Force One, and eating chicken salads like he was running for Congress instead of a second term."

"Well, he better, what with the convention on top of us," Lane said.

"You'll see," Harry said. "And watch your friend Hawley when it happens. See if *he* survives!" Thompson lifted his glass to his lips as he studied Lane Whitney's face. "He's still your friend, isn't he?"

Lane shrugged his shoulders.

"In spite of all that happened?" Harry persisted.

"Let's not go dragging that up again, Harry," Lane said.

"You least of all," Jeff added, eyes suddenly hard.

The three men sat quietly as a young black waiter brought them another round. Gloria Whitney's presence was strong at the table, and Harry felt the oppression within him. "I still can't figure it," he said, as though speaking to himself. "Why . . . why . . . ?"

"Harry! Forget it!" Lane said slowly, emphasizing each syllable.

"But why?" Harry persisted.

"I said forget it!"

Harry shook his head solemnly. "But her going there, to his place—that's what gets me," he persisted. "She wasn't just driving around—"

"Come on, Harry! She knew you went bananas anytime she mentioned Hawley's name. Face it, man, you led her on for a long, long time—"

"Now wait a minute, Lane!" Harry said, putting his drink down.

"Bullshit!"

Jeff Whitney reached a hand across the table and held his brother's arm. "Easy, let's all take it easy."

"The thing is she didn't drive all the way to Hawley's just by accident. *That's* what really bugs me. You want to know the truth—"

"She wanted you to know," Lane said angrily. "I was *there* at your place, pal, remember? Remember how she breezed in and went straight for you. Remember how you reacted?"

Harry Thompson slid back into his chair. He didn't like remembering that last visit and his coldness to her. "You got it wrong, that's all I have to say. That goes for the two of you."

"What it all boils down to is, you let her down, Harry, like Lane said."

"I didn't chauffeur her to Hawley's," Harry retorted.

"Harry, she just wanted to make you jealous."

"She succeeded, Lane. She probably also succeeded in putting an end to Mr. Hawley, no matter how he slices it."

"That doesn't follow, not for me it doesn't," Lane said. "Hawley's no fool."

"He's through. Gloria was his Achilles' heel."

"Harry, just maybe Gloria was *your* Achilles' heel," Jeff said. "If you'd treated her right that last meeting—Lane's filled me in—"

"Nobody's my Achilles' heel, pal. And let's be honest: your sister popping in—uninvited, I might add—thinking she could just drop in and shoot off her mouth every time she had a case of the hots—"

"Back off, fellow," Jeff said, his face flushing.

"I'm telling it the way it was with her. I'm the one who *knows!* Popping pills whenever she got herself all charged up—"

Jeff Whitney's hand whipped out across the table and caught Harry in the mouth. For a moment the three young men sat motionless like a stone tableau.

"Now just—just—a minute!" Harry sputtered, wiping a trickle of blood from his lips. "If you think you can—"

"Can it, Harry. And one more remark about Gloria and I'll finish the job on you, you understand? I came here tonight expecting you to really have the guts to say you were sorry. You left a message with my father about apologizing about *something*. You don't want to remember because you don't choose to remember because you're gutless! Sit and stew in your own guilt!" Jeff picked up his Navy cap and stood up. "Don't ever talk to me anymore about who survives—you, Hawley, or any other son of a bitch! It's Gloria who didn't survive! And she should have." He tapped his brother's shoulder. "You coming?"

Lane looked across the table at Harry Thompson. He shook his head and said, "Jeff wanted to be your friend—all you had to do was to keep your goddamn dumb mouth shut."

Harry held the handkerchief close to his cut lip. In a muffled voice he said, "Fuck off, both of you. And you can calm down, Commander. You just hit the wrong fellow if you don't want to freeze your ass off in some Antarctic supply base. And the same goes for you, Lane. Gloria was your sister, okay." Tears began to well up in Harry's eyes. "I loved her. She knew it. She knew I'd miss her—more than anyone else, and that includes the two of you."

The Whitney brothers stood together, coldly eyeing Harry Thompson's mournful face. "Bastards," Harry said, looking up at them. They turned away abruptly and left him.

20

His back to Betsy, the President quickly riffled through a pile of newspapers spread out on a table behind his desk in the Oval Office. She sat before the desk, patiently waiting for him to dictate. "The way this Sherwood fellow writes you'd think no one ever sees me, I'm in hiding—as though a President, any President, can remain out of sight."

"He's not a George Will. Nobody believes *his* column, Mr. President."

"But they read it," Thompson said irritably as he tossed the paper into the wastebasket. "What's worse, they hear it on television. Such rubbish! Every day reporters see me coming into this office. That's a legacy from Ronald Reagan, and not a bad one. But they still insist I'm hiding."

With that he rubbed his hands together, sat down at his desk. "Now, to a special mission, Betsy." He smiled as he pressed a button that summoned Henry Kraus. "We're going to do a letter. The one I started some time ago, if you remember, the one I wanted Mrs. Curtis to write. She either couldn't write it or didn't want to, no matter. It's *going* to be written. You're going to make an original, Xerox one copy, and bring them *both* to me. You understand? Both."

"Yes, sir."

"And then you're to destroy your notes." He saw the look of surprise on Betsy's face.

"This is going to be a personal note for one other man's eyes *only*. Mr. Turgenev's. The copy will go in my private safe."

At that moment Kraus entered the office.

"Henry, I want you to call the Soviet embassy. Speak only to the ambassador. I want you to advise him that Betsy King will be coming over, in about one hour—no, make it two—in exactly two hours, to hand deliver a letter that she will place in his hands only. I want him to send it pronto by his number-one courier. I want it handed *directly* to Mr. Turgenev. Is that clear?"

"Yes, Mr. President," Kraus said, wondering whether, as Chief of Staff, he would be taken into the President's confidence regarding the nature of the letter.

"Thank you, Henry."

Kraus stood silent, surprised and vexed at the abrupt dismissal. The President turned his attention to Betsy. "Now, Betsy," the President said, "maybe we can change the world today. Let's you and I get to it." With that he stretched his hands behind his head and said, "My dear Nikita . . ." Then, noting Kraus standing in the doorway, he said, "What is it, Henry?"

"Tom Latham wanted to know if you'd made your decision."

"Decision?"

"About Admiral Hornwell's visit last night. Red Dye Day?" he added helpfully.

Thompson looked puzzled. "Red Dye . . . ?" he scratched his chin. "No, no. I haven't. I haven't had time to think it out. I may want to go over it with Tom later."

"Tom seemed to think the matter was urgent. He wanted to remind you that Admiral Hornwell was insistent, even to the point of demanding—"

"I know, I know," Thompson said, waving him off, "everybody's problems are urgent. We'll get to it. You tell him that. Meanwhile," he said, pointing to Betsy King, "Betsy and I have something *I* think is urgent. Okay?"

Kraus nodded and left. "Now, Betsy, where were we?"

"My dear Nikita."

"Yes, yes. My dear Nikita . . ."

☆ ☆ ☆

Seated in his sumptuous New York office overlooking Central Park, Joe Gratton squinted through the thick lenses of his glasses as he read the tearsheet handed to him by Wally Courtright, the scrawny tough little Irishman who headed Federal Broadcasting's news department. "I'll be damned!" Gratton said, as he slid his glasses to the top of his head. "That prick Vance! Son of a bitch! What do you make of this, Wally?"

"He's certainly singled us out, boss."

"Bastard!" Gratton grumbled as he pulled his glasses back down and read from the text. " 'The network policy of pandering to the lowest common denominator in audience taste—' " He glanced up at Courtright. "Now, there's an original charge, as though we haven't heard the same garbage every few years— 'participated in by all of the networks, with, perhaps, the programs of the Federal Broadcasting Company leading the way—' How in the hell do you like that?"

"He's an obvious candidate now, and he's out for headlines," Courtright said.

"Well, he's cut himself off from *this* network," Gratton said, "and if our competitors down the street will stop kissing ass, he won't find too many welcome mats out there, either."

"I wouldn't count on them, Joe," Wally said.

Gratton loosened his tie as he picked up a carafe and poured himself a drink. "Figures. Little pricks'll sit back and enjoy watching Vance hold the soles of my feet to the fire—you can count on it. Ever since we started getting top ratings."

"What about your friend Hawley? Any help there?"

"How? They got him boxed in. Thompson's dumping on him. Vance looks like he's got the President's blessing."

"What about the party? Hawley's pretty popular."

"So's the President, unfortunately," Gratton grumbled. "I'm sick and tired of these goddamn politicians—remember that lying white-haired son-of-a-bitch Tom Dodd, who got himself censured, and rightly so?—all of them rehashing the same tired complaints." Suddenly, Gratton slapped the top of his desk. "Got it! Got it!" He clenched both fists. "Maybe Mr. Hawley *can* do us a little favor. We've been doing a fair amount of nice little things for the White House for some time. Things they're interested in, particularly the First Lady. That Arts Committee. Beautifying Washington—"

"Yeah, and the special on the old houses off Lafayette Park—"

"Right. Now I've got something better than that, a hell of a lot better," Joe said. "The series Hawley himself once suggested on the story of the First Ladies, hosted by her nibs herself. Get it?" Gratton rubbed a hand over his fleshy face, a malicious smile creasing it. "Yeah, I'll call Mr. Hawley. He's going to like this. The First Lady's a natural on television, trained to it. She does it—we promote the bejeezus out of the series, and the Senator? Attacking us? He'll be sitting there in his own fucking stew, serves him right!"

Courtright nodded appreciatively.

Gratton poured a second glass and pushed it to Courtright. "Let's you and me drink on this, Wally. Only thing we have to worry about is her nibs balking at the timing. But maybe not."

"Even if she stalls, it can't stop us publicizing our *intentions* to do a First Ladies series. That's got to eventually involve her," Wally suggested.

"Good thinking. I'll talk to Hawley. He's got to like this. It puts Mr. Vance on the spot—on the defensive—criticizing the only network that's promoting the First Lady."

☆ ☆ ☆

The President stared with intense irritation as he observed a team of workmen putting the finishing touches on the modest renovating that returned Kathy's sitting room to its former traditional status as the First Lady's bedchamber, and his shoulders sagged as new furnishings were carried past him. Retreating into his own study, he was surprised to find Kathy seated across from his desk, waiting for him.

"I don't mind saying it's painful, watching those men down the hall, Kathy."

"I'm sorry, Stephen, but I think it's for the best—for both of us."

"The best," he repeated as he made his way to his chair, sitting down and letting his head rest against its back.

She'd been holding a hand-painted Civil War lead soldier she'd given him. Then, as she put it back she said quietly, "I've done some thinking, Stephen. I'm not a professional politician, you know that. But I do know something about politics, if only from a woman's intuition. And one thing I know: Clifford Hawley's done his best for you. And I don't think you're being fair to him. That's what I came to say."

Thompson's head snapped forward, the veins suddenly throbbing. "Fair ... best ... fine words. But these are attributes that don't necessarily carry weight in a political world."

"Stephen, I only know the good he did for you in the past, the way he worked—"

"Please," he said, raising a hand, cutting her off. "I'd like you to stay out of this, Kathy."

"I simply wanted you to know how I feel, that's all."

"I already know how you feel. I remember your recommending him to me—"

"I was one of many," she reminded him. "Won't you reconsider your decision?"

"That decision's been made." They stared at each other for a moment, then Thompson suddenly chuckled. "He sent you, didn't he?"

Kathy drew herself up in her chair. "I saw him last night at the Kennedy Center. On business, Mr. President, official business. On the Arts Committee, to which you appointed me. And him."

"He sent you, Kathy. And if he didn't send you, he enlisted your support. He's contacted people all over town trying to enlist their support, but it won't do any good." He took out a key and opened the center drawer of his desk, extracting a folder. "You're too young to remember Senator Joe McCarthy holding up a batch of papers, like this," he said as he waved the folder over his head, "telling his adversaries—the whole world, for that matter—that what was in those papers would bring down the State Department because he had a secret list of 205 known Communist sympathizers. Claimed he had their names." Thompson paused momentarily, then lashed out, eyes fixed on Kathy. "Maybe Mr. McCarthy didn't have all the facts *he* should have had, but *I* do. I have enough. In these papers that I am holding—"

"Stephen, I can't bear it, the way you look at me, as though I were—" her shoulders shuddered as she stopped speaking.

"Enemy? Is that the word?"

Kathy looked at him in astonishment. "No, that isn't the word! Oh, Stephen, has it come down to that? I'm your enemy?" She paused for a moment, shaking her head. "What I was saying was that you look at me as though I weren't your *wife*, as though I have no concern for your health ... When I know you should cut back and get more rest—"

"Play into their hands, that it? I have no time for that, Kathy."

Then, marshalling his strength, his voice firm, he added, "Now, let me continue. This man McCarthy had a special technique—baffled his enemies for years. He'd make a charge, and then while the debate was on to force him to reveal his facts, he'd make another charge—he kept everybody off balance. In this case, like I said, I know how Mr. Hawley's emissaries are racing around town—passing the word about my questionable capacity—"

"I don't believe it!" Kathy said.

"Doesn't matter. When reckless charges are made against you, you have to prepare a response. I have in my hands—" again he lifted the papers "—sworn allegations that Gloria Whitney did not leave the Vice President's home that fateful night until long *after* Mr. Hawley returned—"

"That's not true, Stephen, and you know it!" she exclaimed, leaping to her feet.

An ugly grin cut across Thompson's pale lips. "I didn't say it was. But these are statements made by people who *swear* they were present—"

"Who?" she demanded.

Thompson deliberately placed the papers back in the center drawer, turned the key, and then threw open his hands. "Employees."

"They're lying!"

"Could be. I didn't say they were anything but allegations. But they fit in with the coroner's report—his new study on the time of Gloria Whitney's death—"

"Stephen, I don't want to believe you'd lend your name to such ugly fabrications! You know they're not true!"

"I repeat, I haven't said they *were* true. They're just allegations as of the moment. Nothing's been proven. Nothing's been publicized. No one's been charged, yet," he added grimly. And then his voice hardened. "But when these allegations *are* made public, along with a dossier of other alleged charges of influence peddling, financial benefits, and the like—Mr. Hawley will have no alternative—"

"I can't believe you would allow yourself or anyone else to use such tactics, Stephen. Why?"

"You want a motive?" Thompson shot back. "I intend to continue in this office. I intend to win reelection. And I'll do whatever is necessary to block Mr. Hawley. And block him I shall! And you, Mrs. Thompson," he said with emphasis, "you may take back that message!"

"And you would deliberately ruin Clifford Hawley in the process?"

He studied her face for a moment before replying. Then he said softly, "Before he ruins me," he said, "yes."

"Do you know, as a fact, that he's actually plotting against you?" she asked.

"A man full of contemptible plans doesn't go around advertising them."

She shook her head with impatience. "But how do you *know*?" she persisted.

Thompson chuckled. "I know, Kathy, because I have friends. I won't be surprised when he springs his scheme, whatever it is—"

"*If* he springs it—isn't that what you mean?"

"When," Thompson snapped. "You mark my words, Mrs. Thompson, when the time comes he won't say a word to you, either. But he'll stoop to low tactics, of that you can be certain."

"And is taping conversations a low tactic, Stephen?"

Thompson flushed.

"Would you stoop to that?" she said, pressing him.

"*I* wouldn't," he said sharply.

"And your subordinates?"

"They know I would disapprove of that. That I *do* disapprove. Does that answer your question?" He watched her, waiting for her response.

"I don't know," she said, finally.

"It's clear to me," the President said as he continued to study Kathy's face, "that you may not be able to make a choice of *whose* ruination you prefer to see—"

"Neither!" she exclaimed vehemently. "Neither!"

The President nodded. "I'd prefer it that way myself, but matters have moved along too far. It's not that you *may* have to face that choice, Kathy, it's that you *must*."

☆ ☆ ☆

Hawley, about to sit down to breakfast at his home, stood transfixed as he stared at the newspaper headline detailing the brutal physical attack on Vivien Lessing in her Bel-Air home. Shock and anger surged through his body as he instantly thought of Daniels and Daniels' assurance that she wouldn't be a "problem." The thought had no sooner occurred to him than an usher hurriedly entered the room, picked up a telephone from its corner stand, and advised him that Daniels was on the other end. "Hawley here," he said, his voice edged with anger.

"Mr. Vice President," Daniels said politely, "there's a story in this morning's paper—"

"I've seen the headline, Richard." Hawley's voice came across hard and cold.

"Don't jump to conclusions, sir," Daniels said placatingly. "I have one of our best men on the job—"

"If he was in any way involved—"

"Sir," Daniels said cutting in, "Frank Taggart's *here*, here in town, been here for *weeks*," Daniels emphasized, "and right now he's on his way out to the coast to find out exactly what did happen."

"You don't *know?*" Hawley asked.

"Correct," Daniels replied smoothly.

"This is the kind of event that could derail—"

"No way, sir. And if I may make a suggestion, no contacts, no messages—"

"I can't ignore this, Richard," Hawley protested.

"Flowers, then. Once. But nothing else. Simply stay out of it. It's none of your affair, and I recommend you keep your distance."

Hawley reflected for a moment. "And you were surprised, Richard?"

"I was surprised, yes," Daniels echoed, "but we'll find out what really happened. Count on it."

21

Standing at a window in her Geneva hotel, Alice Curtis pulled the heavy drapes apart to look out at the gardens below. "Ralph, why would the President insist on writing a letter to Turgenev at this particular time?" she asked, turning to face Saunders as he tamped tobacco into his meerschaum pipe. "And Voroshilov *knows*, you're sure?"

"That a letter exists, yes," he replied. "But he wouldn't volunteer anything beyond what he's already said. So I think he's as much in the dark as we are."

Alice frowned. "You think Voroshilov really thinks that we don't know, either? Do you think the rest of them know?"

"The Russians?" Ralph shrugged. "I doubt it. Voroshilov was told something, obviously. When he took us aside, I suspect his team may have been as surprised as we were; I think all they know is something's up, period. You know their mentality: 'Theirs not to make reply, theirs not to reason why, theirs but to do and die.'"

"You're speaking of the English."

"Russian diplomats are exactly like British soldiers in following orders."

There was a tap on the door. "Come in," Alice said. Carolyn Hemsley, Mrs. Curtis's assistant, entered. "Mr. Voroshilov's aide just called. The ambassador's on his way to Moscow, he said, but he'll be back in twenty-four hours, forty-eight at the most. That was the message. Except that he did want to remind you that you left suddenly a week or more ago and were gone for more than forty-eight hours while *they* had to wait."

"Anything else?"

"That was it."

"Thank you, Carolyn." Alice turned to Saunders as Carolyn let herself out. "You remember how Voroshilov said that the message—how did he label it?"

"A message for mankind."

"Yes. That the President's message for mankind had impressed Mr. Turgenev—*how* he didn't say—but he did say it would be reviewed."

"By every man in the Politburo, you can be sure," Ralph said.

"But he stressed the confidentiality of it," Alice said.

"All the more reason he'll share it with his closest advisers," he said dryly.

"The problem," Mrs. Curtis said, "is *we're* the ones left in the dark. By our own President. Why?"

"I'd say we were put there deliberately," Saunders replied, "maybe even with a touch of indifference." He puffed on his pipe. "Not like the President."

"Could he have skipped Mr. Clauson? Mr. Jaggers? Could he have bypassed all of Defense, Admiral Hornwell? All of State? Every desk?" Alice asked, perplexed.

"They've *all* been skipped," Saunders replied. "Otherwise we'd know *something*."

"But why?"

"Politics?"

"Not with disarmament talks, Ralph."

"Really, Alice," he said with a smile, "a man sends a letter to another man about 'a message for mankind' and you don't think politics is at work? Can you visualize the impact? The President of the United States, the President of the Soviet Union? The two of them meeting by some lake? In some woods? In an old palace of the Czar? Two human beings seated in isolation with no one there but their interpreters, settling all of the problems of the world, five billion people waiting for them to come out and declare peace for the next millennium?"

"Bush tried it once, started it as a matter of fact, in the winter of '89. But before he did he took care, quietly consulting some of his key advisers." Alice looked at her watch. "I must talk with Secretary Jaggers."

Ralph Saunders put another match to his pipe. "I suspect you'll find he'll be as surprised as we are," he said, puffing away vigorously.

☆ ☆ ☆

At the close of the day, the members of the Committee met in their Virginia retreat at the urgent request of the Secretary of State, and on this occasion he had insisted that the Vice President attend the meeting. An ominous black sky had hovered over Washington all during the afternoon, and a heavy downpour had followed the rolling waves of thunder interspersed with flashes of lightning.

It was Daniels who opened the meeting. "We have two items on the agenda." He turned to Hornwell. "Admiral?"

Hornwell cleared his throat. Briefly, he recounted his efforts to get the presidential authority to implement Red Dye Day.

"You mean he heard you present the facts and he sat there doing *nothing?*" Secretary Clauson was fuming.

"The President said he wanted to think about it," Hornwell replied reluctantly.

"What's there to think about?" Clauson demanded. "The NSC, the Pentagon have approved the plans, this Committee approved the plans—"

"Admiral Hornwell," Daniels said softly, "do you have a recommendation?"

Hornwell swallowed hard as he stared across at Hawley. "We must have authorization. I could go back," he added lamely, "perhaps with Secretary Clauson, Secretary Jaggers, both. Perhaps I didn't make the facts clear enough."

"We need that decision," Clauson said, "and we need it now!"

Daniels raised a hand. "You're right, Mr. Secretary, but before we set our course regarding Red Dye Day, let's hear from the Secretary of State. Mr. Jaggers?"

Jaggers brushed his moustache and then presented the gist of a conversation with Alice Curtis. "That's it, gentlemen. The Soviets have the President's letter. Mr. Turgenev and his key men know what's in it. Ambassador Voroshilov surely knew something about it, too, when he spoke with Ambassador Curtis. The only ones who *don't* have a clue are the Americans. Including this Committee."

It was Daniels who spoke first. "The President sent a letter to the Soviet President. Without consultation with you, Mr. Secretary? No consultation with the Secretary of Defense? The Vice President? The Chairman of the Joint Chiefs? The President's Chief of Staff, Mr. Kraus?" Daniels stretched his hands on the table and looked around the table. "What isn't clear," Daniels said, "is what prompted the President to torpedo his own team in Geneva. And most of all, how could the President short-circuit the decision-making process of his own Administration?"

Anthony Clauson broke the silence. "Let's label this for what it is, a very improper, very irregular, very impulsive action." His genial expression was absent as he continued, the words spilling out. "What in the hell's going on here! No decision on Red Dye Day! That's something of extreme urgency! We have people who spend their lives trying to figure out what the Soviets think! Churchill spelled it out over forty years ago and it's as true now as it was then—the Russians? 'A riddle wrapped in a mystery inside an enigma.' Bush never really knew Gorbachev, we don't know Turgenev. Here we are, we have a National Security Adviser, a Senior Director on Soviet Affairs, every think tank on call! Ever since Director Webster the CIA has its own strategic planning office concentrating on the Soviet Union and nuclear proliferation! We have other teams of experts—Curtis, Saunders, all of their backup technical people—sitting in the midst of negotiations where every goddamn 't' that's crossed, every 'i' that's dotted, needs confirmation from Moscow, or from here, before there's any movement." Clauson hammered the table as he lashed out. "First he can't make a decision! Then he sends out a letter on his own initiative? What in hell has gotten in the President? Has he lost his senses?"

Oliver Moran reached out to squeeze his arm. "Tony, hold on, let's all stay calm—"

"Calm?" Clauson said. "I'm calm, Oliver. But I'm also goddamn mad!"

Moran said, "Other Presidents have written letters to various world leaders, we know that. But they've also done it with advice from the NSC, or the Cabinet, or the White House staff. This is different. Secret. At least secret from all of the President's own advisers. Very unusual." Moran paused for a moment and then went on. "What concerns me at the moment is that it could break into print. Not from our side, but from the

Soviets'. This was a one-to-one message, and now Mr. Turgenev has the ball. He can run with it if he chooses to . . ."

"He's had Voroshilov leave Geneva," Jaggers said. "They'll talk. The Politburo will talk."

"And the United States government is totally in the dark!" Clauson interjected angrily. "Nobody in the Congress knows! Nobody in the Cabinet! Nobody on the President's staff! Nobody negotiating in Geneva! Gentlemen, we don't have a one-man government! Even Turgenev talks with his peers!"

Daniels turned toward Hawley. "Mr. Vice President?"

Hawley felt all eyes turn on him. He knew that what he said could measure him for his ability to analyze a problem quickly, to offer a solution, and to provide leadership. "I believe we should proceed carefully but with dispatch." He glanced across at Hornwell. "The problem is that even with the best of intentions—the President's intentions—this government faces the possibility of a major embarrassment—the option to capitalize on that, unfortunately, left open only to Mr. Turgenev, unless—" Hawley stopped for a moment.

"Unless?" Jaggers echoed.

"Unless we checkmate him. And that's a move only the President can still make. I believe that the Secretary of State should seek a meeting with the President. I'd suggest contacting Henry Kraus tonight to set the time."

"And the object of that meeting, Mr. Vice President?" Daniels asked.

"To persuade the President that it's vital that the contents of his letter be made available to the Secretary and, through him, to Ambassador Curtis, who must be armed with the same information as Ambassador Voroshilov. At the very least our people in Geneva must be on equal terms with their counterparts."

"And if the President refuses to meet with the Secretary of State—?" Jaggers asked, turning to Daniels, feeling that he, himself, was the chief member slighted by the President.

"I suggest you ask the Admiral," Daniels replied.

"Mr. Daniels," Hornwell said, "unless and until the President of the United States breaks a law or commits an act that is clearly unconstitutional, I serve him!" Then, leaning across the table, he said pointedly to Daniels, "If this letter is so critical, why don't you do as the Vice President suggests, contact him *tonight!*"

Daniels nodded. "A good suggestion, Admiral," he replied

coolly, "because I'm not at all certain that we want to wait for an illegal or unconstitutional event to take place." He turned to the others. "If I judge the sense of this meeting, I must conclude that we agree that we do have two extremely serious issues here." He turned to Jaggers. "Mr. Secretary, perhaps you should undertake to discuss this with Mr. Kraus and see if the President might meet with you and Secretary Clauson despite the hour—and if not tonight, first thing in the morning?" He glanced at each of the members of the Committee, then pointed to his left. "Mr. Secretary, you know there's a direct telephone link to the White House in that office. Would you now please make that call, sir?"

☆ ☆ ☆

At the very moment the Committee was about to go into its session, another meeting was taking place at the White House. Henry Kraus had done his best in recommending to the Senator from Kansas that he defer his request until the morning, but Vance had been insistent.

"The President has had a strenuous day, Senator," Kraus had said, stretching his legs across the edge of his desk in his own office. "I really would repeat—"

"This can't wait, Henry. A decision must be made this evening. I'm sorry."

Kraus was annoyed. He hated to intrude on the President after his last scheduled appointment. What also irritated him was the simple fact that he had to pay more attention to Senator Vance these days.

"Henry," Vance said, half whispering, "this matter involves the First Lady." He noted the impact on Kraus as Kraus's legs slid off the desk.

"Could she be helpful?" Kraus ventured.

Vance shook his head energetically. "No, no, no," he said hurriedly. "This isn't anything I'd care to discuss *with* her." Then he added, "It's a matter that only the President can handle, *must* handle, Henry. That's all I can say. Now, Henry," he said, pointing to Kraus' phone, "if you would be so kind . . ?"

"I'm not at all certain that this is the time to do this, Senator. I know the President. I know how fatigued he can be—on some days." His eyes went to Vance's. "You insist?" Vance simply nodded.

☆ ☆ ☆

The two of them were finally together with the President in his study. Vance outlined the nature of the hearings he was about to begin on the subject of sex and violence on television. And in his heart he hoped the matter of the convention might arise, too. He knew this was an opportunity to zero in on the Twenty-fifth Amendment—and another might not arise in time.

"I like your doing that, Senator," Thompson said. "My son's got a little group of concerned people who might assist you and your staff."

"Thank you, Mr. President," Vance said. "I would welcome their assistance. In fact, Harry has already been helpful."

"Good, good."

"It's what Mr. Gratton—he's the head of Federal Broadcasting—is planning that has me a bit disturbed. We're going to invite him into a hearing within the next ten days. We'll issue a subpoena for him and some papers. But I just learned that his network is planning to do a series of specials—you'll understand how fortuitous this all sounds, and you'll understand why I had to bring it to your attention at the very first opportunity—the series is to be built around the subject of the history of our First Ladies. And, of course, it goes without saying," he continued, as he noted a scowl cross the President's face, "they will certainly want the First Lady to participate. My contact has advised me that an invitation will be issued tomorrow."

"Damned clever of Mr. Gratton," Thompson commented. "And your concern—I understand it. With Mrs. Thompson on their network, your investigation . . . it's very obvious. You're in the very unenviable position of investigating a network that's been smart enough to cozy up to the White House. Isn't that it?"

"Precisely," Vance said.

Thompson looked across the room at his Chief of Staff. "Henry?"

"It could be very awkward," Kraus agreed. "The White House cooperating with the network. The Senate investigating that network."

"Investigating them for promoting gratuitous violence and exploitative sex at times when a large portion of the television audience is made up of young people," Vance added.

"Well, sir," Thompson said. "The First Lady is simply not

going to be available. Henry, you can speak to her Chief of Staff, what's his name?"

"Sheridan. Russell Sheridan."

"That's the fellow," Thompson said. He poured himself a glass of water and shook out a pill from a small vial. As he put it to his mouth, he said to Vance, "Helps keep the old motor perking."

Vance was pleased. He decided to push one more point. "I don't want to underestimate this Gratton fellow, Mr. President. He was once Mrs. Thompson's employer." Again he noted a sign of irritation on the President's face.

"Well, he isn't now!" Thompson said. An aide appeared at the doorway. "What is it, Simon?"

"A call for Mr. Kraus, sir."

"Well, it'll have to wait, thank you," Kraus said.

"They said it was most urgent, sir."

Thompson pointed to a phone. "If you want to, Henry, or there's a phone in the corridor . . ."

Kraus asked, "Who's calling?"

"Secretary Jaggers, sir."

Thompson scowled again. "Jaggers, eh? I can guess what that's all about. Go on, Henry, go on, take it."

"No, it can wait. Tell him I'll call him back," Kraus said to Simon as he withdrew.

Thompson stood up, Vance rising with him, satisfied that his message had gotten through, but hoping the meeting could be prolonged. Thompson obliged him. "No hurry, Senator. It was good of you to come by, to let us know. And Henry will instruct Mr. Sheridan that Federal Broadcasting's invitation has been rejected. By the White House. That ought to put a little crimp in Mr. Gratton's plan."

The President sipped some more water. Vance was now determined to take the leap and raise the issues that had been discussed with Hornwell. It would be difficult, but it had to be done. He listened politely as the President rambled on.

"Amazing," Thompson was saying, "the little games people want to play. The hordes of people clawing at you for attention, approval, do this, do that. Jaggers calling Henry. Margaret would have made mincemeat of him. You never met her?"

"No, I regret that, Mr. President."

Thompson stopped for a moment, placing both hands on his desk. "Margaret helps me frequently. Great head on her shoulders." Vance looked first at the President and then at Kraus, trying to conceal his astonishment at the President's remarks. Thompson chuckled again. "I try to get her to stop smoking. That's her one vice. But that's far outweighed by her brilliant mind . . . We both like the Hornwells. Good bridge players, both of them."

Vance glanced again at Kraus, but Kraus's enigmatic face gave no clue as to whether he, in turn, was puzzled by Thompson's non sequiturs or his reference to Hornwell's wife as Vance was: it was public knowledge that the Admiral had been a widower for many years. The Senator quickly concluded that this was an experience not at all uncommon to Kraus.

At that moment Thompson dropped into his chair, placing a hand to the back of his head, beginning to rub it. "A touch sore," he said. Kraus got up and came around the President's side of the desk. "Henry," the President said as he tried to form each word carefully, "you sig . . . press . . ." Kraus reached under the edge of the desk and pushed hard on a buzzer.

"Commander Jensen will be right here, Mr. President," Kraus said. Then he looked across at Vance.

Vance immediately caught the signal and got up from his chair. "Mr. President," he said, feeling the need to escape as quickly as he could, "my thanks for your seeing me. And my apology for dropping by so late."

Thompson lifted a hand in acknowledgment, a faint smile on his face. Vance nodded and took his leave. Now he understood Kraus's reluctance to hold a late meeting. More than that, he felt new misgivings about Thompson's health, and with it a concern about his own prospects for being on the ticket if—and it was a big if—the President could be held together for a few more weeks.

☆ ☆ ☆

Jaggers' failure to reach Kraus was received with irritation by the Committee, but a few minutes later the phone rang in the outer office. An aide beckoned to Jaggers. Hastily leaving the Committee room again, Jaggers picked up the phone in the outer office. It was Kraus. "Henry, I very much appreciate your returning the call so quickly," he said.

"What can I do for you, Mr. Secretary?"

"It's most important, Henry, that I see the President. Tonight, if possible. If not tonight, the first thing in the morning. The very *first*."

"Fine, Mr. Secretary," Kraus said, "we can discuss it then."

"I don't mean to be rude, Henry," Jaggers argued, "but I don't want to discuss it with you in the morning. I want an appointment," he insisted. "This matter is most urgent. Secretary Clauson will be joining me."

"Clauson?" Kraus echoed.

"Mr. Kraus," Jaggers said, "we have two very major issues to take up with the President that require immediate—I want to emphasize, *immediate*—attention. There's the matter of Red Dye Day. I'm sure your deputy has filled you in on Admiral Hornwell's visit—"

"He has," Kraus said.

"And the letter, Henry."

"The letter," Kraus repeated.

"The one to Mr. Turgenev," Jaggers said.

"Oh," Kraus said, pausing a moment. "*That* letter."

"The matter of the letter is critical, Henry. Red Dye even more."

Kraus paused again before responding. "Commander Jensen is with the President at this very moment, Mr. Secretary," he confided.

"Oh? Is the President ill?" Jaggers asked, concern in his voice.

"I'm sorry. I can't discuss it any further, Mr. Secretary. Except we can take it up again in the morning."

Jaggers wanted to pursue it further, but after a moment's reflection he said, "All right, Henry. I'll be in touch first thing."

☆ ☆ ☆

The President was unavailable all day. No word leaked from the White House that he was ill beyond a terse statement that he was indisposed, that his appointments had been cancelled and were being expedited by Kraus as Chief of Staff. Everything was being handled in a routine fashion through the bureaucracy of the White House itself. The news, though, had a major impact on members of the Committee.

But it was Clauson who furnished the final element that triggered Daniels into action. Vance, as Chairman of the Senate Armed Forces Committee, had a scheduled conference with the Secretary of Defense at the Pentagon that morning.

"I appreciate your coming over, but I could just as easily have come to your committee room or your office, Senator," Clauson said as he shook hands with Vance.

"You're there frequently enough, Mr. Secretary. It's high time I returned a visit." He crossed the impressive room to look at a large globe, moving it about slowly. "This is just about the only one in Washington that has every new country marked." Taking a chair opposite Clauson, he then said, "I won't waste any time. You know, of course, I was with the President on a trip out west—"

"I read about it," Clauson said politely.

"He handled it well. But seeing him last night—" Vance shook his head.

"You saw him last night?" Clauson said, making every effort to conceal his surprise.

"Late," Vance nodded. "I had a political matter to take up with him, a trifling matter," Vance said, almost apologetically, "but I was struck—" Vance stroked his chin, shaking his head in quiet disbelief.

"Yes, Senator?" Clauson pressed him on, eager to hear more.

"It was his behavior that puzzled me—you're probably much more accustomed to it than I. I had the feeling that, on occasion, his mind simply wandered between different times, you understand?" He stopped for a moment.

Clauson signified his awareness, inclining his body forward.

"A curious mixture, as it were, as though . . ." Vance hesitated again, then said, "There was a moment when he talked of Mrs. Thompson, the *first* Mrs. Thompson—she's been dead for quite a time—"

"I've heard him speak of her," Clauson said politely.

"Yes, of course, but in the present tense? It was most disconcerting. Henry Kraus was there, but he seemed not to be as—how do I say it?—*astonished*—that's the word. It happened right at the very end of our meeting."

"The President's been bothered by an occasional touch of aphasia," Clauson said reassuringly. "He's made no secret of that."

"But last night," Vance continued, "it was more than a word. It was as though he had the present and the past muddled up as though they were identical." He stopped abruptly. "I'm probably making too much of it, Mr. Secretary."

As soon as Vance left, Clauson lost no time in passing the gist of his meeting with Vance to Daniels. And it was Daniels who immediately canvased the group and set up an urgent personal meeting with Hawley.

In Hawley's upstairs office at the vice presidential residence

Daniels said, "It's come down to this, Mr. Vice President. The President's showing signs of impending disability. He won't acknowledge it. I know how much you want to have the unanimous approval of the Committee before any action is taken."

"That's always been my position. And it's the right position, Richard."

"But we have to get down to basics and judge present circumstances," Daniels said. "For example, Red Dye Day is critical. We know that the Kremlin, naturally, is fully aware of the President's cancelling his appointments. We know the Soviet fleet is making a series of unusual movements, notably in the Mediterranean and the north seas. Those movements have to be checked. The Kremlin also knows what's in the President's letter. We, on the other hand, have no knowledge of its contents." Daniels paused to light a cigarette. "We simply cannot permit the government of the United States to appear to be headless," he said, resuming his argument, "especially when a presidential response is required and none is available. The action required of us may be very temporary, and let's hope it is. But it *is* legal. It *is* constitutional. Most of us say it's necessary. What we propose doing is to protect the office."

"Admiral Hornwell?" Hawley asked.

"He knows we can't wait. Hornwell did everything he could to get the decision from the President. I've talked with him— that was very clear in our conversation. For the first time, I'd say Admiral Hornwell shows far less resolve than before, far less opposition to action the rest of this Committee can take—"

"Would he support the Committee?"

"I think he'll abstain."

"So he won't acknowledge the immediate necessity for decisive action on our part, that it?"

"He knows action is necessary. By abstaining he'd be giving his approval—*his* way. I don't believe he'll try to block the rest of us." Daniels snuffed out his cigarette as he watched Hawley. "You're the only one who can set the wheels in motion. You, Mr. Vice President, have a decision to make on your own."

As he sat in the afterglow of a setting sun, its waning strength leaving a shaft of deep shadows across the floor, Hawley saw the image of a wounded lion lurking in the darkness, heard its growl as it licked a gaping wound. In that same swift flight of imagination he pictured the President, seated in his White House upstairs office, thinking perhaps of Hawley as some scavenging predator slinking about, out of reach, waiting to test his ebbing strength. He wanted time to make a final evaluation. "I'd like to take one more crack at Hornwell," he finally said.

"Done," Daniels replied.

"I'll give you my decision tomorrow."

"Time is of the essence," Daniels said.

"Tomorrow," Hawley repeated.

As Hawley escorted Daniels to the entry hall he put aside his temptation to ask about Vivien Lessing, especially on deciding that he'd give priority to using Daniels' services in running down a question that had been gnawing at him from the moment Kathy Thompson had confided her suspicion that her phone calls had been intercepted or even taped.

Daniels listened impassively to Hawley's brief explanation. "That shouldn't be too difficult a matter, Mr. Vice President," he said. "We ought to be able to find the tapes—if there are any," he added.

"I don't want any but your most trusted people involved in this," Hawley warned. "No written transcribing . . ."

"We'll get the answer to your basic question, Mr. Vice President—do such tapes exist? Once we know that, the question of their disposition can be evaluated. Meanwhile, we'll just look into it."

22

Hawley's car approached the parking area at Philadelphia's winding Wissahickon Creek in Fairmount Park; from it he observed his father waiting patiently at the park guardhouse for him, pipe in hand as usual. They greeted each other warmly and made ready to start walking down the gravel road, Hawley's Secret Service escort following some paces behind.

After walking along in silence for some moments, enjoying the steep rock-strewn scenery on both sides of the creek, Hawley said, "We used to do most of our walking on the other side."

His father chuckled. "You probably still could. You remember how I always had a lot of trouble on the narrow path over there, climbing over all those fallen logs and dead leaves? Not to mention the gradual rise of the path—never liked heights. You always liked to clamber up the damndest, most precipitous routes and I simply *had* to follow." Then, after taking a long pull on his pipe, he added, "You seem to be on one of those precipices again. Want to talk about it?"

As they hiked along, Hawley filled in his father on recent events. "That's the situation in a nutshell," he said, resting his hands on the rustic wooden railing of a small bridge crossing the creek. "Leaving me with this question: What's the best thing to do for the country?"

"Really? Is that the real question?" His father shook his head. "I don't think so. The way I see it, the question is: What is best in the interest of Clifford Hawley? And I might add further that what may be in *his* best interest may just coincide very nicely with the best interest of the country."

"And the answer?" Hawley asked.

His father puffed on his pipe. "Survival," he said.

"Isn't that just reducing everything to personal ambition?"

"No, not solely. But in the words of maybe the smartest politician who ever lived—" He smiled as he looked into his son's questioning eyes. "No, not Franklin. Not Lincoln. Not even Franklin D. Roosevelt or Lyndon Johnson. William Shakespeare's the man I have in mind. Stop and think of Shakespeare's advice in *Julius Caesar:*

There is a tide in the affairs of men,
Which, taken at the flood, leads on to fortune;
Omitted, all the voyage of their life
Is bound in shallows and in miseries.

"That's your answer, son. And the alternative is a lifetime obsession with the unanswerable question of what might have been." The professor paused to relight his pipe. "Politics, Clifford. The President's given you three weeks. You can't wait that long. Like your friend Gratton, was it, who told you he's thrown down the gauntlet? Okay. You either let it lie there, or you pick it up."

"And fling it back. That it?"

The old man shrugged. "The President made the first move. You're fond of telling me Washington is just one big jungle. Nice figure of speech. Well, now it's your move. Think about it. And one more thing. Nothing wrong with ambition, not your kind. You've been backing it up by doing your homework, studying, meeting with men and women who can contribute to your own development, your heavy reading—"

"I've tried to keep up with your recommendations."

"Okay. Like I just said, it's your move."

Hawley sat in the darkness of his library, brooding over all of the recent events now pressing in on him, the stinging rebuke— more an ultimatum—from the President, his father's sobering advice, the decisions he felt weighing in heavily upon him.

To do nothing was to allow himself to be manipulated, to

be moved about at another's whim—worse, on that man's misguided judgment. It pained him to think that the man whom he so greatly admired now viewed him, for reasons that still eluded him, as utterly expendable. To resist meant to face what his opponent—for he'd had to acknowledge that the man whom he'd helped ascend to the presidency was now the man who would propel him into obscurity—had thus far failed to do on a matter of extreme national urgency. Red Dye Day *had* to be implemented. There had been enough waffling. Any further delay could jeopardize national security. A President's chief responsibility was to protect and preserve the nation, and that protection, in a time when minutes counted, required leadership and decisive action.

And, too, he was forced to admit, when such action was necessary to preserve one's own place, the proof of leadership was to be measured by that same standard: weigh all of the options and then make a decision.

He reached for the phone and called Daniels.

"Yes, sir," Daniels said from his cold and cheerless office, "I've been sitting waiting for word."

"What about Hornwell?" Hawley asked.

"He called me not ten minutes ago. Said he'd been reviewing all of the issues."

"And?"

"Without going into every detail, the main point is this: he said he wouldn't play the role of obstructionist."

"And your interpretation of that, Richard?"

"He's not with us. He's not against us. He abstains. As I've said before, that to me is his way of giving you the green light." He paused for a moment. "It's your call, Mr. Vice President. Are you ready to make it?"

"I am," Hawley quietly said. "Let it begin."

☆ ☆ ☆

Hawley looked at his watch, pushed back the chair in his office, and headed across the Capitol corridors toward the Speaker's office. It was seven o'clock, the agreed-upon time for him to join the meeting. The Capitol was quiet, the tourists had left, only a few officials were working in their offices. He nodded politely to the security officers stationed inconspicuously in the building.

As he walked on the glazed tiles, passing the Old Senate

Chamber and striding under the Rotunda, fleeting images of great events and great personages drifted through his mind. He remembered Nixon's moving speech when Eisenhower's plain military-issue coffin rested on the Lincoln catafalque; he had watched and listened as a youngster. He remembered Nixon telling the nation how he had asked each member of the Cabinet to visit the dying President.

And now, moving at a measured pace, he knew that another President's Cabinet was to be asked to pass judgment on an issue never before raised in the history of the country—the necessity of removing an ailing President from office—and he, Clifford Hawley, was the instrument through which this momentous issue was now moving inexorably to a decision. Nixon's tribute over Eisenhower, he thought, was the last time that ill-fated Vice President would be remembered for eloquence. Hawley found himself thinking of the words he might use one day as he, too, would speak over the body of his predecessor and then rebuked himself for giving thought to such a macabre image.

Hawley paused as he entered the outer area of the Speaker's suite of offices on the House side of the Capitol. He knew that for the past two hours, behind the heavy doors of the Speaker's inner office, four men had been locked in discussion and were now waiting upon him—Richard Daniels; Edward Jaggers; the Speaker of the House, Alfred Hackett; and the President pro tem of the Senate, David Carson.

A uniformed guard rapped on the door once and pushed it open. Clifford Hawley stepped into the Speaker's stately, high-ceilinged office. As the door quietly closed behind him, the four men in the room rose to greet their visitor.

No one spoke for a few moments; it was apparent from the grave features of each of the four men that a decision had been made; they knew they were standing in the presence of the first Acting President of the United States. All that remained to make matters official was the fulfillment of the mandatory requirements of the Twenty-fifth Amendment.

Hawley stepped forward and with a gracious smile moved toward the Speaker. Alfred Hackett, like John McCormack and Tip O'Neill before him, was a product of Boston, a fighting, red-haired, hard-drinking, hard-talking politician. What he lacked in the dignity of the Lodges, the Lowells, and the other Boston Brahmins he made up for in the inviolability of his word, his trust, his honor. Normally, at the end of the day, cronies of the Speaker gathered in his office to have their jokes and jibes and their first cocktails of the day; on this day there was no sign of levity, no sign of liquor.

Hawley turned to David Carson, the white-maned Senator from Montana. Carson was the conscience of the Senate, a man who had inherited the integrity of his ancestors, pioneers who'd crossed the country in covered wagons a hundred and fifty years before and had absorbed some of the grandeur and bearing of that once-untamed land. Again there was the solemn handshake, the silent acknowledgment that a great decision had been made.

Edward Jaggers crossed before the Speaker's desk and for a brief moment placed both hands on Hawley's shoulders. Then he reached down and picked up a letter from the Speaker's desk and handed it to Hawley.

Hawley saw that it was a letter bearing his own official letterhead. It read: "To the Speaker of the House of Representatives, the Honorable Alfred V. Hackett, and the President pro tempore of the United States Senate, the Honorable David B. Carson: Be it known that I, Clifford D. Hawley, Vice President of the United States, do hereby solemnly swear that the President of the United States, H. Stephen Thompson, is unable to discharge the powers and duties of his office, and that I do now, with the approval of the majority of the principal officers of the executive department, whose signatures along with mine attest to this act taken under the authority of the Twenty-fifth Amendment to the Constitution of the United States of America, assume forthwith the powers and duties of the office as Acting President." The four men remained silent as Hawley slowly pondered the words.

It was Daniels who finally spoke. "We have some matters to discuss, gentlemen." He pointed to a chair and waited for Hawley to take his place. "The date on the letter, the signatures of the Cabinet—the presentation to President Thompson. Some can be obtained tonight—"

Carson put up a hand. "No, it mustn't be that way. They must meet, as a group, feel free to debate, then sign."

Daniels lit a cigarette. "We can't risk that, Senator."

"Until morning? Is there risk in waiting until morning?"

"President Thompson could make his mind up to dismiss quite a few members of the Cabinet, and where, I ask, would that leave us?" The Senator frowned and was about to speak as Daniels continued. "We can't risk it, Senator, just can't risk it. We already know *some* of their plans." He turned to Hawley.

"None of us knows the President's *intentions*. The President—he still has capacity to take action—" He let the sentence hang there, waiting on the others.

"I withdraw my objection," Carson said.

"I recommend that the date be as of tonight," Daniels said, lifting his head and blowing a small circle of smoke over the Speaker's desk. "Any objections?"

The group turned their attention to Hackett. "None," he said, as he pressed a buzzer. A middle-aged secretary responded to his summons. "Date it tonight," the Speaker said as he handed her the letter.

Daniels resumed the initiative. "Secretary Jaggers has given me a list of the members of the Cabinet with whom he conferred today. He will personally visit each man; each man has assured the Secretary he will be at home tonight. I have a car waiting—and a backup car as well in case of an emergency—and the driver has mapped out the route for speed of contact—"

He stopped speaking as the Speaker's secretary returned with the document. "I have an officer in the car who will call ahead to each member of the Cabinet whose signature we must have, advising him that the Secretary of State is on his way." Daniels reached over for an ashtray. "Any questions, gentlemen?" There were none. "In that case, gentlemen, I think the Vice President should now sign the document."

"No," Hawley said.

Daniels' hand stopped as he was about to snuff out his cigarette, his head cocked toward Hawley, a look of disbelief on his face.

Jaggers had half risen in his chair.

"Don't misunderstand me, gentlemen," Hawley said, breaking the tension and placating them. "I *will* sign. I think, though, that the document needs one additional paragraph."

"It's legal just the way it is," Jaggers insisted.

"It's not the legality I question. It's the spirit. History must know that in taking this unprecedented move, we did so with honor and with respect to the office and to the man who occupies it."

"What are you suggesting?" Jaggers asked.

"Something brief. Something that says, 'The undersigned look forward to the day when the President shall be fully able to resume the powers and duties of his office.'"

"That's in accordance with the Amendment. No problem," Daniels said.

The Speaker sent for his secretary and Hawley dictated the new paragraph.

"Most commendable, Mr. Hawley, most commendable," Senator Carson said. "The President should know that this was your suggestion."

"It may be helpful with one or two Cabinet officers on the borderline," Jaggers added.

The Speaker studied the paper as his secretary returned it to him. "It would be better, of course, if the Cabinet vote turns out unanimous," he said.

"By getting the signatures of the eight who *are* absolutely firm on this *first*—then the others seeing that—it could be unanimous," Daniels said.

"These are honorable men and women, Mr. Daniels," Carson said, "and you have to be prepared for some of them in all good conscience to decline."

"They'll want to serve in the Acting President's Cabinet," Daniels answered imperturbably. "Believe me, when they see the first signatures—"

"Mr. Daniels is right," Hackett said. "And now, Mr. Vice President," he said as he handed Hawley a pen, "your signature."

☆ ☆ ☆

The black limousine rolled quietly through the early-morning fog that enshrouded Washington, the four men in it as locked in their personal thoughts as the immobile figure of Lincoln barely visible in the swirling low clouds. Daniels sat hunched in a corner of the car, eyes closed. Jaggers, in the middle, toyed with his Phi Beta Kappa key dangling from a gold chain stretching across his vest—a formal touch to his clothes even in summer. Alfred Hackett stared out the edge of the window, in his hand the briefcase that held the document that would end the presidency of H. Stephen Thompson, signed by ten of the thirteen members of the Cabinet. David Carson, nervous, kept running his hands through his white hair and studied the back of the chauffeur's head.

It was eight o'clock.

Hawley sat at his desk in his White House office. It had been agreed that he would remain there while Jaggers, Carson, and Hackett called upon the President to present him with the momentous decision taken the night before. As he listened to the cheerful chirping of birds outside, he wondered, lugubriously, if vultures ever sang.

Henry Kraus had been surprised to see Hawley, the first time in weeks Hawley had occupied his White House office so early. When Hawley passed him in the corridor, Kraus had barely greeted him, smugly enjoying the fact that he had a closer intimacy with the President than did the Vice President. Kraus headed toward his own office, more spacious, more impressive than the Vice President's, occupying the large corner suite at the end of the long corridor leading to the Oval Office of the President.

It was 8:10 in the Oval Office. The President, as it had happened so often before, had thrown off his indisposition and now sat behind his desk, sipping a cup of hot coffee. Tom Latham stood before the French windows leading to the Rose Garden. Thompson picked up the paper on his desk, and held it out toward Latham. Latham strode over and read it, nodding his head with satisfaction. As he finished, Kraus entered the office. Latham greeted him and turned to Thompson. "When does this go to the press, Mr. President?"

"After this meeting." The President rose and stretched himself. "Everything set with the press, Henry?"

"All set."

"Nothing's leaked?"

"No, sir."

"Good."

"This is a first in our history," Latham said.

"An unfortunate necessity," replied the President.

"Will you reappoint any of the members of the Cabinet?"

"Two or three, maybe four. But seven will be dismissed for sure. You and I know who they are," Thompson said.

"They'll never know what hit them."

"They'll know," the President chuckled. "And the phones will ring, oh how they'll ring. They'll want to explain."

"I can hear some of the snivelling right now," Kraus said.

It was 8:15. Daniels and his group entered the north entrance foyer of the West Wing of the White House. George Kane, the President's Appointments Secretary, met the visitors with his official smile. Daniels slipped off to his right and headed to Hawley's office. Kane, a young lawyer, his thinning blond hair neatly parted and trimmed, led the rest of the party through his office down the main corridor to the Oval Office.

"This way, gentlemen. The President's expecting you." He rapped on the door and then pushed it open. Jaggers, Hackett, and Carson entered. The group was surprised to find Thompson looking fit, hands in his coat pockets, standing before his desk.

"Gentlemen," the President said affably as he offered his hand to each of his visitors. After the amenities, he waved the group to seats across from his desk, then walked over to Latham, took the paper from his hand, and joined the others.

"How are things on the Hill?" he asked as he let himself slip into a wing chair, turning his attention to Carson.

"Fine. Fine, sir," the old Senator replied, sitting across from Thompson in a companion chair.

"You're looking well, Senator."

"Comes from having the right genes, Mr. President. The right mother and the right daddy. They both went past ninety-five. I'm seventy-three, so that gives me, let's see—"

Thompson said, "At least three more six-year terms."

Carson's eyes widened with surprise at the President's alertness and he smiled, pleased at the compliment. "If the voters can stand it."

There was a sound of polite laughter.

Hackett, seated on a red and blue striped sofa, looked down at the briefcase on his lap, then glanced over at Jaggers sitting beside him. Jaggers' eyes were fixed on the briefcase as Hackett opened it and took out the fateful document, letting it rest on his lap.

The President sat straight in his chair, his eyes searching the faces of each of his visitors. It was Carson who spoke.

"Mr. President, my colleagues and I have come here on a most important mission. I am here in my official capacity as President pro tempore of the Senate." He drew himself up as he looked at the impassive face of the President. "An important mission," he repeated, "and a delicate one."

The chimes of the grandfather clock that stood behind Carson's chair sounded the half hour.

Thompson spoke kindly. "Go ahead, David," he said.

The Senator edged himself forward. "I'm pleased, Mr. President, that you find me looking fit. I find you looking the same."

"Thank you, Senator."

There was a beat in which the two men smiled benignly at each other. "Looking fit, however, Mr. President, doesn't necessarily mean that one *is* fit. I, for one, could never carry the burdens of your office. They're almost too much—for any man."

"You would manage if it were your duty, Senator."

"Duty. Now there's a four letter word that would take a book to explain. A man's duty. Mine. Yours."

Thompson's eyes had begun to narrow. "I know mine, Senator. Now there must be a reason—a very good reason—that brings the three of you to this office so early. I don't want to be rude or impatient, but would you mind getting on with it?" The President glanced over at Kraus and then back at Latham, who stood behind the President's chair.

"Of course, Mr. President. The Committee has been meeting—"

"The Committee," Thompson said, the throbbing veins of his temples beginning to show. "Yes, I understand the Committee has been at work. Devilish work I might add—if that's the subject of your meeting."

Jaggers spoke. "The Committee has its duties, Mr. President, even as you have yours." Jaggers waited to see if the President would respond; he noted the slowly rising pinkish hue of Thompson's neck as the color advanced over the collar line. He continued speaking. "The Committee has been charged with many difficult tasks—" he stopped as the President began to chuckle. The sound of his throaty laughter startled the visitors.

"Gentlemen, I don't mean to be rude. I know all about your difficult tasks—your duties—the Committee's duties," he emphasized, a touch of sarcasm creeping into his voice.

Suddenly his mood changed as he snapped out his response. "You've been engaged in conversations—it's the Committee I'm referring to—conversations full of—" his hands flew up as he searched for the right words "—chicanery, that's what, chicanery. And per . . . per . . ." He turned to face Latham, his lips twisting, trying to form a word—seeking his help . . . "per . . . per . . . what is that word, Tom?"

Latham leaned down. "Pernicious?"

Thompson nodded and turned back to the group. "Yes, pernicious. That says it nicely." He held up the paper in his hand and waved it at them. "This announcement is going to the press this morning. Mr. Kraus will present it at a special briefing. You can read it, Mr. Secretary. It will spare us any further conversation. And it says it all. Everything." His hands shook as he passed it over to Jaggers. "You can read it aloud, Mr. Secretary."

Jaggers cleared his throat. "Gentlemen, this is the President's statement, dated"—he glanced up—"as of this morning."

"That's right," Thompson said, "this—very—morning."

Jaggers exchanged looks with Senator Carson and Speaker Hackett. "The statement reads as follows," Jaggers went on.

"'The President has accepted, as of this date, the resignation of his Cabinet—'" Jaggers stopped, looking up at the President.

The President spoke. "And if you're concerned about the convention and the election, don't be. The public will know only one thing. And that's that the President, for good and solid reasons, is cleaning house—he's going to take a bipartisan approach in his second term as we face our problems at home and our adversaries abroad. I think that says it all, gentlemen." Thompson stood up and started toward the door that led to his private working office.

It was Speaker Hackett who spoke. "One moment, Mr. President. I'm afraid that your press release is not the end of this subject." Thompson turned, his eyes glowering with anger. "I'm sorry, sir, but we must continue this meeting."

Thompson stood still, the rubbing together of his finger's the only other visible sign of the anger he was suppressing. "Say what you have to, Mr. Speaker."

"I'd like to suggest that you sit down, sir—"

"Get on with it!" Thompson said brusquely.

"I have a document here in my hand, Mr. President, a document signed last night—last *night*," he repeated with soft emphasis. "I'd like to discuss it with you."

Senator Carson rose from his chair and extended both hands. "Please, Mr. President?" He pointed to Thompson's chair.

Thompson inhaled deeply, lifted his shoulders, and walked back to his chair, sitting on its edge. Carson nodded to Hackett. "Proceed, Mr. Speaker."

"A great deal of conscientious thought—debate, too—has been taking place, Mr. President, on many subjects—"

"I sense that loyalty is not one of them, Mr. Speaker."

"Quite to the contrary, Mr. President. The Committee, I am told—"

"They know nothing of fealty, nothing." Thompson turned his attention to Jaggers. "Mr. Jaggers? Do you, sir?"

Jaggers flushed as he removed his glasses. "Mr. President," he said slowly, "I do—to the Constitution of the United States. I've taken an oath to defend it, to protect it." He stopped for a moment to contain his own inner anger. "Mr. President," he began again, softly, "there is no personal oath in our government, no act of fealty as you describe it, to any official. Respect, yes. Loyalty, yes. Honor, yes. But an oath, an act of allegiance—that, sir, is given only to the Constitution, to the law of the land. Never to a person."

The room went silent for a moment. Then Carson spoke,

his voice, too, soft, conciliatory, kind. "Not even to the President of the United States, sir, because we are, above all, a country of law." He leaned forward from his chair. "Mr. President, not since those terrible days when another group of honest men called upon a President—around whom, one could say, perhaps a bit dramatically, that coils of mistrust, dishonor, and malfeasance had brought the government to a grinding halt—called upon that President, in the hope that he would assess his position—"

"Are you comparing me to *that* man? To Nixon?"

"Not at all, sir, not at all. Just to the fact that circumstances have dictated that this group, like the other, had to consider their responsibilities to the nation, to champion an action which hurts them as human beings, and which, I must emphasize, believe me, wounds each of us."

"I sense, though, that I am the one you would call upon to do the bleeding," Thompson said contemptuously.

"These are times of enormous responsibility, Mr. President, times when executive actions may be required upon a moment's notice—"

"Are you suggesting that I've been incapable of making such decisions," Thompson said, as beads of perspiration broke out on his forehead, "that I've made errors, confused my associates?"

"Sir, we've been impressed with your skill and with your leadership. But that is the past. That's yesterday."

"And what of today, Senator?"

Carson glanced at his colleagues, Hackett picking up the cue and, with it, the paper in his hand. "Mr. President, you're a man who understands duty, no one denies that. But there are decisions to be made—"

"Mr. Speaker, are you trying to force me to name a justice to the Supreme Court? Don't you realize the time needed—"

"It's not that, sir, not that alone I might add. It's a matter of far greater urgency. The matter of Red Dye Day. That demands—"

"I've said it has my attention," Thompson thundered.

"It requires decision, Mr. President," Hackett said quietly.

"And you're setting yourself up to judge me on when I must make that decision?"

"Sir, it's been your inability to *do* so that accounts for our being here."

"And you're going to tell me how to run this office, you—all of you, your Committee—"

"I'm afraid there's a deeper concern, Mr. President. You are, if I may be permitted to say so, a man whose physical condition is—and the Committee has access to official medical reports—somewhat less than—"

With a sweep of his hand, Thompson brushed a Chinese porcelain vase, full of flowers, from the small mahogany coffee table between his chair and the sofa on which Hackett was sitting. "So it's come to this! To this! You're now sitting in judgment upon my health! Placing yourselves above my doctors!"

Jaggers reached out to calm the President, but Thompson pulled back from his touch. "History is full of treachery, and it's no wonder, Mr. Jaggers, that you want to split hairs on the difference between fealty and loyalty since you possess neither—"

"Mr. President!" Jaggers exclaimed in protest, his voice shaking with outrage.

"I have your resignation! You're free to leave!"

Jaggers' portly frame quivered as he said, "I shall, Mr. President, but first we have a mission to conclude. Mr. Speaker, I suggest that you now show the President the paper in your hand."

Hackett stretched forward and passed the document to Thompson. As the President read it, he slowly struggled from his chair. Then, suddenly, he fell back, face ashen, the paper slipping to the floor. Latham picked it up, directed by a signal from Hackett, and read it, too. Slowly, he passed it over to Kraus.

The President's voice was suddenly weak. "I know all about that Amendment. You shall have my written declaration as to my fitness this afternoon—this afternoon, gentlemen."

Senator Carson walked over to the President, placing his hands on the wings of his chair, hovering above him, and talking quietly. "It won't do, sir. The Cabinet will refute it—"

"The Congress—the Congress—" Thompson muttered. "They—the Congress," he repeated, looking past Carson to Kraus and Latham. "The Congress . . . the Joint Chiefs . . . as Commander . . ." His eyes closed as he continued to mutter, "The Congress . . ."

"No, Mr. President," Carson said quietly. "To place this before the Congress would be disastrous, dangerous."

Thompson opened his eyes. "The Amendment states the Congress—it can be assembled—"

"Yes, that is correct, sir. The Congress can be assembled within forty-eight hours after receiving the declaration from the Cabinet and the Vice President that, in their judgment, the President is still unable to discharge his duties, and the Congress can then debate the issue for twenty-one days."

Thompson propelled himself forward. "And if the Congress votes on the issue—it would require a vote of two-thirds—two-thirds!" he thundered, "to sustain the charge that the President is unable to discharge his duties! Do you think this Congress will place Mr. Hawley above *me!*"

"No, Mr. President," Carson said quietly, "they will place the *country* above you. The *country*, sir."

Thompson's jaw went slack, his eyes taking on a glassy look. Hackett joined Carson. "Mr. President, the Cabinet and Mr. Hawley—and it was at Mr. Hawley's request—earnestly want you to return to your duties. You need rest, time to recover—"

"Do you realize, Mr. Speaker, what this action does to my campaign? Have any of you thought about that? It hands the presidency over to the opposition!"

"With this temporary arrangement and with a much-needed rest, Mr. President, you can still be nominated—"

"You don't believe that, Alfred," Thompson said, his eyes beginning to water.

"I do, sir," Hackett said, but without conviction. "Mr. Hawley will want your counsel, Mr. President, he will seek it. The country needs a united government, Mr. President. Acceptance, your acceptance—this can be your greatest contribution."

Thompson placed his hands on the arms of his chair and lifted himself laboriously to his feet. He appeared tired, a bewildered look sweeping across his face. "I'm to be carted out—"

"Not at all, sir," Carson said. "The Acting President expects you to occupy the White House throughout your entire term of office . . ."

Kraus moved in close to the President. "Sir," he whispered, "the date on your release about the Cabinet, move it back, sir!"

The President shook his head. "No, we can't do that, Henry. Not that." He turned to the others. "Destroyed. He's destroyed me—by *one* day," Thompson murmured as he moved away, his shoulders sagging. "By *one* day," he repeated. He turned to look at the assembled group. "Jackals!" he spat out as he left the room, shaking his head.

It was Hackett who retrieved the President's press release.

"I think this had best be destroyed." He looked at the others and then at Kraus. "Henry?"

Kraus reached out for the paper and slowly tore it to pieces.

Hackett stood before him. "The right thing, Henry, the right thing's been done here this morning. Hard. Sad, too, but still the right thing."

"The press has been waiting for an announcement," Kraus reminded the group.

Hackett responded. "Keep them locked up with the press secretary. They'll have their announcement." Kraus started out. "Oh, and one more thing, Mr. Kraus. Gather up any copies of that release about the Cabinet and destroy them. All of them. Including the secretary's notes."

"Yes, sir, I shall."

"I think, now," the Speaker said, "that we must call upon the Acting President."

23

Thompson steadied himself as he entered the family quarters of the White House, closing the door of the upstairs study slowly behind him, compelled momentarily to lean against it for support. A few seconds later he lurched across the room, maintaining a precarious balance by holding on to the room's furnishings as he maneuvered his way to sit behind the desk. He placed his elbows on its top and held his head between his hands, his body quivering as he fought to contain his emotions. He had an almost uncontrollable urge to yield to tears.

A light tapping on the door steeled him to regain his composure. "Yes?" he called out.

Johnson, a White House usher, opened the door partway. "Chief of Staff wishes to see you, sir."

Thompson raised a hand. "No one, Johnson, no one."

Kraus stood at the door. "Sir, there is still time," he began.

"Later, Henry, later," Thompson said. "I must do my own thinking."

"You still have the power, Mr. President," Kraus insisted, "and Senator Vance has it in the Senate," he added.

"Later, Henry. Johnson?" the President said, pointing to the door. "I am not to be disturbed. No calls, no visitors, no one." You understand?"

"Yes, sir," Johnson said, and then as an afterthought, he added, "Mrs. Thompson? Your son?"

"No one, Johnson, absolutely no one. That's an order."

Johnson nodded, quietly closing the door.

The President reached across the desk for his water carafe. His right arm trembled. He suddenly found that his fingers would not move. He slumped back into his chair, fear and perplexity creasing his brow as he concentrated all of his effort on moving his hand.

☆ ☆ ☆

Joe Gratton stood at a bay window in his New York office looking down at the crowded street below. At a tap on his door, he growled, "Come in!"

Wally Courtright strode in, holding a fax.

"That it?" Gratton said, reaching out for it.

Courtright passed it over as Gratton scanned it, crumpled it, and threw it in a wastebasket. "Son of a bitch never called me."

"Hawley?"

"What the fuck keeps a Vice President so goddamn busy?" he snarled in anger. "And who the Christ is this Sheridan? Never heard of the bastard."

"Russell Sheridan? The First Lady's Chief of Staff. Used to be a teacher, communications at UCLA, before that a reporter on the *Times*. L.A. *Times*. Runs her office in the East Wing. Knows his stuff, Joe."

"Well, we'll see about that. I'm not taking *his* word about anything." He kicked the side of his desk as he sat down. "Your offer to the lady was the right ticket, Wally, no criticism there. How in the hell could she say no?" Gratton rubbed at his fleshy face. "Our Washington people know this Sheridan?"

"Sure. But if he turns *my* request down, he's not going to reverse himself for a White House correspondent."

"Hawley could do it."

"Hawley could do it," Courtright agreed.

Gratton's eyes narrowed as he grappled with the rejection. "Something funny about this. This is a big project. The White House comes out looking very nice. Good timing with the convention a matter of a few weeks. Why would Sheridan say no?"

"Beats me, except, maybe . . . I'm just guessing. Could there be a Vance connection?"

"Vance," Gratton nodded. "But how could he get wind of this? Your story on the series hasn't broken yet."

"Slated for the Sunday papers," Courtright said.

"We have a chatterbox feeding inside stuff to Senators?"

Wally Courtright shrugged. "Joe, all of our people in Washington shoot the breeze. Trade. You know the game."

"Vance. It has to be Vance," Joe said. "He's positioned us to be fried on his hot seat. He had to pick up something from Tom Collins, maybe Hank Roberts, any one of our reporters."

"The First Lady may never have seen our message," Courtright volunteered. "Pressure. Vance covers his flanks. Smart Senator. But I don't think a Senator can push on Sheridan. Not even Vance."

"Balls," Gratton said sneeringly. "Senator Vance is *it*. Somebody tipped him, and we know he's thinking of a big grandstand act with me as special attraction. Okay. Sheridan may not kowtow to a Senator, but how's about the President?"

"Vance getting the President to put the kibosh on us? Not a bad scenario, Joe."

Joe flipped his intercom. "Mary, did you try the Vice President again?"

"We left another message, Mr. Gratton."

"Bastard," he growled. "Now, here's what I want you to do, Mary. Get me Mrs. Thompson at the White House." He flipped off the intercom and looked at Wally. "I'm not one of the lady's favorite courtiers, but if she's there I think she'll take a call from me. We can at least try an end run on Mr. Sheridan, and since I never called her before, maybe she'll talk. I've got no sure alternative."

☆ ☆ ☆

Frederick K. Vance sat in the sunlit morning room of his white Colonial home on the fashionable outskirts of Chevy Chase, glancing at the front page of the *Post* as his wife, Elizabeth, in a flowered peignoir, studied him over the rim of her cup of coffee.

"Something's bothering you, Freddie. You're not reading the paper."

"You have the bluest eyes in all Washington, Elizabeth," he

said, pushing the paper away, "and the most observant. They go with your robe."

"And that isn't the answer," she said chidingly.

"All right," he replied. For the next ten minutes Elizabeth Vance listened in silence to her husband's account of his meetings with the President and with the Admiral. When he finished, he simply said, "Now you know."

"I remember how excited we were when you spoke to me from Nebraska," she said, reaching over and pouring herself a fresh cup of steaming coffee, then, as Vance lifted his cup toward her, filling his.

"I was. I still am," he said, helping himself to cream and sugar.

"Then, what is the question?"

"All right. The question is: knowing the various circumstances—" He paused momentarily. "That means," he continued, ticking off each item on his fingers as he spoke, "knowing the President's state of health, knowing the Admiral's concern about the Twenty-fifth Amendment, knowing—or suspecting—some of the activities of the Vice President, knowing all these matters, does the Senator from Kansas put his personal future ahead of the country's need, or does he put the country's need ahead of his personal ambition?"

His wife folded her napkin neatly and placed it on the table. "Why is it that men always want to make such simple decisions so complicated?"

"Elizabeth," he said gently, reaching across the table to take her hand, "because there are such peculiar matters as principles, honor, commitment—"

"Do you believe Mr. Hawley's thinking like that while he's busy plotting his every move right now?"

"He's not doing it alone."

"You have the trump card," she said, tapping the table.

"The President."

Elizabeth Vance smiled complacently. "The President."

Vance pulled out a cigar, bit off the end, and took his time lighting it, letting the flame of the match barely touch it as he rotated it gently from side to side. "Elizabeth," he said as he smiled enigmatically.

"When you pronounce my name like that, I know I'm not going to like the rest of it," she said, arching her eyebrows.

Vance pushed his chair away from the table, resting it on

its two back legs as his hands gripped the table edge. "Would it surprise you to know that I'm considering whether I should have a talk with Admiral Hornwell or one with Mr. Hawley?"

"Really, Freddie," she said, a note of annoyance in her voice.

"The President's interest in me . . . okay, let's admit his obvious interest. But there's no absolute guarantee," he began. "And he's not a well man, Elizabeth."

"He looked well at his last press conference."

"Makeup," Vance said. "Covers his pallor and the circles under his eyes. But Elizabeth," he said, "some of his answers? Didn't you notice they weren't responsive to the questions, that his mind wandered?"

"He's still President, Freddie."

Vance shrugged. "I must admit I'm in a quandary." He took a long drag on his cigar.

"Freddie," she said, pulling back and standing before him with her arms crossed. "Do you really think that Mr. Hawley is sitting in his office thinking about—what was your list—principles, honor, commitment? Or is he trying to figure out what he has to do to hold on to his job, or, worse for you, get a better one?"

Vance reached up and took his wife's hand. "You're probably right, Elizabeth."

"I *know* I'm right. It isn't the Admiral or the Vice President you want to see. Freddie," she said, slipping behind him and rubbing his shoulders, "you want to see the President. It's all so easy. You don't deal in speculating on this or that, no fretting about all the 'what ifs'—you concentrate on only one thing."

"And what is that?"

"The now. This moment." She moved around to face him. "It's called reality, Freddie," she said.

☆ ☆ ☆

Hawley's White House office was quiet, the men in it aware that new forces were entering the political arena. Jaggers sat apart from the others, still stung by the President's attack. Carson and Hackett huddled together in whispered conversation. Daniels, cigarette dangling from his lips, leaned his lanky frame against the pale blue wall in the rear of the office, observing and listening. Kraus was seated before Hawley's desk, looking up at the man whom only an hour before he held in amused contempt. The rest of Thompson's immediate staff was gathered outside in small groups, wondering what was going on inside Hawley's office.

Hawley was advising those in the meeting that the members of the Cabinet would be gathering within the hour and that he would be speaking to the nation from the Cabinet Room later in the afternoon. He had ordered Kraus to put the networks on standby notice.

Lane Whitney, coming in through the West Wing, made his way to his own office, a cubicle near the Vice President's. His secretary pointed a finger toward the door of the Vice President's office.

"They're all in there, Lane," she whispered. "It's topsy-turvy time. Everyone in the White House press room is demanding to see this one, that one. We're like the eye of a hurricane in here. But back *there*," she pointed in the direction of the Press Secretary's office, "I hear it's a madhouse, a crazy pushing yelling match. They want Kraus, they want Hawley, they want Daniels, you name them."

"They're in there?" He glanced at Hawley's office.

"Everyone. Hawley and a flock of biggies. The Secretary of State, the Secretary of Defense—"

"Jaggers? Clauson?"

"The Speaker, Senator Carson, Mr. Daniels—"

"All of them? In there?"

"With the Vice President. And Henry Kraus."

"What the hell's going on?"

His secretary shrugged her shoulders. "Something big, *very* big, that's for sure. They were all with the President first—most of them—except Hawley. And he's been asking for you, so maybe you'd better go on in."

"Christ! You come in late once in four years and miss the revolution."

Lane entered the crowded room as Hawley was concluding his remarks. "And let's all remember one thing, and it's very important to friend and adversary. It's this: this government will continue to function as it has been functioning under President Thompson. His team remains intact. Every man and woman will remain in his post, performing his duties." He peered over the heads of those before him. "Lane?"

"Yes, sir," Lane said, inching forward.

"I'd like you to go to Harry Thompson and have him set

up a meeting with the President. He's the best one to do it. I'd very much like the President to participate on television with me, in the Cabinet Room. We'll prepare a few words for him if necessary—" He turned to Kraus. "Henry, can you handle that?"

Kraus nodded.

"Just a few words that acknowledge that we're proceeding constitutionally, and that at an appropriate time he fully expects to resume his office. Is that clear?"

"Clear," Kraus repeated.

"I'll want to review it . . . and I'd like to see him."

"Yes, sir."

Hawley looked about the room and then said, quietly, "I'll need the help of all of you. Mr. Clauson?"

"Sir."

"Red Dye Day. Let it begin as soon as I'm sworn in. Check Hornwell."

"Should we raise the alert status of our forces?" Clauson asked.

"Absolutely not," Hawley replied emphatically. "We do that, the Soviets will respond in kind. We don't want that. What we want is to maintain our normal defense condition. Clear?"

"No alert. Clear," Clauson said, leaving the office immediately.

"Secretary Jaggers?" Jaggers rose and took a step toward Hawley. "When President Thompson joins us, we must make a request for his copy of that special paper, that letter, you understand?"

"I understand," Jaggers said.

"*We* have to know what *they* know. We can't be left in the dark. We must persuade Mr. Thompson of the necessity."

"Agreed. But it won't be easy."

"One way or another . . ." Hawley caught an acknowledgment in Daniels' eye.

Then he turned to Kraus again. "Henry, the press is to be told only that an important announcement will be coming from the White House later today. You're to take no questions . . ." Then, turning to the assembled group, he said, "I know there'll be no leaks." For a few moments his eyes rested on each official in the room. Then he said firmly, "All right. Now let's everyone get on with his work."

On his way out, Daniels stopped for a moment by Hawley's

side. "I'll be back, sir. Taggart's in from the coast. I'll have that report of his," he added, as he leaned in closer to Hawley and whispered, "that . . . incident? Miss Lessing?"

Hawley nodded understandingly, and as the others filed out he signalled to Lane to be seated. "I understand that you, Harry, and Jeff had some unpleasant words recently in a public place." Hawley walked around his desk and looked down at Whitney. "It was about Gloria, wasn't it?" he asked. "And me?"

"About a lot of things," Lane said lamely.

"It's important to me that you all accept the findings—"

"I do, I do," Lane protested, "and so does Jeff."

"Good. But it's even more important that Harry Thompson accept them."

"Intellectually he knows the truth. Emotionally . . ." Lane shrugged.

"I'm counting on you to straighten him out," Hawley said, "and to fill him in on what we're doing today. What we've *had* to do. Tell him as much as you have to—but get that meeting set up. That's it."

As Lane Whitney stood up, his hand on the doorknob, Hawley said, "Lane, you must emphasize to Harry that my assumption of the President's duties is only temporary." He noticed the look of surprise on Lane's face. "You do know what's happened?"

"I do now," Lane said, looking at Hawley with a mixture of awe and a new respect.

☆ ☆ ☆

Seated in his spartan office, Daniels glanced up at Frank Taggart, a thin smile on his face. "Wellman's taken the bait, that it?"

Taggart, his face showing signs of fatigue from his speedy trip to and from the coast, stood before Daniels' desk. "He's sure he has a great story. Exclusive one, sir."

"Anything new on the First Lady?"

"Nothing, he's got nothing. Not yet," Taggart hastily added. "We've kept him too busy. Off balance."

"It's about time to dump on him. Let the other fellows have the story. Little Sammy Wellman won't be considered so reliable anymore. Not to Mr. Chet Gaynor and *Time*." Daniels motioned Taggart to a chair. "You got in to see Miss Lessing?"

"Yes, sir."

"And?"

"I had about three minutes. Three and a half," Taggart said. "Hospital was very reluctant, but we managed."

"Conclusion?"

"She'll be out of things for six months. Minimum."

"Sure?"

Taggart reached into a pocket, extracted an envelope, and placed it before Daniels without comment. Daniels ripped it open, pulled out a photograph, examined it, then laid it down on his desk. "Vivien Lessing?" he asked, looking up again at Taggart. Taggart nodded his head in assent. "They did quite a job. Six months?" he said softly. "Looks more like a good year before this little lady'll be together again."

The two men sat quietly, eyes focused on the photograph of Vivien Lessing, her face and body swathed in bandages. "She have any idea of who did it?" Daniels finally asked.

"No."

"Her studio? The people there?"

"Total blank. Except some vague connection to Vegas, a casino owner. Seems she rejected him a couple of times."

"Anything on him?" Daniels asked.

"Not really. Everyone in Hollywood has that kind of connection. With Vegas, that is. Hotel owners, fellows who flash a lot of cash around, big wheels fronting as land developers, fellows who control the food brokers, laundries, all kinds of hangers-on."

Daniels pushed the photo back toward Taggart. "Whoever did it was professional. Nothing that can't be fixed. She'll work again." He rolled a cigarette. "What'd she say?"

"Very little, Mr. Daniels. She wasn't up to talking."

"She knows where you came from?" Daniels asked.

"Yes, sir."

"You made sure of that," Daniels said flatly.

"Yes, sir."

"Good." After blowing a series of perfect smoke rings Daniels turned again to Taggart. "Frighten her?"

"She's frightened," Taggart said.

Daniels leaned forward. "She got the message."

"She got the message, sir. After she learned I was government she said, 'Tell Mr. Hawley' . . . she kind of whispered it, 'I won't be bothering him again.' That was it. Plus apologizing for even mentioning his name. And we were alone."

"Bright lady. Smart. Somebody saved us a lot of trouble," Daniels said, crushing his cigarette into a filled-up ashtray. Daniels got to his feet, Taggart rising with him. "We'll tell the man *this* problem's not a problem anymore."

As Daniels headed toward his own home, he reflected on the events taking place. He knew that Hawley would be waiting for his report. He figured Hawley would still be furious and that his instincts would still be to be solicitous, to make calls, send flowers, etcetera. But he would talk him out of it. Silence would send the right message to Vivien Lessing.

☆ ☆ ☆

Henry Kraus was surprised to find Frederick Vance again waiting in his office. "Senator," he said, "I'm under a certain amount of pressure right now."

Vance rose to greet Kraus, putting down a magazine he'd been reading. "I persuaded your secretary that it was very urgent. Five minutes, that's all it will take."

Kraus pointed to a chair.

"Thank you. I've done a lot of thinking since seeing the President. I came here on a particular mission this morning, one you may find difficult to believe." Vance pulled out a handkerchief to touch his perspiring brow. "It's all rather bewildering if the truth be known. I came here convinced that I had to see the President—"

Kraus cut in, shaking his head, "Not this morning, Senator. Impossible."

"That's all right, Henry. Believe it or not, it was while I was coming in the West Wing I realized that it wasn't the President I wanted to see."

"Oh?"

"It was the Vice President." Vance noted a subtle change of expression on Kraus's face. "The Vice President," he repeated.

After a moment Kraus said, "That's going to be just as difficult, Senator—"

"Henry. I simply *must* see him," Vance reiterated, a firmness in his voice.

Kraus rocked back in his chair. He didn't like being put in the middle, especially where his instincts warned him he could be the loser no matter which way he turned. But Vance now surprised Kraus by saying, "Mr. Hawley will be pleased with what I have to say, Henry. Let me assure you of that." Kraus looked up expectantly. "Ever since you and I met with the President I've been very troubled. Frankly, I've been unable to forget it."

Kraus continued giving Vance his attention.

"You're wondering what this is all about," the Senator said, shifting about in his chair. "I pretty well know what's in the air, Henry, maybe not the details, but the essence. The Twenty-fifth Amendment, to be precise." He looked steadily into Kraus's eyes. "I'm on the goddamndest mission, Henry. You wouldn't believe it if I weren't here telling it to you myself. And I can promise you, Mrs. Vance wouldn't believe it after our breakfast talk because I've done a complete reversal. I'm here to help Hawley." He shifted closer to Kraus. "What I'm saying, Henry, is that in a showdown . . . where the Congress is involved . . . where the Senate has to act . . . this Senator will be in Mr. Hawley's corner." He sat back. "Now you know why I want to see him."

Kraus looked across at Vance with new respect. "I must admit I'm really surprised," he said.

"No more than I," Vance replied.

Kraus stood up. "Okay. Come with me, Senator." As they left the office together, Kraus said, "I think Mr. Hawley will be as surprised—and pleased—by your words as you probably will be by his."

☆ ☆ ☆

Lane raced down to the White House gymnasium, where Harry Thompson and Jeffrey Whitney were fencing. He stepped in close, trying to interrupt them as Jeff suddenly pressed Harry in a series of swift, savage lunges, pinning him to the wall. Harry removed his mask in anger. "What in the hell's gotten into you, Lane? Can't you see what we're doing?"

"I've got to talk to you."

"It'll have to wait," Harry retorted curtly. Then turning to Jeff and raising his foil, he said, "Shall we?"

Lane put both hands up to stop his brother. "What I have to say, it *can't* wait."

"For Christ sake!" Harry said with annoyance.

"I want you to listen, both of you."

Harry, ignoring him, turned his attention again to Jeff. "Look, locked up in a submarine you're bound to get rusty. What kind of space do you have? You're good, but that move just now—even with Lane's help in distracting me—you're forgetting the play in your wrist. That's where it counts—like this," he said, demonstrating a swift parry.

"Harry! Hawley wants you to set up a meeting with your father! Goddamn it, listen!"

Harry brought his foil down, the tip resting on the floor. "Is that all?" he asked, a smile of contempt on his face. "Is that all Mr. Hawley wants? He can't get through to the old man with the staff, with you, with Kathy? He has to have *me*?" Harry turned again toward Jeff, foil raised. "Shall we?"

"He's not begging, Harry. He's—he wants him to go on TV this afternoon."

Thompson let his foil down again. "What in the hell are you talking about?"

Lane took a deep breath. "Harry. Your father—" he stopped speaking, shaking his head in wonderment.

"My father, what?" Harry Thompson grabbed hold of Lane's lapel. "All right, my father, what?"

"Harry, look. I just left Hawley . . . Hawley, the Cabinet, the Speaker, the President pro tem . . ." He paused again for a moment. "They've *done* it, Harry," he said softly.

"What do you mean, 'done it'? Done what? Who?"

"They've taken over, Harry. It's the Twenty-fifth Amendment, that's what."

"The Twenty . . . Son of a bitch!" Harry shouted. "The bastards! Those goddamn bastards!"

"They want your father—they had a meeting with him, maybe a half hour, an hour ago—they want him to go on television with Hawley—"

"On television? What?! To give them his goddamn blessing?" He threw his mask to the floor and clenched a fist. "Those goddamn bastards!" He began to pace the floor, marshalling his thoughts. "My father has remedies. *I* know the law! *I* know that Amendment! I know all the rules! I know them all! Congress has something to say—"

"It's done, Harry, I heard it." He took a step toward Harry. "They won't let him, Harry. The Speaker and old Carson, they said it couldn't be done. It's all a matter of national security—his health—"

"National security, my ass!" he shouted, cutting the air with his foil. "You're talking dirty tricks—well, it won't work!"

Harry flung the foil on a bench. "My old man's never walked away from a fight yet. He's the President. Fuck them! Health or no health, he's going to fight!" He picked up a towel, wiped his face, and started out of the gym, calling out over his shoulder to Lane. "Yeah, I'm going up to see my old man all right. But, Mr. Whitney, it's not to get him to see your Mr. Hawley—"

"Wait a minute!" Lane said following him. "He's not my Mr. Hawley any more than he's yours. Harry, listen to me. What he is, is Acting President. Until the President's health is back. He told me, everyone. Harry, look . . . you *have* to set up this meeting—"

"I don't *have* to do anything!"

"What do I tell him?" Lane asked, as he watched Harry's receding figure.

"I don't give a damn what you tell him!" Harry shouted back. And with that he was gone.

24

While her husband was being confronted by the Speaker of the House and the President pro tem of the Senate, Kathy Thompson was in her own office, listening to Joe Gratton's explanation of his proposed series on the First Ladies. Her initial reaction to Gratton's call and his request for her participation had been affirmative, but that reaction was soon replaced by one of outrage when Gratton advised her that her Chief of Staff, Russell Sheridan, had earlier rejected the proposal.

Sheridan, summoned to her office shortly after Gratton left, his eyes looking owlish behind his heavy lenses, had done his best to assuage Kathy's feelings. "As I've said, Mrs. Thompson, we deal with many requests for your services. Almost every day one of the networks, some television station, some paper or magazine contacts us, usually through the press secretary, and we deal with them."

"But this request came directly to you."

"This one came to me."

"And did you refer it to Maxine Stuart for her reaction?"

"No."

"May I ask why not?"

Sheridan scratched at his chin and smiled as he said, "Maxine reports to me. I'm not required—" There was a suggestion of patronizing indulgence as he shrugged his shoulders, indicating no further explanation was required.

Kathy persisted. "You rejected it just like that?" she asked with a snap of her fingers.

"Not at all, Mrs. Thompson, not at all. We evaluated it very carefully. We considered your schedule as well as what's in the pipeline. The convention for one thing."

"With no discussion with me? None with the press secretary?"

"Correct," he said, concealing the irritation he felt at the continued cross-examination. He decided to deprecate Gratton's offer. "Federal Broadcasting's not exactly an NBC or a CBS, Mrs. Thompson."

"That story in the press, about the Senate committee investigating the networks, Federal Broadcasting in particular, did that play a part in your rejection?"

Sheridan smiled in what he hoped was not too unctuous a manner. "That kind of thing isn't helpful, Mrs. Thompson," he said.

"Are they *guilty* of something, Mr. Sheridan? Even before the investigation begins?" Sheridan shook his head and was about to speak when Kathy continued, "And what about the merits of the idea, quite apart from the Senate hearings?"

"I don't think the two can be completely separated, Mrs. Thompson," Sheridan began. "It gets rather complicated . . ."

"But the idea of doing a history of the First Ladies . . . it is a good idea, isn't it? Wouldn't women all over America be interested in such a series?" Sheridan nodded his head in agreement. "And wouldn't they be surprised," Kathy went on, "if the current First Lady ignored such a series?"

Sheridan smiled. "I don't think they'd do the series without your participation. They'd want White House cooperation, help from the Archives, the Smithsonian . . ."

"Am I to assume, then, that you're in favor of killing it . . . the whole idea of a series on the First Ladies?"

"Well, no, not exactly," he said floundering, "it's only a matter of timing . . . your time . . . the whole backdrop of the upcoming campaign . . ."

"And the upcoming Senate hearing . . . on television?" Kathy persisted.

"Well, now, that *is* a factor, of course," Sheridan said reluctantly.

"I'm not naive, Mr. Sheridan," Kathy said sharply. "That *is* the real issue, isn't it?"

Sheridan paused, then grudgingly acknowledged, "It is *an* issue, Mrs. Thompson."

"And your rejection of Mr. Gratton's request . . . that's tied to *that* issue." Sheridan remained silent as Kathy waited. Finally, she broke the silence. "You were told to say no to Mr. Gratton, weren't you? Not to complicate Senator Vance's investigation. Am I right, Mr. Sheridan?"

"Mrs. Thompson," he began, removing his glasses, and fighting back his own personal concern, "there are matters in the White House—"

"Am I right, Mr. Sheridan?" Kathy asked, her tone now bristling.

Sheridan sat up straight and took a deep breath. In a slow and deliberate fashion, he adjusted his glasses, and then, looking directly at Kathy, he said, "Part of my job is to be responsive to the chain of command at the White House—"

"You report to this office only, Mr. Sheridan," Kathy replied.

Sheridan nodded agreement. "Yes, of course. Of course. But when the *President's* Chief of Staff . . ." he lifted both hands. "Well, in that case the prudent thing is to give any such suggestion a certain degree of proper weight." He stopped talking as he waited on her.

"I think I understand," Kathy said coldly as she rose.

Sheridan stood up and said, with a touch of condescension, mistaking her courtesy for surrender, "I thought you would, Mrs. Thompson."

"Yes," she said, speaking incisively. "I *do* understand. Now, I trust *you'll* understand. You're to call Mr. Gratton the moment you get to your office and advise him that the White House is reviewing his request and that *this* office looks with favor on my participation. Thank you, Mr. Sheridan. That will be all," she said, dismissing him.

☆ ☆ ☆

Kathy Thompson strode along the broad corridor of the second floor of the White House toward Thompson's office, determined to find out the whole truth about the pressure placed on Sheridan. She glanced at a news release her secretary had pressed into her hands. "You may already know about this, but if not, I thought you might want to see it," Anne said as Kathy started off. Kathy was both surprised and puzzled to read the announcement of the resignation of the Cabinet. At the door to the President's study Johnson, the white-haired black usher, intercepted her and bowed politely. "The President gave orders, Mrs. Thompson, not to be disturbed."

"Well, I have to see him, Johnson."

"He gave his orders, ma'am. Firm."

"Yes, I heard you, thank you, and I'll take the responsibility." Johnson frowned as she placed her hands on the doorknob. "I'll explain it, Johnson," she said as she entered the President's study.

As she closed the door softly behind her, she saw that the President's big chair was turned so that its back faced her. Seeing his right hand hanging limply across the arm of the chair, she paused for a moment, feeling her heart pounding, glancing again at the release announcing the dismissal of the Cabinet.

"Stephen," she said softly, announcing her presence.

The President's chair slowly swung around. Kathy was shocked at his appearance, the lines in his face looking deeper, his eyes more sunken in their sockets. His tie hung loose from his collar.

"Stephen, are you all right?"

"I was not to be disturbed, Kathy. I gave orders."

"I'm sorry. If you'd rather I leave—"

"No one obeys my orders anymore, Kathy, no one. Not even Johnson out there."

"Please don't blame him. He wanted me to stay out, Stephen. Are you all right?"

"Under all the circumstances, as right as I can be," he said, finally looking up at her.

"I'll get Jensen."

"No, it's not necessary. I just need some time to think. To think things through." He spied the paper in Kathy's hand. "What's that you're holding?"

She placed it on the desk. "Your order about the Cabinet."

Thompson smiled as he pulled it toward him with his limp hand. "You won't have to make that choice, Kathy. Frees you from deciding."

"I don't understand."

He looked up at her wearily. "Between Mr. Hawley and me," he said with a sigh.

"Stephen . . ." she hesitated for a moment, about to protest. "Why do you keep raising that subject, Stephen?"

A wave of anger swept over Thompson's face, and looking at her long and hard, he said, "I sense your choice, Kathy. I have for some time. And now, under the present circumstances," he said, his voice stern and emphatic, "I think you should leave." He leaned on the top of his desk, pushing himself up. "Kathy, I have some very serious thinking to do, and I don't believe you have anything so urgent that it has to be discussed here today."

"But we do, Stephen," she started. "I just had a rather unpleasant experience with Russell Sheridan. What I'd like to talk to you about is—"

Suddenly the door to the study flew open and Harry Thompson, struggling to shake off Johnson, barged in.

"Sorry, Dad, I have to talk with you!" he shouted, wrestling with the usher. "You can't take this lying down! I won't let you, the country won't let you! You can stop Hawley right now!" He tried to pull himself free. "And tell this joker to get away from me!"

Thompson gave his assent as Johnson released him and left the room.

"I've heard all the news, all the bullshit about national security," Harry went on. "How Hawley wants you to go on television with him, so that everything looks neat, peaceful, legal." He leaned across the desk. "I'm supposed to bring you around, set up a meeting so the son of a bitch can come up and talk things over while he's pushing the knife in deeper!" He moved around the edge of the desk. "You don't have to do it! You don't have to cooperate for *one single moment!* You can jail the bastard! For committing high crimes! High misdemeanors!"

"And the President pro tem of the Senate? The Speaker? A majority of the Cabinet? Maybe jail all of them?" The President slumped down into his chair.

"Yes! Every last one of them! You've got Hornwell! You've got the military! There's a thing called martial law! There are troops minutes away! Tanks! You can round them all up in an hour!"

Thompson raised a hand.

"You're the President, goddamn it!" Harry shouted, as he bent closer to his father. "What are you going to do?!"

Thompson pulled his handkerchief across his lips, then shut his eyes momentarily.

Kathy broke the silence. "Will someone tell me what's going on?"

Harry turned around, surprised. Then he looked at his father. "You mean she doesn't know?"

The President smiled. "Call it my own little personal joke."

"Well, that's *some* joke!" Harry shouted as he turned to Kathy. "They're downstairs, the bastards! They're trying to take over!"

"Who? Take over . . . what?" Kathy demanded.

Harry snorted. "I thought you were bright, Kathy. Take over, yes! Mr. Hawley! Your good friend—your *special* friend—remember? You'll find them all downstairs, sitting in the Oval Office, trying it on for size, figuring it's theirs! Go on down and tell them they have another thing coming! Tell them there's a thing called the Constitution! *This* President's going to fight them tooth and nail!"

"Harry, calm down, please," the President said, extending both hands, "calm down."

Kathy looked across the room at the President. "You *knew*, Stephen, you knew all this when I came in? And you were egging me on, trying to make me choose?" She shook her head in disbelief. "That was beneath you. Shabby. And I'd only come to talk to you about a television series I was asked to do." In that split second she realized how academic it was to be talking about a series to be hosted by the First Lady. First Lady? With a defiant toss of her head, she turned about, went to the door, and said, "I don't think that matters now. Besides I have some very serious thinking to do of my own."

"Still the high and the mighty," Harry said with contempt, watching her leave.

"Temper won't solve anything," the President said evenly. "I have to recognize the best course. The best course, Harry. The one that stands the test of common sense." He made an effort to pick up a carafe. "Harry, could you please pour me a glass of water?"

Harry noticed his father's trembling hand as he held the glass and slowly drank. The President set it down on his desk, saying, "Margaret—she had common sense. Did I ever tell you . . ."

"Dad, please! For God's sake, stay on the problem! It's urgent!"

The President looked up at his son. "I'm aware, I'm aware. I know I sometimes wander. It's only letting private thoughts escape . . . that's all they are . . . they get insistent . . ."

"You were talking about the best course." Harry pulled a side chair closer to his father's desk. "You're the President. They're afraid to act without your participation—"

"No, son, they've already taken the real action. All they want now is some window dressing."

"Well, you don't have to give it to them," Harry said, clenching his fists. "You fight them, that's what. Some of them will weaken on the spot. The Speaker—"

The President raised both hands. "Harry, hold it! Hold it! What I'm trying to do is sort out all of the options—" Then, sensing Harry about to protest, the President, raising his hands again, cut him off. "Harry, you go downstairs. You tell them . . . tell them—" Thompson stopped abruptly.

"Tell them what!"

"My message. It will be coming—it will be in the best interest of the country. Tell them that. Just that. There's to be no television. Not today, not tonight. None."

"You'll fight them?"

"I need time to think, to review every alternative—" The President smiled. "The Twenty-fifth Amendment works for the President, too. Go on, Harry. Deliver my message."

"Dad, you can't delay—"

"I know, son, I know." He lifted a faltering hand. "Go."

☆ ☆ ☆

Hawley felt awkward as he and Vance approached the butler standing to the side of the door to the President's study on the second floor of the White House, remembering the unpleasantness of the last confrontation and Thompson's icy demand for his resignation.

Now, again Johnson shook his head, "I'm sorry, Mr. Hawley, I got my orders. Direct from the President."

Hawley patted the butler's broad shoulders. "That's all right, that's all right, Johnson. Would you mind telling *Mrs.* Thompson that we'd like to visit with *her*?"

"Yes, sir, I'll do that, sir." He pointed toward the entrance to the East Sitting Hall. "If you'll wait in there, gentlemen. Won't take a minute," he said, hurrying away.

Hawley stood quietly at a window looking out toward the Treasury Department and then gave his attention to a Cassatt hanging above a newly covered striped sofa. He turned when he heard Kathy enter. She nodded politely to Vance, then seated herself in a small armchair close to the window, some distance from him. Hawley pulled over a matching chair to sit near her, Vance discreetly moving farther from them out of earshot, picking up a small painting resting on an easel atop a mahogany desk to study it close up.

"I have to see him, Kathy," Hawley began, speaking softly, aware of her high state of tension.

"He won't see you, Cliff," she said. Then, first glancing swiftly at Vance's back, she whispered, "Why didn't you tell me? Why did you keep everything so secret, right up to the last minute? I don't understand. Why? *Why?*" she insisted.

Hawley reached over to pat her hand solicitously.

She withdrew it instantly. "Don't treat me as a child, Cliff. Just answer me. A few days ago you came to me for help. I offered it to you. And then—" she stopped abruptly. "I don't understand."

"I couldn't, Kathy," he murmured.

"You *couldn't!* But yet you *could* ask me—"

"Kathy," he said, interrupting her, "it would have been unfair—"

"Unfair!" She retreated against the back of the chair, struggling to keep her voice under control. "You call what you . . . you call *this* fair? Keeping me in the dark? I have to be the last person to know?"

"I couldn't tell you, Kathy. I couldn't put you in the middle between the President and me. *That* would have been unfair. Unthinkable," he said, adding, "Kathy, I couldn't tell you because I couldn't ask you to share such a secret—"

"No, you were more afraid I wouldn't *keep* it."

"I couldn't put you in that kind of position. I couldn't ask you to make that kind of choice."

Tears formed in her eyes. "What's to become of *me?*" she asked.

Hawley felt embarrassed and uncomfortable; the timing was all wrong for such a discussion, and he had to acknowledge to himself it was a subject he hadn't fully explored. What, indeed, *was* Kathy to do?

"Kathy," he whispered, trying to come to grips with her feelings, a tone of urgency in his voice, "nothing's going to change. Not right away. The President will occupy the White House. I'll want to confer with him, get his advice. *You'll* be in the White House. And when the President notifies the Congress that he's prepared to resume his duties, that there's no inability—"

"And if he *can't* resume his duties? Then what?" she asked, her voice muffled. "You carry him out?!"

Before he could answer, they were interrupted by the sound of something falling. The painting had slipped off the easel as Vance sought to put it on the desk. "Sorry about that," he said, setting it back in place. "Clumsy of me."

Kathy stood up. "We've been rude to you, Senator, and I apologize."

"Not at all," Vance said. "Mr. Hawley thought I might be helpful if we met with the President together."

Suddenly they became aware of Thompson's presence at the entrance to the room. Hawley took a step toward him. "Mr. President, I came upstairs to ask Kathy to intercede. Senator Vance and I would like to have a quiet talk with you so that—"

Thompson shook his head, his lips pressed tightly together, the muscles of his jaws bulging from angry internal pressures. Glancing contemptuously at Vance, he mumbled, "*Et tu*, Senator." Abruptly, he turned away from them, heading back to his office.

"Mr. President . . ." Hawley said as he took a few steps to follow him.

"Don't, Cliff. Let him be, please," Kathy pleaded.

The three of them stood together, watching the President vanish behind the door to his office. "We *must* see him, Kathy."

"All right, I'll try," she said. "I'll try to bring him to you."

Kathy hurried down the hall and entered the President's study to find Thompson seated behind his desk, his face ashen.

"He wants it all, doesn't he? The President's title, the President's power, the President's house, the President's wife."

"Stephen, please don't say things you'll regret. He came up wanting to see you."

"But first he had to see you—to lay another claim."

"Stephen! He couldn't get by Johnson! He asked me to intercede!"

"And you were willing?"

She sat down in a chair facing him. "I don't know what I think."

Thompson's eyes narrowed as he studied her. "And what does that mean?"

"Stephen, what are you going to do?"

"And if I told you," he said, pointedly, "would I then be telling Mr. Hawley?"

"No," she said, quietly. "And you don't have to tell me. You assumed I knew what was going on, that I was aware . . . But I knew nothing. Here I sit, right in the center of the White

House, and I know no more than all the millions out there. It's incredible, it's humiliating, and it's true. Stephen, I'm your *wife*. How could you keep me in the dark?"

The President leaned back in his chair, touched by her words. "What would you have me do?" he said quietly.

"Why do you ask? You wouldn't follow my advice," she said.

"You've been telling me for some time about the strain of the office, that there are others who can do this job, isn't that right?"

"Yes. Yes, I have," she acknowledged, "but—" Kathy called upon all of her resources—her past experience as a television news reporter/interviewer, capable of thinking quickly on her feet as a complex story unfolded, often moving in contradictory directions—to find the right response. She knew, almost at once, as she searched Thompson's face, that she would jettison all past thinking. Everything had come down to survival, and she would not jeopardize the little security that she still had by allowing herself to be cannibalized by others in the jungle world of politics. She rapidly reviewed the meeting with Hawley. In countless discussions he'd had to be part of, she had been stunned to learn, her fate had never been among his considerations. She'd felt used before. Now it was worse—she'd been ignored. If Stephen Thompson were not to continue in office, if Hawley had not a single word to offer about her future, she had no alternative except to protect herself.

She was the First Lady.

For her to remain First Lady, Thompson would have to resist.

Finally, she spoke. "You don't have to agree to Mr. Hawley's claim."

"You've read the Twenty-fifth Amendment?" he asked.

"You suggested it a long time ago. And Harry suggested it as well," she replied, "in that very nice manner of his, right here in your study just a little while ago."

"So he did, so he did." Thompson eyed her cagily.

"There's nothing in that amendment, Stephen, that says how much time a President is given to notify the proper authorities that he's ready and able to discharge his duties . . . that could be tonight, that could be a month from now, that could be on the eve of the convention . . ." She let Thompson think about the point, then continued. "And Mr. Hawley would have four days to respond negatively . . . if he elected to, if he insisted you were wrong."

"You've read the Amendment carefully, I can see."

"Yes, and if he does respond negatively, then it goes to Congress," she said.

"Correct. And they have twenty-one days to decide the issue."

"And it would take a two-thirds vote of both Houses to reject the President. That means *he's* the one who needs the vote." Kathy paused for a moment. "*You* only need one-third of both Houses to remain in office."

Thompson nodded, impressed. "You're something of a political strategist, Kathy."

"You can do it, Stephen. If you *want* to."

"One-third I could muster—more," he said, with a smile.

The door of the study opened and Harry Thompson looked in with Johnson hovering behind him. "It's all right, Johnson," the President said. Harry's face revealed his confusion at seeing Kathy back in the room. "Come in, Harry. Kathy and I are reviewing the situation." Harry was also surprised at his father's relaxed attitude. Then glancing at Kathy, the President added, "We've been studying the options."

"Oh?" Harry said, pulling a chair up to the desk.

"I know what *you* think, Harry," the President said.

"Fight back, that's what I think."

"They have their arguments."

"You're President. You were elected President. The country's not about to support a power grab."

The President paused to pour himself a glass of water. "Now I'd like to know what Kathy thinks."

"I think we know what she thinks," Harry said smugly.

"Let her speak for herself," Thompson said.

Kathy spoke softly. "I have my concerns. I've voiced them any number of times. I've worried about the campaign after the convention. About four more years. What those years can do. I've had my own conversations with Jensen." She looked over at Harry. "But we aren't talking about four more years. Not now. Not today."

"I am," Harry snapped.

"What we're talking about *first*, though is staying in office. That means Stephen rejects Mr. Hawley's declaration." Kathy noted with pleasure the look of total astonishment on Harry Thompson's face. And in that moment she thought of Hawley again, of how he'd dismissed her in his calculations, of how he'd overlooked the fact that the President still had power. Hawley and the others, she felt, were underestimating him.

And underestimating her.

She might not love Thompson as she once did, true enough, but *with* him she was First Lady. And that was something, something she knew now she prized more than ever, something to hold on to.

"That gives him six more months *if* he doesn't run, is that what you're saying?" Harry asked.

"And four more years if he runs and wins," Kathy said.

"You want him to *run?*" he asked, again visibly surprised at her position. "I thought . . . What about his health that you're always prattling about? What about his taking all of the pressures?"

Kathy looked at him coolly. "I have a solution," she said.

The President's eyebrows shot up. "Well," he said, as he rubbed his hands together. "And what can that be, Kathy?"

"It will sound crazy at first. But it makes sense. The Vice President—"

"Hawley?" Harry interjected.

"The *new* Vice President. Senator Vance, whomever Stephen wants, the new Vice President is a man of ability, stature, experience."

"Vance," Harry said. "Okay, assume it's Vance."

"Vance, then. If at any time during the second term, if at any time Stephen actually *does* feel the burden is too much, why then, he makes an arrangement with the Vice President." She enjoyed watching Harry's face as he tried to keep up with her solution. "They wind up switching jobs," she said.

"Switching jobs?" Harry repeated, incredulous.

"Why not?" Kathy shot back. "Who could be a better backup to a new President than one who's already served and whose only reason to relinquish the office is to reduce his own burdens? Meanwhile, he's there to help, to advise the new President, without the responsibilities. Remember, both men are elected. The people will find it easy to accept. That's my solution."

"Ingenious, I'll have to admit," the President said. "That's never happened, of course, except the time Ford wanted something like that when Reagan was running. But Ford made so many demands he couldn't swing it."

"You could," Kathy said.

"Provided I declare there's no inability on my part," Thompson replied. *"Provided,"* he repeated.

"You're not going to let them go *ahead?"* Harry said, standing before his father and pointing down toward the West Wing.

"Let them go on television and lie to the people? When all you have to do is walk in on them?"

"They've set their course. I'm going to rest now, do some real hard thinking myself. And then set *my* course."

"You'll think of what I said?" Kathy said.

"I'll think of everything," the President replied, "everything," he repeated as he searched their faces. "For the first time today I'm feeling all right. I'm feeling fine," he said as Kathy and Harry exchanged puzzled looks.

☆ ☆ ☆

Hawley and Daniels stood together by a window in the Vice President's White House office, looking out across the roadway to the Executive Office Building.

"You may just have to do it without him," Daniels said. "Not as good to be sure, but good enough."

There was a light tap on the door, and Tom Latham edged in. "Mrs. Thompson's secretary's outside, Anne Koyce. Wants to see you. Says it's urgent."

"Show her in." Latham opened the door and beckoned to Anne.

Anne walked in breathing heavily as Latham closed the door behind her. She smiled at Daniels and then, speaking rapidly, said, "I'm a little winded rushing from the East Wing. You'll have to excuse me." She paused to get her breath before continuing. "Mrs. Thompson asked me to run over."

Hawley pointed to a chair as Anne sat down, catching her breath.

"Thank you, thank you," she said, inhaling deeply. "Mrs. Thompson's waiting for you in the Monroe Room, upstairs. She said it's extremely important. She's talked with the President. She wanted you to know that. And that before you do anything, like on television, she has to see you."

Hawley glanced at his watch and looked over at Daniels. "We have time," he said.

"Not much," Daniels said. "Where's President Thompson now?"

"He's resting," Anne said.

"You just saw her," Daniels reminded Hawley.

"Yes, but she must have some kind of message. I have to see her, Richard. I don't want anything to be said later, that

I was too busy, too eager to rush things. You understand what I'm saying?"

"You've got the press room bursting, ready to knock down doors. Whatever's to be done should be done as quickly as possible before those know-it-alls begin filling their air with all kinds of speculation."

"It'll be fast," Hawley said.

"Surgical," Daniels added. "Best way."

"Surgical," Hawley repeated as he stared at Daniels. "I understand," he finally said. Then thanking Anne, he hurried out.

☆ ☆ ☆

Kathy Thompson was waiting in the Monroe Room, its green velvet wallpaper a handsome, rich background for its historic pieces of furniture. She was seated in the corner of a small striped sofa, its back against a window overlooking the South Lawn. Hawley pulled up a hand-carved side chair.

"I appreciate your coming, Cliff. I had to see you before you did anything."

"We're going on television, Kathy, and very soon. We have to."

"I've talked to the President," she said, ignoring his statement. "Both Harry and I. The President's not going to join you downstairs."

"I know that. We've already received his message, Kathy. Harry delivered it to Henry Kraus." He was inwardly impressed with her change of attitude and her deliberate effort to hold on to her inner reserves; he wanted to be helpful, courteous, even more, but he'd resisted those natural impulses as he'd begun to feel the pressure of events. "I don't have much time, Kathy."

Kathy Thompson drew herself erect in her chair, the tension showing in that move. "You can't do this, Cliff. I can't let you."

"Kathy, it can't be stopped."

"It *can!* It has to be. It's never been done before. There've been other Presidents in far worse condition—McKinley. Garfield. I know my history, Cliff. No one took over. No one. What happened was that their key men—men with integrity, loyalty—pitched in, that's what happened."

Hawley was stung. "And all of us? We're something else?"

Kathy saw the sudden hurt in Hawley's eyes. "No," she conceded, "but they gave their Presidents support, they protected them. They didn't push them aside."

"Hold it!" he said. "There was no constitutional provision back then. That only came along in 1967. It could have been used, Kathy, if it had been available, and if it had been available it should have been used."

"If you use it, I'm afraid you'll kill him."

"That's not true," he said sharply. "What would kill him, if you feel we have to debate the subject, is the job itself. It *is* killing him. He's demonstrated impaired judgment. That's why the Committee had to make its decision."

"He's not going to accept this. He doesn't have to. And where will that leave you and all the rest?"

Hawley stared at her, instantly concerned. "Has he told you that?"

Kathy didn't want to admit that she didn't know, but she sensed Hawley's anxiety. "I'm certain that he won't accept this," she finally said.

"A little while ago you were almost in tears, wondering what this action would mean—to you. You've spoken more than once to me about the impossible strain the President's under, his age, his health." Suddenly, a new thought struck him. "Tell me, Kathy, are you more concerned now about *your* role than his?"

"I resent that, Cliff," she said angrily. "You've already told me you couldn't trust me with your secret. But as long as you've asked me, I'll ask you again. Did you give one moment's honest thought about me, about *my* life, while you were planning all of this, you and your Committee?"

He knew he had to terminate the discussion. He could not allow himself to think of their past, let alone the future, nor would he be anything less than frank.

"No," he admitted, "the Committee never discussed it."

"And you?"

"No." He stopped for a moment, then said, "Our preoccupation is not with personalities. It's with the nation's security."

"So I'm left to think for myself. Whenever I've asked Stephen to think of me, he talks of duty, his duty. And now you. You talk of national security. Big words, Cliff, but I deserved better from you. You told me that Stephen demanded your resignation. I was appalled. I told him so. I'm a human being, Cliff. And so is Stephen. Don't do this to him." She paused for a moment.

"Once, I asked you, before I married Stephen, 'Do I lose you?' Remember?"

Hawley nodded. "At Ed Jaggers' place, Leesburg. I remember, yes . . ."

"'I'd never lose you. Never.'" They sat quietly examining each other. "Those were your words, Cliff."

Hawley broke the silence. "There's nothing more I can say. Unfortunately, this is not a time for personal feelings. I have my duties, Kathy, as the President has his. I'd like to have your affection. To keep it. But, if necessary, I'll settle for your respect—I want it—"

"That's an odious word under the circumstances."

She stared at him, pained, but he would say no more; he could say no more. He reached over and gripped her arm. Then, abruptly, he released her and walked briskly from the room.

He glanced down the broad corridor, noticed the fresh flowers that made even the center hall resemble a handsome room with its bookcase, side tables and desks, and its large comfortable chairs and potted plants. As he walked down the broad stairway to the first floor, he felt for the first time that he was, in fact, President of the United States.

25

The East Room of the White House, its chandeliers sparkling from the lights within, was crowded with dignitaries hurriedly assembled for the swearing-in ceremonies. Hawley wanted everyone with political importance to be present, and the White House machinery, orchestrated by Kraus and Latham, had brought in all the members of the Supreme Court who were available together with the Cabinet, congressional leaders, the dean of the embassy corps, the brass of the Pentagon, the heads of various federal agencies, and key members of the press. The ceremony, originally planned for the Cabinet Room, required the grandeur of the East Room.

Hawley had taken time to contact his parents, Joe Gratton, and Felicia Courtney. All of them were present, lined up with others to greet him. He mingled with them, and as he walked by, he found Felicia standing quietly at the end of the line.

"You knew a lot more than you told me that night in Alexandria," she said, speaking out of earshot of the others. "I'm not that impressed with you being a President," she added.

"Oh?"

"I'm more impressed with my being a prophet."

"Oh? Any more prophecies?"

"Questions," she said, looking about the room. "Will President Thompson attend?"

"No."

"Will he fight you?"

"I don't know."

"Harry? Kathy?"

"Harry's been an aide. He'll show, I think, maybe reluctantly. Kathy? No. Not without the President."

"I admire her for that." Then, her attitude changing, she said, "Now you have some chips, remember?" she asked.

"Where we play fox and lion," he replied, "but it'll have to wait for now." Their eyes met for a moment as Hawley smiled and then turned from her to greet Chief Justice Whitney.

Television cameras ground away as the Chief Justice administered the oath of office. Behind them were the famous full-length portraits of George and Martha Washington. As Hawley stood at a podium to address the nation, his eyes spotted Harry Thompson. He wanted to believe his presence was a tacit sign of family acceptance, if not approval, of his decision. And in deference to Harry, whom he deliberately singled out with a compassionate reference to the special circumstances in which he had assumed the role of Acting President, Hawley kept his remarks brief.

"The work, the dreams of President Thompson must go on," he said. "We take note of his steady dedication to duty..." he added, glancing at Hornwell seated behind the Cabinet. "... The work he began will be the work we'll continue ... and complete, if necessary," he said, aware that the members of the press would leap on that as a declaration of his candidacy to succeed himself. "The important point is that the Constitution of the United States was tested today—and the Constitution worked. The baton has been passed ... *that* is the American way. God bless you all."

He stepped to the front row, shaking his father's hand, kissing his mother, and threading his way through the group. Members of the Cabinet and others eagerly surged forward to congratulate him, Jaggers and Hornwell first.

"Admiral Hornwell met with Secretary Clauson on that matter of Red Dye Day, and Navy and Air Force planes are all in place awaiting your orders," Jaggers said, pressing Hawley's hand.

"Good. You notify the Soviet ambassador."

Then Hawley moved toward Hornwell, grasping his hand.

"Red Dye Day, Admiral. Implement it immediately. At the same time notify NATO headquarters."

"Aye, aye, Mr. President," Hornwell said as he took leave.

Jaggers turned to Daniels. "Mr. Hawley's made his first decision. Red Dye Day's now operative—finally." Then, nodding to Latham, he said, "The President should have acted, Tom."

Latham agreed. "Admiral Hornwell did his damndest."

Jaggers shrugged. "If he'd succeeded . . ." He observed Hawley shaking Senator Vance's outstretched hand. "None of this would have happened."

The three watched as Hawley signalled Vance to accompany him to the Oval Office.

☆ ☆ ☆

"A day to remember," Hawley began, as he pointed to the sofa in the Oval Office. "Fred, I want you to know your coming in today was generous, surprising under the circumstances. Kraus admitted *his* surprise—now I can finally admit to mine."

"Thank you," Vance said. "I must confess it wasn't exactly planned. I convinced myself that President Thompson could hang on, perhaps take a much-needed rest after the convention . . ."

"You weren't alone," Hawley said, adding, "The President obviously thinks very highly of you. Your future is still ahead of you, Senator."

"I appreciate that, too," Vance replied, accepting Hawley's statement as a winner's patronizing, conventional compliment. "You stay in the Senate long enough you can shoot for Whip or Majority Leader."

"Fred," Hawley said abruptly. "Let me ask you—how important is your inquiry into network programming?" He could see that Vance was thrown off balance by the sudden change of subject.

Startled, Vance could visualize a grinning Joe Gratton standing immediately behind Hawley. "Not too important," he began, "to me, that is," he sputtered. He decided he didn't relish having his surprise decision to support Hawley suddenly become an action that would trigger a series of political confessions on his part. The whole investigation had been a Harry Thompson ploy with his Washington Six, and now he could easily dispense with it.

"Investigating the networks on the eve of a convention just

isn't good politics," Hawley said, burrowing in as he seated himself across from Vance. "We'll need them. All of them."

"Yes," Vance replied, raising both hands in a gesture designed to downplay the importance of his investigation. "It could be put off," he said, but detecting no enthusiasm on Hawley's part to a mere delay, he added, "We could just let it all wither away."

"I don't want you to abandon something you feel has great public merit," Hawley said disarmingly, "though your time might be better occupied with other matters."

Pure tactics, Vance thought. He'd caught the meaning of the whole discussion about television, but no matter how he accommodated Hawley, he knew he was being advised that he wasn't to consider the wiping out of the Gratton investigation any claim to some future obligation on Hawley's part. Vance fell back in his corner of the sofa, a little dubious. "I've really taken up enough of your time, Mr. President. You must have a lot on your mind . . ." He began to feel uncomfortable.

"The convention's coming up, Senator," Hawley said. "I believe the President had you very much in mind."

Vance was suddenly even more uneasy. He regretted voicing his interest in being the new Whip. "Yes, well, all that's quite academic, now. The President was a certainty for renomination . . ."

"I was going to allow my name to be placed in nomination, no matter what the President planned . . . as Vice President," Hawley added.

"Yes, of course."

"You can be sure of one thing, Senator. From the moment your name surfaced, the President had the FBI conduct a thorough investigation on you. Kraus would have ordered it on his own. You understand all that, of course?"

"Of course, sir."

"It would have been a struggle between us, uneven I think." Hawley rose from his chair, indicating as he did that he wanted Vance to remain seated. He took a few steps toward his desk, glanced back at Vance over his shoulder. "I don't think being Whip or Majority Leader is in the cards for you, Fred."

Vance shrank within, his fears confirmed that he had spoken too frankly of his immediate ambition in the Senate hierarchy. "It's not that you aren't qualified, Fred," Hawley continued, "it's just that this is one of those moments I was talking about a couple of minutes ago. You deliberate weeks, even months.

It's just a question of 'the best laid plans of mice and men . . .'" he glanced again at Vance.

"Yes, I know," Vance murmured unhappily.

"You deliberate for months," Hawley repeated, "and then you take action on a moment's notice." When he began to chuckle, Vance yearned to escape. "You can get up now, Fred. You and I are going down the hall for a minute and we're going to give Henry Kraus his second shock of the day." He came over to Vance with an outstretched hand. "Don't you understand, Fred, what we've been talking about? You *do* know how the Twenty-fifth Amendment works, don't you?"

"Yes, of course."

"Well, sir. Assuming that President Thompson does not contest this decision, and assuming I'm the party's nominee—two fairly large assumptions—I'm going to ask you to be my running mate," Hawley said. He saw the shock register on Vance's face. "It was President Thompson's wish. Now it's mine."

"I don't believe this," Vance finally said, his voice choking with emotion.

"Elizabeth will," Hawley said, chuckling again. "Now let's go see Kraus."

☆ ☆ ☆

Hawley's next visitors in the Oval Office were Jaggers and Daniels. Daniels immediately informed Hawley that agents, under the combined authority of the National Security Agency and the Committee, had found the copy of the letter addressed to Nikita Turgenev. It was marked "For Mr. Turgenev's eyes only," addressed to "The President of the Soviet Union." The envelope was secured by a presidential wax seal.

"President Thompson has been officially notified of these actions," Daniels said. "We sent Henry Kraus to advise him."

Daniels handed the letter over to Hawley, who immediately picked up a letter opener and cut through the seal. He walked over to the French doors leading to the Rose Garden and quietly read the letter as Jaggers and Daniels sat patiently waiting. Then he returned to his desk and said, "I think, perhaps, the best way to handle this is for me to read some of this to you, give you copies later. Agreeable, gentlemen?" Jaggers and Daniels nodded their approval.

"Okay. It starts out, 'My dear Nikita: As my first term draws closer to its end, I have begun to give deeper consideration to what kind of legacy I can leave to the people of my country.

I have no doubt that the same consideration is frequently on your mind.

"'Our two countries are still the two chief guardians of the peace. I believe that we each can readily admit that there is no sensible, acceptable alternative to this joint role.

"'Perhaps now is as good a time as any to indulge in what some might characterize as wishful thinking. My country will soon be involved in a political contest. I believe, judging from the record of my Administration as it is reflected in the polls taken here, that we will be returned to office. Should I become disabled or be incapable of finishing my prescribed term for any reason, I would expect that my successor will find these personal proposals worthy of discussion with you.'"

Hawley stopped for a moment and noted the look of surprise on the faces of his associates. "The President clearly had some concern about his future."

"And counting on his successor to implement his wishes," Daniels added.

"He asks," Hawley said, "questions on how we, together, can create a better world, refers to, and I quote, 'these mechanisms which are designed to destroy each other.'"

"Mechanisms? Well, now, that's a novel way of describing nuclear stockpiles," Jagger interjected.

"He goes on," Hawley said, returning to the letter, "to write about 'the industrial-biological-scientific complex that challenges the existence of our species, and that threatens to affect the fate of mankind more profoundly than nuclear power,' and he proposes some steps we might take that would move us closer together."

"I'm afraid there's already a *lot* of wishful thinking in that document," Jaggers said.

Hawley nodded his agreement. "Let me read this next part. He writes, 'I do not want to spell out the myriad of details that each suggestion I offer is certain to create; for example, I'm aware, of course, of the various cultural and especially the scientific exchange programs we share with each other here and in space, and the growing tourist activity in both of our countries. But I'm not thinking simply in terms of tourists, but as participants *within* each other's society. I would like to see the same number of Americans and of Soviets settle, for a respectable amount of time, in each other's country. How many and for how long? Perhaps as many as one hundred thousand from each side for a starter. Annually. Perhaps for a stay of three years or longer. People from all walks of life, men, women, children, a veritable cross section of your vast country and ours.'"

"A hundred thousand? Annually? On each side?" Jaggers shook his head. "That's totally unrealistic. Good Lord, did he stop to think of the logistics! Did he know we only had fifty or so of their students in '88? A hundred *thousand*, living *here*? I'd say that's a bit preposterous!"

"Hold on," Hawley said. "He goes on about housing lawyers with lawyers, police officers with police officers, teachers with teachers, and so on. And he suggests that some of the Soviet citizens who come here might work in our plants, attend some of our schools, live on our farms, etcetera. And we, in turn, have the same privileges in the Soviet Union. And then he writes, 'We start off with some basics. Everyone must eventually return to his own country, unless there is absolute mutual agreement to make exceptions. For example, I think that neither side should place any obstacles in the way of marriage if that is the wish of any couple, and they should have the right to choose where they want to live. We should agree not to proselytize; our purpose should be to inform, to educate, to illuminate.

"'Think, if you will, eventually, of as many as one million Soviet citizens in our country at any given time committed to a stay, and one million Americans in yours. Think of this as a ten-year experiment, of the impact of such an experience on millions of other Soviet citizens and millions of Americans. And as the years pass, the numbers could increase.

"'Further,' the President writes, 'I would like to see all space colonization, from this point on, conducted jointly, from lift-off to actual settlement on the planets, moons, and space stations. I would like to see citizens from other countries invited to participate in our joint colonization efforts.'

"Then he talks about a new agency, something on the order of the International Atomic Energy Agency, in Vienna, its sole function perhaps the dismantling of six nuclear weapons daily on each side, doubling that effort in due time and so on. That all of this should be carried on in all other nuclear states— whether they are signatories to the Nuclear Nonproliferation treaty or not—at a scale commensurate with that established by the United States and the Soviet Union, that this is a way to end the specter of nuclear proliferation in Brazil, Israel, Iraq, and so on."

Hawley looked up at Daniels and Jaggers. "Let me read the end. 'Finally, I would suggest that certain elements of the leadership of both countries, at appropriate times—myself, for example, at the end of my term as President—be part of the group settling for a reasonable period in each other's country.

"'These suggestions, Mr. President, are designed to reduce tensions, to give more meaningful direction to our coexistence. Such a start would permit us to devote some attention to the issues raised at the beginning of this letter. Think, sir, of the legacy that we can jointly bestow not only on our citizens but on the future of mankind.

"'The Red Army and the United States military must be the guardians of world peace whether the target is a local war, an act of terrorists, or the still loathesome work of the drug cartels. The exchange of citizens among all nations—and we two set the example—can be the prelude, eventually, at some time in the future to open borders. These actions will sow the seeds for One World, which, of course, will ultimately require some levelling down for some nations and some lifting up for others. The process will, admittedly, take time, but these suggestions, once you embrace them, might serve as starters.

"'May I suggest that if there is even a modicum of interest on your part, we entrust to our negotiators at Geneva, Mr. Voroshilov and Mrs. Curtis, the task of devoting some time to exploring the practicalities of implementation? Sincerely, H. Stephen Thompson.'"

Hawley sat back in his chair, pensive, as he waited on Daniels and Jaggers, Jaggers speaking first. "Mr. Turgenev won't do anything on this until after the election this fall."

"If then," Daniels added.

Hawley passed the memorandum to Jaggers. "A copy of this should be sent to Alice Curtis at once."

Jaggers stroked his moustache. "Well, now I know why the President felt he couldn't discuss this with the Cabinet as well as his staff and the Joint Chiefs. Who would have endorsed it?"

As Daniels lit a cigarette, he said, "I have to agree with the Secretary. And especially if we've been at Geneva all these years with so little progress to report, how much progress do you think we can make—and in how little time—on total joint space colonization, on the logistics of who will be included in those thousands and thousands of Russians? No members of the KGB? Of how we check their arms and biological research?"

"You're not bound to any of this," Jaggers added, raising the letter.

"Of course not, but I wouldn't want to repudiate it out of hand, either," Hawley replied.

"Mr. Turgenev will save you that embarrassment," Daniels said. "When Mrs. Curtis puts these questions to Mr. Voroshilov it will die in Geneva," Jaggers predicted.

"If it hasn't already been murdered in Moscow," Daniels concluded.

"You're probably right, both of you," Hawley replied. "This letter was, in one sense, maybe a symbol of a presidency gone a bit awry. No consultation with anyone, the Secretary of State, the Secretary of Defense, the Joint Chiefs, the Congress—the Committee. No matter how meritorious the proposals, there are established procedures that protect each of us, including the President."

"He may have meant well," Jaggers volunteered, "but he should have remembered the Iran-Contra affair. Good intentions don't add up to good government."

Looking across the desk at a portrait of a smiling H. Stephen Thompson and a radiant Kathy Thompson photographed on their wedding day, Hawley couldn't help thinking how much had changed in just a few brief years. "This letter was one of the President's last official acts," he said, "one in which he was reaching for what many a politician would describe as an impossible dream. Even Eisenhower was accused of being unrealistic when he proposed our actually exchanging blueprints of our military establishments with the Soviets, plus a mutual right to exercise aerial reconnaissance over each other's borders. The Soviets reflected that. But dreams, gentlemen, yes, even impossible dreams, these are the stuff accomplishments are made of. By the poets, by the Einsteins, by the great builders. Without the dreamers, where *would* mankind be?"

Neither Jaggers nor Daniels responded.

"One time, while I was on a political trip," Hawley went on, "I was in Rushville, Indiana. I stopped at the gravesite of a man who wanted to be President. Wendell Willkie. He had the dream of One World, as I recall. On a marker there, right by his grave, I never forgot some words he wrote. He believed in America, he said, 'Because we have great dreams and because we have the opportunity to make those dreams come true.' Those were his words. And it may be that President Thompson is pointing the way with his own impossible challenge. Remember Kennedy's dream of putting a man on the moon? We have only to remember that an impossible goal in one generation is what often makes for a remarkable achievement in another."

"I like your words even better than Willkie's," Jaggers said as he rose from his chair. "I'll see that a copy goes out to Mrs. Curtis at once," he added, pocketing the Thompson memorandum.

Daniels lingered behind as Jaggers left the Oval Office. "On the matter of the White House tapes," he said, glancing up at Hawley, "Mr. Taggart's been our point man. The NSA and the Signal Corps have been very cooperative. Except for one chap. Rossmore. Know him?"

"No," Hawley said.

"Harry Thompson's key man. Taggart's team has located all the sites and they have the tapes. Most of them."

"The others?" Hawley asked.

"They're all coded automatically, sequentially, with location, time, dates. But there are a couple missing." He looked at his watch. "Taggart's with Rossmore right now, at the CIA," Daniels added. "I'll stop by and have a look-see."

"We have to find them all," Hawley said quietly.

"Yes, sir," Daniels replied as he headed for the door, adding, "including copies, if any."

26

Henry Kraus and Hugh Riley, Hawley's Chief of Staff, had feverishly worked out Hawley's schedule for his first day as Acting President. Hornwell was one of the last visitors to the Oval Office along with Jaggers, both men reporting on the impact of Red Dye Day. Hours earlier, the Soviet ambassador had suggested that the time had come, perhaps, when both sides should seriously consider a cooling-off period in the underseas games in order to avoid unanticipated results.

"What he said," Jaggers reported, "was that this undersea battle we've been waging for so many years has been remarkably secret on both sides and any public disclosures might result in creating the very conditions the games were designed to prevent."

"Meaning?" Hawley interjected.

"Some unpredictable action by some American—even some Soviet skipper—who, maybe, under considerable pressure from the strain of these constant war games, might persuade himself that some preemptive strike would be in his country's best interest."

Hawley turned to Hornwell. Hornwell's face creased into a confident smile. "Anything's possible anywhere, but the price extracted would be immediate. They know *we* know where *they* are, and *we* know they know where *we* are. Any such move would be an invitation to presumed self-destruction on either side. They also know we actually *do* have real superiority in our technological edge. I think it's safe to say that deterrence still works. And our deployment of space defenses—modest as they are—could handle an unstable commander's full complement of missiles."

"Red Dye Day ended their short-lived celebration of superiority," Jaggers added as he glanced at Hornwell.

"It's one of those events we can each take some pride in, but it's a mighty small circle that'll celebrate," Hawley replied, nodding toward Hornwell. "Admiral," he continued, "I know you have a scheduled commitment with the Joint Chiefs and I salute you and each of them for the speed with which you effected all of the details connected with Red Dye Day. Well done, sir."

Hornwell stood up, saluting Hawley. "One day your decision will be in the history books and provide the full explanation of the responsibilities you had to assume."

"Thank you, Admiral," Hawley said as Hornwell left the office.

"He's come around," Jaggers said. "You thought he would."

"Kraus says the networks, the wire services, reporters from everywhere, are screaming for a face-to-face press conference."

"Too soon," Jaggers said, "but maybe a few carefully selected reporters here in the Oval Office might be a useful way for you to counter such a demand."

"Maybe," Hawley said. "On the other hand, I don't want to rush things and find myself in a position of saying one thing only to have Mr. Thompson making a contradictory statement a few minutes later. Meanwhile, Senator Vance is working with the Speaker and the President pro tem. If I'm to believe Vance, if the issue is drawn, it could be a close call. By the way," Hawley added, "Kraus is upstairs with Thompson at this very moment."

"Kraus is still Mr. Thompson's man," Jaggers said, preparing to leave. "Might have been better to have included Hoberman. The Attorney General's a persuasive man, and the President respects him."

"He's up there, too," Hawley broke in. "Explaining the difference between inability and disability. Everyone's been talking about disability, but as you know, the word in the amendment is *inability*." Hawley pointed to the ceiling. "Here I am, Mr. Secretary, in the Oval Office, Acting President. Upstairs, the elected President. At this moment, who's *really* in charge?"

Jaggers reflected for a moment at the door, then said, "When all's said and done, if he'd wanted to make a direct confrontation, he would have challenged you right here, in this very office. He chose not to."

As Jaggers left, Tom Latham ushered in Hawley's next visitor, Everard Meade, a tall, balding onetime professor of political science at the University of Virginia. Catapulted into the governor's chair some years later, he had continued his political activities running the party machinery. Sitting down and placing both hands on Hawley's desk, Meade asked, with characteristic bluntness, "What goes with the man upstairs?"

"Can't answer that, yet," Hawley said.

"He can really screw up the convention," Meade said. "And if he insists he's capable of discharging his duties, who's to determine if he's right or wrong?" Without waiting for Hawley's response he said, "For sure the country would demand he undergo some tests, physical *and* mental. And then the Congress has twenty-one days to arrive at a decision, assuming you hold on." Meade shook his head. "What a way to launch our campaign."

"Not a cheerful picture."

"Sir, the mistake was made four years ago. The President was sixty-six years old then. Popular, seemingly in tip-top physical shape, that great voice—all big assets. Then to balance the team, you. Young, vigorous, perfect partner. Four years later? You're still young. And the President?" Meade sat back in his chair. "You can't fight the actuarial tables. The lessons were there for everyone to study, to take a little extra look down the road. Actually we saw it in Reagan—too old from day one. Even with his laid-back style—over the years some of those press conferences of his were downright embarrassing, assistants scurrying around explaining his gaffes, his confusions, even his downright ignorance. Not to mention his forgetfulness. Remember his taped testimony at the Poindexter trial? His inability to remember the name of his chairman of the Joint Chiefs, Vasey, plus maybe a hundred other areas where he blanked out?" Meade shook his head. "Incredible," he said, "and that's why I say I don't think you'll be seeing a presidential candidate in the next century running for office who'll be much past seventy when he *finishes* his second term."

"Ineligible at sixty-two, say, that it?"

"Won't surprise me. There's plenty of talent between thirty-five and sixty-two. I've been studying the subject. Our Founding Fathers. Practically all of them took office when they were fifty-seven or -eight, and that includes Washington. Adams was the oldest of that crowd. Sixty-one. And Reagan the oldest ever. Seventy-three going into his second term. If President Thompson resumes this office, he'll have tough sledding for a second term."

"If," Hawley repeated.

"Let's hope, for the sake of the party, Henry Kraus gets the right answer."

"For the sake of the country," Hawley said.

"Amen, Mr. President."

☆ ☆ ☆

As Hawley and Meade were meeting in the Oval Office, Daniels sat in his own office, his legs resting on his plain wooden desk. Seated across from him, Jeb Rossmore was determined to retain his own equanimity. Taggart, arms akimbo, stood off to the side against the wall, somewhat behind Rossmore, but in Daniels' line of sight. Taggart felt pleased that in quickly filling in Daniels on the results of his interview of Rossmore, Daniels had not once interrupted him. That was a sign of having won Daniels' approval.

Daniels leaned back in his chair, hands clasped together behind his head, and nodded toward a batch of notes lying on his otherwise clean desk. "Any quarrel with Mr. Taggart's review?"

"None, sir," Jeb replied.

"You haven't told the whole story, Lieutenant," Daniels said coolly.

Rossmore frowned. "I've answered every question put to me."

"I daresay. But you also withheld information. That means to me that you failed to speak with candor."

"I haven't told any lies if that's what you're implying."

"It's not what I'm implying."

"I answered every question he put to me," Jeb repeated, glancing back at Taggart. "Ask him."

"I've heard his report and I've skimmed his notes. But now I'm going to ask you a couple of questions myself—"

Rossmore suddenly clenched the arms of his chair. "I'm not

sure you have the authority to be asking me *any* questions, Mr. Daniels."

"I have the President's authority."

"Not President Thompson's," Rossmore said belligerently.

"The *Acting* President's, to be sure. Mr. Hawley. The man who was sworn in just a few hours ago by the Chief Justice." Daniels suddenly pulled his feet off the desk, hunched forward, and in a firm voice said, "Your integrity is at stake here, Lieutenant. Your honor as a West Pointer. If you don't answer to me—as the President's emissary in this matter—you'll be answering to the Department of Justice. Do you understand?"

"On what basis?"

Daniels fixed his eyes on Rossmore. "Lieutenant, you are holding government property."

"Property?" Rossmore echoed.

A thin smile crossed Daniels' face. "You understand English, sir," he said, picking up Taggart's report. "Mr. Taggart asked you if there was anything else you cared to add and you politely replied, 'No, sir.' Isn't that correct?"

"Yes, sir," Rossmore said glumly.

"But you *had* something more to add, didn't you?"

"Like what?" Jeb responded challengingly.

"Like *where* are the missing tapes?"

"I answered that."

"Sort of," Daniels said, fingering Taggart's notes. "I saw your answer a moment ago . . . here it is," he added, studying the papers, then looking across at Rossmore. "Your response: '*Are* there missing tapes?' Remember saying that?"

"If you say so," Jeb said, pointing to the papers.

"Not if *I* say so, Lieutenant. Those were *your* words. Now, let's stop the trying to be clever and ducking answers."

"I've answered everything," Jeb insisted.

Daniels smiled. "Your way. Now, do you want to speak with full candor?" A moment later the smile suddenly vanished and the words shot out with a sudden toughness. "Do I have to drag an answer out of you?"

"I don't take kindly to threats, Mr. Daniels," Rossmore retorted.

"Where are the missing cassettes, Lieutenant?"

Jeb Rossmore slowly pushed back in his chair as he kept his eyes fixed on Daniels. "I'm not sure," he finally said.

Daniels leaned in closer. "Well, now, that's a better answer. At least now you admit some cassettes *are* missing." He began rolling a cigarette. And as he finished, he said, "So you're not sure. Okay. You're not sure." He lit the cigarette and blew out a perfect ring of smoke. "Where, Lieutenant, do you *think* they are?"

"I'd just be guessing."

"Good. Go on."

"They could still be in the White House," Jeb said, shrugging his shoulders.

"In whose office?"

"Maybe the Signal Corps."

"They're not there. Go on."

"I don't have them."

"We know that." Daniels' hands went behind his head again. "Anyone listen to those tapes?"

"They were the President's," Jeb replied.

"Did *he* listen to them?"

"I don't know. I don't think so."

"How would you know *that*, Lieutenant?"

Rossmore shifted in his chair, plainly uncomfortable. "I was told."

"You were told," Daniels repeated as he looked at Taggart, shaking his head. Then he returned his gaze to Rossmore. "Okay, you were told. The sixty-four dollar question, Lieutenant Rossmore. Who told you?"

There was a long pause before Rossmore spoke. "Harry," Jeb murmured.

"Thompson? Harry Thompson? That it?"

"Yes, sir."

"And does he have the tapes?"

"No, sir. Not all of them."

"Well?"

"Now that I think more about it, they aren't in my office—"

"Your White House office—" Daniels said, interrupting him. "You have another office?"

"Another office?" Jeb asked.

"Another office," Daniels repeated patiently. "Maybe at home?"

"At home." Rossmore took in another deep breath before speaking. Then he said, "Yes."

Daniels looked over again at Taggart. "Would you care to place them in Mr. Taggart's hands yourself, or do you want Mr. Taggart to find them on his own?"

"He can have what I have."

Daniels blew out a fresh series of smoke rings. Then, turning his attention to Jeb, he said, "I want you to know you've done the right thing, Lieutenant. I understand your reluctance. Anyone else hear those missing tapes besides you and Harry Thompson?"

"Maybe. Possibly Lane Whitney."

"You like Harry Thompson and Lane Whitney?"

"We've been close friends for years."

"I happen to know that the Acting President and the Secretary of State are considering an important mission for young Mr. Thompson. That's because of his interest in minorities—blacks, Hispanics, Indians. You're familiar with that interest?"

"Yes, sir."

Daniels studied his young visitor. "Would you like to be part of that mission?"

"If Harry wants me—if the government assigns me—except—"

"Except what?"

"I'm not sure about the tapes, how Harry'll feel about my surrendering them."

"Anything on those tapes damaging to Harry—or to President Thompson?"

"No, sir."

"To anyone else?" Daniels asked softly.

Rossmore hesitated. "I think—others would have to judge that," he said.

"Of course. If Harry doesn't know you surrendered the tapes—"

"I'd have to tell him."

Daniels smiled. "Candor, sometimes. That it?"

"I'd just have to," Rossmore insisted.

"All right. And the mission?"

"If I can be useful, fine, sir."

"Thank you," Daniels said as he rose. "Now let's you and Mr. Taggart go get the tapes, Lieutenant."

27

Harry Thompson gazed at his father across the table in the upstairs dining room of the White House. "I saw Henry Kraus for a minute," he said. "Told me he'd just left you."

"Briefed me," his father replied.

"Very courteous of him," Harry said sarcastically.

"He had no hand in any of this, Harry. He sits on the National Security Council, but this was the work of the Committee. The Attorney General made his position clear, too."

"Both pretending to be figureheads, I'll bet," Harry commented.

"They were," the President said, toying with his food. "Kathy sent in word she'd join us a bit later."

"For once we're in agreement. I mean Kathy and me." Then, eyeing his father, he added, "Except I wouldn't trust her." He saw the immediate impact of his words. "You don't, do you?" His father quietly set down his fork. "You don't, do you?" Harry persisted.

The President sighed. "I *can't*, if that's any satisfaction."

"Did you tell Kraus where you stand? Isn't that what he really came up to find out?"

The President sipped a glass of wine. "Brought me a message from Chairman Meade."

"Mr. Meade was conferring with Hawley at the same time. I saw him going into the Oval Office."

"No surprise there. Mr. Meade suggested I consider withdrawing my name before the convention."

It was Harry Thompson's turn to set down his fork. "He asked for *that?*"

"That was his message," the President said.

"And your response?" Harry asked.

The President smiled. "Seems like the whole world's waiting for my answer—"

"Well, it *is*," Harry said. "I hope you told him that you're going to notify the Speaker that you *have* no disability—"

"Inability," the President said, correcting his son.

"The same."

"Not exactly," the President said. "Hoberman was quite specific."

"You're not going to let a dictionary definition dictate your response, are you?" Harry inquired.

Thompson began to chuckle, and then, as though Harry wasn't present, he went on, "I can see them turning to one another, trying to establish how this whole mess developed, why no one spoke out in my defense. Where was Hornwell? Where was the National Security Adviser? Why didn't they have the courage to come in and talk to me, do things manfully, openly, honorably? Why the rush? Why on the eve of the convention?" Suddenly, his eyes narrowing as if focusing on some visible menace, he slapped the table with his right fist. "A grab for power, that's what it is! Power! Dog eat dog! Margaret would know how to handle this! How to put the heat to them! By God, she's right, Harry, she's right!" he exclaimed.

As he raged on, Harry became alarmed at the sudden twitching of the President's facial muscles, the stiffening and curling of the fingers on his right hand. He got up from his chair and hurried around to his father's side. "Dad! Hey, please! Take it easy!"

But the President ignored him. "You'll see, Harry. I've worked it out. Your mother always was sharp! Intellectual! Give her the facts, set out the problem, she finds a solution!" He stopped talking, aware of Harry's arm around his shoulder. "Why are you . . . why aren't you having your dinner?" he demanded.

"I will, I will," Harry said, reassuring him. "It's just that . . . are you all right?"

The President looked down and studied his twisted fingers. "It's nothing, nothing."

"I'll call Jensen."

"It's nothing!" Thompson insisted. "Now go sit down!" He paused a moment, breathing heavily. "It'll go away, you'll see. Look. Already," he said, raising his hand, his fingers gradually straightening out. "See?"

"I see, but, Dad, that could be a symptom of something deeper. You're under too much of a strain—"

"Of course I'm under a strain! But I'm here, Harry! Here! Fully aware!" He put out both hands and lifted his wineglass to his lips. "You're not to worry. *They're* to worry. They think I'm through. I'm not!" Slowly he placed the glass on the table, shutting his eyes and resting his head on the back of his chair. "Sit down, Harry," he murmured.

Harry Thompson returned to his chair, his eyes still fixed on his father. For the first time, he acknowledged to himself that his true awareness of the real state of his father's health was the result of his father's determined and successful effort to conceal it. Perhaps, he had to admit, the Committee knew more than he did. If his father could talk to him about his mother as though she were alive and present, could he have done the same with others listening? *That* had to be alarming, even frightening. His thinking was interrupted by Kathy's appearance. At that moment, the President, opening his eyes, straightened his shoulders as she took her seat.

"I'm sorry to be late, Stephen," she said. "I'm really not very hungry. I've already told them to just bring me a salad."

"I'm glad you could join us. Harry and I have been having an interesting conversation. Reviewing their . . . what shall we call them, shenanigans?"

"I've been watching television. There's a lot of confusion. A lot of special programming. Everyone being interviewed. Members of the Cabinet. Congress. People from every think tank in the country. . ."

"All regular programming cancelled?"

"No. There were one or two regular programs running."

"Their ratings winners," Harry commented, contemptuously. "Typical. The world could be ending. Rome burning. But the show goes on. Gratton's world."

"Yes, but most of them are off. I asked about it," Kathy said, as her salad was set before her. "Thank you, Mildred," she said to the waitress. Then, quietly, "Have you made your decision, Stephen?"

"You still want me to make a fight for it?"

"Need you really ask?" she replied.

"Just wanted to be sure," the President said.

"*I'm* not sure," Harry said with some emphasis.

"Oh?" Kathy looked up, surprised. "I thought . . . weren't we in agreement earlier?"

"I'm just not sure now, that's all," Harry said, staring hard at his father.

"Well," the President said, "if you two would hold to a firm position, it would help *me* make my *own* mind up."

Turning to Harry, Kathy asked, "What's given you second thoughts?"

"What if my father really isn't all that well, Kathy?"

"But he is. Look at him."

The President smiled.

Harry persisted. "But what if the doctors know. . ." Then looking again at his father, he said, "What if *he* knows, what if the medical records indicate that while he *looks* well—"

Kathy looked at her husband. "Stephen?"

The President rubbed his hands together. "Fascinating, listening to each of you. You've each switched positions, do you realize that? Harry, in just the last few minutes. Quite a contrast, Harry, to your earlier behavior. 'Arrest them! Call out the troops! Forget the Constitution!' And you, Kathy, for weeks urging me to step aside, let others come forward, I'm *not* the indispensable man. Whenever I mentioned the word *duty* you scoffed. Now, tell me, both of you . . . whose advice am I to follow?"

Kathy broke the silence. "*They* changed the rules of the game, Stephen, and that's why *I've* changed my opinion. What they've done is outrageous and unforgivable. Not one of them had the decency to come forward and discuss his concerns, lay out the options for you. No, they simply conspired—I can't think of a kinder word—they conspired to find a pretext to achieve their ends, ends to which I know you would never voluntarily have surrendered."

"Well said, Kathy," the President acknowledged.

"You're forgetting one thing," Harry interjected, facing Kathy. "My father's physical condition. They knew about it. Hornwell's on the Committee. He went to Bethesda with my father. Whatever that report said, they know."

"It was made public," Kathy replied.

"Sure," Harry responded, "those parts Jensen and my father's other doctors *wanted* made public. Isn't that true, Dad? The country got only what *you* wanted it to know. But the Committee? Wouldn't they have the power to get it all, an actual copy of the whole report?"

"They could have gotten it, yes, Harry," the President admitted.

"Then who's right? Kathy? Or me?"

Thompson pushed himself away from the table. "We won't know that for some time, son."

"Are you just going to sit? Wait? Let them cart you out, is that it?" Harry said, testily.

The President flushed. "No one's going to cart anyone out. I'm not dependent on Mr. Hawley's largesse to stay here in the White House. It's the President's home, not the so-called Acting President's. Besides, the *real* White House is where the President says it is."

"And what does that mean?" Harry asked.

The President stood at the door and smiled. "You'll have the answer in just a few hours."

☆ ☆ ☆

Harry Thompson had gone from the White House to sit at his special window nook in the dark, intimate Round Robin Bar of the Willard Hotel, to be alone and to think. It had been Gloria's favorite cocktail spot, and his weekly Friday visit had taken on the form of a regular ritual in her memory, even to the setting of a glass for her. A red rose was always in place in the bud vase, and the bartender never hesitated to signal anyone who wished to join Harry of his desire to be alone for a private quarter hour.

After a while he slipped out of the bar, the small vase in his hand, and went upstairs to a room the hotel kept available to him. There, chin resting on folded hands, Harry sat back in an old walnut armchair he'd pulled up toward a window, peering through lace curtains to an unobstructed view of the Washington Monument.

He thought of Hawley sitting in the Oval Office and of Kathy upstairs, each, perhaps, wondering what was on the other's mind, he, Harry, certain that Hawley would have been startled by Kathy's determination that his father hang on to his office.

That determination had not only surprised him, but even confused him.

A knock on the door interrupted his reverie. He glanced at his watch—early, but it could be Lane Whitney, perhaps Jeb Rossmore. Harry was wrong on both accounts. Framed in the doorway, slumped forward in his familiar stance, a smile on his face, was the tall, imposing figure of Richard Daniels.

"May I come in, Harry?"

Thompson opened the door wider to admit his unexpected visitor. As he closed it, he surreptitiously glanced down the hallway.

"No one with me, Harry," Daniels said casually as he entered the room and placed his hand on the back of the chair Harry had turned to the window. "Nice view." He turned the chair about and let his rangy figure ease into it. "You do move around, Harry."

"If you don't mind my asking, what possible difference does it make to you where or how I live, Mr. Daniels?"

Daniels raised his hands in sham protest. "None. It just makes it harder to find you when I want to see you."

"I don't think finding me is so hard. My friends always know where I am."

"If I were one of your friends—"

"Your business doesn't really allow for friends, does it?" Harry replied mockingly.

Daniels shrugged and reached into a pocket, bringing out a crumpled pack of cigarettes. As he started to light up he turned to Harry. "Mind?" Then, looking at him with his searching gray eyes, he said, "I'd like to hear all the tapes, fellow. The White House tapes. I think you know what I mean."

"You mean you *want* all the tapes."

"That's another way of saying it."

"The Signal Corps has the tapes, Mr. Daniels."

"Not anymore."

"I'm surprised to hear you say that. The President asked me to set that system up some time ago. Are you on some official mission, Mr. Daniels?"

"Let's say I'd like to see a bright young lawyer play things smart. Let's say I already have most of those tapes." Daniels stood up and let his hand rest momentarily on Harry's shoulder. "With the exception of one or two. That's what brought me over for a visit."

Harry glanced at his watch. "I don't want to appear inhospitable, but I *am* expecting a visitor."

Daniels' manner remained friendly. "I like you, Harry, all the Thompsons. I admire your father. As a matter of record I was reappointed by him to my post."

"On the recommendation of Mr. Hawley, as I recall."

"Correct. I've been privileged to share the confidence of Presidents." He placed his hand on the doorknob. "You're young, and that's sometimes an advantage. Not always. But let's make one thing clear," he said, his voice hardening, and then, as though he were reading Harry's mind, adding, "this is not a game, Harry, not one of your fencing matches. I'll go further. We're in the process of collecting the tapes. Matter of fact, by now that collection's taken place. I know you have one or two of the missing pieces."

"Why would you want them?" Harry asked.

"We like to have things neat and precise. No loose ends." As he exhaled some smoke, Daniels said, "What makes you want to hold those tapes, those particular tapes, Harry?"

"I think the President has his rights in this matter. I believe he'd have a very good case—"

"Executive privilege?"

"That and private property taken from the private quarters of his residence, do you follow?"

"I'm not a lawyer, Harry. You are. But this isn't a legal matter—"

"Yes, I know how the CIA sometimes works, Mr. Daniels," Harry said with a disarming smile.

There was a light tapping on the door.

"Excuse me, do you mind?" Harry said, moving over past Daniels to open the door. Standing there, the bright hall lights of the hotel corridor reflected on the military insignia he wore, was Jeb Rossmore. "Come in, Jeb. Been expecting you. This is the Director of the CIA, Mr. Daniels. Lieutenant Rossmore."

"Sir," Jeb stammered.

"I'm glad to see you again, Lieutenant," Daniels remarked as he took Jeb's extended hand, and then looking across at Harry, he added, "I'll say good night for now, Mr. Thompson." As he stood framed in the doorway, he added, "I think the Lieutenant can fill you in," then, directing his remarks to Rossmore, "and, Lieutenant, I hope you can arrange to bring in Mr. Thompson's tapes to Mr. Taggart in the morning."

☆ ☆ ☆

The turmoil created by the Committee's action was evident in the banner headlines of newspapers, the concentrated coverage of events on radio and television, the public statements made in the White House press room by Henry Kraus, the well-orchestrated appearances of the Secretary of State, the Secretary of Defense, and the Attorney General on all of the networks' regular and special-news programs. But if the lights were on late into the night in the West Wing of the White House, there were no signs of panic or confusion.

On his own, Hawley had stepped into the White House briefing room, simply to offer reassurance to the nation that his actions were only temporary, and that he fully expected, in due time, that the President would resume his office. Meanwhile, he declared with confidence that the business of the country was in the hands of the President's own men. "We are, after all, President Thompson's team, elected *with* or selected *by* him," Hawley said, determined to project an image of a calm transfer of power. "Trustees in the very best sense of the word. And rest assured, the President will be consulted . . . *is* being consulted on all substantive matters that come before this Administration." He smiled and waved off reporters' questions as he returned to the Oval Office.

Some time later, in the drawing room of the Vice President's residence, along with Jaggers, Clauson, and Daniels, Hawley was surprised to receive a message from Henry Kraus. "He's just received a call from the Secret Service—" Hawley paused for a moment. "Gentlemen, President Thompson's moved out of the White House."

"Moved?" Jaggers exclaimed, standing near the room's fireplace. "Where to?"

"To his Kalorama place." Hawley glanced at his watch. "It's nearly midnight. Of course his home's been secured since the last election. Secret Service, the Signal Corps, it's always been kept in a state of readiness."

"It could be a sign he's accepted the inevitable," Jaggers said.

"I agree," Clauson remarked, "because if he actually intended to resist Mr. Hawley's elevation, I should think that would be better done by his remaining right there *in* the White House."

"Maybe he thought this might minimize some of the pressure," Jaggers volunteered, "both being there in the same place. . ."

"I don't think so," Daniels said. "The pressures won't go away no matter where he goes. The press, the TV cameras, none of that's going to let up. Matter of fact, his moving out simply adds to the suspense." All eyes turned to Hawley.

Hawley spoke up. "After my meeting with Mrs. Thompson I can't see that she'd *want* him to make this move—"

Daniels got up from his chair to go to a side table, pouring himself some coffee. "Unless she's planning to commute daily to *her* office," he observed over his shoulder.

"She's the First Lady, still is, and there are demands on her time every day. Groups calling her, luncheons—plus the commissions she sits on," Hawley interjected. "And if she continues *her* normal schedule, *that* might be a sign that President Thompson *will* contest the decision."

"It's obvious he deliberately scheduled that move to escape the eleven o'clock news on the East Coast," Jaggers said.

"He's playing the fox not wanting to be devoured by the wolves," Hawley said. As he noted Clauson's puzzled expression, he explained, "One of Machiavelli's principles at work." Then turning to the group, he added, "We're all speculating, of course, but by morning every spare camera in Washington will be in the Kalorama district. And I sense something else very clearly. At some point he'll be wanting to see me. I think that's one of his purposes, to show the nation that *I'm* calling on *him*."

"The whole nation's waiting to see the two of you meet," Jaggers agreed, "that's really the main point."

"And our position will be that we are always ready, willing, and able to do just *that*," Hawley replied.

☆ ☆ ☆

Kathy stood at the entrance to the impressive wood-panelled dining room of Thompson's Kalorama estate. There were dark circles under her eyes, induced by the strain of the overnight decision to move from the White House. As her eyes swept the room, they flashed open disdain at the sight of prim Betsy King seated at the President's right, taking dictation. "Good morning, Mrs. Thompson," Betsy said, with her usual touch of excessive deference.

Thompson looked up from his desk, nodded, and invited Kathy to join them as a maid walked in with a breakfast tray.

"Thank you, Stephen, and good morning Miss King," Kathy

said coldly. She continued standing quietly by one of the carved wooden columns that framed the entranceway.

"Won't you join us?" Thompson asked.

"I'm having breakfast at my office with Anne Koyce."

Thompson frowned. "I'd rather you didn't go there, Kathy. Especially this morning. I'm told there are more than a hundred reporters milling around outside here at the main gate."

"I have a car waiting," Kathy replied. "I'll get through without any trouble."

"They'll flash the word to their counterparts and you'll have the same kind of reception at the White House."

"I have my work to do. I told you that last night."

"And I have mine," Thompson emphasized, his eyes narrowing, "which I'm doing *here*. I thought we settled all this when we drove over last night."

Pronouncing each word with icy precision, and looking directly at Betsy, Kathy said, "I don't think this is the proper forum for us to debate this matter."

Betsy instantly pushed away her chair. "If you'll excuse me, Mr. President, I left my other pen in my bag. It's in the library." As she passed Kathy, she said, "I always have two when I work with the President. I'm getting forgetful."

"Well?" the President said, after Betsy disappeared. "*Now* you have the proper forum."

"I never liked this room, Stephen. These dark mahogany walls. That huge armoire. So depressing."

"It was owned by Maximilian. Quite a history to it."

"Perhaps there is," Kathy said wearily. "But to me it's a symbol of defeat. He was a loser."

"And because I own it," Thompson said coldly, "that makes me a loser?"

"If you stay here, yes."

As Thompson picked up his orange juice and sipped it, he asked, "Are we to go over all of that again? We're here, Kathy. We're staying here."

"*You* are, Stephen. I'm going to my office."

"You do that, Kathy, you complicate matters. I'm here working out a decision—handling White House business—"

"And Mr. Hawley? Sitting in the Oval Office? Your office? What is he doing?"

"Thinking. Just like me. Okay, he's made his move. Now he has to wait. He has to wait until I make mine."

"And I'm to sit upstairs, in my room. Watching TV, reading a book, telephoning friends? That's what you'd have me do?"

She shook her head. "I told you yesterday I wouldn't do it." She took a step toward him. "Stephen, don't you see? Sneaking out of the White House, at night—how it makes you look like you've given up?"

"Is that a fact? Perhaps you're not aware. Mr. Kraus is here. The Attorney General's here. Admiral Hornwell *will* be here. I've advised Kraus to have the Secretary of State here at one sharp. The Majority Leader will be here at two. Does that sound like giving up?" He pushed back and placed both hands on the edge of his desk. "The White House, Kathy, is where the President is. Camp David. A hotel in Santa Barbara, Key West, or even in the air. We're tied into 1600 Pennsylvania Avenue. There's a hot line here. Instant communication with anyone, anywhere. All *they* have is an office. If I choose to occupy the White House itself next week, that'll be *my* decision. In the meantime, they're in the West Wing of an empty building. Period."

"Aren't you forgetting that the White House is a symbol to the people? That's where *they* think the government is, there and at the Capitol, not in your private home." She still remained standing, framed in the doorway. "What it's come down to is, have you made your decision, Mr. President? About the amendment? What you're going to do about it?"

"No, I haven't. But in the meantime, I'm still running the executive branch of this government, Kathy."

"I don't think so, Stephen. The papers don't think so. The TV reporters don't. That's why you should have confronted them."

"And created a bigger crisis?"

"Indecision creates crisis," she replied. "And isn't that exactly what prompted Mr. Hawley and the Cabinet to correct?" she added chidingly.

"And your going to the East Wing won't contribute even more confusion?" he retorted sharply.

"I don't intend to talk with the press. I've already instructed Maxine Stuart, who knows how to handle reporters. And Mr. Gratton is meeting me there. We're going to discuss that TV series on the First Ladies. The one you so eagerly wanted me to do," she added, with a touch of sarcasm in her voice.

Thompson got to his feet, the veins in his temples beginning to throb with repressed anger. "I can prevent your leaving this house or the grounds!"

"*That*, Mr. President," Kathy said, instantly flaring back, "would create more problems than it would solve! Someone's got to show all of them how *we* feel. Mr. Daniels! Mr. Hawley! All of them! You always claim you have your duties, Stephen." As she started from the room, she said, "I'm still the First Lady, Stephen. And I have *mine*," and with that she was gone.

☆ ☆ ☆

Gratton sat comfortably hunched up in a corner of a big wing chair in Kathy's East Wing White House office. The business arrangements of Kathy's participation had been quickly settled. "We have film on all the First Ladies of this century," Gratton said.

"And I've seen dozens of old photographs, and artists' drawings of all the others. And it's marvelous what a clever director can do with still pictures," Kathy said.

"Some things you may want to use live actors," Gratton suggested.

"Yes, I think so. Even something about them *after* they left the White House. Sarah Polk, for example. When the President retired to Nashville—I was reading about it only last month—he died barely three months after he settled in their new home. And *she* lived on there for forty-two more years, almost into the twentieth century! Think of that! There are dozens of stories like that, inspiring ones—Eleanor Roosevelt, of course, Rosalynn Carter capturing Jimmy when she was only seventeen. Lovely stories about so many of them."

"I see you've already been doing your homework."

"Every First Lady reads about her predecessors. It's part of the job."

Gratton eyed her over his coffee cup, remembering the moment soon after he hired her when he'd patted her buttocks as she left his car; he chuckled inwardly at incidents that would never get into the history books. He wondered about the woman he was observing, and the Acting President of the United States.

"I love history myself," Gratton said, "which, of course, is one of the reasons we wanted to do this series—"

"And to give Senator Vance's committee a little friendly nudge," Kathy said with a smile.

"Oh, that, too," Gratton acknowledged. "But I still have printer's ink in my veins, and your being here, that's a story. Do you have any idea what it's like back there?" he said, pointing to the west side of the White House. "Your leaving last night was big news. The President's whereabouts is big news. So?" he squinted at Kathy, pushing his glasses to the top of his head. "The big story is, who's in charge? The whole world's wondering! Yesterday Mr. Hawley claims the President is unable to discharge his duties and he's taken over—temporarily, he says. *He's* sworn in. The President's *son* was there. That makes things look official, gives credence. Says something to the man on the street. But then, comes this morning. And your being here, *that* says something, too. Quite the opposite. The First Lady's on the job." Gratton edged forward. "So, now, I ask you, what's the President trying to say?"

"I think when you read the President's schedule today, you have your answer."

"That's one answer. But he has to give an answer to the Speaker and the President pro tem—but when? When does he do that?"

"There is no precise provision for that in the amendment, Mr. Gratton," she said.

"You sure?" Gratton asked, pulling down his glasses and extracting a paper from his inside jacket pocket. "I've got a copy of the amendment right here. . ." Gratton fingered the paper. "No, nothing . . . you're right . . . nothing as to when the President must respond. . ." He looked up at Kathy again as he pocketed the paper. "The most popular piece of paper in the country today," he said, slapping the left side of his chest. "Says only 'when'—that's the key word, 'when' . . . when the President claims no inability exists. Well," he said, scratching his forehead, "so he doesn't say 'when' exactly. He just performs his duties . . . his way of saying there *is* no inability." Gratton stopped for a moment, studying her. "He knew, of course, you were coming here?"

"Of course," she said smoothly. "And there's something else. I'm really surprised no one realizes that the President's already answered."

"How's that?" Gratton asked.

"He's indicated that he intends to run for a second term, hasn't he?"

"Yeah, you're right, you're right," Gratton admitted.

"And I like being First Lady," she said bluntly. "Doesn't that answer your question?"

At that moment, after a quick knock on the door Anne Koyce pushed in halfway. "Mr. Hawley's outside."

"Bring him in, Anne," Kathy said, "bring him in."

Gratton turned and stood up as Hawley entered. "Joe dropped by earlier, told me he was meeting with you. Congratulations on the TV series. I hope I'm not interrupting. . ."

"Take my chair. We've finished our business," Gratton said.

"Yes, please, sit down," Kathy said.

Kathy walked Gratton to the door, and as it closed behind him she leaned against it momentarily. "Well," she said, "and what brings you all the way over to the East Wing?"

Hawley smiled. "Heard you were in. I've never been here before. And I wanted to come by and say welcome."

"Cliff, those are very pretty words. It's your actions that matter." She walked across the room and seated herself.

"They aren't directed at you, Kathy."

"I just happened to get in the way of the bullet, that it? Wounded by a ricochet shot?"

"There are no bullets. No shots. No ricochet."

"You weren't aiming at me, I'll grant you. But what you've done, Cliff. . ." She shook her head in disbelief. "When you once said I'd always have you, and you'd have me . . . Did you ever ask yourself as what? . . . spoils of war?"

Hawley frowned. "Kathy, we've been through this. The Cabinet voted for it almost to a man. The Committee of the National Security Council endorsed it. The Speaker—"

"And you couldn't wait, you *wouldn't* wait," she said bitterly.

Hawley stood up, chagrined. "I made this visit on my own initiative. I wanted to encourage you to stay, and, when the President's fit, to encourage *him* to return—" He started to the door.

"Am I to deliver that message?"

"Yes, you can deliver that message," he said sharply, turning as he placed a hand on the knob. "A long time ago we talked about our lives, moving on parallel lines. If you're on parallel lines, you may, one day, ultimately return to the point of origination." He stared hard at her. "Do you understand what I'm trying to say?"

She smiled. "Cliff, you were always good with words. But I remember someone, a writer I think, commenting about someone else's work. That there was much in it that was original and much that was good. The problem was, he said, that what was good wasn't original and what was original wasn't good. Somehow, it seems to fit here."

Hawley gritted his teeth. "Then we'll use a favorite word of yours . . . *kismet* . . ." he said. "We'll just have to leave it at that for now, and wait and see."

☆ ☆ ☆

Hawley sat in a pensive mood back in the Oval Office, still stung by his meeting with Kathy. Flanking him were Speaker of the House Alfred Hackett, Daniels, Jaggers, Hornwell, and J. C. Hoberman. He had briefed them on his short meeting with her.

"She never gave even a hint that Mr. Thompson was sending an official response to the Congress?" the Attorney General asked.

"Not a word, J. C." Hawley replied. He picked up a slip of paper on his desk. "Joe Gratton saw her before me and left this little note. It says, 'Tell Mr. Hawley the lady said I like being First Lady and that's a quote.'"

"That says something," Hoberman said.

"That she likes her own status for sure," Daniels commented. "Maybe even to coming to the White House on her own, and *not* with the President's approval."

It always annoyed Hawley to have Daniels speculating about Kathy Thompson. He turned to Alfred Hackett. "How do the members of Congress feel about the executive branch seeming to operate in two places at once?"

"Unacceptable," Hackett replied, pushing his hand through his thatch of red hair. "My recommendation is that President Thompson be notified that the only way in which he can exercise executive power, on his own," he emphasized, "is to follow the procedures of the Twenty-fifth Amendment. That automatically requires that he declare himself fit. The Congress and the executive branch of the government will then have their own options to exercise."

The others waited on Hawley's response.

Hawley was quick to set the right parameters. He spoke with authority and decisiveness. "We know Mr. Thompson's already summoned the Secretary of State and the Speaker to his home for a two-hour meeting. Those two must carry the Speaker's very precise message to President Thompson."

"I think, sir," Hoberman interjected, looking across at the others from his position near the fireplace, "that it would be helpful if I let Mr. Jaggers, the Speaker, and the Chief of Staff have a written statement from the Justice Department supporting that position."

"I'll buy that," Hawley said. As he stood up to end the meeting, there was a knock on the door. Tom Latham walked in and handed him a note. Hawley read it with a smile. "We're all being summoned, he said, looking up and raising the note. "The President has asked me to call on him at 5:00 P.M."

Then, turning his attention to Jaggers and the Speaker, Hawley added, "You two are to advise the President that you will always accommodate reasonable requests—on the proviso that he understands that no directives he gives you have any standing unless, and until, such directives are approved by the Acting President. In short, gentlemen, he can give advice. He cannot give orders."

"I'm not sure it's proper—your calling on him," Jaggers said. "*You* are the Acting President, and he should be the one—"

"Hold it," Hawley cut it. "Remember, we said we'd be accommodating. I will see him after the Attorney General's given Kraus *his* message, and after you and the Speaker have made *your* positions clear."

"Maybe by then he might just conclude that it's best that he step aside, officially, at least for the time being," Jaggers conceded.

"Don't let it surprise you if he resists," Hornwell countered. "You have to remember he told me he'd run for a second term, and if he means to do that, then he *must* resist."

"And if he resists?" Hoberman asked, looking at the Speaker.

"He only needs that one-third of the Congress to support him to stay in power," Hackett said, shaking his head worriedly.

"And the chances?" Hoberman persisted.

Hackett shrugged. The room was quiet until Hawley spoke. "Gentlemen, Mr. Thompson must make the next move. I believe in the end—after all of you have done your part today, and as I've said from the beginning—he'll come down on the side of common sense. He'll see his place in history, his record, and above all he'll recognize his duty and the national interest. He'll abide by the amendment in spirit as well as to the letter."

"You may be forgetting one element," Daniels said.

"What is that, Richard?"

"*Mrs.* Thompson. She's already voted to stay in office. He could have stopped her. He didn't."

As the others left, Daniels lingered behind for a few moments to brief Hawley on his meetings with Rossmore and Harry Thompson. "I have one more suggestion about Harry Thompson," he said. "I think it could be smart, politically speaking, for you to separate Harry from his father, capitalize on his having been present at the swearing-in ceremony."

"What's your suggestion?"

"Simple. You give Harry an assignment that adds further

proof that he's accepted your role no matter what his father decides. An assignment may in fact help settle the President's mind." Daniels watched Hawley carefully as he pressed on. "I've already talked to Mr. Jaggers. About a mission, not anything permanent, maybe a week, ten days. Plenty of areas touch on Harry Thompson's interests in Central America—maybe Venezuela, Colombia. State has those kinds of missions coming and going all the time. Could you spare him?"

"I understand, Richard. Yes, I could spare him for those few days."

Daniels nodded. "Good, sir. I'd also include this Lieutenant Rossmore on the mission as well. Maybe Lane Whitney, too. Giving Lane a little visibility, letting the nation see him accept your new role can be helpful in that sensitive area as well. Besides, the three of them are good friends," Daniels added as a clincher to his argument.

"Good idea, Richard. And you've already worked it out with Mr. Jaggers?"

Daniels smiled as he crossed over to the door. "We were just waiting on you, Mr. President." He scratched an ear. "On the question of the tapes. We have most of them."

"Oh?" Hawley remarked.

"Two are missing. But we're quite certain we know who still has them."

"Sure?"

"We'll soon find out. Count on it."

28

Henry Kraus stood near the closed doorway to President Thompson's library. "He's had a long day, Harry, and a tough one. I wouldn't press him too hard about any decision today."

Harry Thompson tapped Kraus's shoulder in a friendly fashion. "The old man's obviously still got reserve power. When I read his schedule for today it made me think maybe, just maybe it may be *me* giving him the wrong counsel. Maybe Kathy's right. Maybe she went down to the East Wing just to show him."

"He told me your position and hers. Now, if you begin to waffle—"

"Who's waffling?" Harry demanded.

"If you change your mind, it's all going to be more and more confusing to him. He's asked Mr. Hawley to come by at five o'clock. He wanted you with him. Doesn't that tell you something?"

"And Kathy?"

"Not Kathy, Harry. You. He knows where you stand. Or at least he knew this morning."

"But I saw that schedule, one meeting after another—that's pretty convincing evidence. And it's not for me to say to a

President, father or no father, 'Okay, step down, you had your day, step aside.' I admit I felt that way yesterday, even this morning—"

"Nothing's changed, Harry," Kraus emphasized.

"Maybe he has."

Kraus pushed open the door. "You'll be the judge."

Harry entered the spacious room with its hand-carved fruitwood bookcases, filled with first editions and leather-bound volumes, its darker wood-panelled walls, its French casement windows and their lead panes that looked out on the formal gardens. The President was standing near a baronial stone fireplace, looking up at a Cortez he preferred over greater names in the art world. "Given to me by my old associates at the law office when I first went into government."

Harry was determined to keep his father's mind focused on the matter that had to be resolved. "Chief of Staff just told me you're meeting Hawley."

Thompson glanced over at the towering grandfather clock. "He'll be here in a few minutes. I wanted you as a witness." He stood gazing at the etched brass pendulum, his hands moving in rhythm with its movement. "Been like that myself these past couple of hours, first on one side, then on the other." He turned and pointed to a manila folder on his desk. "Contains some special findings on Mr. Hawley. You're to hold on to that. Go ahead. Take it." Harry reached down and picked up the material. "The proof's in there—if it's ever needed. Mr. Hawley knows about it. Some of it may be pure gossip, rumor mongering, I'll admit that." Then moving over to take a seat behind the desk, he added, "But not all of it."

"You've had a heavy schedule today."

The elder Thompson pulled a blue silk handkerchief from his breast pocket and dabbed his forehead. "Yes. They're forcing the issue. All of them."

"How?"

"With procedural rules. It's demeaning," the President said, shaking his head in disapproval. "Downright demeaning! I'm free to give advice! But no orders! Jaggers and the Speaker were their messengers."

"They're in murky water."

"If I were to challenge them," the President said.

"*If* you were. . . ? Is that a decision?"

The President gazed up at the elaborate coffered wood ceiling. "No," he said, softly. "And you, has your position changed?

I know Kathy's. She gave me hers by going to the White House when I asked her not to."

"She shouldn't have done that," Harry said. "And I'm sorry, but I still say she can't be trusted. You know it. I know it." Harry noticed the President wince. He decided to press on. "Maybe she just wants to be within easy walking distance to Mr. Hawley?"

"That's enough, Harry!" the President snapped. "That's a subject I don't want to discuss or debate, do you understand?" The two sat in silence, Harry satisfied he'd made his point, the President quarreling within himself, vexed he could be consumed by jealousy based only on a fragment of one intercepted call. For days he'd been deeply troubled, half wishing he knew more—if there was more to learn—rather than being victimized by his own imagination. He fought his daily suspicions and his troubled sleep. Now, as he'd worked out his position vis-à-vis the presidency, *that* would be his real answer to Hawley and to Hawley's future.

"It's been a hard day," the President finally said. His voice began to rise in anger. "To have to fight for one's authority! To have a handful of willful men—" Suddenly, he fell back in his chair, gasping for breath. He stretched out a hand, but it fell limp on the desk. "The pills, Harry," he muttered as his eyes focused on a small vial next to a brass inkwell. The President's head came forward as he raised his eyes looking up at Harry. "Harry, get them . . . two of them. . ."

Harry sprang into action, ripped off the top, and dropped the pills into the President's outstretched hand. Then he hurried to a side table, poured a glass of water, and held it to the President's lips as Thompson placed the pills in his mouth. A moment later, eyes shut, breathing stertorously, the President rested his head against the back of the chair.

"Maybe you should cancel this meeting," Harry said, standing near his father, concern showing on his face.

"I'll be all right. Just sit down." He paused to take a deep breath. "I'm to breathe in deeply . . . exhale slowly . . . relax all the muscles . . . breathe in again. . ." His eyes flashed opened. Then a moment or two later he said to his son, "When the time comes . . . one day, not soon, don't worry . . . just remember, I want to be in Arlington. No eternal flame, not that. No carved words, not that, either. But words, yes. My voice . . . two or three lines from my best speeches, you pick them out, Harry. . ."

"Dad," Harry barely whispered. "Please..."

As the President finally relaxed, his pallor gradually gave way to a healthy hue. "You won't have to do this for quite a time, maybe a long time. Just wanted you to know. The details are in the safe in this room. Just remember that, all right?"

The phone on the desk rang. "Answer it, Harry."

"Yes?... Just a moment," Harry said into the phone as he looked across at his father. "Hawley's car just came through the gate."

"Fine, fine. Tell Kraus to bring him in as soon as he arrives. And one more thing. Tell Kraus to pass the word to Kathy that Hawley's here."

"Why? Why do you want her to know?"

The President chuckled. "Let that be one of my secrets for the day."

☆ ☆ ☆

It was Kraus who swung open the door to the Thompson library when Hawley and Lane Whitney were ushered into the President's presence. As it closed, Hawley stood at ease, determined to wait for Thompson to make the first move. Both men eyed each other warily; Hawley saw in Thompson's stretching himself to his full height, together with the forceful jutting of his jaw, the taut posture of a wounded lion gauging the presence of an unwelcome intruder on his turf.

Thompson, on his part, made a quick and calculated judgment on the appearance of Hawley at his estate. He counted it a small victory, a recognition that his powers were still to be reckoned with, despite the words he'd heard from Jaggers and the Speaker earlier in the day. His hands clasped behind his back, he continued to stare at his visitor for a few quiet moments, and then, with a slight nod of his head, indicated a chair before his desk.

Although no words had been spoken, Hawley noted that the President had by that action, at the very least, accorded him a courtesy lacking in their last face-to-face meeting. "Thank you, Mr. President," he said, sitting down as Thompson, too, took his own seat.

"I summoned you here for a special purpose... sir," Thompson said, after a beat.

Again, Hawley sensed another subtle, if grudging, acknowledgment that their relationship had assumed a new dimension.

Nodding politely, he continued his resolve to wait upon Thompson to disclose the reason for the summons. It was not long in coming. "I've made some decisions, Mr. Hawley. I'm aware of yours, your instructions to government officials to ignore my orders. This meeting should not detain us very long." Thompson sat in silence for a few moments before going on. "I've asked Harry to take some notes."

Hawley said, "I've asked Lane to do the same. After our meeting, the two of them can work out a joint record both of us can approve. They've done that sort of thing together before."

Thompson looked up at Harry standing behind him. "Harry, you work that out." Then he turned his attention to Hawley. "As I said, I've made my decision, Mr. Hawley, and I wanted you to hear it directly from me."

Hawley observed the wry smile on Thompson's face, then noticed the flicker of surprise in Harry's eyes at his father's announcement, immediately inferring that Harry might be in the dark as to his father's intentions.

"Nothing that has happened in these past few hours, Mr. Hawley, has altered the views I expressed to you at our last meeting."

Hawley felt a flush of irritation. He had not made this conciliatory gesture just to review the past; his only interests were in the present and the immediate future.

"Everything I felt that justified my request is in that packet Harry's holding," Thompson said, pointing to it without taking his eyes from Hawley's. "I've considered all of the options open to me. One of them is that under the terms of the amendment I can send a written notification to the Speaker and to the President pro tem that I'm fully capable of discharging my duties and that no inability exists. Until such time as I send such notice, under the amendment, you, as Vice President, can function as Acting President. Correct?"

Hawley returned the baleful stare of Thompson's cold blue eyes, still fixed on him. "Correct," he murmured.

"I'm disappointed in you, Mr. Hawley, but I'm not surprised."

Hawley held his feelings in check, committed to his decision to hear Thompson out and to maintain, if at all possible, every accommodating courtesy he could offer. "My disappointment, Mr. Hawley," Thompson continued, an accusatory tone in his voice, "stems from *your* failure, and that of many in the Cabinet, and of others as well—admittedly all trusted advisers," he added with a touch of contempt, "to come to my office and to present your misgivings about my ability to do my job. You have acted in a totally insensitive manner, without the slightest personal consideration." He let himself rest against the back of his chair, his penetrating eyes still fixed on Hawley.

"We discussed that, Mr. President," Hawley said, "but deemed it inadvisable since you could have dismissed the Cabinet—as we now know you intended."

"Yes, and Mr. Bromley, *your* Mr. Bromley, in Commerce," Thompson added sarcastically, "would have been first, let me tell you. And after him. . ." but Hawley had momentarily stopped listening.

It was the President's singular emphasis on Bromley's name that triggered an instantaneous recall in Hawley's mind of how he had tossed out the name in a private meeting with Daniels as the ideal Cabinet official to leak word that he, Bromley, would favor an open contest for the vice presidential nomination, with Hawley battling the President's presumed choice to supplant him, Vance. In that moment he once again heard Daniels' voice questioning him. "Bromley? You sure?" and his own response that, yes, he knew Bromley was with him, could be trusted. Hawley had now to consider whether Thompson's reference was a mere coincidence, or whether, in fact, it had been deliberately given to Thompson by Daniels himself. Worse, he wondered whether Daniels, who had once remarked that every man has his Judas, was now, in truth, Hawley's. Hawley tensed as he returned his attention to Thompson. He would deal with the Daniels question later.

Quietly, Thompson was saying, "Take Eisenhower. His men rallied to his support when he had a heart attack. His Vice President—Richard Nixon—played a respectful and helpful role. His Cabinet stood behind him. His press secretary, Jim Hagerty, was his chief spokesman. Eisenhower!" he snapped, suddenly pressing forward in his chair. "Down with a heart attack! Unable to function! But still—Mr. Hawley—still President of the United States!"

"True, but there was no Twenty-fifth Amendment in existence at that time, Mr. President," Hawley replied softly.

"And do you think that Mr. Nixon would have presumed to declare himself Acting President—over General Eisenhower?"

Hawley was inwardly pleased at the President's challenge and at his question. Quietly folding his arms, noting, even as he spoke, a twitching of the muscles at the corners of Thompson's lips, Hawley said, "Mr. President, if the amendment had been in existence at that time, it would have been Mr. Nixon's duty—his sworn *duty* as Vice President—to uphold the Constitution by exercising section four of the Twenty-fifth Amendment."

"And declare himself Acting President, that it?"

"Together with the support of a majority of the members of the Cabinet, yes, sir," Hawley asserted, "until the President could himself declare that no inability existed."

The President glanced up at his son, turned to look at Lane, and then resumed his concentration on Hawley. "Let me ask you, during Ronald Reagan's stays in the hospital with serious operations, did Mr. Bush presume to make himself Acting President?"

"No, sir," Hawley said, "though you'll recall, I'm sure, he did serve for a few hours as Acting President at President Reagan's direction."

"Yes, informally. And for most of that time Reagan was hospitalized, in fact immobilized. And, may I remind you, still running the country!"

"But in control and recovering every day, Mr. President," Hawley said. Then deciding the moment was right to go on the offensive, Hawley burrowed in. "Those operations *improved* his health, Mr. President. They were debilitating, agreed. But his physical condition sustained him, and his mental acuity. . ." Hawley paused, deciding to let that word reach Thompson's consciousness without his being compelled to issue a more provocative statement.

Thompson bristled as he understood Hawley's reluctance to speak out. "What about it?" Thompson shot back. "Well, say it! Say it! His acuity, his mental acuity—his awareness! His thought processes! His ability to reason, to reason and take action if needed! What you're implying is that mine . . . mine . . . are faulty! Isn't that it? That maybe I might even be senile?!"

"No, Mr. President, no. But I don't believe that you and I, alone, can properly find a mutually satisfactory way to resolve *that* question."

"That *is* the issue, isn't it?" Thompson's eyes narrowed. "My reasoning power? My ability to make decisions?" He let a few moments pass. Then, with a disarming smile, he asked, "Have you ever seen me in such a condition?"

"Mr. President, I consider you to be a man of great intellectual power, the equal of any of your predecessors, the superior of most of them. No one questions that. But the issue isn't intellectual ability, Mr. President. It's something quite different—not intellectual ability, but intellectual quality."

"And what is the difference between ability and quality?"

"Sir, I don't have to remind you that we live in an unpredictable, hostile world and that at any given moment the United States can find itself in immediate crisis, one created by internal or external forces. We've had four Presidents assassinated, two of whom died within hours, one in a week or so, Garfield lingering on for ten weeks. There have been assassination attempts—FDR, Truman, Ford, Reagan. The Twenty-fifth Amendment protects us from uncertainty inherent in that kind of internal crisis. In other periods of our history, external conditions may have deteriorated over a period of time, maybe weeks, even months, as with the Japanese before Pearl Harbor, but no such extensive time frame exists any longer—"

"For our adversaries as well as us," the President cut in.

"Precisely," Hawley said, welcoming the intrusion. "Signals could be misread. Computer terminals might give erroneous readings. Malfunctions."

"That happens from time to time, on their side *and* ours."

Hawley agreed. "But a new configuration of such errors could occur—one never before recorded," he emphasized. "Given the state of the arts in computer technology, it is possible that a launch-on-warning stage could be reached."

"And you believe, I'm to conclude from this little history lesson," Thompson said, rising from his seat and peering down at Hawley, his voice building to a crescendo of anger, "that I'm so disorganized, so disoriented, in fact so deranged that I would lack the ability to make a sensible judgment, in *time*? That it?!"

"Mr. President, no one questions your sanity—"

"Well, now, that's a generous admission—"

"Your sanity's not in question, Mr. President," Hawley interjected as he sat back, composed, staring up at his taut antagonist, "nor your intelligence, your intellect, your reasoning power—none of that. What *is* in question, sir, is whether all of those attributes are at your beck and call every instant of every waking moment."

"And what makes you think they aren't?" Thompson retorted. "Have I ever once—just once—failed to meet a crisis in the Oval Office? Have I ever once—just once—failed to give specific orders to subordinates when an instantaneous decision was required? Can you name one example?"

"Sir, I can," Hawley said calmly.

An infuriated look darkened Thompson's face as he took out a handkerchief to wipe his brow. "When?" he challenged.

"Red Dye Day, to be precise. But the issue isn't the past, Mr. President," Hawley said after a deliberate pause, again stressing his words. "The issue is the reverse, the *future*. And the present. There have been indications, observations on the part of others, men and women close to you—"

"Name them!" Thompson demanded.

Hawley looked across at Harry Thompson, standing behind the President. "This is not the forum, sir, in which that issue can be decided."

"You want it to go to the Congress, that it? You insist on it!" the President said, the veins now beginning to throb ominously at his temples.

Hawley felt pressures building within himself, too. He'd seen Harry make his notes as well as Lane. The President had made his case, so far, with confidence and skill, and Hawley had to do no less. "If it must go to the Congress, Mr. President, only *you* can make that decision."

"Do you have any doubt that, if I make the effort—that I can't persuade one-third of the members of the Congress to support me, enough to terminate your actions?"

"I understand the numbers, Mr. President, but I hope that matter is never put to the Congress."

"If you're satisfied upon my declaration to the Speaker that no inability exists, then it *will* never go to the Congress. That's *your* decision."

Hawley, looking directly at Thompson, said, "Mr. President, a majority of the Cabinet will reject your declaration."

"And you?"

"I, too, regretfully, will reject it. I must," Hawley said.

"So, it's finally come down to you and me. A short time ago I demanded your resignation. What you'd really like is mine," Thompson said, making a great effort to suppress his anger. "You won't get that, Mr. Hawley."

"I'm not asking for it. I'm hoping, along with the entire country, that you'll return to duty soon."

"I'm touched by your good wishes, Mr. Hawley. But let me say it straight out. You won't be the President, Mr. Hawley. Acting President—that's all. For a few weeks or months at most. A footnote in history. Far less important than our other unelected Vice President and President, Mr. Ford."

"There is a difference, sir. Mr. Ford was *appointed* Vice President. I was elected."

"To be sure," Thompson said, taking a few steps toward the fireplace, "and I think I may have helped bring that about," he added with a touch of irony. "And, of course, you must also want to know what the party and I are planning for the convention?"

"I do," Hawley said, now resolved to force Thompson to provide answers. "Sir, are you prepared to take your decision to the people, to a press conference where the sole subject will be your ability to respond at a moment's notice to any crisis the country faces?" As he observed Thompson about to speak in defiance, Hawley pressed on, pointing a finger directly at him. "Let me ask you, sir, are you prepared to meet with a panel of experts that Congress is most certainly going to establish before it votes on whether to accept your assurances or our objections? Panels that most certainly will be on every television station in the country? Mr. President," he added, leaning toward him, "are you prepared to undergo the physical and mental tests that Congress will insist be undertaken? Do you really want to be the subject of such scrutiny? Such debate? Most important," Hawley paused briefly before proceeding, "do you really think that the best interests of the United States are served by a public struggle for authority? And can we—can *you*—permit it when it's *your* authority—not mine—that is the subject of such crucial concern that most of your advisers recommend it be replaced?"

Thompson surprised everyone in the room by saying "Well said, Mr. Hawley, well said."

Hawley was startled by Thompson's reaction. "Be at ease, Mr. Hawley," Thompson said, returning to his chair. "When you came into this room, I told you that I'd made my decision. I told you that one of the options open to me is to make my declaration to the Speaker that no inability exists and that I am perfectly capable of discharging the obligations of my office. Now, let it be noted for the record, by Harry and Mr. Whitney, that I believe that I *could*—utilizing all of the energy I possess—continue in office. But I recognize, too, that the national interest is *not* served by a public dispute between the two highest elected officials in the land. Quite to the contrary. That would raise issues that may confuse our friends overseas, as well as encourage recklessness on the part of our adversaries.

"Furthermore, I've no doubt, sir," the President continued,

"that I *could* win the vote of one-third of the members of Congress in a showdown with you." Thompson straightened his shoulders as he went on. "Another President said it well, nearly seventy years ago. Calvin Coolidge. He could have been elected a second time. Instead, he said, 'I do not choose to run.' You recall that bit of history, I'm sure." Then, lowering his voice, he said, "And I, sir, do not choose to contest your role as Acting President."

The room was silent except for the rhythmic sound of the grandfather clock, its measured beat audible in the sudden stillness. Harry Thompson stood as if made of stone, Lane Whitney stared at the President with astonishment. Hawley sat quietly, his mind accepting the President's surprising announcement, but on guard for some qualifying condition.

Thompson's voice was firm. "I am not withdrawing, Mr. Hawley," he said, "because of any lack of confidence in my ability to win congressional support. I am doing so because I recognize better than any other person alive that the unseemly public debate to which I would have to submit myself, the harassment that your supporters—even you—would mobilize on your behalf, all of this would drain my strength and deplete the physical and mental resources that I have held in reserve in order to handle the very crises you predict may arise." He paused for a moment. "You see, Mr. Hawley, I know that if I won, it could cost me my life." Thompson stopped, an ugly grin crossing his face. "You understand the consequences of that?" Without waiting for a response he said, "You'd succeed me. And Mr. Hawley," he added, his rich voice now falling to a whisper, "I said you would never be President of the United States. Acting President? At most a few months—and always subject to the possibility of my submitting a positive declaration on my ability to discharge the duties of the office. But President? Never."

Hawley stood up, aware that the meeting was over.

"I will confer with the Cabinet from time to time," the senior Thompson continued, "with the Joint Chiefs, with the congressional leadership. Here. At my home. Mr. Hawley," he said, drawing himself erect. "We shall not likely meet again. And now, sir, good-bye." He walked around his desk, opened the door, and left the room.

Henry Kraus appeared at the open doorway. "Sir," he said to Hawley, "I tried to arrange your return by air but Secret Service recommends against it because of unexpected traffic at this hour. They have backup cars to help speed you back to the White House."

"Thank you, Henry."

Harry Thompson had been a pensive observer of the exchange between his father and Hawley. He felt a sense of betrayal, but he also recognized the finality of his father's surprising decision. In the few moments that elapsed between his father's surprise announcement and his abrupt termination of the meeting, Harry had quickly reviewed his own options. His mission to destroy both Hawley and Kathy had failed. One thing, though, had had an impact on him—he'd been impressed by Kathy's own moves, her determination to cling fast to her own prerogatives, her ability to thwart all of his own efforts to capitalize on the President's jealousy as a means to eliminate her and to ruin Hawley. Kathy had, moreover, shown surprising agility in altering her own position vis-à-vis Hawley, and now, if only as a means of personal survival—and a chance to remain close to the center of power—Harry Thompson would do no less. To succeed in whatever role the future would offer him, he, too, would bind himself to Hawley's rising star, holding to himself his secret animosity, the seeds of which had been sewn in him long ago by the words and actions of Gloria Whitney. Revenge, now to come later, would still be his ultimate purpose; he would bide his time, and meanwhile stake a new position in the jungle world of Washington politics.

As Hawley nodded to Harry and turned to leave, Harry intercepted him.

"If it's all right with you," he said politely, "I'd like to take you up on your request, join you and Lane and work out a report—whatever."

Hawley studied him, momentarily surprised.

"And one more thing," Harry said, firming up his own private decision as he handed the manila envelope his father had given him over to Hawley. "I don't think I really want to hold this."

"Are you sure?" Hawley said.

"I'm sure," Harry replied smoothly. "I think my father was being fair, of course, from *his* point of view. Frankly, I'm glad he's made a decision." Harry Thompson paused as Hawley nodded understandingly. "I just wanted you to know, hearing both sides, I think *you* were fair, too." Harry Thompson extended his hand.

Hawley took it, gripping it firmly. "Welcome back, Harry," he said.

29

Harry Thompson, seated in the middle of the presidential limousine beside Hawley, was struck by his silence. He turned his attention to Lane Whitney as they respected Hawley's brooding and together began quietly to compare their notes. They had no way of knowing that Hawley was now pondering the vexing question of how to handle the issue raised by the elder Thompson's reference to Bromley. In a quick assessment of pros and cons he had to acknowledge that Daniels had been the chief adversary to the continuance of the Thompson presidency.

Perhaps, Hawley mused, Daniels had kept open a slender channel into the Thompson White House, insurance, as it were, all the while he was helping to maneuver Hawley's elevation. The possibility that Daniels was serving two masters could not be tolerated. Another cautionary passage in Machiavelli floated through his mind: "It is far safer to be feared than loved." In the end, he would have to teach that lesson to Daniels. That was the price of living in the jungle.

Kathy Thompson was seated in the back of a White House limousine as it sped out to the Kalorama area of Washington. The call from Henry Kraus had been brief but unsettling. She felt she had been abused by the two men who most mattered in her life. Her husband had defied her and seemed to be taking peculiar actions on the spur of the moment; Clifford Hawley had left her unprotected, uninformed.

After opening a compact to adjust her makeup, she smoothed down the blue linen skirt of her suit, wondering if she and Hawley were to meet, wondering what had induced the President to have Kraus pass on his cryptic message to Anne Koyce: "Tell Mrs. Thompson that Mr. Hawley's visiting the President—the President wants her to know." Why and what did Stephen want her to know? When she phoned him to find out, she was told he couldn't be disturbed. Was he looking to her for support in his effort to stay in office? If so, she knew she would give it to him.

She let her mind drift back to the brief meeting she'd just left with Felicia Courtney. Felicia had been tipped about the television series Joe Gratton had agreed to do on the First Ladies, and had called to congratulate her and to offer to do a cover story in her magazine. But the interview had quickly focused on the mind-boggling events of the past forty-eight hours. She had been pleased at Felicia's immediate assumption, after seeing her functioning in the East Wing, that the President would make a fight for his office. She was also curious as to whether Hawley had given Felicia any prior indication of his own plans.

"Not a word, Kathy, not a hint," Felicia had said.

That pleased Kathy; at least Hawley had played no favorites.

What annoyed her was Felicia's rambling on that she'd always enjoyed Hawley's company. "But then," Felicia had said, "he's always been something of a womanizer, don't you think?"

"Womanizer? It's not a very nice word, Felicia."

"Oh, come on, Kathy," Felicia replied. "All those dates with that Vivian Lessing? Although his apparent indifference—"

"Indifference?" Kathy interjected.

"Indifference. Coldness. Call it what you will. The girl's brutally assaulted, she'll be weeks in a hospital, he dated her, and nothing."

"What does that mean, nothing?"

"He never went out to visit her for one thing, and from everything we've learned at our shop there's been no contact. Nothing. And she herself won't talk about anything. Odd."

"She's frightened after that horrible experience."

"By something, yes. By someone, maybe," Felicia said, then added, "and there were other starlets in his life. We have their names in our files. A Hollywood writer, too—the one who wrote some miniseries. Not to mention Gloria Whitney—"

"He never had any relationship with Gloria," Kathy said sharply.

"Maybe not, but we'll never know for sure." Then, looking up from the pad on which she'd been taking notes, Felicia said, archly, "And you, back in your reporter days. You're in our files, too."

"I don't know what's in them, but it can't be of much value," Kathy said. "We were just friends."

"*That* doesn't sound like Cliff Hawley."

"Perhaps you know him a lot better than I do," Kathy said with a cold smile.

"I doubt it. But of course, he could be a lot more interesting now." Suddenly, Felicia lifted a hand toward Kathy. "I'm sorry. I really am gossiping. I'm very thoughtless, when here you are, First Lady, with the President being placed in such an awkward position . . . honestly, Kathy, I think it's remarkable your being able to carry on. I really do."

"The President's carrying on," Kathy said, "so why shouldn't I?"

"Why shouldn't you, indeed!" Felicia said. "Perhaps I'll know more after tonight."

"Tonight?"

"Yes. I'm dining with Cliff, at least I think we are. We've had this date for over a week. Unless, under the present circumstances, he has to break it." She closed her notebook.

It was at that moment that Anne slipped Kraus's message to Kathy, Kathy crumpling the paper. "I'm sorry, Felicia. Something urgent's come up."

"No problem," Felicia said. "We were all finished anyway."

Now, as her car approached the entrance to the Thompson estate, Kathy saw the newly erected barricades hastily thrown up by the Secret Service against potential terrorist attacks as well as to block out reporters and cameramen. As her car entered the driveway, another car was just pulling out from under the porte-cochere. In that fleeting instant, she saw Hawley seated in the back of his car with Harry Thompson beside him. When she saw Hawley lift an arm in recognition, she nodded, thinking of parallel lines going in opposite directions. She wondered if it was an ill omen as she hurried into the house.

In the very chair Hawley had vacated only minutes before, Kathy sat across from her husband looking at his drawn face.

"You wanted me to know Clifford Hawley was with you."

"Yes, I did."

"I just saw him leave," she said. "I couldn't get here any quicker."

"I didn't want you here any quicker, Kathy," Thompson said.

"Oh?" She was puzzled by the almost sly smile that creased his face. "I don't understand, Stephen," she said.

"I only wanted you to know we were meeting. I invited him here."

"Am I to ask why? The purpose?"

Thompson chuckled. "You're to do exactly that, Kathy. Because I wanted you to know it's too late."

"Too late?" She looked at him, puzzled.

"You would have argued against me, Kathy. Now do you understand?"

Kathy felt a twinge of alarm. In that instant she knew that H. Stephen Thompson had voluntarily stepped down. He would be President in name only. She would be First Lady in name only. "Why, Stephen?" she demanded.

"Your favorite word these past few hours, Kathy. Duty. Duty," he repeated, as he settled back in his chair.

"You haven't resigned?" she blurted out.

"No, I'm still President." Thompson chuckled. "At least in name."

Kathy's eyes revealed her uncertainties. "If you're still President . . . Stephen . . . but President in name . . . doesn't that mean you've given up?" she asked, hesitatingly. "Because if you had asked me to come out, to *be* with you—"

"And you would have talked me out of it, right?" he asked, a mocking grin on his face.

"I would have tried! Yes!" She stood up, suddenly angry. "You've thrown it all away? You're going to just roll over, let them come in, do nothing?"

"Bravo, Kathy! Bravo," he said, clapping his hands halfheartedly. "A little while ago I was applauding Mr. Hawley. He made a fine speech, too. And so have you. But it's too late now."

Kathy Thompson fought to regain her composure and to reason matters out. "All right. You didn't want me here when you were meeting, all right. But you wanted me to rush over after you were certain it was all over. Is that it?" Kathy said, nervously biting her lip.

"Yes, that's it, Kathy," Thompson replied calmly. "It's something of the sort Ulysses S. Grant did to *his* wife when a delegation of Cabinet officers pleaded with him to run for a third term. The story has it that Mrs. Grant, intensely curious about that delegation, as it took its departure, begged her husband to tell her what they'd come in for. But Mr. Grant took his own sweet time, slowly lighting up a cigar, making absolutely sure enough time had passed so she couldn't go chasing after them to try to reopen the whole thing. She wanted him to run, all right, but that was really because she didn't want to give up being First Lady." He paused for a moment. "You see? You understand?"

"You didn't give up because of *me*?" she exclaimed.

"I think you like the role, Kathy. But, no. Not just because of that, that's a small part of it. I'm just not going to protest the decision. It all boils down to this, Kathy: I'm not going to run for a second term."

"Why, why not?" she asked, slipping back to her chair.

"Because I intend to *live*, Kathy. Hawley is a caretaker. Nothing more. You'll be a former First Lady. Nothing more. Nothing less. What this adds up to is that we have each other." Thompson settled back again in his chair. "We have each other," he repeated with a raspy laugh.

"I'm beginning to understand," she said, shaking her head. "And you really must be ill, Stephen, she said, "talking like that."

"Perhaps so. But I'll carry on—they'll actually be doing my work," he said, continuing in a suddenly cold tone, "and Kathy, deserting a President, the first to be displaced *legally* for inability to do his job? Or an ex-President, not in the best of health? It wouldn't do to try to divorce me because you'd only destroy yourself. And your place in history."

"What makes all of this so really painful is that you've been planning it," Kathy said bitterly.

"Mr. Hawley would like to have my endorsement to be elected," Thompson went on, ignoring her charge, "but I will say *nothing* prior to the convention. It may well be that his term as Vice President *and* as Acting President will expire with *my* term. And with yours. And since I don't intend to let Mr. Hawley become my successor, I will play my cards when and if I have to. And then what?" Thompson asked, a puzzling look in his eyes.

"And then what?" Kathy echoed.

"We'll see what kind of cards the good Lord's dealt each of us. There's only one thing I'm determined to do, Kathy."

"What?"

"To live a long time. With a beautiful young wife pledged to take care of me, here, right here."

Kathy fought back angry tears of frustration. "Stephen, I never knew you hated me."

"I don't hate you, Kathy. Not at all," he said protesting, a softer tone suddenly in his voice. "Perhaps—who can predict these matters?—we may, in time, be able to get to know each other again. I would hope so," he added placatingly.

He paused for a moment and then went on with a sad smile. "I believe Mr. Hawley wanted the wife of the President as well as the office." As Kathy started to rise in protest, Thompson waved her down. "Well, he's just not going to get her. Because, like I say, I intend to live for a very long time."

☆ ☆ ☆

Felicia Courtney sat before her white dressing table brushing her hair in long, easy strokes. It was midnight. She removed her makeup and studied her reflection as she resumed the gentle, rhythmic movements.

She was pleased that Clifford Hawley had kept his word. Their meeting had been brief, but that it had taken place at all seemed proof enough that she was a player now in the big leagues. Hawley had phoned ahead and had started to explain that the demands of his new role made it impossible to keep the dinner date. When she instantly settled for a quick cocktail, he accepted.

Felicia led him to her Shakespearean room. "I'm sorry, I didn't have time to change," she said as she poured Jack Daniels on his ice.

He held up a hand. "That's fine, fine. Plus a little more ice."

Felicia took a pair of silver tongs from the bar. "Two cubes? More?" she asked, holding the tongs in midair.

"Two will do it." He picked up a swizzle stick and stirred his drink, then lifted it toward her, touching his glass lightly against hers. "I like your outfit. Green. Your color. You were wearing green that day I bumped into you at the Four Seasons."

"I remember. A suede suit. That would be much too hot today. Kathy Thompson said she liked it, too. This one, this afternoon."

"Oh? You were with her?"

"Went calling at the East Wing. She's going to do something on television . . . historical, the role of the First Lady."

"So I've heard," he said.

"Bother you?"

"No. Why should it?" he said easily.

"Just seems to emphasize there are two different White Houses at work. Hers. Yours."

Hawley sipped his drink. "Felicia," he said, "Kathy *is* the First Lady."

"But not yours," Felicia said, "Mr. . . . ?" Then looking at him over the rim of her glass, she added, "should I address you now as Mr. President?"

"Not here," Hawley said.

"Well, then," Felicia went on, "is she going to represent you on your official duties, presiding over state dinners, White House social events, that sort of thing?" There was a mischievous glint in her eyes as she waited for his response.

"Frankly, I haven't thought about that, Felicia. But, no, I don't think that would be appropriate. I might call on my mother," he said. Then, as an afterthought, "Protocol will have some ideas. You have any suggestions?" he asked, setting his drink on the counter.

"I don't think that should be my role," she replied. "Making recommendations—about others. As a publisher, well, maybe yes," she added, "but as a woman, no. That's definitely not my kind of game."

Hawley dropped another cube of ice into his drink.

"Aren't you impressed that I predicted this move?" Felicia asked.

"Any more predictions?"

"You'll do whatever is right for the country. And you'll do whatever is best for Cliff Hawley."

"Are they compatible?"

Felicia shook her head in mock disbelief. "Cliff, all of your moves have been correct. Of *course* they'll be compatible. And something else just crossed my mind." She paused for a moment, setting her drink on the bar. "Kathy Thompson," Felicia said, with a twinkle in her eye.

Hawley sipped his drink without responding.

"She's part of the equation, Cliff. It's fairly well known you introduced her to Mr. Thompson when you were in the House. It's in our files. What isn't in our files is *before*."

Hawley stared back at her with no change of expression. "Before," he repeated quietly.

"We know she interviewed you. It was printed in some magazine, not ours. She never sold anything to us when she was a reporter. But somewhere, Cliff, in some ways, she figures. Yes," she said with conviction. "Kathy Thompson figures, doesn't she?"

Hawley smiled. "More fiction there than fact," he said, now wanting to drop the subject.

"Once, on a date, you asked me, speaking of yourself, of course—'Which am I, the hunter or the hunted?' Well, I looked something up after that date. I knew I knew it, but I couldn't put my finger on it. It's Tennyson, of all people. He's the one who said 'Man is the hunter; woman is his game.' Good?" she asked. "And with your chips? Doesn't it make sense! *You*, Cliff, are the hunter. And we—Kathy, myself, and Lord knows who else—*we* are the game. Yours." Felicia smiled as she freshened their drinks. "Another prediction," she said. "Everyone . . . who's really in the know . . . knows that the President is ill, worn down—"

"But not worn *out*," Hawley insisted.

"Time's against him in any event," she replied. "And as a player in the game, Kathy brings something unique to the table. Experience. She's *been* First Lady. I'm sure she'd like to do it for at least four more years." She picked up her glass and raised it toward him. "Cliff. You could make me a prophet again."

Hawley sipped his drink, eyes fixed on hers. "If someone like *you* stayed in the game," he said, "no one could tell what's ahead."

"Like me?" Felicia asked as she walked around the bar and stepped up to him. Slowly she raised her arms and draped them around his neck. "I *am* in the game, Cliff."

☆ ☆ ☆

Edward Jaggers stood in the elaborate formal reception room of the State Department where he had been briefing Harry Thompson, Jeb Rossmore, and Lane Whitney. "The plan, gentlemen, was to have someone from the Latin American desk handle this assignment, but it was one of President Thompson's final recommendations—seconded by Mr. Hawley—that some bright young men could do what formal diplomacy might handle in a straight—let us say, routine—fashion. That impressed me because human rights deserve human representation, and the government of Chile will respond better to your presentation of our case than that of a career officer from State." Glancing at Harry and Lane, he added, "I'm very grateful Mr. Hawley is willing to spare you two for a week, particularly with the convention coming up. You each have a briefing book to study. And of course the ambassador will handle all the formal business matters."

Harry Thompson looked back into the friendly eyes of Edward Jaggers as he took his hand. Despite his father's low opinion of Jaggers, he had come to like him. During the difficult times he'd endured with the death of Gloria he'd found Jaggers to be sympathetic and attentive, even to the point of hosting two private lunches, one at the State Department and the other at his home, offering his counsel in furthering young Thompson's Washington career.

The assignment particularly appealed to Harry since he wanted to do whatever he could to champion one of his father's programs; moreover, he saw the assignment as an opportunity for the future. Looking back at Jaggers, he felt the warmth of Jaggers' hands pressing his own. "I wish you great success," Jaggers said to him as he reached out to grasp the hands of Lane Whitney and Jeb Rossmore. "All of you, have a fine trip."

They were driven to National Airport. The driver, cleared from the State Department, headed toward an Air Force plane, but Harry issued new instructions. "Out to the edge of the airport, driver," he said. "We're using my plane."

A few minutes later the three sat in Harry Thompson's Lear 35—a plane his father had bought some time before his presidency. After Harry completed his own routine check, it was Lane Whitney who began to express some doubts about the mission. "It's the suddenness of the whole damned thing that's bothering me. And now you switching planes—I don't get it."

"I like to do my own flying," Harry Thompson said as he sprawled comfortably in the pilot's seat. "You ought to know that."

"Yes, but the secrecy of the whole business. Why? And then I ask, why us? Why us *three?*"

Jeb said, "Look, having a President's son—that's something

pretty special. The State Department's pretty fussy about who goes on diplomatic missions, hush-hush or otherwise."

"Yeah, but even that bothers me," Lane said.

"You're suddenly getting bothered by nothing, Lane," Harry said. "Just figure you're getting a little vacation from the new man in the Oval Office."

Lane Whitney ran a hand through his hair. "Yeah, but we know that man doesn't make a move without figuring out every angle, and there has to be an angle somewhere, except we haven't found it. Our being away, especially with the convention, it's puzzling. He welcomes you back, Harry, then bingo, it's off to Chile."

Jeb's tongue flicked across his lips. "Lane may have something there. Could just be."

"Well, spill it, Jeb," Harry said.

"Well, I've been thinking . . . Daniels was questioning me about the tapes. Like he wanted to know if you had heard them, and I told him yes."

"So?" Harry chuckled. "We'd agreed on that, Jeb. You'd be very proper, but you'd force him to extract any information. No volunteering, right?"

"Right. Matter of fact, now that I think of it, he did volunteer something about how he and Jaggers had a mission for Harry, and would I be interested in being part of it."

"Holy shit!" Lane shouted. "*Daniels* is part of this deal?"

"Right," Jeb said.

"Any anything else?" Lane demanded.

"Well, yeah. He also wanted to know if anyone else besides Harry and me heard the tape."

"And did you tell him?" Lane shot back.

"I told him the truth. I told him you'd heard it, too."

Lane Whitney stood up. "Jesus H. Christ!"

"What's eating you, Lane?"

"I'm getting off this plane, that's what!" He started to reach down to pick up a small satchel.

Thompson sat up. "Have you gone off your rocker? What in the hell's the matter with you?"

Whitney reached up and pulled out a raincoat from an overhead locker. "I'm telling you, I'm getting off this fucking plane. And Jeb, if you've got any brains, you'll get off with me!"

Jeb started to chuckle. "I'm copilot. You suddenly afraid of me not being able to get you across the Andes?"

Whitney looked down the length of the aisle away from the

cockpit. Then leaning close, he spoke to Harry in a tense whisper. "Look, chum, we're the only three who heard those goddamn tapes. The three of us. Just *us*."

"So?"

"Don't you see? Those tapes are hot. H-o-t, hot, and you know it! They can burn them, erase them, do what they want, but *we* heard them and *they* know. Now *I* know. It's no coincidence that we're here on this assignment."

Harry chuckled. "Sure, they get us together and blow up the whole plane. Just like that. Only we're not *on* their plane."

"With Daniels in this? The guys got brains and a thousand spies! You think he couldn't have figured this out?" Harry Thompson burst out laughing. "Laugh, Harry. I'm getting off."

"Three experts from the State Department brief us, the Secretary meets us . . . and Mr. Jaggers believes we're going in an Air Force plane—with an Air Force crew—"

Lane's voice dropped to a whisper. "Hey guys, remember studying the old U-2 affair? Remember how an American plane supposed to be out of range of Soviet guns suddenly gets in a jam, can't reach its altitude, gets brought down? Who handled that plane? Wasn't it the CIA?"

"Oh, come on," Jeb said.

"Somebody wanted to shaft Eisenhower's meeting with Khrushchev—and if you remember that, you'll remember the meeting was torpedoed in Paris."

"So?" Thompson said.

"So when the CIA wants something to happen, they have their ways."

"Daniels just figures to have his CIA henchmen blow up an Air Force plane, the three-man crew and us, that it?"

"But not me!" Lane said, as he started down the aisle.

Harry Thompson reached out to grab his arm. "For Christsake, Lane, you're letting your nerves get to you. We're not *on* that plane."

"I don't care!"

"We've outfoxed him if the bastard had any such crazy ideas. We have clearance, the flight plan's been filed. Our first leg's Caracas. No sweat, no problems."

"Outfox Daniels?" Lane shook himself free of Harry Thompson as the two of them moved down the aisle. "You want to be a sitting duck, you go ahead! Me, I'm resigning this commission."

Harry stood at the door as Lane started down the steps. "And you want to see the Secretary of State blow his stack?"

"Fuck him," Whitney said.

"Lane! Come on back here!" Thompson shouted as he stood framed in the doorway.

"If you're smart, Harry—you too, Jeb—you'll both follow me!" Whitney called back as he hurried across the field.

30

Kathy Thompson paced her elegant white and gold bedroom in the Kalorama mansion, reviewing the events of the past forty-eight hours. Her husband had made his decision without consulting her; he had made it in a calculating manner designed to make her role meaningless, untenable. And then there was the sight of Clifford Hawley, the momentary glance they'd exchanged from their cars. As she opened the French windows that looked down on the manicured lawn, she remembered his assertion that even when they were moving in opposite directions, there would come a time when they'd arrive back at the starting point.

It was possible, she said to herself, observing her own image reflected in the windowpanes of the doors, that they *would* one day arrive back at the same place at the same time. But, she asked, could they pick up the pieces and resume something they'd each pushed aside years earlier?

For a split second she saw the image of Felicia Courtney. Felicia, she had to admit, could be a formidable rival. Then she let herself relax because *she* knew Clifford Hawley better than Felicia—how cautious he was. And he would be even more cautious now. She knew, better than anyone else, how he had planned his own career, how he had willingly let another man claim *her*. She reasoned that his ambitions had propelled him to his target, the presidency. Now he would want it in his own right. Stephen Thompson could refuse to endorse him, but under the circumstances of the Twenty-fifth Amendment, Hawley might be able to convert that opposition to an advantage. He was clever, confident, and in the end he would have his way. Of that she was sure.

As she wrapped her arms about herself, she knew what she would do. Despite her husband's seemingly cruel pleasure at seeing her career end along with his, she would resist his decision. She would return to the White House daily. She would exercise all the privileges of being First Lady. *Her* role wasn't dependent upon the amendment. The President was being displaced; but the First Lady would carry on.

Moreover, she would return home to the Kalorama estate each and every night, making certain she'd be perceived as a woman dedicated to serving the public in her official role, and serving, too, as the eyes and ears of her ailing husband.

And she *would* be seeing Clifford Hawley. She might be in the East Wing and he in the West Wing, but they'd be sharing the same building; she enjoyed knowing he'd feel their proximity even if they *were* at opposite ends. There would be messages dealing with official White House business. Each had a Chief of Staff who would act as intermediary. There were telephones—and there'd be no taping.

She went inside and stretched out on her bed, pleased by her ruminations. Stephen Thompson had made his move, rejected her advice, thought he had ended her career. But she would prove him wrong. Thompson had eliminated himself, not her. Yes, time, she felt, was on her side, not, as he claimed, on his. She knew she had some cards to play.

☆ ☆ ☆

It was their first meeting since Hawley had talked with the President, and Hawley felt an unexpected agitation as he paced behind his desk waiting for Daniels to enter the Oval Office. As Latham swung open the door, Daniels bowed politely.

"Come in, Richard," Hawley said.

Daniels waited for Hawley to be seated behind his desk. "Glad to see Harry Thompson getting in line," he said, taking out a cigarette. Then, as he struck a match, he added, "Still, I wouldn't count too much on him." He glanced at his watch. "Their plane should be taking off about now."

"Oh? I didn't realize their mission was taking place quite

so soon," Hawley said, "but his father's decision surprised Harry. I'm certain of that."

"Maybe. But it didn't take him very long to make *his* decision to jump *your* way," Daniels remarked drily. "And if there are any tapes at his place we'll find them during his absence. If necessary, that'll include the Kalorama estate."

"Yes," Hawley said, and then wanting to change the subject, he added, "As I told you on the phone earlier, the President's not going to challenge our decision. He's going to sit back, keep me dangling."

"Make a move if he feels he wants to, that it?"

"That's it," Hawley said. "And no participation in the convention. I don't know what else is in his mind or heart."

"I do," Daniels said. "It's something called silent murder. There's nothing more dangerous than a wounded adversary." He blew two smoke rings. "He's sitting back waiting for his kind of revenge."

"He's already having it, holed up where he is," Hawley said.

"Gives with one breath, takes back with the next. He wants to keep you off balance. And you have to remember that young Harry might be a fifth columnist."

"Could there be others?" Hawley asked, looking squarely into Daniels' eyes.

Daniels shrugged. "You don't always find out, not that kind of thing," he replied easily. "But if and when you do," he added, snuffing out his cigarette in an ashtray on Hawley's desk, "you eliminate him, like that."

"No explanation? No confrontation?"

"Not if you're certain."

"And if you're uncertain?"

Again, Daniels shrugged. "You don't take chances. In your position you can't afford to have doubts. About anyone," he said.

"Harry expected the President to come out fighting at one point," Hawley said. "He told that to Lane and me quite openly, admitted he was for it at first."

"And just changed his own mind like that?" Daniels said, snapping his fingers.

"No. It was his father who changed it. Not in words, but in his actions. Harry saw him close up and not in full control for the first time, and that alarmed him. Must have."

"Hasn't seemed to alarm the First Lady, and she has to have seen it more than he. I think she'll be in her office every day.

Matter of fact," Daniels said with a thin smile, "your working with her, giving her an assignment or two, might make good political sense."

"Undercutting President Thompson?"

"Why not?" Daniels replied, shrugging his shoulders.

Hawley smiled inwardly. It was clear that Daniels was dropping his last ties, if there were any, with President Thompson. He nodded in agreement. "Yes," he said rising, "an interesting thought."

☆ ☆ ☆

The President's son was missing. For the first twenty-four hours there had been more than hope, there was optimism, but as the hours passed, a wave of pessimism swept through President Thompson's estate, the White House, the city, the nation.

Every detail of Harry's mission had been examined, and the cold truth could not be pushed away. The plane had taken off routinely and been passed along by one air-traffic center to another all the way down the East Coast. It was the Miami traffic-control center that had the final report on the whereabouts of the plane. A traffic controller had followed its flight path for only a few minutes when it disappeared from his screen.

At first it was not considered significant. Planes moving east disappeared if they were two hundred miles out simply because they were moving behind the horizon, reappearing minutes later as their course was corrected.

Harry Thompson's flight plan had been filed within a few minutes of clearance, and the plane was on course heading toward Caracas for refueling. There was speculation that at the high altitude the plane was capable of reaching, trouble had suddenly erupted, leading to a violent descent, but no radar control center reported any plane making a dangerously rapid drop in altitude.

In the end, though, that became the generally accepted explanation. The plane had veered some two hundred miles off the coast: that—and the absence of finding any debris after a seventy-two-hour search by teams of military ships and planes covering hundreds of square miles—indicated that the plane had either exploded in the air or had developed engine trouble that dropped it from its 51,000-foot altitude to ground level with dizzying speed. Impact on the surface of the ocean would have smashed the plane into thousands of fragments.

The absence of any radio contact added further evidence that a fatal accident had occurred so quickly that the occupants of the plane had had no time even to send out a distress signal.

☆ ☆ ☆

The small group assembled in the Cabinet Room included Hornwell, Daniels, Jaggers, Clauson, and their key aides. Lane Whitney sat apart from the others as Hawley conducted the impromptu meeting. "I'll be concentrating on the convention activities a good deal of the time," he said, "and I'm glad to announce to the group that Lane Whitney will be working as closely with me this time as he did in the last election. We're all glad you're here, Lane." There was a general murmur of agreement as Hawley went on. "One more item—President Thompson's private letter to Turgenev. I thought all of you should know that Mrs. Curtis has had a response from the Soviets in Geneva. Mr. Secretary?" he nodded toward Jaggers.

"For all practical purposes the letter's been tabled. Mr. Turgenev indicated that some elements might be studied and pursued after our election, depending on the next President's interest."

"And Turgenev's real interest?" Clauson interjected.

"Minimal."

"Good. At the very least," Clauson went on, "that indicates that he has no desire to do or say anything that could be interpreted as Soviet interference in the election process. I see that as a positive sign."

"Admiral Hornwell?" Hawley asked, turning toward him.

"Mr. Turgenev's met you more than once. He scarcely knows your potential opposition. He's done the right thing, the proper thing. It clearly shows his respect for, and acceptance of, your role as Acting President."

Hawley acknowledged the compliment. "We'll let the National Security Council study all of the implications in President Thompson's ideas," he said, "and, as you know, I see merit in some of them. And those I intend to pursue after the election."

Hawley rose and shook hands with those closest to him as the meeting began to break up. When Daniels lingered behind, momentarily, Lane Whitney approached him. He held out a cassette. "I think you should have this, Mr. Daniels," he said, passing it to him.

Daniels pocketed the cassette.

"There are no other copies." Whitney took a deep breath, then added, "I can promise you that."

"Thank you, Lane. I know Mr. Hawley will be appreciative. I think we can say this particular incident is closed?" Daniels said, in his usual interrogative fashion.

"Yes," Lane said, shaking his head sadly. "I only wish it could have been closed before—" he stopped, checking his emotions before proceeding. "Only did it *have* to happen, Mr. Daniels? Did Harry have to die in exchange for that?" he pointed to the pocket holding the cassette. "Harry *and* Jeb?" Pain stared from his eyes.

"You can be proud of them, Lane," Daniels said firmly, placing a hand on Whitney's shoulder.

"If they'd only taken the Air Force plane . . . maybe. . ."

"That was Harry's decision not to. We're happy that *you* made *your* decision—as it turned out, the right one."

"I only wish I had given the cassette to you before the plane took off," Lane said as he continued to search Daniels' eyes.

Daniels returned the gaze impassively, then, tapping Whitney's shoulder twice, nodded and moved away.

☆ ☆ ☆

Hawley had returned from the special services conducted in the resplendently gothic Washington Cathedral to honor President Thompson's missing son. He'd been struck by the pallor and the gauntness of H. Stephen Thompson and the attentive manner in which Kathy, dressed in a somber but fashionable outfit, had taken her place beside her husband as they stood silently acknowledging the sympathy of official Washington.

All of the familiar faces were there—the Joint Chiefs led by Hornwell, the Cabinet by Jaggers, the leadership of the House and Senate, the Chief Justice and his associates. Hawley noticed the firm grip Thompson placed on Daniels' left arm as he grasped Daniels' outstretched hand. When Hawley reached Thompson he merely murmured, "Mr. President," as he offered his hand, aware that Thompson simply let his own rest without movement in his. Turning to Kathy, Hawley bowed, and when he extended his hand to her he felt her instant firm grip and caught the sign of a slight smile hovering on her lips.

Back in the Oval Office he asked Senator Vance, the Secretary of State, and Henry Kraus to join him for a brief conference.

Hawley knew each of them was curious as to the nature

of the unplanned meeting. He wanted it to hit them with surprise, and he wanted no tedious debate. The subject was one that had been gnawing at him for some days and it had to be excised expeditiously. For a fleeting moment he saw images of Vivien Lessing and her battered body, of Harry Thompson and his ill-fated plane, and once again he heard President Thompson's reference to Commerce Secretary Bromley, a subject he knew he'd raised in confidence only with Richard Daniels.

Now it was time for action. "I've been doing some thinking about the National Security Council," Hawley began, "and, in particular, the operations of the Committee. I think the system might well need some fine tuning." Hawley noted the immediate impact those words had—Vance's raised eyebrows, Jaggers reaching up to stroke his moustache, Kraus fumbling with the knot of his necktie.

It was Jaggers who, as usual, made the first response. "Could be," he said carefully, well aware that the system was, in fact, now *going* to be changed, and that its most powerful member, Richard Daniels, had not been summoned to the meeting, a factor he knew had to be present in the minds of the others. He had made his own position clear by his cagey acknowledgment that Hawley's idea, whatever it might be, could well be desirable. He would let the others carry the ball. "What do you think, Henry?"

Kraus knew he couldn't pass the ball to Vance because Vance had never participated at the NSC, an executive arm of the President. And he welcomed Hawley's initiative because he'd always felt that the Committee had preempted his own role as Chief of Staff as well as that of his predecessors. "I don't think either body should ever meet for substantive decisions without the presence of either the President or the Vice President," he bluntly stated, "preferably the President."

"Senator Vance?" Hawley asked.

Vance smiled. "Its evolution—I'm referring to the Committee—has occasionally raised some questions in both Houses, but it does seem to me that its findings should always be subject to the same system of executive review we've given the NSC ever since the Irangate embarrassment." He glanced across at Kraus. "The Chief of Staff makes a good point."

Hawley nodded agreement. "I concur. I'd like the three of you to give this some further thought, to confine the discussion to yourselves only, and to give me a recommendation right after the convention." As he rose from his chair, the others stood up. "Thank you," he said, and as they started to the door, Hawley beckoned to Jaggers. "Mr. Jaggers, if I could take another minute of your time."

When Kraus and Vance left, Hawley stood near the French doors leading to the Rose Garden, his back to Jaggers, who remained near the presidential desk. "Mr. Daniels has been a tremendous asset to the CIA and to the Committee."

Jaggers knew he was obliged to respond. "For a long time, sir."

"A very long time," Hawley repeated as he turned to face him, pointing to a sofa. Jaggers settled into one of its corners as Hawley walked about the room in a measured way. "I've been doing some thinking. There'll be some minor action at the convention. Meade informs me that it's possible that the governor of California wants his name presented to the convention."

Jaggers shook his head. "Wouldn't have a chance."

Hawley smiled. "True, but governors of the state of California believe they govern something like the equivalent of a nation. They like to point out that their gross national product is larger than all but maybe seven or eight countries in the whole world."

"True, but it's still a state, not a country."

"Mr. Daniels has to have an assignment of importance." Hawley glanced down at Jaggers. "He's earned it."

"Of course," Jaggers said, absolutely delighted that Richard Daniels' powerful talons were about to be clipped.

"Would you have a thought on this?" Hawley asked.

Jaggers stood up. "Only one, sir."

"And that is?"

"Whatever the assignment, the change should be instituted without debate. Public or otherwise. Even Mr. Daniels would say this is the kind of action that should be surgical."

"I agree," Hawley said.

The two men were silent for a moment, each preoccupied with his own thoughts. Then Hawley said, "He's had a great deal of useful experience in foreign affairs," he commented.

"In a pragmatic way, yes," Jaggers responded, "but he's no student of history, especially of the movement of ideas."

"He should be on an assignment where he can feel he *can* make a contribution—"

"Yes, and because of his special knowledge, the CIA and so on, it has to be secure. His safety is of vital concern. He knows so much . . . Western Europe, Canada, maybe Mexico. Even Latin America."

"Perhaps NATO?"

"Perhaps NATO. Yes, a possibility."

Hawley rubbed his hands together. "Good thinking, Ed. You and Henry work on the specifics." Hawley took a few steps to his desk, his action signalling the end of the meeting.

Jaggers stopped at the door and said, "If he wants to see you?"

Hawley shook his head. "No debate, no appeal, Mr. Secretary. Surgical. Your word, Mr. Jaggers."

"No. Daniels' word," Jaggers emphasized. "He wrote the book on matters like this."

☆ ☆ ☆

Three weeks later, Hawley sat in the presidential suite of the Blackstone Hotel in Chicago watching the evening proceedings, with him in the handsomely furnished room a handful of visitors including his parents, Elizabeth Vance, Hugh Riley, Chief of Staff to the Vice President, and Alex Broome, television adviser to the Acting President. Secret Service men stood in the foyer. All eyes were glued to the television set as Senator Vance, smiling and lifting an arm to the cheering audience, approached the rostrum to deliver the first of several nominating speeches.

Hawley turned to Elizabeth. "You'll want a cassette of this for your family records."

"Oh, they've been taping every moment of the convention back home," she said beaming, eyes fixed on her husband.

At that moment Everard Meade, chairman of the party, entered the room and, smiling perfunctorily at the assembled guests, leaned down to whisper confidentially to Hawley.

Hawley looked up with surprise. "Here?" he said softly. "She's here?"

Meade glanced at the door at the far end of the room. "In there."

Hawley rose from his chair as the others, puzzled, looked at him. "I have to step out for a moment—"

"But you're about to be nominated, Clifford," his mother said, looking up at him in astonishment.

"I'll have my own tape," he replied good-naturedly. Then, striding briskly to the door, he paused, hand on the knob, and whispered to Meade, "She give you any idea of why?"

Meade shook his head. "Just said it was important. Had to see you."

"Okay." As Hawley pushed the door open, he said to Meade, "You'd best stay back with the others." Then, closing it behind him, and looking across the suite's elegant, small library, he observed Kathy Thompson by the pink marble fireplace. For a moment there was silence.

"I had to come, Cliff," she finally said.

"I'm glad to see you," Hawley replied, still unsure of himself. "Surprised, but glad."

Kathy studied him. "Are you?" she asked, a quizzical look on her face?

"Yes, of course," he said, indicating a chair.

"I'd rather stand for the moment."

"You said you had to come," Hawley repeated.

"I've thought it all out, Cliff. All of it."

Hawley looked at her, admired the confidence in her manner, the classic beauty of her face and figure, aware of the grace and self-assurance that had become part of her in her role as First Lady.

"I'm not here to play games," she said, "unless you want to characterize my offer..."

"Offer?"

"Yes, offer. Unless you want to characterize it as something like a game—maybe chess? I know you play," she added with a smile.

"Not in a long time," he said.

"You're always playing chess, Cliff, that's what handling power is all about. You're a king," she said, and as he seemed about to protest, she said, "And a king has power, lots of power. But even a king is vulnerable. Which is why he surrounds himself with knights and bishops and pawns, a lot of pawns." She paused. "Stephen is a king, too."

"Two kings. All right, I'm with you," he said.

"And all of the others are just players, totally expendable. In chess, all the players have one simple function—protect the king." Again she paused for a moment. "I've come to do just that."

"I'm not sure I follow you."

"Oh, but you do, Cliff. Two kings. One queen. Doesn't that help? And look, Cliff, I know *I'm* expendable. Which is precisely why I've come to make my move." She stopped momentarily, staring at him fixedly.

"Go on. I'm listening."

She took a deep breath, then said very deliberately, "I've come to second your nomination."

Hawley was stunned. "Now I think we'd both better be seated," he said, pointing to one end of the sofa as he sat at the other.

"It will checkmate Stephen. End of game. His game."

"Maybe you'd better spell it out, Kathy."

"But you already know. I can see the wheels spinning."

"Well, then help me see them."

"Stephen has kept his own counsel, you know that. He's kept you in a state of suspense. Your opposition. Everybody. Everyone wants to know whether he will declare himself able to resume his duties, take over his office, throw a monkey wrench into your campaign at the moment of his own choosing. Right?"

"He could do that, yes," Hawley replied. Then, after a moment's pause, he added, "I thought you wanted him to do that if he could."

"I did."

"And now?"

"I have to checkmate him—and in chess that's the one major thing a queen can do. She can stop a king. This is *more* than Stephen and it's *more* than you. The country deserves the best from each of you, and if the best can't be forthcoming from each of you, *voluntarily*, then I have to do my part, make certain that no last-minute monkey wrench wrecks everything."

"How do you propose to do that?"

"Cliff, Stephen couldn't sustain a whole campaign. Harry recognized that. Though he wanted his father to fight you, in the end he came down on your side. And even before Stephen could campaign he'd have to meet the challenge of the doctors, not to mention you, the Cabinet, the struggle through the Congress, and all of the steps in the Twenty-fifth Amendment. And if he were—let's assume it for the moment—victorious, his victory would last for only a month or two at the most while all around him the party, you and your campaign, would turn to dust." She reached over to press his arm. "Cliff, when I second your nomination I do it in Harry's name as well as mine. The President's son. The President's wife. We *both* endorse you." She extracted a piece of paper from her pocketbook. "It's short. I've written it out. The Thompsons—we've come to endorse your nomination. And *that*, Mr. Hawley," she said, edging forward, "that's checkmate."

Hawley looked at her, a sense of admiration and total surprise overtaking him, an awareness that her daring and imaginative analysis, backed up by her personal support at the precise moment when it would strike the nation with its greatest impact, had to give his campaign a momentum that could not be stopped. He wondered about her motivation and quietly asked, "Kathy, what does all this do for you?"

She sat back in the corner of the sofa. "I don't know. I haven't thought that out. *This* is as far as I've gotten. I only know I'll return to Washington as quickly as I can. Tonight." She passed the paper across to Hawley and he glanced at it.

Hawley looked up at her. "Does he know?"

"I couldn't risk telling him. He'll know when the world knows."

Hawley stood. "You wait here. I'll get Meade. He'll take you down to the podium and arrange for your introduction." A sudden thought stopped him at the door. "Kathy, I think you should plan to be here tomorrow."

"I have to return tonight. I *must*."

"We'll handle that. But tomorrow I'd like you back here."

"Why?"

"We pick the Vice President. And right after Senator Vance is nominated I'm going to the podium to deliver my acceptance speech. I want you there between us to raise our arms. Will you do it?"

"If I came this far—"

"Good. I'll send Meade in to escort you over to the rostrum."

☆ ☆ ☆

H. Stephen Thompson, highball in hand, sat in the semidarkness of the drawing room at his Kalorama home staring at the television set, watching the parade of political nabobs seconding Senator Vance's nomination of Hawley. Betsy King and Henry Kraus were the only others in the room. On the screen, the governor of California was winding up his remarks.

Thompson chuckled as the network anchorman's face filled the screen for a moment and then the picture abruptly cut away to an interview on the floor of the convention. "Fellow knocks himself out to make what he thinks may be a speech that will project him into the limelight for the next convention and then *boom*, he's cut off by some network producer and left there all alone droning away to an inattentive gaggle of conventioneers.

"Says something about the power of the networks. They decide who gets seen, who doesn't." At that moment the anchorman reappeared on the screen. "There are only three or four of them and fifty governors and they can even cut away from the governor of California if they want to—"

"Which apparently they're doing," Kraus said as the camera suddenly swung from the governor's face to the rear end of the speaker's platform. As it did, they heard the anchorman's voice rise in a tone of excitement, heard him saying, "We've just gotten word, even as the governor of California is coming to the end of his speech, that something unscheduled is about to happen ... and you can see *that* word has been spreading throughout this hall ... suddenly all those inattentive convention delegates ... just look at them ... they're rising in their chairs, as you can see ... Now you can see Everard Meade, the chairman of the party, and he's coming up the stairs of the speaker's platform, yes, and he's reached over and is helping someone up the rear steps ... yes!! ... Well! ... ladies and gentlemen, this is the *big* story of the convention! ... There she is! The First Lady! ... Yes, it's the First Lady! ... She's making her way down from ... listen to that welcome!"

As the camera caught the smiling Kathy Thompson moving toward the podium with a tremendous roar of welcome from the thousands in the convention hall, H. Stephen Thompson, scowling, rose halfway in his chair, staring with dismay and disbelief at the image on the screen. His highball glass slipped from his outstretched hand as he suddenly fell back. "Turn that sound down!" he thundered. Kraus hurried to the television set and Betsy King retrieved the fallen glass.

Thompson sat glaring at the now almost silent screen, his chest heaving as he watched the images of the cheering conventioneers intercut with the smiling and waving image of his wife. "Now, Henry, we know, *now* we know why we weren't able to reach her earlier. They covered for her, that secretary of hers and that Chief of Staff—" he stopped, groping for his name.

"Sheridan, Russell Sheridan," Kraus said.

"Bastard!" Thompson muttered between his clenched teeth. Then venting his anger he struck the arm of his chair with his fist. "Bastard!" he repeated vehemently. Betsy King brought over another drink and set it gently on the table next to him.

"Turn up the sound," Thompson grumbled. Betsy pressed the remote control and Kathy's voice filled the room.

"I speak not only for myself but also for Harry Thompson,"

she said as the crowd roared. "Together we felt that Clifford Hawley would carry on the great work started by my husband, the work that will lead America forward into the twenty-first century. . ." Again she was stopped by a tremendous roar of approval.

Thompson, giving his attention to Kraus, and shaking his head in consternation, said, "The one thing I never thought was possible, the one thing I never contemplated, *this* move. *This* move," he repeated. "I want to get the full text of her remarks. . ."

"I'll have it for you, Mr. President," Betsy interjected, taking down every word of Kathy's speech. The three of them sat in silence as Kathy spoke on. In a few minutes her speech was over, the anchorman busy at once analyzing its contents and impact.

Thompson sat quietly observing the network pundits. "You can turn the sound down, Betsy," he said, "and check Chicago, find out when she'll be home." As Betsy quietly left the room, Thompson turned to Kraus. "She's really boxed me in. Taken the Thompson name and handed it over to Hawley."

"Not, however, if I may say so, without including very generous references to your own achievements and the record of your Administration," Kraus murmured.

"Yes, to be sure, yes, she did do that," Thompson conceded. "But that's what I mean when I say she's boxed me in. Whatever plans I may have had—" Thompson rose to his feet. "I'll be in the upstairs study, Henry. If you could be so good as to stay until she returns—just explain that I'll be waiting," Thompson said as he headed toward the great stairway of the house, slowly making his way up its broad, heavily carpeted stairs.

☆ ☆ ☆

It was after midnight when Kathy entered the study. Thompson had spent the time quietly analyzing his position when she'd finally appeared. He rose to greet her and pointed to a chair across from him. "You made history tonight, Kathy."

"I did what I felt I had to do," she said simply.

"And finally made your choice."

As Kathy bristled at the words, Thompson extended a solicitous hand toward her. "No need to start defending your actions, Kathy. While you've been flying east I've been doing my own review, right here, all by myself." He gritted his teeth, straightening himself in his chair. "I have to say it. I have to commend you—" again he raised his hand to keep her from interrupting his thoughts, "what you said, the way you said it, the all-inclusive manner in which you wove yourself, Harry, and this Administration into one neat little package, all for the purpose of endorsing that man." He stopped for a moment and spoke again with grudging admiration. "Politically, quite a job."

"Are you being sarcastic, Stephen, or am I missing something?" she asked.

"Only your apparent inability to understand that I honestly recognize the brilliance of your tactics—whatever their ultimate motive might be—your understanding of the impact of the political effect of your appearance. The words, if they were yours—"

"They were mine alone," she interjected.

Thompson bowed his head toward her. "All the more impressive. I'm afraid you don't really understand what I'm saying."

"I wasn't expecting compliments, Stephen."

Thompson smiled. "Well, then, perhaps you might be more appreciative since I mean every word I've said. That isn't to say I'm happy about the turn of events, but I'm a realist. As I told Henry Kraus earlier, you've boxed me in—"

"I would have fought for *you* if you'd been willing to fight for *yourself*," she said.

"I have to say now I really believe you would have," he said. "But I won't speculate on what might have been." He sighed and murmured. "It's over."

Kathy looked at her husband, impressed with his calmness and his civility when she'd expected a bitter confrontation. "Why are you being so generous, Stephen?"

"Because I admire brains, Kathy, even an opponent's brain. Mr. Hawley's, for example. I told you I applauded the speech he made to me in this house right in front of Harry." The moment he mentioned his son's name he stopped, abruptly clasping his hands together. "Harry was worried about me," he said softly, "about my ability to carry on—" He stopped and stared at Kathy. "We're going to be together a long time, Kathy. I may not have been able to cope with a campaign, but I think I can cope with the role left to me, elder statesman, attentive husband. *That's* what's left for me." Then, abruptly bringing the subject back to the moment, he said, with a smile, "Tomorrow?"

"Tomorrow?" Kathy repeated.

"You'll be flying back to return to the podium. To cap today's events. To stand right between Mr. Hawley and Mr. Vance."

"Are you going to try to stop me?" Kathy asked.

"Not at all, not at all," Thompson said. "If I did that, it would be self-defeating. No, I salute you, Kathy, for your political skills. Yes, I'll be watching. And yes, I'll be waiting, for your return. And when all is said and done, Kathy, as between *us*, you and me, there are no losers. No winners, either. We are simply left as we are—with each other."

Epilogue

Upstairs, for the first time, Hawley stood at the window of his bedroom in the White House, sensing a chill in the air and pulling the collar of his robe closer. He glanced behind him, examining the room, aware that this was once a room shared by Kathy with H. Stephen Thompson. Now he wondered at what they, north of him, still in their Kalorama estate, were thinking on this, his first night as President in his own name.

Thompson had had his own small vial of revenge, if it could be called that—he had let Hawley drive out to the estate only to send word down that he was indisposed, and that he would not be participating at Hawley's inauguration. And Kathy, Hawley knew, had had to remain behind—there could be no choice between an ailing husband, if, indeed, he was ailing, and Hawley's own inaugural.

Again, Hawley looked out the window, thinking of the deceptive stillness of the city and the placid calm of the Potomac River. And he knew that beneath the quiet and murky water was evil and decay, a turbulence that infected the majestic and peaceful environment of the capital. He knew no man was free of the inner fears and anxieties the city spawned. At that moment the wind rustled with a menacing sound that seemed to sweep through the grass and the underbrush, through all the distance between Arlington and the White House, an ominous growl vibrating at its edges as though a nighttime predator were prowling the city. As he let his imagination run, he thought he could even hear the quick, stricken cries of its victim, and the snarling grunts of scavengers waiting in the distance. All of it he sensed was part of the Potomac Jungle. The Thompsons, father and son, had been part of that world. So was Daniels. Kathy and Felicia. Harry and Gloria. All of them. And so, he had to admit, reluctantly, was he.

And then in the darkness of the night he observed the gleaming white shaft piercing the sky, honoring George Washington. Its clean lines symbolized for him the ever-present challenge that rose above the clamor and the clawing of the jungle below. He recognized the contributions and the virtues of H. Stephen Thompson, understood the pain the President had to feel in his inability to continue to lead. Even though Thompson's passing the torch had been reluctant, it had been passed. Now, he, Clifford Hawley, was the latest soldier in that small battalion of men who felt the burden and the challenge of White House duty.

For a moment he thought of all the females in his life—and the one special woman. He would now necessarily compartmentalize her in his mind. Love and personal happiness might eventually have their moment, but as with other men he would have to wait on events to shape his ultimate decisions.

He returned to his desk and picked up a copy of the private letter Thompson had sent to the Soviet President. Challenging ideas there, seeds to be studied, developed. He had taken that letter to the convention, pledging it first as *Thompson's* vision, then his. There was irony in his public support of Thompson's secret letter—a letter that had helped trigger the move that undermined Thompson's own presidency and that now was, in fact, a piece of *his* ticket to the nomination and the presidency itself.

As he studied the letter, he tightened the collar of his robe, again feeling a chill in the air. He felt a new resolve to serve the people of the United States, and he vowed to proceed with courage and hope alike. His objective would be to root out the jungle where he could, tame it and clear it whenever it showed signs of reemerging; he would prepare a vision for America that would spur every man and woman to contribute his best, but in so doing he would never forget that though he would try to project himself as his country's leader, he would never forget, either, that, for the moment, he was also, now, the master of the Potomac Jungle.